HOUSE
OF
SECRETS

HOUSE OF SECRETS

CHRIS COLUMBUS   NED VIZZINI

Jasper

HarperCollins *Children's Books*

First published in Great Britain by HarperCollins *Children's Books* in 2013
HarperCollins *Children's Books* is a division of HarperCollins*Publishers* Ltd,
77-85 Fulham Palace Road, Hammersmith, London, W6 8JB.

The HarperCollins website address is: www.harpercollins.co.uk

1

ISBN 978-0-00-746583-5

Chris Columbus and Ned Vizzini assert the moral right
to be identified as the authors of the work.

Printed and bound in England by Clays Ltd, St Ives plc

MIX
Paper from
responsible sources
FSC C007454

FSC™ is a non-profit international organisation established to promote
the responsible management of the world's forests. Products carrying the
FSC label are independently certified to assure consumers that they come
from forests that are managed to meet the social, economic and
ecological needs of present and future generations,
and other controlled sources.

Find out more about HarperCollins and the environment at
www.harpercollins.co.uk/green

For Monica,
whose love of books
and reading inspired this adventure
– C.C.

For my son, Felix,
whom I trust will enjoy this one day
– N.V.

Brendan Walker knew the house was going to be terrible.

The first tip-off was the super-cheerful tone the estate agent, Diane Dobson, used with his mother.

"It's *truly* the most *amazing* house, Mrs Walker," Diane chirped on speakerphone. "The perfect place for a sophisticated family like yours. And it's just gone through a major price reduction."

"Where is this house?" Brendan asked. Aged twelve, he sat next to his older sister, Cordelia, playing *Uncharted* on his much-loved PSP. He sported his favourite grass-stained blue lacrosse jersey, torn jeans, and weathered high-tops.

"I'm sorry, who is that?" Diane asked from the dashboard of the car, where an iPhone sat in a holster.

"Our son, Brendan," Dr Walker answered. "You're on speakerphone."

"I'm talking with the whole Walker family! What a treat. Well, *Brendan*" – Diane sounded as if she expected to be commended for remembering his name – "the house is located at one twenty-eight Sea Cliff Avenue, among a stately collection of homes owned by prominent San Franciscans."

"Like Forty-niners and Giants?" asked Brendan.

"Like CEOs and bankers," corrected Diane.

"Shoot me."

"Bren!" Mrs Walker scolded.

"You won't feel that way once you've seen the place," said Diane. "It's a charming, rustic, woodsy jewel—"

"Whoa, hold on!" Cordelia interrupted. "Say that again?"

"With whom am I speaking now?" Diane asked.

With whom? Seriously? Cordelia thought – but the truth was she also used "whom" in her more intellectual moments.

"That's our daughter Cordelia," said Mrs Walker. "Our eldest."

"What a pretty name!"

Don't 'pretty name' me, Cordelia wanted to say, but as the eldest she was better than Brendan at being tactful. She was a tall, wispy girl with delicate features that she hid behind a dirty-blonde fringe. "Diane, my family has been looking for a new house for the last month, and in that time I've learned that estate agents speak in what I call 'coded language'."

"I'm sure I don't know what you mean."

"Excuse me, but what does that mean, 'I'm sure I don't know'?" piped up Eleanor, aged eight. She had sharp eyes, a small, precise nose, and long, curly hair, the same colour as her sister's, that sometimes had gum and leaves in it, if she'd been adventurous that day. She tended to be quiet except in moments when she wasn't supposed to be quiet, which was what Brendan and Cordelia loved most about her. "How can you be sure if you don't know?"

Cordelia gave her sister an appreciative nod and continued: "I mean that when estate agents say 'charming', Diane, they mean 'small'. When they say 'rustic', they mean 'located in a habitat for bears'. 'Woodsy' means 'termite-infested'… 'Jewel', I don't even know… I assume 'squat'."

"Deal, stop being an idiot," grumbled Brendan, glued to his screen, irritated that he hadn't thought up that line of reasoning himself.

Cordelia rolled her eyes and went on.

"Diane, are you about to show my family a small, termite-infested squat located in a bear habitat?"

Diane sighed over the speakerphone. "How old is she?"

"Fifteen," Dr and Mrs Walker said together.

"She sounds thirty-five."

"Why?" Cordelia asked. "Because I'm asking pertinent questions?"

Brendan reached over from the back seat and ended the call.

"Brendan!" Mrs Walker yelled.

"I'm just trying to save our family some embarrassment."

"But Ms Dobson was about to tell us about the house!"

"We already know what the house is gonna be like. Like every other house we can afford: bad."

"I have to agree," Cordelia said. "And you know how much it hurts me to agree with Bren."

"You love agreeing with me," Brendan mumbled, "because that's when you know you're right."

Cordelia laughed, which made Brendan smile despite himself. "Good one, Bren," said Eleanor, giving her brother's uncombed hair a quick rub.

"Kids, let's try to be positive about the house," said Dr Walker. "Sea Cliff is Sea Cliff. We're talking unobstructed views of the Golden Gate. I want to see it, and I want to know about that 'reduced' price. What was the address?"

"One twenty-eight," Brendan said without looking up. He had an eerie ability to remember things; it came from memorising sports plays and game cheats. His parents joked that he would end up a lawyer because of it (and because he was so good at arguing), but Brendan didn't want to end up a lawyer. He wanted to end up a Forty-niner or a Giant.

"Plug it into my phone, will you?" Dr Walker waved the phone in front of Brendan while he drove.

"I'm in the middle of a game, Dad."

"So?"

"So I can't just *pause*."

"Isn't there a pause *button*?" Cordelia asked.

"Nobody's talking to you, Deal," said Brendan. "Could you guys just leave me alone, please?"

"You're already practically alone," said Cordelia. "You always have your head buried in your stupid games, and then you get out of going to dinner with us because of lacrosse practice, and you refuse to go on trips… it's like you don't even want to be part of this family."

"You *are* a genius," said Brendan. "You guessed my secret."

Eleanor swooped in, grabbed the phone and plugged in the address – but she did it backwards, putting the street in first and then the number. Cordelia started to give Brendan a nasty retort but reminded herself he was at that "awkward" stage for boys, the stage where you were supposed to say horribly sarcastic things because you looked so gawky.

It was the house that was the real problem. Even Eleanor was suspicious of it now. It was going to be old enough for people to have died in. It was going to be falling apart and have crooked shutters and a layer of dirt an inch thick and an overgrown tree out the front and a bunch of snoopy neighbours who were going to look at the Walkers and whisper, "Here are the suckers who are finally gonna buy this thing."

But what could they do? At eight, twelve and fifteen, Eleanor, Brendan and Cordelia were each absolutely sure that they were at the worst possible age, the most powerless and unfair.

So Brendan gamed and Cordelia read and Eleanor fiddled with the GPS until they pulled up to 128 Sea Cliff Avenue. Then they looked out of the window and their jaws dropped. They had never seen anything like it.

Sea Cliff was a neighbourhood of mansions on hills, most built right up against the sunny street with its row of young trees trimmed into perfect leafy spheres. But the house the Walkers were looking at was set back, perched at the edge of the cliff from which the neighbourhood took its name, so far back that Brendan wondered if it was half supported by stilts. An expanse of emerald lawn buffered it from the street, with three wide pine trees that kept the grass in shadow. The house itself had gold and tan trim accenting the royal blue that wrapped around its slatted sides. An impeccably groomed pebbled path slalomed through the trees to the front door.

"I've biked by here tons of times, but I've never seen this place," said Cordelia.

"That's because you never look up from your stupid

books," said Brendan.

"And how do you figure I'm reading when I'm on a bike, genius?"

"*Audiobooks?*"

"Guys, no fighting in front of the estate agent," Mrs Walker said under her breath. She had already called Diane Dobson back to apologise for how Brendan had hung up on her, and now they saw a woman who looked like Hillary Clinton standing at the front of the path. "That must be her. Let's go."

The Walker family stepped out of their Toyota, bumping into one another. Diane greeted them, wearing a finely tailored, coral-coloured suit, her hair lacquered into a blonde helmet. She made the house look even more impressive.

"Dr Jake Walker," Dr Walker said, reaching out to shake hands. "And this is my wife, Bellamy." Mrs Walker nodded demurely. Dr Walker didn't bother to introduce his offspring. He hadn't shaved that morning, even though he used to make a point of telling his children how men who didn't shave every day lacked discipline. But he wasn't the man he had been back then. Diane eyed the family's second-hand car.

"Can we keep our horse here?" Eleanor asked, tugging Dr Walker's leg.

"We don't have a horse, Nell," he laughed. "She's going through a horse phase," he explained to Diane.

"But it's perfect, Daddy! You said I could get a horse on my next birthday—"

"That was if we got a country house, which we're not getting, and you can't keep horses in the city."

"Why not? There's lots of places to ride them! Golden Gate Park, Crissy Field… You think I don't remember things you promise—"

Mrs Walker knelt and took Eleanor's shoulders in her hands. "Honey, we'll talk about this later."

"But Daddy always—"

"Calm down. It's not Daddy's fault. Things have changed. Why don't we play a game? Here, close your eyes and tell me what kind of horse you want in your wildest dreams. Come on, I'll do it with you."

Mrs Walker shut her eyes. Eleanor followed. Brendan rolled his eyes instead of shutting them, but he was tempted, deep down, to join in. Cordelia shut hers – in solidarity with her sister and to annoy Brendan.

"And… open!" Mrs Walker said. "What kind of horse is he?"

"*She*. Calico. Light brown with white spots. Her name's Misty."

"Perfect." Mrs Walker hugged her daughter tight, stood up and went back to looking at the house with Diane Dobson, who had waited patiently for the family to work out their very obvious issues.

"Delightful, isn't it?" the estate agent said. "A completely unique construction."

"There are some things about it that concern me," Mrs Walker said. Brendan saw that she was entering negotiation mode, where she used her charm and poise to make people do things. Standing in front of the home, she looked strong and beautiful, more confident than she had been in months. Brendan wondered if it might be fate that had brought them to this house.

"What concerns you?" asked Diane.

"First of all," said Mrs Walker, "the house is on the edge of a cliff. It seems very precarious. And what would happen in an earthquake? We'd slide right into the ocean!"

"The house emerged from the quake of 1989 without

a scratch," Diane said. "The engineering is superb. Come inside; let's take a look."

Intrigued, the Walkers followed her up the path towards the house, past the big pine trees. Brendan noticed something odd about the lawn. It took him a minute to realise… there was no For Sale sign. *What kind of house goes on sale without a sign?*

"This is a three-storey, Victorian-style property," Diane declared, "known locally as Kristoff House. It was built in 1907, after the Great Quake, by a gentleman who survived it."

Dr Walker nodded. His family, too, had survived the Great San Francisco Earthquake generations before. They had moved away, but work had brought Dr Walker back. Work he no longer had.

"Two eighteen!" Eleanor said, pointing at the address hanging over the front door.

"One twenty-eight," Cordelia corrected gently.

Eleanor huffed and looked down at her feet. Diane continued her monologue on the front steps, but Cordelia hung back and knelt beside her sister. This might be a "teachable moment", as Cordelia's English teacher

Ms Kavanaugh liked to say. Since one of the effects of Eleanor's dyslexia was that she read things backwards, Cordelia figured there must be a simple psychological trick that could get her to read perfectly. They just hadn't found it yet. Brendan lingered, eager to see Cordelia fail.

"Can you try reading it backwards?" she encouraged.

"It's not that simple, Deal. You think you know everything!"

"Well, I *have* read books about this, and I'm trying to help—"

"Then where were you at school last week?"

"What? What're you talking—"

"This stupid substitute teacher in my stupid English class called on me to read from *Little House on the Prairie*. And I couldn't do it."

As she said the words, Eleanor remembered that day at school. Ms Fitzsimmons had been off sick, and Eleanor had been too scared to tell the sub teacher that she had problems reading, so she went in front of the class and held the book and waited for magic to happen. She thought maybe somehow, just once, magic would happen and she'd be able to read a sentence the right way. But the words looked as mixed-up as they always did – *not backwards, Cordelia,* she thought, *mixed-up* – and when she tried to read the title, the first four words came out right, but the last one came out like a swear word. The whole class laughed and Eleanor dropped the book and ran out of the room and the sub teacher sent her to the principal and everybody was still calling her that swear word.

Cordelia spoke in a quiet voice: "Oh, Eleanor… I'm so sorry. But I can't be with you in class."

"No, you can't! So don't pretend you can *fix me!*"

Cordelia winced. Brendan, amused by her failure, prepared to deliver a cutting remark, but before he could—

"What's *that?*" Eleanor exclaimed.

Brendan and Cordelia glanced over in time to see a figure streaking from one of the pine trees to the side of the house. A flash of shadow. Too fast to be a person. A car honked on Sea Cliff Avenue behind them.

"That was probably just the car's shadow, Nell," said Brendan. "Jumping from the tree to the house."

"No, it wasn't. It was a person. And it was bald," insisted Eleanor.

"You saw a bald guy?"

"*Girl*. An old woman. Staring at us. And now she's behind the house."

Brendan and Cordelia glanced at each other, each expecting the other to be making a '*silly Eleanor*' face. But they were both as deadly serious as their sister.

They looked at the side of Kristoff House. The silhouette of a dark figure stood there. Watching them.

Brendan took a deep breath and tried to stay calm, strong. The figure remained still. "Hello?" he called, stepping off the path and pulling Eleanor with him, Cordelia following close behind. "Is someone there?"

He was trying to use his toughest voice, but it cracked – more *Sesame Street* than Schwarzenegger. He cleared his throat to cover it as he and his siblings crept to the side of the house.

The figure was nothing but an old statue. A Gothic angel, looming two metres tall, carved from grey stone stained with streaks of green and black. It had wings folded behind it and arms stretched forward, with the right hand broken off. Its face was worn down, chinless and lipless, eroded by decades of San Francisco wind and fog. Mossy patches covered its eyes.

"Beautiful," said Cordelia.

Brendan wiped his forehead, surprised to find it covered in sweat. It was stupid, but he'd expected to see the person Eleanor had described: a bald woman, a crone. His imagination ran away with him a little and he could even picture this woman pointing a crooked finger and hissing, "Here are the suckers who will finally buy this house!"

"See, Nell? It's just a statue. There's no one here," Brendan said, putting his hand on Eleanor's shoulder.

"She went somewhere."

"It was the light. It played a trick on you."

"No, it didn't!"

"Let it go. You're scared."

"Not, as scared as you," said Eleanor, moving Brendan's hand away and pointing at the sweaty spot he had left on her shoulder. Before Brendan could protest, another hand reached out from behind and grabbed his neck.

4

"Help!" Brendan screamed, whirling around and shoving with all his might.

"*Oof!*" His father hit the ground.

"Jeez, Bren, what's the matter with you?" said Dr Walker, hoisting himself to his feet and rubbing his tailbone.

"Dad! Don't sneak up on me like that!"

"Come on. Mum and Diane are waiting for you guys. We're going to check out the inside of the house."

The Walkers followed their father. Brendan felt a chill breeze as he approached the door with the 128 on it – but then again, the house *was* half off a cliff. The stone angel had so fascinated him that he'd almost failed to notice: the far side of Kristoff House was supported by metal stilts anchored in boulders far below on the beach. And hanging under the house were dozens of barrels.

"What are those…?" Brendan started to ask as he entered.

But he was silenced by the sheer beauty of the interior. Mrs Walker, too, was amazed; she had totally dropped negotiation mode. She was busy ogling antiques and checking her reflection in polished banisters. Dr Walker let out a low whistle. Cordelia said, "Wow, you could call this a great hall and not even be ironic."

"You are indeed standing in the front or 'great' hall," Diane said. "The interior has been impeccably restored, but the previous owners kept the original touches. Not bad for a termite-infested bear habitat, huh?"

Cordelia blushed. The room was filled with red-on-black and black-on-red Greek pottery (*reproductions,* Cordelia thought, *because the originals would be priceless),* a cast-iron coat-rack with curlicues, and a marble bust of a man with a wavy beard, which screamed *philosopher.* All of it was lit by spotlights, like in a museum. Brendan wondered how it was possible, but the place seemed twice as big inside as it looked from outside.

"This house was built for entertaining, from the time it was constructed," Diane said with a wide sweep of her hand.

"Who entertained here?" Cordelia asked.

"Lady Gaga," deadpanned Brendan, trying to hide his unease. *First no For Sale sign, then a creepy statue, now a house with an antique shop inside…*

"Bren," Mrs Walker warned.

Diane went on: "No one's had a party here for years. The previous owners were a family who paid for the restoration. They lived here briefly, but wanted a change. Moved to New York."

"And before that?" Brendan asked.

"Unoccupied for decades. Some of the cosmetic touches fell into disrepair, but you know these old houses were built to last. In fact, this one was built to float!"

"What?" Brendan asked.

"Are you kidding?" said Cordelia.

"The original owner, Mr Kristoff, wanted to make sure his house would survive an earthquake like the one he'd just been through. So he underslung the foundation with air-filled barrels. If the Big One comes and the house falls off the cliff, it's designed to hit the ocean and drift away."

"That is *so cool*," said Eleanor.

"No, it's absurd," said her father.

"On the contrary, Dr Walker – they're doing it now with homes built in the Netherlands. Mr Kristoff was ahead of his time."

Diane led the Walkers into the living room, which had a stunning view of the Golden Gate Bridge. That didn't seem right to Brendan – he thought it was on the opposite side of the house – but then he realised that they had turned around, doubling back from the great hall. Crystal vases, alabaster sculptures and a mounted suit of armour had distracted him… and so had the stone angel he knew was out there, reaching out her broken hand and staring with mossy eyes.

The living room had a Chester chair, a glass coffee table with driftwood for legs, and a Steinway piano. "Is the furniture for sale?" Mrs Walker asked.

"Everything's for sale." Diane smiled. "It's all included in the purchase price."

She moved on with all the Walkers except Brendan, who lingered by the view of the bridge. Growing up in San Francisco, he'd got used to seeing it every day, but from this angle, so close he was almost beneath it, the bridge's salmon colour struck him as unnatural. He wondered what the house's original owner, Mr Kristoff, had thought of the bridge when it was first constructed. Because if the house was built in 1907 – Brendan's mind quickly accessed dates and facts – then it was standing thirty years before the bridge was built, and the view back then would have simply been a great expanse of ocean, framed by two giant rocky outcroppings. Was Mr Kristoff dead by the time the bridge went up?

"Hello?" Brendan suddenly asked, realising he was alone. He rushed out of the living room to find Diane and his family.

Meanwhile, Cordelia was thinking about Mr Kristoff too. She'd heard that name before, but couldn't think where. It taunted her as she entered the next room, which she knew by smell alone: dust, musty pages and old ink.

"Welcome to the library," Diane said.

It was stunning. A vaulted ceiling spanned books stacked on mahogany shelves that reached all the way up the walls. Two brass ladders ran on casters to enable access to the shelves. Between them, a massive oak table lined with green-glassed bankers' lamps split the room. A few gleaming dust motes circled the table like birds on updraughts.

Cordelia absolutely had to see what books were on the shelves. She always did. She poked her nose up to the nearest one and realised where she'd heard of Mr Kristoff.

5

Cordelia could read anywhere. She had been reading on the car ride to 128 Sea Cliff Avenue even though she was sandwiched between her siblings going up and down San Francisco hills with a dyslexic in charge of the GPS. "Losing yourself in a book is *the best*," her mother always said, and Cordelia had a feeling her grandmother had said the same thing to Bellamy as a young girl.

Cordelia had started early, embarrassing her parents in a fancy restaurant at the age of four by reading a newspaper over an old lady's shoulder, causing the woman to shout, "That *baby* is *reading*!" As she got older, she moved on to her parents' collection of western literature: the Oxford Library of the World's Great Books, with their thick leather spines. Now she was into more obscure authors, people whose books she had to find in first edition or old paperbacks with names like Brautigan and Paley and Kosinski. The more obscure the better. She felt that if she read a writer that no one had heard of, she kept him or her alive single-handedly, like intellectual CPR. At school she got in trouble for sneaking books inside her textbooks (though Ms Kavanaugh never minded). In the last year she'd discovered a man whom Robert E. Howard and H. P. Lovecraft had cited as an influence, quite prolific, who'd written adventure novels in the early twentieth century.

"'Denver Kristoff'," she read from a book's spine. "Diane: the Kristoff who built this house was *Denver* Kristoff, the writer?"

"That's right. You've heard of him?"

"Never read, definitely heard of. His books don't even show up on eBay. Fantasy, science fiction… instrumental in the work of the people who later invented Conan the Barbarian and our modern idea of the zombie. Never got much critical acclaim—"

She had to stop speaking because of Brendan's exaggerated gagging.

"Will you stop that?"

"Sorry, I'm allergic to book geeks."

"Dad, we could be living in the home of a well-known obscure writer!"

"I'll take that under advisement."

Diane led the family out of the library (Dr Walker practically had to drag Cordelia) and presented a pristine kitchen, the most modern room they had seen so far. New appliances glittered under a sprawling skylight. It looked like a place germs would be afraid to enter. An impressive array of knives, in order from smallest to largest, hung magnetically over the stove. Eleanor asked, "Can we make cookies here?"

"Sure," Dr Walker said.

"Can we make *only* cookies here?"

"Viking, Electrolux, Sub-Zero," Diane checked off, leading the family past the stainless-steel, double-doored fridge. Brendan wondered if there might be something weird inside it, like a head, so he peeked… but he didn't see anything more disturbing than clinical emptiness.

Diane took the Walkers upstairs. The contemporary decor of the kitchen was instantly lost in a spiral wooden staircase that Eleanor insisted on climbing up and down and up again. The spiral stairs were wider than any the Walkers had ever seen; they served as the main stairs between the first and second floors. Upstairs, a broad hallway ran the length of the house, ending at a bay window and another, smaller staircase that led back down to the great hall.

The walls featured old portraits, in colour, with a faded pastel tint. In one, a grim-faced man with a square beard stood next to a lady in a frilled dress gripping a buggy. In the next, the same lady looked over her shoulder on a wharf as men in newsboy caps eyed her. In a third, an elderly woman sat beneath a tree holding a baby in a dress and bonnet.

"The Kristoff family," Diane explained, noting Brendan and Cordelia's fascination. "That's Denver Kristoff" – the man with the square beard – "his wife, Eliza May" – the woman on the wharf – "and his mother" – the woman under the tree with the baby. "I forget her name. Anyway. The pictures are just for show. When you move in – *if* you move in – you can put up pictures of your own family."

Brendan tried to imagine Walker photos on the wall: him and Dad at a lacrosse game with Dr Walker holding the stick incorrectly; Cordelia yelling at Mum because she didn't want her picture taken without make-up; Eleanor crossing her eyes and smiling too wide. If you took stupid pictures and added a hundred years, did they end up looking eerie and important?

"There are three bedrooms on this floor," Diane said. "The master—"

"Only three? You guys promised me I'd have my own room," Brendan said.

"The fourth is upstairs. In the attic." Diane pulled a string on the ceiling. A trapdoor swung down, followed by steps that folded out to lightly kiss the floor.

"Cool!" Brendan said. He climbed the ladder hand over fist.

Cordelia entered one of the bedrooms off the hall. It wasn't the master (which had a king-size bed and two bedside tables) but it was a nice-sized room with fleur-de-lis wallpaper. She said, "I'll take this one."

"Then which one is mine?" Eleanor asked.

"Guys, this is all hypothetical…" Dr Walker tried, but Cordelia pointed Eleanor to the third bedroom, which was more of a maid's bedroom – or a closet.

"I'm stuck with the smallest?"

"You are the smallest."

"Mum! It's not fair! How come I get the little room?"

"Cordelia's a big girl. She needs space," Mrs Walker said.

"Hear that, Cordelia? Mum says you need to go on a diet!" Brendan called from the attic.

"Bren, *shut up*! She means I'm *older*!"

Alone, upstairs, Brendan smiled… but then the attic began to hold his attention. It had a rollaway bed set up by the window, a bureau with various ornaments on top, and a bat skeleton on a shelf jutting out of the wall.

The bat skeleton was mounted on a smooth black rock with its wings outstretched. Its head tilted up like it was catching bugs. It was one of the creepiest things Brendan had ever seen… but he wasn't scared. He pulled out his phone to take a picture.

"Brendan, apologise to your sister!" Mrs Walker yelled, and Eleanor joined in: "Yeah, Bren, get down here!"

Of course when he wasn't scared of something, there was no one around to be impressed. Brendan descended the ladder. Cordelia glared at him.

"I'm sorry," he said. "You don't need to go on a diet. But – look what they have upstairs! I took a picture—"

Cordelia grabbed his phone and deleted the photo.

"Hey!"

"Now we're even."

"You didn't even look at it!"

Diane tried to hide her exasperation with a smile. "Shall we continue?"

The family followed her down the hall, passing a knob sticking out of a square cut into the wall. "What's that?" Eleanor asked.

"Dumbwaiter," Diane said curtly.

They reached the end of the hall. "That's it," Diane said, glancing out of the bay window at the Walkers' used Toyota, then back to Dr Walker. "You haven't asked the critical question."

"The price," Dr Walker said dolefully. Truth was, when he'd heard "rustic" and "charming", he'd thought the same thing as Cordelia: that the house was a fixer-upper he could afford. But two storeys plus an attic, fully furnished, with a library and bridge views, in Sea Cliff? This was a five-million-dollar residence.

Diane said, "The owners are asking three hundred thousand."

6

Brendan saw a look of disbelief ripple across his father's face. Then Dr Walker pulled himself together and put on his business voice. It was good to hear. Brendan used to hear it often, when his dad did interviews or advised other surgeons, but for the last month, since 'the incident', Dr Walker hadn't had occasion to make those sorts of calls. Now he spoke with purpose.

"Ms Dobson, we'll take it. Please draw up the papers and we'll close as soon as possible."

"Wonderful!" Diane opened a silver case to give Dr Walker a business card. Mrs Walker hugged her husband.

Eleanor asked, "What's that mean? We got the house? We're going to *live here*?"

Brendan stepped forward. "Why is it so cheap?"

"Bren!" Mrs Walker snapped.

"It's the same price as an apartment. Less, even. It doesn't add up. What are you trying to pull?"

"Your family's inquisitiveness is welcome," said Diane. "Brendan, the owners are trying to liquidate their investment. Like many families they've fallen on hard times, and they're willing to drop the price to get out – especially if it means helping others in a tough spot. You may have noticed that there's no For Sale sign on the lawn. The owners aren't looking to sell to any family – they're looking for the *right* family. A family in need."

She smiled. Brendan hated being the object of her pity. It would have been one thing if she only pitied him – that he could deal with – but she pitied all of them. And that was because of his father. It was so embarrassing. Dr Walker was trying to do it all backwards: reverse-engineer his reputation by getting an impressive house to land an impressive job at an impressive hospital with an administration that was impressed by his renown and willing to overlook 'the incident'. But he couldn't even impress this estate agent. Brendan felt like he'd be better off on his own, or maybe at boarding school like some of his friends. But there was no way his parents could afford boarding school.

Diane led the Walkers downstairs, through the great hall, to the front entrance. "I think you'll find Kristoff House a wonderful home."

"We shouldn't take it," Brendan whispered to Cordelia. "You know Dad's not thinking right these days. There's something fishy here."

"You're just scared."

"What? Me? No."

"Sure you are. You don't want to live with that creepy angel on the lawn."

"Excuse me? There was a bat skeleton in the attic and I wasn't scared of that."

"So? Doesn't prove anything. Nell, wasn't Bren scared of that statue?"

Eleanor nodded.

"I rest my case."

There was no way Brendan was going to let Cordelia have the last word. As his family walked out of the front door and headed down the pebbled path, he split off and ran to the stone angel, pulling out his phone to take another picture. He'd put his arm around the thing and grin and show the world he wasn't frightened of a hunk of rock with moss accents.

Except the stone angel wasn't there.

Brendan suppressed the urge to call out. Maybe he was just confused. Maybe the statue was on the *other* side of the house. But no: he remembered the broken hand was the right hand, and that it was a few inches from the exterior wall. *Who moved the statue?*

Brendan knelt to investigate the pine needles that carpeted the ground. There should have been a clear imprint where the base of the statue had been, where the needles were flat and damp, maybe with pill bugs scurrying around, but it looked like the statue had simply never been there—

Suddenly a face appeared. Inches from Brendan's own, hissing, its voice like a swarm of wasps leaving hell.

"You don't belong here."

She was a bone-white old woman, as tall as the stone angel, bald, with cracked lips pulled back over brown teeth. She stared at Brendan with glistening steel-blue eyes. She wore dirty layers of rags and no shoes; her toenails were amber, encrusted with soil. She was the crone that Brendan had feared, but a hundred times worse, and when she spoke, her breath was fouler than six-month-old compost.

"*Leave this place!*"

She wrapped her hand around Brendan's wrist. It felt like a rope. He tried to pull away, but she held him fast… and then she looked into his eyes. "Who are you?" she asked more quietly.

"B-Brendan Walker," he said.

"Walker?" she repeated.

Brendan had never been so scared. Not scared stiff – beyond that, scared into action, like someone had shot a spike of adrenalin into his back. He twisted and wrested his hand free. He ran, spit flying out of the side of his mouth. "*Mum! Dad!*"

Surely they'd seen her: she was a six-foot baldy with the body-mass index of a skeleton; she'd be tough to miss. He reached his family back at the Toyota after running across the lawn, which suddenly seemed to be the size of a football field.

"Bren, what's wrong?"

"Are you OK?!"

"I – you guys – you didn't—?" Brendan looked back. Suddenly the whole scene looked much smaller and safer to him. It couldn't have been more than twenty metres from the pavement to the house. The whole time he'd been running, his heart pounding in his chest, still seeing the old crone's face in front of him… that had been only seconds.

And the woman was gone.

The sun had moved. The side of Kristoff House was bathed in shadow. The stone angel might have been there or it might not. Shadows hid all sorts of things.

"Brendan…? Did something happen?" That was Cordelia. She was looking at him seriously; she knew he was freaked. Brendan started to explain – but what would be the point? He couldn't prove anything. He didn't want to sound like a little kid.

"Nothing," he said. "I just… I thought I lost this."

He turned on his PSP. He had never been happier to see the title screen of *Uncharted*. Back in a world that he understood and controlled, he slipped into the car.

A funny thing happened to Brendan on the drive back from 128 Sea Cliff Avenue. Every second that he put between himself and the old crone, he became more and more convinced that she hadn't been so scary after all. Dressed in rags, barefoot, with bad teeth… obviously she was a homeless lady. The more Brendan thought about it, the more it made sense: She lived in the yard. *That* was why the price was so low. She'd been spying on the Walkers, and she'd hidden when they'd spotted her – that was the darting shadow that Eleanor had seen. She loved the angel statue – she was obviously mentally disturbed; maybe she talked to it – and so she moved it (*never mind how*) when she saw Brendan and his sisters investigating. Then, when she had the chance, she sneaked up on him to scare him, to drive his family away. And she asked his name because… because she was crazy! What other reason did there need to be?

Brendan kept telling himself this as he went through the hypnotic motions of gaming, and soon he was not only convinced that the old crone wasn't dangerous or supernatural (*supernatural, come on*), but he was determined to go back and drive her from the property. After all, Brendan Walker wasn't somebody you could just push around. He was practically JV lacrosse.

The Walkers had been renting since 'the incident'. Their new apartment was much smaller than their old house, especially the kitchen, which was more of a corner than a room. That meant less cooking and more cheap takeout. The night after seeing Kristoff House, Dr Walker convened a family meeting over Chinese food in the living room.

"So what's up?" Brendan asked.

"I just want to make sure you're all comfortable with our decision to buy Kristoff House."

"You mean *your* decision," said Brendan. "We had no part in it."

"Fine," said Dr Walker. "But speak now if you have a problem."

"If we moved in, wouldn't it be Walker House?" asked Eleanor.

"I think we should call it one twenty-eight Sea Cliff Avenue, its proper address," said Mrs Walker. "Otherwise it sounds like we're moving into something that belongs to someone else."

It does belong to someone else, thought Brendan. *The old crone.* But he didn't want to sound scared. He said, "I like it fine. Better than this dump."

"I like it too," Eleanor said. She was using a sauce-dipped spring roll to gather up as much shredded carrot and celery as possible; it looked like the spring roll was wearing a wig. "The faster we move in there, the faster we can get Misty."

"Nell, how many times do we have to go through this—"

"But Mum *said* I could get her. Mum made me picture her—"

"You'll get your horse some day," Mrs Walker said, "if you eat your spring roll and stop playing with it."

Eleanor tackled the spring roll in four huge bites. She looked at her mother and spoke with a full mouth: "Do I get my horse now?"

Everybody laughed – even Brendan. You'd have a hard time getting them to admit it, but the Walkers liked dinners this way, quick and greasy, instead of with cloth napkins with rings.

"What about you, Cordelia?" Dr Walker asked.

"Let me show you something." Cordelia ducked out of the room and returned with an old book. It had a black cover, no dust jacket, and gold lettering nearly worn off the spine.

"*Savage Warriors* by Denver Kristoff," Cordelia announced. "First edition, 1910. I took it from the library. And look!" She pulled out her MacBook Air. "On Powell's Books they're selling this for five hundred dollars! So that library alone is worth, like, the closing cost of the house!"

"Cordelia," Brendan said, "you *stole* from the Kristoff House library?"

"You don't steal from libraries. You borrow. Not that you would know."

"No, your brother's right," said Dr Walker. "It's not our house yet, and you shouldn't have taken that—"

"That's right you shouldn't!" Brendan stood up. "Somebody might be really mad at you for stealing! You ever think of that?"

"Seriously, Bren?" Cordelia smirked. "Since when do you have a moral compass?"

Brendan didn't answer – partly because he didn't know what a moral compass was, partly because he was terrified of the old crone. Maybe she was a homeless lady, but maybe she wasn't. Maybe she *lived* at 128 Sea Cliff Avenue. Maybe she didn't take kindly to curious girls stealing books from her library. Brendan almost spoke up then about seeing her, about how he could still feel her hand around his wrist, about how that wrist felt *cold* even now, about how she had said "Walker" like it meant something… but he didn't want to be made fun of. He would handle the crone himself when they moved in. Like a man.

"Sorry," he said. "It's just… it's not right to steal."

"That's true," Dr Walker said, "and Cordelia, you'll be putting that book back next week."

"What happens next week?"

"We're moving in."

9

Spartan Movers was a removal company in San Francisco, the name of which was a source of huge embarrassment for Cordelia. "Why don't we just go with Low-rent Movers?" she asked her mum. But when she saw the truck, she realised it wasn't *spartan* like self-denying; it was *Spartan* like a citizen of ancient Sparta, with a plumed helmet for a logo.

The Spartan truck pulled up in front of Kristoff House, and a trio of burly men got out. The Walkers were already there, eager to get their stuff moved in. Brendan was more eager than anyone: he had visions of turning his attic bedroom into a teenage man cave where he could happily ignore the rest of his family. He started trailing one of the removal men as the man carried a bag of lacrosse equipment into the house.

"That goes in my room, the attic," Brendan said.

"No problemo," said the man, eyeing Kristoff House. It looked the same, except the lawn needed mowing. Brendan's dad would probably make him do it.

"Nice place," the man said. He was clearly one of those people who liked to talk. "Most folks are downsizing these days. But you guys are moving up."

"*Back* up," corrected Brendan as they walked down the path. When Dr Walker looked over, Brendan gave a big smile, pretending to help the mover with the bag. "We used to live in a place like this."

"What happened?"

"There was an incident," said Brendan, before realising he'd said too much.

"Oh yeah? What kinda incident?" asked the man. "Your old man was running schemes on the stock market and he got caught?"

"No."

"He did time in the joint for tax fraud?"

"Oh, no—"

"Did he wear a scuba suit to check the mail? Was he riding his bicycle naked in circles? What?"

Brendan stopped short: "Yes. Yes, you totally nailed it. Riding his bike naked in circles."

The removal man nodded and frowned as if he knew Brendan didn't want to hear any more from him. They moved into the kitchen… and Brendan's mind went back to the day that had changed everything.

Dr Walker had been a surgeon at John Muir Medical Center. His speciality had been gastric bypass surgery; he'd been heading for a senior position – but then one day he fell asleep in the break room during a shift and woke up standing over a patient, holding a bloody scalpel.

He had carved a symbol into the man's stomach.

It was an eye, with an iris and pupil in the centre and half-circles above and below.

Brendan had come home from school and found his mother and sisters in tears. His father couldn't remember disfiguring the man's stomach; Dr Walker had been taking sleeping pills to help him rest, and they had made him sleepwalk.

The patient had sued, of course. Dr Walker had lost his job. The lawsuit was still pending, and the Walkers had spent so much money fighting it that they'd been forced

to sell their old home and their two cars. It was so weird
– so crazy and unlikely – that Brendan still had trouble
believing it had really happened, even though he was living
with the results.

"You know, I heard weird stuff about this place," the
removal man said as they walked along the upstairs hall,
past the portraits of the Kristoff family.

"What?" Brendan asked.

"Maybe I'm no Harvard grad, but I'm a real good
listener and an even better eavesdropper. And I heard this
house was cursed. That's why the last family left."

"You believe in that stuff? Curses?"

"In San Francisco? With all kinds of hippies and freaks
running around? Anybody could get cursed."

Brendan had a question, but he wasn't sure if he could
ask it without sounding crazy. He pulled the string so the
attic stairs came down and went into the attic with the
removal man.

"Where you want the hockey stuff?" the mover asked.

"Lacrosse," Brendan said. "Put it anywhere." The man
put it by the window. Then Brendan said, "If this place is
cursed, how do I fix it?"

The man didn't seem to think that question was weird. "Best way to fix a curse is to find the person who set it up," he said, shrugging. Then he left Brendan to think about the old crone.

Out on the pavement, the removal man returned to the Spartan truck for his next item: a white trunk with bands of riveted bronze. It had rounded metal corners and the faded initials *RW* stencilled over a hefty lock.

"What's in that trunk?" Cordelia asked. She was standing outside with her father.

"Just some old family records," said Dr Walker. "You never noticed before? I've been lugging them around for years. Master bedroom!" he told the removal man. Two hours later the Walkers had settled in, hardly daring to believe that this was their new home. Since the purchase price had covered the furniture, everything inside was as beautiful as when they'd first visited: the pottery, the suit of armour, the grand piano… The Walkers' belongings seemed out of place, unworthy of their new surroundings. Even the box of groceries that they brought from their old house didn't seem to belong in the shiny kitchen. After making her family take a self-timed photo with the

Golden Gate Bridge in the background, Mrs Walker let her kids wander while she made tea in the stellar kitchen and her husband dozed beneath a sunbeam in the living-room Chester chair.

Cordelia went to the library to return *Savage Warriors* to the shelves, but was surprised to see there wasn't any space for it, as if the other books had multiplied in its absence. *Oh well,* she thought, putting it on the table and taking down a book called *The Fighting Ace.*

Eleanor went upstairs and bravely passed under the creepy old pictures, moving to where Diane Dobson had pointed out the dumbwaiter. She pulled the handle in the wall; it opened like a mailbox. She was just tall enough to see a small compartment hanging on what looked like two bicycle chains. She wanted to climb in, but she knew that her mother would have a fit, so she tossed her dolls inside the dumbwaiter and tried to figure out how to make them go down to the kitchen.

Brendan grabbed a lacrosse stick to use as a weapon and went outside to investigate the stone angel. He was sweating nervously and hated himself for it as he crept around the side of the house. He came to where the statue had been…

And it was still gone. Pine needles and twigs lay over the area in uniform distribution.

It was her, Brendan thought. He had no idea where the thought came from, but he knew he was right. He remembered how the angel had been missing a right hand. He tried to remember which hand the old crone had grabbed him with. He would put money on the left. *Eleanor saw her, and she turned into stone to hide herself. Now she could be anywhere.*

Brendan scanned the property. He didn't hear anything but a babbling squirrel and the irregular sibilance of cars passing on Sea Cliff Avenue. After a few minutes he decided he wasn't doing anything useful and made his way back inside.

She was right there, in the great hall, talking to his family.

"W hat are you doing here?" Brendan demanded, brandishing his lacrosse stick like a two-handed axe. "Leave my family alone!"

"Brendan!" his mother snapped. "Have you lost your mind? Put that *down*!"

The old crone turned to face him. She wasn't dressed in dirty rags any more. She wore a loose polka-dot dress and a floral bandanna that hid her baldness; her teeth were freshly cleaned and polished, almost white. She carried an apple pie in her left hand; her right was tucked into her dress pocket. "What's wrong, son? You seem troubled."

Brendan gritted his teeth. "You bet I'm troubled. Now drop the pie, put your hands over your head, and get out of our house—"

"Brendan! Give me that lacrosse stick! *Immediately!*" his father ordered.

"Dad, this old bag's evil. I'll bet she spiked that pie with arsenic—"

"You're playing too many video games. *Hand over the stick!*"

Silence gripped the room. Brendan gulped and gave his dad the lacrosse stick.

"Now apologise," ordered his mother.

Brendan took a deep breath, refusing to make eye contact with the old woman, and said under his breath, "Sorry."

"You're more than sorry. You're grounded for a month. You can't just *threaten* people," said his father.

"I'm not sure she's a person," Brendan mumbled.

"Bren," Cordelia said, "she was *introducing* herself. She's our next-door neighbour."

"Great."

"I apologise for my son's unconscionable behaviour," said Dr Walker, putting the lacrosse stick against a wall. "Brendan, go to your room; we'll discuss this shortly. Ma'am, we never had a chance to get your name."

"Dahlia Kristoff," the old crone said. "And please don't worry about your son. I understand about young boys. Especially these days. So many stimuli."

"Are you related to Denver Kristoff, the writer?" Cordelia asked breathlessly.

"He's my father."

Was your father, Brendan thought as he mounted the back stairs, *unless he's like two hundred.*

"I'm a fan," Cordelia said. She held up her copy of *The Fighting Ace.*

"It's so nice to meet a fellow bibliophile. Did you get that from my father's library?"

Cordelia nodded, a little embarrassed – but then again, it was her library now.

"I remember when he finished it. I was born here. See that old joker behind you?" Dahlia nodded to the philosopher bust in the great hall. "Used to call him Arsdottle. Never could pronounce his name correctly."

"How long did you live here?" asked Cordelia.

"Oh, not too long," replied Dahlia. "I've moved around a bit. Europe, the Far East… I've lived in places you wouldn't believe. But I could never get Kristoff

House out of my soul."

"Where do you live now?" Eleanor asked. "One thirty or one twenty-six?" Cordelia gave her a squeeze. She was getting better with numbers.

"Aren't *you* a precious one!" said Dahlia. "One thirty, the fine painted lady next door."

"The purple house with the white trim?" asked Mrs Walker. "It's beautiful."

"Thank you. And you are… *Walkers*, correct?" said Dahlia.

"How did you know that?" asked a slightly unnerved Dr Walker.

"The neighbours," replied Dahlia. "They like to talk. But they didn't tell me your Christian names—"

"She's lying!" Brendan called from the staircase where he'd been spying. "Don't listen to her—"

"Brendan. To. Your. Room," Dr Walker said. "I'm sorry, Mrs Kristoff—"

"Miss Kristoff."

"*Miss* Kristoff. We are the Walkers, yes." Dr Walker put on his business voice. "I'm Jacob. This is my wife, Bellamy; our daughters Cordelia and Eleanor; and…

um… Brendan… who is apparently refusing to leave the staircase."

"That's right!"

Dr Walker sighed.

"Such a pleasure," said Dahlia. "So what are you children 'into'?"

"Excuse me?" Dr Walker asked.

"What are your enthusiasms and interests? Isn't that how the young people put it today?"

"Reading," said Cordelia.

"Horses," said Eleanor.

"And your brother? What about him? Is he more adventurous?"

"None of your business!" Brendan yelled. "Why are you guys letting her stay here! You should be kicking her—"

"Brendan! I've got this," Dr Walker said. "I don't want to be rude, Miss Kristoff, but we have dinner to get to. We do look forward to being your neighbour. And we gratefully accept your pie."

Dahlia handed Dr Walker the gift and looked at each of the Walkers in turn. There was nothing in her eyes but equanimity.

"I know I ask too many questions. It's only because I don't have many friends left. Or much time."

"Oh, I'm sorry!" said Mrs Walker. "Your health…?"

"It's nothing to worry about. Nothing lasts forever. I shouldn't have even mentioned it! Please, enjoy your pie – and your evening."

With that she left, closing the door behind her.

"What a strange—" Cordelia started, but her father said, "*Shhh.*"

"What?"

"When you say goodbye to a person, you always wait ten seconds before talking about them." He counted down: "Two… one… go."

"What a *freak*," Brendan said, rejoining them. Dr Walker sighed at the futility of sending his son to his room. "I bet she isn't even sick. And you better throw that pie away. Definite anthrax alert."

"For once, Bren, I agree with you," said Dr Walker, dumping the pie in the trash.

"Hold on!" said Cordelia. "You guys aren't being fair. She could just be senile. She's obviously not really Kristoff's daughter. He built this house in… Bren?"

Her brother thought for a moment. "1907."

"Right, so what is she, a hundred?"

"If she was born here, she could be as old as a hundred and six. And you should see how she looks *before* she takes a shower. And gets teeth-whitening strips." Brendan was wondering how he would sleep tonight. Forget the lacrosse stick – he needed a flamethrower.

"She *was* a little creepy," Mrs Walker said. "I don't like the idea that she used to live here."

"Don't worry, it'll sort itself out." Dr Walker put an arm around his wife. "Let's just be thankful that the move is over and get dinner." He kissed Mrs Walker on the cheek.

"Who wants to try our new pizza place?" Mrs Walker asked. "It's called Pino's." She was already looking at her phone. "It's supposed to be delicious."

"I'm going upstairs," Cordelia said – and then, in a whisper to Brendan, "to find out a little more about Dahlia Kristoff."

"I'll come with you," Brendan whispered back, surprised at his sudden urge to work with his sister.

"No, you've got to talk your way out of being grounded," Cordelia said, leaving Brendan… who looked up to see his parents standing over him, ready to have a long talk with him about threatening people with weapons.

Upstairs, Cordelia took down a picture from the wall: the faded image of the elderly woman, who Diane Dobson had said was Kristoff's mother, holding a baby. She went to her room, got a nail file, and came back to the hallway. She used the nail file to open the frame, moving very slowly and carefully. Finally she got the picture free. On the back of it, perhaps in Denver Kristoff's own handwriting, it said: *Helen K w/Dahlia K, Mother's 70th, Alamo Square, 1908.*

Cordelia flipped the picture over to look at the baby: the infant Dahlia Kristoff. Her eyes had the same steely intensity—

"Cordelia!"

She nearly jumped out of her skin. It was her mother from downstairs. "Pizza's here!"

Cordelia shimmied the picture back into the frame, which was a very painstaking process that left her pizza downstairs almost cold by the time she got to it. She found her family on the living-room floor, digging into a pepperoni pizza without plates, pouring cups of soda for one another. Dr Walker had hooked up the TV and ordered an on-demand movie: the Marx Brothers' *Duck Soup*.

"The Marx Brothers? Again? We always watch the Marx Brothers!" argued Eleanor. "Can't we watch something in colour? Where the people are still alive?"

"It's a family tradition," said Dr Walker. And he was right. Whenever the family had something to celebrate, they'd order up a Marx Brothers classic. The opening credits for *Duck Soup* began to roll.

"What'd you find?" Brendan whispered to Cordelia.

"Dahlia Kristoff is in one of the pictures upstairs. And if that picture is dated correctly, she's a hundred and five years old."

"Did you see her hands in the picture?"

"Yes, why?"

"Because somewhere along the way she lost one. I have to tell you something, Deal. I didn't want to say, because I was embarrassed, but—"

But the doorbell rang.

11

"Probably a noise complaint from all your arguing," Dr Walker joked to Eleanor. He left his family and went to the great hall. He opened the front door without using the peephole. He was used to living in safe neighbourhoods.

Dahlia Kristoff stepped in swiftly. She wore her polka-dot dress, but no hat or shoes this time. She was completely bald. Dr Walker drew back from her splotchy red skull and yellow toes.

"Excuse me – *hello?* Miss? You can't come into my house!"

"*Shut up!*" Dahlia hissed, striding towards the living room.

Dr Walker followed, pulling out his phone to dial 911, but suddenly the phone jumped from his hand. It flew through the air and cracked against the philosopher bust, as if it had been snatched up by a powerful gust of wind. When Dr Walker retrieved it, it wouldn't turn on.

"Dad, who was it?" Brendan called, but instead of his father, Dahlia Kristoff stepped in. He froze.

"My God," Mrs Walker said, "what are *you* doing here? How dare you barge into our home—"

"*How dare you consider this your home?*" Dahlia shrieked, and then the transformation began.

Brendan backed up against the driftwood-legged coffee table, watching it all in slow motion. It was like IMAX 3-D but way better (and way worse). The old crone threw her hands up. Just as he'd suspected, her right hand ended in a knobby stump. Dahlia arched her back, stretching, stretching, as if to crack the bones in her spine, and then two grey *wings* sprang from the neck of her dress!

Brendan was terrified, stunned, and amazed all at once. His world had just got a lot bigger. But all he could think was: *I'm not gonna let this freak hurt me. And I'm not gonna let her hurt my family.*

Dahlia Kristoff's wings unfurled behind her to spread across the room. They weren't like angel wings; they were dusty and greasy-looking, filling the air with the stench of sulphurous rot.

"Mum, what's happening?" Eleanor cried.

"I don't know, honey," Mrs Walker said, grabbing her youngest with one hand and the cross around her neck with the other. Dahlia laughed – a breathy cackle, a skeleton's laugh.

"Get out!" Dr Walker yelled, crashing into the room, but the crone swung a wing and slammed him across the back, knocking him into the piano with a cacophonous *dong*. On TV, Groucho Marx slid down a fireman's pole.

Brendan tried to run for a weapon, but now Dahlia was flapping her wings, whipping the air up in the house, keeping him off balance. He stared at her. Something horrible was happening to her face. The fine blue veins under her old pale skin, which had been notable to begin with, rose to the surface, bulging as her wings beat. Soon they were joined by her red arteries, protruding from her face like lines of bark on a tree. Brendan thought she might explode and drench them all in blood.

"*You!*" Dahlia said, turning to Cordelia. "You stole from my library!"

"I was just – borrowing—" A gust of wind knocked

Cordelia against a wall. The contents of the room were swirling in a spiral now – a pizza box, cups of soda, a Pino's menu, the TV remote. Brendan had to clutch the couch to stay upright.

"*For the honour of my father!*" Dahlia Kristoff howled. "For all the evil done upon him by the Walkers! For the disturbance of the great book! For the craven consultation with Dr Hayes! For Denver Kristoff, who lives again as he lives always! A life for a life, the Wind Witch has spoken, let a page torn be a page reborn!"

Slam! The shutters closed on the living-room windows. Brendan heard them slam in the kitchen and library too. Then the glass coffee table rose and hurled towards him. He ducked, but it spun towards Mrs Walker. She was kneeling, praying. It smacked her in the head.

"*Mum!*" Brendan yelled. His mother hit the floor, covered in broken glass, bleeding from her forehead.

"Get down!" Dr Walker screamed to his children as he lunged towards his wife. But the Chester chair got him – the same one he'd been sleeping in that afternoon – hitting his skull with a nauseating *crack*. He slumped over. For some reason Brendan flashed to his mother asking Diane Dobson

Is the furniture for sale? and Diane saying *Everything's for sale.*

The Wind Witch – that's what she had called herself; *the Wind Witch has spoken* – blew Mr and Mrs Walker into a corner. They lay unconscious against each other. Brendan, Cordelia and Eleanor were far away from them, by the piano.

The foundation of Kristoff House began to shake.

Brendan wondered if it would tip over and slide into the ocean. The television tilted up and flew at him, the Marx Brothers looking demonic until the cord came out of the wall and they disappeared. The TV shattered on the wall behind him, sending shards of plastic and LCD whirling around – "*Nell, close your eyes!*"

Brendan's younger sister was curled into a ball. Books were flying into the room now from the library, clobbering Brendan and his sisters, attacking like those terrible birds in that Hitchcock movie Brendan had seen once. Each time a book neared him, its pages open and fluttering, he heard *voices* inside, gibbering in aged accents, demanding to be released.

"*Deal!*" Brendan called. All he cared about was surviving – and making sure his family survived. His parents were unconscious on the other side of the room; he couldn't help them at this moment. *But I'm supposed to protect my sisters.*

He couldn't see Cordelia. The wind was all-consuming; the debris blinded him to everything. He squeezed his eyes shut, rubbed them, and forced them open. Right in front of him floated three books, leather volumes that suddenly seemed to grow, expanding from hardcover-size to almanac-size to encyclopedia-size. *Impossible!*

Brendan screamed, but he could no longer hear himself, and then he saw that the room was larger, the ceiling now twenty metres from the floor and rising every second, as if the house were warping and stretching. And then, while the Wind Witch rose to the ceiling and stared down from a towering height, like an avenging angel sent by the wrong side, one last thing entered the room: the bookshelves from the library. Massive, sickeningly heavy even without the books, they slid in one after another, levitating higher and higher, swirling to an apex above and crashing down – and then all was black and silent.

Brendan came to in a pile of rubble that used to be his new living room. He struggled out from under the heavy shelving that lay on top of him and checked himself for crippling injuries. He felt like he'd been put in a bag of rocks and shaken, but aside from cuts and bruises he was OK.

He looked around the living room. It was like the pictures he'd seen of that horrible tsunami in Japan, where a slew of debris was thrown across the land. What used to be individual chairs and tables and books was now a foot-deep pile of scrap. The shutters were still closed.

"Mum?" Brendan called. "Dad?"

He saw part of the pile move. It looked like a mound with an earthworm underneath. Brendan ran over as Cordelia reached an arm up and dragged herself out.

"Deal! Are you OK?" Brendan asked.

"I think… I blacked out. What about you?"

"I blacked out too… after a lot of insane stuff. These books grew in front of me – they were massive – and then that… I don't want to say her name…"

"Witch. Wind Witch," said Cordelia. "That's what Dahlia called herself."

"Right, fine. That Wind Witch flew up to the ceiling and knocked me out. Where are Mum and Dad?"

Cordelia's eyes got very big. She started to call desperately: *"Mum! Dad!"*

Brendan joined in: *"Mum! Please! Hello? Where are you?"*

No answer. Brendan's eyes welled up, but he didn't let any tears fall. "What about Nell?" he asked.

"Nell! Eleanor!" Cordelia began. They stumbled over broken furniture, searching and calling, pawing through piles of splintered wood, trying to avoid slicing their hands on shattered glass. Brendan felt guilty – what kind of older brother was he? He hadn't even been able to keep his little sister safe.

A musical *plink* made him turn his head.

"What was that?" Cordelia asked.

It came again, a tiny chime, like a muted string being plucked. Brendan and Cordelia moved towards it. "Nell?"

"Mum?"

"Dad?"

They reached the wreckage of the Steinway. It wasn't as ruined as the rest of the furniture; although its legs were snapped off, it still had its sinuous piano shape. The *plinks* were coming from inside. Brendan and Cordelia lifted together...

And there was Eleanor, curled up on the strings. She picked at one. "I think that's an A."

"Come here, you." Cordelia offered Eleanor a hand while Brendan held the piano open. Once she was out, her brother and sister hugged her so hard that they all fell over.

"Did you black out?" Brendan asked.

"No, I was awake the whole time."

"What did you see?"

"That... *angel thing* rose to the ceiling, the whole house got really tall, and everything went black."

"That's what we saw! You *did* black out!"

"No, I was awake. It was the *world* that went black. *She* made it happen. I *told* you I saw her when we first looked at the house, and you didn't believe me, remember? And now look what happened!"

"How do you know it was her?" Cordelia asked. "It could've—"

But Brendan interrupted his sister: "I saw her too. The Wind Witch."

"What? When?"

"When I freaked and said it was 'cause I lost my PSP? I saw her. She grabbed my hand and… she asked me my name."

"Bren!" Cordelia shoved her brother. "Why didn't you tell us?"

"How was I supposed to tell you? Would you have believed me? No, you would've told me I was trying to get attention."

"No, I wouldn't! I listen to you – *when you actually have important things to say*. Which is very rarely—"

"*You're* the one who got us into this situation, Cordelia. *You* stole from the library—"

"I *borrowed*—"

"She specifically said, 'You stole from my library!' Do you remember that, or were you already blacked out?"

"Stop fighting!" Eleanor yelled. "Where are Mum and Dad?"

Brendan and Cordelia had to catch their breath. "We don't know," Brendan admitted.

Cordelia struggled to keep her face composed so she wouldn't scare Nell. "They're gone."

"Then let's find them," said Eleanor.

They started looking by the wall where they had last seen their parents. There was a streak of blood on the paint, but otherwise no sign. Eleanor started to cry when she saw the blood. Cordelia put an arm around her. The siblings made their way into the great hall. It was as unrecognisable as the living room, with the coat-rack sticking out of a wall and the pottery reduced to jagged jigsaw chunks.

"Arsdottle's fine," said Brendan, looking at the philosopher bust.

"Because the Wind Witch liked him when she was a girl," Cordelia said. "She spared him."

They spent a quiet moment staring at the implacable bust – and then entered the library. Cordelia cringed. It was bare now, with the shelves gone, the ladders smashed and the long table split in two. The books had mostly sailed into the living room, but some were still there, strewn around with their covers open. Cordelia picked one up.

"Guys, it's *The Fighting Ace*! This is the book I was reading when the Wind Witch attacked. Isn't that crazy?"

Brendan wondered briefly if it was one of the three books that had expanded in front of him, but they had bigger problems now. "Who cares?"

"*I* do," insisted Cordelia. Brendan snorted and led Eleanor towards the kitchen. Cordelia carefully found her place in the novel and salvaged a sliver of wood for a bookmark. No matter how bad things got at Kristoff House, with *The Fighting Ace* she could escape.

The kitchen showcased more destruction: the fridge was dented and leaking; a burner grate from the stove had smashed through a cabinet and destroyed the dinnerware; a family-size box of Cheerios had spilled its guts into the sink. The kids ran upstairs, frantically calling for their parents, but there was no sign.

The second floor was also in ruins, with two exceptions. The pictures in the hallway were in perfect condition. That made sense, because they were of Dahlia's family; she wouldn't hurt them. But Cordelia discovered something in the master bedroom too: the white-and-bronze *RW* trunk.

"Bren? Nell? Look. Everything is demolished, but this trunk is fine."

"Maybe the Wind Witch protected it," said Brendan. "Maybe there's something inside she wanted to keep."

"Or," said Cordelia, "it's magical. Guarded by a ward."

"A what?"

"You know, like a magic symbol that protects something."

Cordelia paused. "What about 'RW'? Who do you think he is?"

"Maybe it's a *she*," Eleanor said.

"Rutherford Walker," said Brendan, recalling the name. "Dr Rutherford Walker, to be exact."

"Who?"

"Our great-great-grandfather. Dad told me his name once."

Cordelia was impressed. "You remembered from hearing that once? How come you don't have better grades?"

"Because at school there's nothing worth remembering."

"Well, this trunk could be a clue," said Cordelia. "Remember what the Wind Witch said: 'For the evil done him by the Walkers—'"

"'For *all* the evil done *upon* him by the Walkers—'"

"Bren, she was talking about revenge. And *him* was her father, Denver Kristoff. It must be revenge for something that happened decades ago. Maybe Kristoff started a blood feud against us."

"Why would he do that?"

"I don't know; why does anybody start blood feuds?"

"Maybe that old bag was *crazy*. She said a lot of stuff back there. 'The craven consultation with Dr Hayes'? Who's he? What's that even mean?"

"I don't know... but our family used to live in San Francisco."

"And you think some relative of ours just happened to know the guy who built this house?"

"Not just some relative. Dr Rutherford Walker, our great-great-grandfather, who owned this trunk. What did Dad tell you about him?"

Brendan sighed. "He was the one who settled here. He jumped off a boat when it anchored in the bay, because San Francisco was so beautiful. And he stayed."

"Maybe Dahlia Kristoff fell in love with him."

"Like he'd date a bald chick."

"She wasn't bald *then*, obviously—"

"Guys!" Eleanor yelled. "We're *supposed* to be looking for Mum and Dad!"

"We are, Nell— just help me get this trunk open—"

"No! We have to find them *now*!" Eleanor's mouth trembled. "Aren't you worried that they're *dead*? Didn't you see that table hit Mum and that chair hit Dad? And there's *blood* on the wall downstairs? I don't want to be an orphan! I want Mum! *I want Mum!*" Her face collapsed into angry angles. She doubled over, crying, pressing her fists into her eyes.

"Nell, it's all right," Brendan said, wrapping her up. "Close your eyes, OK?"

"They're already *closed*!"

"OK, so keep them closed. And… ah… think about a happy time."

"Like before our parents were *gone*?"

"Ah, yes… Deal, a little help?"

"Think about the future," Cordelia said, gently pulling Eleanor's fists away from her face. "When we *find* Mum and Dad."

Eleanor held back her next set of tears. "Are your guys' eyes closed too?"

Cordelia looked to Brendan. He shut his eyes. She shut hers. They all pictured the same thing: their smiling parents, alive and well, occasionally bickering, often annoying, but full of love. "They're closed," Cordelia assured.

"OK, so we're gonna open them, and then we're gonna make it our *mission* to find Mum and Dad. Agreed?"

"Agreed," said Brendan and Cordelia. They all opened their eyes and kept searching.

They didn't find anything in the other bedrooms or bathrooms (Eleanor did pull her dolls out of the dumbwaiter, which pleased her), so the only place left was the attic. Brendan pulled the string, brought down the steps, and led them up.

"What time is it?" Cordelia asked. The attic was a wreck. The rollaway bed was tossed into a corner.

"I don't know, why?"

"Because it looks like daylight outside." Cordelia nodded to the window. The shutters were closed, as were all the shutters in the house, as if the Wind Witch had tried to conceal the mayhem she had caused. Thin shafts of sunlight shone through the slats – and through the translucent white curtains that were on every window.

Did we get through the night? Brendan wondered. He'd never been so happy to think about dawn in his life. He walked to the window – and ducked as a small black shape dive-bombed him.

"A bat!" Brendan yelped. "Watch out, guys!"

Cordelia screamed way louder than Brendan or Eleanor expected, then hurtled towards the attic steps.

The bat, which couldn't have been more than ten centimetres long, plummeted towards her. Cordelia slapped at her face and nearly broke her neck tumbling down the steps before closing the attic door behind her. "Kill it!" she yelled.

"Cordelia?" Brendan said. "It's just a bat! What's your problem?"

"I *hate* bats!" Cordelia answered from downstairs. "Where did it come from?"

Brendan looked at the stand where the bat skeleton had been. Sure enough, the stand was there. But the skeleton was gone.

"Remember that bat skeleton I told you I saw? Well... I think it came to life."

"If it's a magical zombie bat, you shouldn't mess with

it!" Cordelia said, running her fingers through her hair. She was sure she could feel the bat's sinewy wings brushing against her scalp.

In the attic, Brendan motioned for Eleanor to help him. They approached the window as the bat circled frantically. They opened the shutters; sunlight flooded the room. The bat retreated to a corner in the rafters.

"Is it gone?" Cordelia asked from downstairs. "Can I come up?"

But Brendan and Eleanor didn't answer. They couldn't. They were too busy staring out of the window.

A primeval forest lay outside Kristoff House.

Trees with trunks as thick as houses reached up so high that Brendan and Eleanor couldn't see the tops no matter how they craned their necks. Beams of dappled light broke on giant ferns spread like green fans over mossy logs. It looked like the painted background in a dinosaur exhibit, still and calm and even a bit fake. Trees marched into the distance, blending into a uniform brown-and-green curtain.

"Where are we?" gasped Eleanor.

Brendan opened the window. Sounds swept in: caws, chirps and rustlings in the air.

Downstairs, Cordelia noticed that her siblings were unusually quiet, so she went back into the attic to see what was going on. "Hello?" she said, stepping to the window. "*Whoa.*"

The trees started just a metre from the house. Smaller trees stood below them, where the honey-hued light broke through. A thin haze lay at eye level, listing up and down. They could make out the sound of a brook babbling in the distance and, behind the caws and chirps, a loud, grating buzz. The haze entered the attic, carrying a tang of dirt and pine and a balm of sweet flowers and sap.

"Where's our street?" whispered Eleanor.

"Maybe the Wind Witch moved our house somewhere," Cordelia said.

"Jurassic Park?" asked Eleanor.

"Humboldt County."

"Does Humboldt County have *those*?" Brendan pointed to one of the towering trees in the distance. Circling it was the source of the buzzing – a monstrous dragonfly with the wingspan of a condor.

The dragonfly's body was dull green, its wings clear mesh. It drifted up and down as it circled around the trunk, disappearing and reappearing, its purple eyes as big as dinner plates. It was so huge that the Walker children could see its complicated mouth parts twitching.

"Close the window!" Cordelia yelled.

Brendan leaned forward. "It can't hurt us. It's… what's the word? Vegan?"

"*Herbivorous*. Seriously, Bren, close it."

Brendan had another idea: he stuck his second and third finger between his lips and whistled. It was one of those skills he was proud of that his sisters hated.

"Bren!"

"I just want to see if he'll come closer!"

The sound aggravated the bat in the rafters. It dived for the window. Cordelia shrieked as it flew past her and darted outside. The Walker kids watched it zigzag through the mist, threading between the trees – and then the dragonfly whipped out a long tongue and nabbed it.

Eleanor screamed as the dragonfly drew the bat into its mouth and started grinding it into digestible mush. The giant insect buzzed towards the house as it ate, its purple eyes focused on the Walkers like they were next.

Brendan slammed the window shut and they all ran from the attic, not stopping until they got to the kitchen with its comforting (if damaged) stainless-steel appliances. Cordelia promptly opened all the shutters, locked all the windows, and turned to Brendan.

"Not exactly herbivorous," said Cordelia.

"Where *are* we?" Eleanor asked. "Bugs aren't supposed to eat bats! It's the other way round!"

"Obviously it was different in dinosaur times," said Brendan. "I think we were sent back to the prehistoric era." He was reminded of those books Cordelia used to read to him when he was five – the ones with the tree house that travelled through time.

"I don't know if dragonflies ever got *that* big," Cordelia said. "I'm not sure where we are…"

She stopped, noticing a black plastic corner peeking from under the fridge. Her mobile. She pulled it out; it was scuffed but intact. It sprang to electronic life.

"Does it work?" Brendan asked.

Cordelia closed her eyes and made a wish, but when she opened them, she saw what she expected. "No bars."

"Let me see!" Eleanor grabbed the phone and tried Mum, but got CALL FAILED.

Brendan sighed. "That's what you get for not having four-G."

"Maybe the landline works," Cordelia suggested. Brendan took the cordless white receiver off the wall.

He looked at his sisters. They looked like they were about to crack, like they needed some good news. Brendan briefly considered faking a call to 911, so he could give them some hope, but before he could decide if that was a good idea, all the lights in the house went out.

"What did you do?" Eleanor demanded. It wasn't just the overhead lights; the LEDs on the microwave and stove were out too.

"Nothing!" Brendan said, putting the phone back in its cradle. Sunlight slanted through the curtains.

"I was worried this might happen," said Cordelia. "We must've been running on a backup generator since the attack."

"We have a backup generator?"

"We must have *something* – it's probably in the basement. I don't think there's a 'grid' out here."

"So let's start it back up."

"With what, Bren? Generators need fuel."

"Maybe there are fuel cans down there! Come on! We

need to do *something*. Without power we'll starve—"

"But what if there's something *else* in the basement?" asked Eleanor.

"Like Mum and Dad," said Cordelia. The Walkers looked at each other with a mixture of hope and fear, imagining the ways they could find their parents: safe and well… or laid out on the floor, cold.

"We need to be strong, not psych ourselves out," said Brendan, trying to sound brave and unexpectedly pulling it off. "There's gotta be a flashlight somewhere." He rifled through kitchen drawers until he found a Maglite as thick as Eleanor's arm. He tested it – it worked – and shone it on an unadorned door at the back of the room.

"Who's going first?"

"You've got the flashlight," said Eleanor.

Brendan reluctantly opened the door. Rickety wooden steps led down to a cool, cavernous basement that smelled of cedar and dust.

"Was this the part of the house that hung over the cliff?" Cordelia asked.

"I think so. I wonder if the barrels are still there."

Brendan panned left and right so nothing could jump

out at them. Cordelia jammed a shoe in the doorway so they couldn't get locked in.

They went down the steps. Stacks of cans, a wheelbarrow, and a sledgehammer lay in one corner of the basement; a tent and power tools lay in another. Between them was a black box on six wheels, the size of a mini fridge, pressed against the wall and plugged in.

"Is that it?" Brendan asked.

"I think so…" said Cordelia. She hopped on one leg, not wanting to let her single shoeless foot touch the floor, but when it did, she found it wasn't so bad; the floor was worn-down wood, almost soft. Brendan read the yellow sign printed on the box: "'BlackoutReady IPS Twelve Thousand.' That sounds good."

He illuminated the box's control panel; it was completely dead. "Where does the fuel go? Maybe there's a manual."

Brendan whipped around the flashlight, saw something on the floor – and screamed.

He was staring at a human hand.

Brendan jumped, knocking over Cordelia and Eleanor. The flashlight hit the floor and rolled, coming to rest beside a rusted old sewing machine. The beam of light pointed to a mannequin on the floor in a half-finished Victorian dress. The mannequin was missing a hand.

"Nice one, Bren," Cordelia said. She picked up the fake hand; it was made of wax.

"Yeah," said Eleanor. "You're freaking out over a dummy. At least Cordelia got scared of a real bat."

"Whatever." Brendan took the flashlight and refocused on the BlackoutReady, finding the instructions on top. He read aloud, "'The generator will automatically begin recharging through the input plug when power returns.'" He groaned. "*If* power returns."

"What are we gonna do?" Eleanor asked.

"Sit here and wait to get killed by witches or giant dragonflies. Whatever comes first."

"Don't say that! Deal?"

"I don't think there's anything we *can* do."

"No!" Eleanor grabbed the flashlight and pointed it accusingly at her siblings. "We had a mission, remember? To find Mum and Dad!"

"That's right, Nell. But we've checked the whole house, including the basement, and they aren't here."

"What about outside? We haven't looked there yet."

"That's where the giant dragonflies are!"

"I don't care what's out there. We need to search for them while it's still light out. You guys can stay here if you want."

Eleanor stomped up the basement stairs. Brendan and Cordelia glanced at each other and rushed after her; she had the only light.

Back on the first floor, the Walkers opened all the shutters to let in enough light for them to see by. Then, in the kitchen, Brendan insisted on some self-defence measures before the group ventured out. He took a chef's knife from the magnetic rack that was now on the floor, and he outfitted Cordelia with a steak knife and Eleanor with a barbecue fork. "Hold your weapon like a hammer," he instructed, "with the blade pointed up."

"I don't have a blade," protested Eleanor.

"Your fork, then. In a fight you can use your hand to deliver butt-end knife strikes – Nell, that's not funny. Stand with your legs shoulder-width apart. Don't you guys know anything? Ugh, forget it."

Brendan led his sisters out of the kitchen, past the suit of armour that was knocked over in the hall. "Hold on." He went back to the kitchen, grabbed some duct tape, and taped the breastplate around Cordelia. Then he put the helmet on and gave Eleanor the gauntlets, which were big enough to reach from her elbows to her wrists. Thus armed, looking better prepared for Halloween than for a fantastical forest, the Walker children opened the front door and stepped outside.

Brendan squinted in the light. The helmet hadn't been such a good idea: the eye slits were meant for someone with further-apart eyes. He tried to take it off, but it was stuck on his head. Cordelia tipped her head back and saw the tops of the trees, dozens of metres up, against slivers of blue sky.

"Mum!" Eleanor called. "*Mummy!* Are you out here?"

"*Dad!* Hey, Dad, can you hear us?" Brendan said. "We're safe! Kind of…"

For a moment, the birds and bugs dipped into quiet… and then they started up again, filling the void as if the Walkers had never spoken. The children circled the house, sticking together, weapons drawn, calling out as they went. Brendan longed for anything familiar, even the stone angel. He noted the terrifying uniformity of the wilderness that surrounded them. Apart from the distant brook they had spotted through the attic window, there wasn't anything to indicate direction. The only way to tell which way was which was by looking at the shadows of the trees. *And if we didn't go back in time, who's to say we're not in some weird place where the sun rises in the west and sets in the east?*

When the Walkers came back around to the front door, they were no closer to finding their parents, but their calls had attracted something else.

A wolf, over two metres from tail to snout, was sniffing the ground in front of their home.

16

The wolf raised its head, revealing scarred, matted fur and milky, rabid eyes. It growled, stretching the noise out like a fake smile, exposing double rows of wet, razor-sharp teeth. It took a step towards them.

"Bren!" Cordelia whispered. "What do we do?"

Brendan tried to remember what he'd been taught in Boy Scouts about animal attacks – you were supposed to not move, stay quiet, and be calm; the animal wouldn't bother you if you didn't bother it – but that seemed irrelevant under the gaze of this creature, which clearly intended to eat them. All he could do was tense his muscles and gulp. The wolf bent its head over Eleanor. It was fifteen centimetres taller than her; it looked capable of swallowing her whole. The line of its mouth ran nearly all the way up its triangular head. Spittle gathered where its black lips were subsumed by fur.

The wolf sniffed Eleanor. Her breath came in tight jerks. Tears streamed down her face. The wolf opened its jaws. She closed her eyes, hyperventilating, smelling its meaty breath—

And the wolf stopped, cocked its head, and ran off behind the house.

Brendan couldn't believe it. He caught Eleanor as her knees gave out, hugging her with Cordelia, using all his strength to tear off his helmet and kiss her hair.

"What happened?" Eleanor asked. "I thought I was gonna *die*!"

"The wolf must've been scared by us."

"By what, our fierce appearance?" Cordelia said.

"*Maybe,*" suggested Brendan.

"Don't be stupid. It heard something. Listen."

They all heard it now, far off in the woods: hoofbeats.

"Horses?" Eleanor asked hopefully.

The sound grew louder, drumming through the ground into their legs and the pits of their stomachs. "Everyone inside," Cordelia said.

"But Deal," Eleanor began, "I want—"

"*Now.* Someone's coming!"

Cordelia rushed to the entrance of Kristoff House. Brendan followed, dragging Eleanor with him. They slammed the door and turned all the locks. Brendan tried to set the house alarm, frantically pressing buttons on the keypad.

"Bren!" said Cordelia. "There's no electricity!"

"Right, my bad."

Cordelia led them to a window, inched open a shutter, and peeked out.

"What do you see?" Eleanor asked.

"*Shh.*" The truth was that Cordelia found it difficult to describe what she saw without sounding completely insane.

A band of warriors was riding up to the house on horseback. They were muscular and massive and terrifying, from the glinting helmets on their heads to the knifelike spurs that rattled on their leather boots. They had thick, bristly beards and big full-plate armour that made her breastplate look like a toy. They carried swords, axes and bows. Their boots were caked with dried mud… or was it blood?

"How many horses are there?" asked Eleanor.

"Seven, I think, but Nell, that doesn't matter—"

"Let me see!" Eleanor pushed her sister aside. "Oh my gosh!"

Brendan crowded her out. "What is this, *Lord of the Rings*, the reality show?"

The siblings jostled for position, finding a way to all peer out. The warriors dismounted and tied their steeds to trees. They approached the house with caution. The one who was clearly the leader had a maroon feather sticking up from his helmet like a plume of blood. He took off the helmet to reveal pockmarked skin and a scar running from his ear to his chin. When he turned to speak to his men, the Walkers saw the glint of his black, suspicious eyes.

"A witches' den. This was not here yesterday," he declared.

One of his compatriots, a red-haired, red-bearded man, grabbed his arm: "Slayne, m'lord, could be a trap."

Slayne (*good name*, thought Brendan; *he looks like he's slain a lot of people*) grinned, twisting his scar like a second smile, bearing blackened stumps of teeth. "If there are witches… we need to get inside. And quickly kill them all."

"Um, may I suggest we go to the attic?" whispered Cordelia.

The Walkers dashed away from the window.

At the front door, Slayne grabbed the knob, found it locked, and turned to his red-headed number two. "Krom?"

Krom handed him a battle-axe. Slayne swung. The first blow left a gaping hole in the door. The second sent it flying off its hinges.

Slayne and his men entered, on guard.

"A great battle was waged here," said Slayne. He drew his sword, stabbed it through the remains of Bellamy Walker's iPad, and lifted it off the ground. "And at least one of the parties *was* a witch. This appears to be some sort of occult toy for children."

Slayne led the warriors through the living room and library as the Walkers huddled in the attic. They could hear the warriors' clomping boots and gruff voices, but not their words.

"We can't just *sit* here," Eleanor said. "We've got to find out what they want. Maybe they know where Mum and Dad are!"

"How do you propose to find that out?" Brendan asked.

"Watch." Eleanor opened the attic door and started down to the second-floor hallway.

"No, Nell!"

"Stop!"

But it was too late. Eleanor was already opening the door to the dumbwaiter. The warriors were in the kitchen, below her, and sound travelled directly up the hollow shaft. It was like she was in the midst of the warriors as they investigated their alien surroundings.

"This appears to be a witches' torture chamber," Slayne said. Eleanor heard the microwave door pop open. "Possibly a box for shrunken victims." Eleanor stifled a laugh.

In the kitchen, Slayne opened the fridge and paused. Here was a pleasant surprise. His men were all hungry, and the power hadn't been out long. Slayne tossed an apple aside and went for a jar of Hellmann's mayonnaise. Behind him, Krom ripped open a box of Cap'n Crunch, sniffed it, ate a handful, and started pouring it into his mouth: "It'th *good*!" Slayne unscrewed the mayo and scooped out a big clump.

Upstairs, Brendan and Cordelia poked their heads over the attic steps to get a report from Eleanor.

"They're eating our food!" Eleanor said. Then she heard Slayne's voice through the dumbwaiter.

"This white sauce is mine, men. Touch it under penalty of death. It's so good, I do believe, when we return to Castle Corroway, I'll eat my horse with it. He's getting on in years; it's time for a younger steed—"

The men all laughed. That set Eleanor off.

"He can't kill a horse!" she said, climbing into the dumbwaiter, gauntlets on, brandishing her barbecue fork.

"Nell, stop! You can't—" Brendan yelled, but she had already closed the door.

It was pitch-black in the dumbwaiter. Eleanor could hardly move. If she'd been a foot taller, she never would have fitted inside. She twisted to grab one of the bicycle-chain-like cables that the container rode on and pulled one way. The dumbwaiter inched up. So she pulled the other way and started down, moving quickly. The rusty pulleys squeaked. With every foot she descended the voices of the warriors grew louder.

"Hand me that sweetened meal, Krom!"

"Find your own!"

"We could set up camp here and run raids over the East!"

"It could do with a few slaves to tidy up—"

Halfway down Eleanor started to think she'd made a terrible mistake. Slaves? Raids? This wasn't some TV show;

these men would cut her to pieces. But she couldn't reverse course and be a coward. Not with Bren and Deal upstairs depending on her.

The dumbwaiter stopped at the kitchen with a metallic *chunk*.

"What was that?" Slayne asked. Eleanor heard him approach. He was only a metre away, on the other side of the wall – and then he opened the dumbwaiter door.

His black eyes met Eleanor's. He had mayonnaise in his beard. His rancid-sweat smell hit her like a punch.

"Why, it's a little witchling," Slayne chortled to his companions, turning his head—

And Eleanor stuck him in the cheek with her barbecue fork.

"*Raagh!*" Slayne brought his hand to his face, shocked that the girl had cut him. Then he plunged his sword into the dumbwaiter. Eleanor shrank back and threw up an arm—

Clang! The blade glanced off her gauntlet. "*Help!*"

Slayne pulled back for another thrust. Eleanor felt a jolt – and the dumbwaiter began to rise rapidly. The next sword strike hit the wall of the shaft below Eleanor, just missing her. She heard Slayne's bellow of frustration as she moved up in herky-jerky starts until she reached the second floor. Light entered the dumbwaiter… and with it the shadows of Cordelia and Brendan.

"Get out!" They yanked her into the hall. "They're coming!"

A thunderous clamour of metal sounded from the spiral steps. "Kill her!" roared Slayne.

The Walkers ran into the attic, closing the door and locking it. "Nell! What were you *thinking?*" Cordelia demanded.

Eleanor started to explain – when they heard the deep crunch of an axe biting into wood behind them. They turned to see the tip of Krom's axe poking through the attic door. It disappeared and struck again. Chunks of wood fell away, leaving a hole. A sword stuck up and slashed around.

"I'm so sorry! *I'm so sorry!*" Eleanor cried. "*I was just trying to be brave, and now we're all gonna die!*"

Brendan ran to the rollaway bed. There wasn't much time. Krom kept widening the hole – any minute now it'd be big enough to let all the warriors in. Brendan tossed the mattress off the bed and wheeled the metal frame to the window.

"We're too high up to jump. But if we can get to that tree…"

Cordelia and Eleanor understood. They opened the window, and then helped Brendan lift the front of the frame and shove it out diagonally, so it would fit; then they grabbed the back and lifted that too, pushing it out to make a bridge, hoping it would catch against the gnarled bark of the nearest tree.

"Count of three!" Brendan said. "One… two…"

With all their might they heaved.

"Yes!" Cordelia said. The far end of the bed caught. The near end was hooked over the inside of the windowsill. "We did it!"

"You two go first." Brendan glanced back. There was now a huge hole where the attic door used to be. The stairs, which folded up when the door closed, were gone as well – reduced to splinters. Slayne's red feather poked through the hole.

"Krom, on your hands and knees! I need to get up there!"

Cordelia took the lead. She removed her bulky breastplate and stepped out on the bed, teetering back and forth on the springs. She willed herself not to look down. She moved by feel, eyes closed, trusting her balance. The humid air washed across her face as she reached the tree. The thick seams in the bark provided perfect handholds. She started descending.

"Nell!" she called back. "You can do it! Just don't look down!"

But Eleanor, crouching at the foot of the bed frame, had already looked. The fall was far enough to cripple her, if not kill her.

"C'mon!" Brendan urged.

"I can't, Bren!"

"You have to!"

"I can't. I looked down."

"Then look behind you!"

Eleanor glanced back to see Slayne hoisting himself into the attic. She didn't give it another thought; she tore off her gauntlets because they made her arms feel clumsy and ran full tilt across the bridge, nearly slamming into the tree at the other end and starting down as Brendan came across last.

Cordelia stood on the ground, urging Eleanor to jump the rest of the way. Brendan reached the tree and kicked the bed frame aside so no one could follow. Eleanor screamed as it fell, diving off the tree to keep from getting hit. Cordelia darted into position and caught her. The frame crashed to earth, smashing ferns and logs. Brendan reached the ground as Slayne appeared in the window and yelled, "Run, sorcerer's spawn! See how far you get before I gut you!"

Another warrior appeared at the window with a bow and fired off a shot.

The bronze-tipped arrow whizzed past Brendan's ear and thudded into the earth. Brendan, Cordelia, and Eleanor ran through the woods, slipping on pine needles and wet rocks, no idea where they were headed. The journey across the bed bridge and down the tree had left them with bruises and scrapes that screamed at them. Their armour was gone; none of them had weapons. They were terrified and had no idea how to run without leaving a trail. They didn't speak, hearing only their breath – and then another sound. Hoofbeats.

The warriors were mounted and gaining. Cordelia stumbled on a root. Brendan grabbed her before she hit the ground. With a *thunk* an arrow spiked into a tree next to him. Eleanor ran as fast as her small legs could carry her. The thoughts going through the Walkers' heads were less the thoughts of human beings and more the thoughts – *No! Keep going! They're here!* – of hunted animals.

Slayne, in the lead on his mighty horse, expertly twirled a chain-mail net and let it fly at Cordelia, Brendan and Eleanor. It landed on top of them like a spider's web, only a million times heavier. Slayne jerked it, bringing the chains together, and the kids crashed against one another as they were pulled over sharp rocks and sticks and brought to a stop, crying out in pain.

Slayne halted and swung himself to the ground with surprising grace for a man built like an army tank.

He walked in a calm circle around his captives. The Walkers heard his boots, the birds and insects, and their own heartbeats. The other warriors stayed mounted. Suddenly Slayne reached through the net and grabbed Brendan, lifting him by his shirt collar. The chain-mail links cut into his face.

"*Why are you here?*" Slayne demanded, bathing Brendan with a gust of noxious breath.

"I don't… honestly I don't know. The Wind Witch—"

"So you admit to being witches!"

"No, no! Of course not—"

"And the Wind Witch is your mistress?" He nodded to Krom and another of his men, the one who had fired the bow. They both dismounted and stood above Cordelia and Eleanor.

"No, no, she *sent* us here," Brendan said. "We're not—"

"You're trespassing on my land."

"We had no control over that—"

Krom and the other man planted their boots on Cordelia and Eleanor's stomachs. Cordelia felt a bug crawl past her earlobe and thought she might scream.

"Don't – don't hurt my sisters. Please just let us go, and we promise we'll get off your land."

"Do you know the penalty for trespassing?"

"No…"

"For a warlock: death." Slayne squeezed Brendan's throat playfully. "For a witch…" His eyes narrowed. "We have our own ways of killing them."

The warriors, on horseback and foot, had a good laugh at that. Krom knelt to grab Cordelia.

"*Get your hands off her!*" Brendan yelled, kicking. Slayne dropped him – and punched him in the gut on his way down.

Brendan wheezed on the ground, writhing like a fish out of water. Slayne strode to where Eleanor lay trapped.

"As for *you*," he said, kneeling over her, "take a look at your handiwork." He showed her the left side of his face.

"I'm sorry," Eleanor said, seeing the two holes in his cheek, "but you shouldn't talk about eating horses." Cordelia and Brendan looked at each other. Even though

Brendan was just getting his breath back, they managed to share a smile at their sister's bravery.

"For marring me," Slayne said, "there's a special punishment for you. You'll be coming along to deal with someone much less forgiving, much less understanding, than me and my men."

"Who?" Eleanor asked.

"Queen Daphne." Slayne grinned. "She loves little children, even witchy ones. Loves to eat them while they're still alive. And awake. She usually starts with the fingers."

"I've seen her start with the ears. Rips 'em right off their head," added Krom with a thoughtful nod.

Eleanor shuddered on the ground, scared speechless for the first time in her life.

"Wait!" called Cordelia. "Queen Daphne of *where*? Where *are* we?"

"Silence!" Slayne ordered. Krom kicked Cordelia in the stomach. "Don't you dare open your mouth to me."

Cordelia squeezed her eyes shut and tried to block out the pain in order to figure out what she was hearing. These warriors were familiar in some way she couldn't put her finger on. It buzzed in her brain, but there was too much fear and pain in there to let it surface.

Slayne drew his sword and returned to Brendan, who was trying to sit up. Slayne pointed the blade at his throat.

"I—"

"*Shh,*" Slayne cooed, pressing the tip against Brendan's skin. It didn't break, but Brendan knew it would; he could *see* it happening – the thin membrane that separated him from the world would split, and he would die in a place where no one even knew he was. He was surprised to find his thoughts very simple. He didn't see his life flash before his eyes, or start thinking about all the things he wouldn't get to do because he died at twelve; he just thought, *No, no, make it stop, please, God, something!!* And then—

ACK-ACK-ACK-ACK-ACK-ACK-ACK!

Brendan thought it sounded like a machine gun. Slayne looked up. Krom looked up. Everybody looked up.

"A Sopwith Camel!" Brendan yelled.

Brendan had seen the Sopwith in history books about World War One. It was the iconic early British fighter plane – single propeller, two sets of wings. And this one was coming right towards them.

It had torn through the tree canopy, raining down

branches and leaves that were only now hitting the ground. It looked like it was held together with spit and glue. Black smoke streamed from its cockpit. Behind it, through the new hole in the foliage, came bursts of gunfire.

"German triplane!" Brendan called. He'd seen this plane too; it was what the Red Baron flew in old movies, with three sets of vertically stacked vermilion wings and black crosses. The triplane was in hot pursuit. When it became obvious that the Sopwith Camel was going down, the German triplane veered up, made a sharp right turn, and disappeared into the clouds.

The Sopwith Camel arced lower. Its engine whined in the dense air. The warriors stared, dumbstruck; they could smell the smoke now. Slayne pulled his sword away from Brendan's neck and demanded: "What creature of darkness is *that*?"

The Walkers weren't inclined to respond. Slayne's warriors *couldn't* respond, stunned as they were by the spewing, many-winged monster slaloming through the giant trees, smoke heralding flames from its mouth, veering skyward as if attempting to soar, but inevitably listing down – straight towards them.

The warriors dived to the ground. The Walkers huddled inside their net. The aircraft buzzed them, the vibration of its stuttering propeller only inches above their heads—

And then it crashed.

First the two oversize wheels at the front snapped off. Then the fuselage bounced up like a skipped stone and crunched back down. Then the plane skidded forward over rocks and sticks and roots, carving out a trench before coming to rest at a tree twenty metres away. The engine was still running. The propeller turned fitfully.

The pilot crawled out and collapsed. He was covered in black soot, with goggles and a leather helmet obscuring his face, wearing a bomber jacket zipped over a military uniform. He staggered to his feet, thin and miraculously uninjured, and legged it away from the plane.

"Who's that?" Eleanor gasped.

"He looks like… a pilot," Cordelia said, her voice hollowed by disbelief.

"A World War One fighter pilot," said Brendan.

"Watch out!" the pilot shouted to the kids and warriors, throwing himself to the ground.

The Sopwith Camel exploded behind him.

Everyone ducked as shards of plane flew across the forest. Fabric strips rained down, along with a cascade of broken leafy branches. The plane was now a smouldering pit where the cockpit, engine, and propeller used to be.

"I always said too much of that plane was in the front," remarked the pilot in a British accent. He turned to Slayne's men and inclined his head. "What's this? Are we performing a panto?"

The men drew their weapons. Krom said to Slayne: "I

thought only gods fell from the sky."

"He's no god," Slayne scoffed.

"How can you be sure?"

Slayne grabbed the bow from his man and notched an arrow. "Gods don't bleed."

"Now wait a minute!" objected the pilot, holding up his hands—

But Slayne shot an arrow into his right shoulder.

"*Aaaagh!*" The pilot fell to the ground and stared cross-eyed at the arrow, which stuck out of him like a sandwich toothpick. He seized it, snapped the shaft off and tossed it aside, wincing as he jostled a nerve.

"Savages," he spat, heaving himself up and glaring at Slayne, eyes fierce.

"A mortal," sneered Slayne. "You know what to do."

The warriors charged, descending with swords and axes, but the pilot drew a revolver, lightning-fast with his left hand, and squeezed off six crackling rounds—

BLAM! BLAM! BLAM! BLAM! BLAM! BLAM!

The Walkers let out a gasp: not only was the pilot a quick draw, but *every one of his shots hit a man's hand.* The warriors cried out and dropped their weapons, cradling their fingers as blood ran through them. Slayne's grin twisted into an expression the Walkers hadn't seen on him yet: fear.

"*Retreat!* Black magic! Away to Castle Corroway!"

The men raced to their horses, climbed on awkwardly and rode into the depths of the forest, each guiding his steed with one good hand – except for Slayne, who had to keep both hands from shaking.

The pilot reloaded as they receded. He moved slowly, gritting his teeth at the pain in his shoulder. None of the Walkers knew what to say until he finished and aimed his gun at them: "*Sprechen Sie Deutsch?*"

20

"Help us!" cried Eleanor.

"Dude, you'd totally rock *Call of Duty*," gasped Brendan.

But Cordelia silenced them both. "No, we don't speak German."

The pilot removed his helmet and let his goggles hang from his neck. He was just a few years older than Cordelia, she could see now, with shaggy brown hair and deep blue eyes. He reminded her of a young F. Scott Fitzgerald.

"You certainly seem to *understand* German," he said.

"Of course I understand '*Sprechen Sie Deutsch*'. I'm an educated person. Everyone understands that."

"I don't," said Brendan.

"Quiet!" the pilot ordered. "You speak German because you *are* German. Now who were those men?"

"We don't know," Cordelia said.

"And I don't believe you. I think you're Kraut spies."

"Hey!" Brendan said. "David Beckham! We're American. Get it? From San Francisco."

"Is that right? Because I was shot down over Amiens, not San bloody Francisco. Perhaps you've seen the plane?" The pilot nodded to the smouldering wreckage of the Sopwith Camel. The flames hadn't caught against the tough bark of the tree… but they'd made quick work of the wings and tail.

"Anybody with half a brain could see you're not in Germany," said Brendan.

"Course not. Amiens is in France."

"You're not in France, either! Hello? Does France have trees like this?"

"Perhaps I'm in a Gallic hunting preserve."

"Perhaps you're in a special state I've heard of called *denial*."

"Bren! Stop!"

"I say, you do sound like an American," said the pilot. "Only a Yank would attempt such a pathetic joke."

He holstered his gun and started to walk away. He didn't get far before he stumbled and gripped his shoulder.

The blood was still flowing freely, adhering his uniform to his skin. He tried to pull out the broken arrow, but the pain was too intense.

"Come on!" Cordelia said. "We've got to help him."

"No, we don't—"

"Bren, he's hurt. And he saved our lives."

Cordelia pushed at the net until she found an opening. She stepped out and held it wide for her brother and sister. They went (Brendan very reluctantly) to the pilot, who was kneeling on the ground, having torn a cuff off his trousers and tied it around his shoulder.

"What's your name?" Cordelia asked.

"Draper, Miss. Wing Commander Will Draper. Royal Flying Corps, Squadron Seventy."

"I'm Cordelia Walker." She stuck out her hand and spoke quickly. "This is my brother, Brendan, and sister, Eleanor. We can help you, Mr D—"

"Call me Will." Will took her hand and lightly kissed it, managing a winning smile through his pain.

"Oh," she said. "Oh, OK. Oh." She took her hand back and stared at it briefly. "We have a house nearby. Can you walk?"

Will stood, leaning away from the pain, and lurched as his knees buckled. Cordelia caught him and propped him up on his uninjured side.

"Thank you," he mumbled.

The group made its way back to Kristoff House. It was easy to see which direction they'd come – the horses had trampled a path in the undergrowth. Brendan walked sullenly in front, tearing the tips off ferns and disassembling them piece by piece. Cordelia stayed next to Will, supporting his left side, smelling the smoke and sweat and blood coming off him and trying to explain exactly who they were, what decade they were from, and what they were doing here. (Will wouldn't believe a word of it.) Eleanor walked beside them, at one point tapping Cordelia's shin with a twig and mouthing: *You like him!*

In a few minutes, Kristoff House appeared. Will blinked and rubbed his eyes. "Is it possible that arrow was tipped with a hallucinogenic drug? I'm having visions."

"We told you we had a house," Eleanor said.

"But how did it get here? Brought by woodland creatures?"

Cordelia sighed. "I *told* you—"

"It flew in from San Francisco," Brendan said.

"Come off it, I won't be made a fool—"

"We're not making fun of you," said Cordelia. "We don't know how it got here, but it's our house, and inside we've got stuff that will help your shoulder."

Will furrowed his brow. "It's much nicer than my house," he finally admitted, before allowing the Walkers to lead him in.

Soon afterwards they took Will to the kitchen. The sun was lower now; the light coming through the windows was amber instead of yellow. Eleanor found her barbecue fork in the dumbwaiter and declared she was going to search the house to make sure they were safe. Cordelia said that was fine as long as she screamed if she saw anything strange. Eleanor left as Cordelia and Brendan helped Will on to the kitchen table.

"I'll get you some ice to numb the pain," Cordelia told Will. Brendan followed her to the fridge, whispering, "What do you think you're doing?"

"What?"

"Taking in strangers? We're about to spend a night here without electricity. We have limited food. We don't know who this guy is or—"

"Bren," Cordelia said with a smile, "you don't have to be jealous just because he's better-looking than you."

"That's not true! He's not—"

Cordelia raised her eyebrows like, *Really?* Behind her, Will took off his shirt – very delicately so as not to disturb the arrow.

"So?" Brendan whispered. "I'll have a six-pack too when I'm *old*."

"You *wish*." Cordelia opened the freezer and pulled out an ice tray, but it was only filled with water. The shelves inside dripped with melted Häagen-Dazs. "I'm sorry, Will," she said. "No ice."

"Not a problem," shirtless Will said. "Can you please come and help me fetch something?"

Brendan rolled his eyes. Cordelia walked to Will.

"It's for my shoulder, in my right hip pocket. Can you—"

"Sure." Cordelia tried to project an air of confidence, like she was an old pro at dealing with handsome young British pilots. She edged her fingers into Will's pocket, blushing as she looked away from him, and felt something metal warmed by the heat of his body.

"Your gun?" she asked anxiously.

"No, no, gun's on the other side. Go on, you've almost got it."

Cordelia pulled out a sterling silver hip flask.

"There she is!"

It was slim and curved, with a Latin phrase etched on the front. Cordelia squinted at it. Even though she'd only known Will for about thirty minutes, she liked to think of him piloting fighter planes, not drinking. She handed the flask over disapprovingly.

Will took a long pull. As he drank, Eleanor came back to the kitchen from her mission securing the house. Her eyes went wide. When Will rested the flask in his lap, she ran up and grabbed it.

"Hey!" Will said.

Eleanor turned the flask upside down and let all the alcohol drain on to the floor.

"What do you think you're doing?" Will yelled. He lunged at her, but sat right back down – his shoulder hurt too much.

Eleanor handed the now-empty flask back to him. "We used to have this uncle, Pete," she explained. "I mean, we still have him, but he's not the same. He started drinking way too much. One time he got crazy and threw a raw steak at our aunt. So I don't approve of drinking, and you're not allowed to drink if you're in here."

"But it's *my* drink!" Will protested.

"But it's *our* house," said Eleanor firmly.

Will sighed and looked at his shoulder. "Then how exactly do you expect me to manage my pain? If you haven't noticed, I've got an arrow sticking out of me!"

"Right," said Cordelia. "We have to take that out. Any idea how?"

"No! I was trained for war with Huns, not barbarians."

As Will got worked up, his face got pale. Beads of sweat lined his brow. Cordelia felt his forehead with the back of her hand. It was burning up. She became deadly serious.

"Your wound is getting infected. Nell, come with me. Brendan, stay with Will."

"What? What do you want me to—"

"Keep him calm, relaxed. We're going to find out how to treat him properly."

She grabbed Eleanor and left the kitchen.

"You really *do* like him, don't you?" Eleanor asked in the hall.

"No."

"Yes. You're doing that thing where you look away when you answer my questions. That's how I know you're not telling the truth."

"I just want to keep him alive. He's good with a gun and he—"

"Looked away again," Eleanor smirked.

They went to the living room and picked up all the books that had been blown in during the Wind Witch's attack. They brought them to the library (it took a few trips) and tossed them on the floor so all the books in the house were in a central location. It was a mess. Books lay on the floor in literary dunes. Some were open; some had had their covers ripped off. Mixed in with them were the splintered ladders and broken table of the library.

"Now we have to separate the books," Cordelia said. "Put the ones by Denver Kristoff by the door; give the others to me."

"Why are we doing this exactly, Deal?"

"Because maybe one of those books is a medical manual! Can you help? Just look for a *K*—"

"I can read 'Denver Kristoff'!"

"Don't get mad, Nell—"

"I just searched this whole house by myself to make sure it was safe, and you're treating me like a little kid!"

Cordelia smiled to herself. She and Brendan had known the house was OK when they'd let Eleanor go off exploring; they had each checked a floor when they'd gone to the bathroom upon arrival. (Unfortunately, after testing the sinks and determining that the plumbing was as busted as the electricity, they had been forced to go outside.) "I'm sorry, Nell," she said. "Tell me if you find anything interesting, and I'll tell you if I need help."

The sisters went to different corners of the library. Every time Eleanor came across a non-Kristoff book, she handed it to Cordelia. Cordelia was looking for something like *Gray's Anatomy*, but she wasn't having any luck. She wondered how she could open up Will's shoulder, pull out the arrowhead, and sew it back up without a book to guide her. At least she had her memories of her father. She remembered how he used to sit her down at the kitchen table and show her how he performed surgeries, with a plate of lasagne for a patient and a butter knife for a scalpel. "The most important thing," he told her, "is to think of your hands as tools. They're the greatest and most precise tools in the world, but they're just as dumb as a hammer. They'll perform as well as you command them to."

They searched for twenty minutes. Cordelia found books about Scottish armour, Polynesian occult practices and mushroom cultivation, but she didn't find anything that would help Will. Eleanor, meanwhile, pretended that Kristoff was a neighbourhood in Denver, Colorado, and so she was looking for books about Kristoff restaurants and shops; that helped her read the covers fine. For fun she tried to read all of them, and soon she came across something that jogged her memory.

"Hey, Deal! Wasn't this the book you stole from the library?"

Cordelia immediately recognised the first-edition copy of *Savage Warriors*... and then something clicked in her head. The memory that had eluded her when she was captured by Slayne.

Cordelia took *Savage Warriors* and began flipping pages.

"What? What are you doing?"

When she hit page 17, she screamed.

"Brendan! Brendan!" Cordelia ran into the kitchen, waving *Savage Warriors*. Eleanor was close behind. Cordelia was momentarily silenced by the sight of Will, propped up on the kitchen table with some pillows, playing Brendan's PSP.

"What?" her brother asked.

Brendan sat next to Will. The pilot's skin was sickly and pale, but he looked happy. "We're relaxing," Brendan said. Then, to Will: "Get him!"

"Oh!" Will yelled. "How do I get him?"

"Do you really think it's a good idea for him to play… *Red Dead Redemption*?" Cordelia asked.

"He likes it! Gaming is good for people in pain. What's it called? Tempur-pedic?"

"Therapeutic."

"Whatever."

"Give me that." Cordelia snatched the PSP from Will and turned it off.

"Beg pardon!"

"Bren, you need to preserve the batteries in this thing."

"Why?"

"We may need them. And how about you, Will? How are you feeling? Still think you're in France?"

"I'm not sure where I am, Miss Walker."

"I have an idea."

Cordelia opened *Savage Warriors* to page 17.

"Listen: 'They came forth from the forest then, seven men. Born majestic but transformed by time and blood into rootless killers. They rode on great steeds in armour that covered them as casts of steel. They were the Savage Warriors, who lived to sow mayhem and reap plunder. They killed men quickly... and women specially.' Remind you of anyone?"

"Yeah, the dudes who just almost murdered us!" Brendan said.

"That's not all. I *knew* those warriors seemed familiar. Their leader in the book... his name is Slayne."

"Like the guy whose face I messed up!" exclaimed Eleanor.

"Guys: *we're trapped in a Denver Kristoff book.*"

"The writer who built this place," Brendan said to Will. "Wait – Deal, shouldn't you have figured this out before? Didn't you *read* that book?"

"I skimmed it, Bren, OK? I have a lot of books to read."

"This is preposterous," said Will. "Whoever heard of being trapped in a book?"

Instead of answering, Cordelia handed Will another book.

"*The Fighting Ace,*" said Will. "What's your point?"

"Open it and read. Out loud."

Will started with page 1: "'He was destined to end up as rugged as they come, but as he walked across Farnborough Airfield on April 22, 1916, Officer Cadet Will Draper was nothing more than a boy who wanted to fly.' Now hold on a minute! What's the meaning of this?"

"Uh, *you?*" Cordelia said.

Will continued to read. "'Before he boarded the plane, Officer Cadet Draper removed a silver flask from his pocket. He took a long drink, then glanced at the engraved inscription, *Per Ardua ad Astra,* and thought of the day his brother Edgar gave it to him...'"

While Will read, his voice got smaller, and then he dropped the book as if it had burned him. Brendan looked at Will's empty flask next to him. *Per Ardua ad Astra.*

"What does it mean?"

"Royal Flying Corps motto," said a trembling Will. "'*Through Struggles to the Stars.*'"

"Big deal. I'll bet everybody in the Flying Corps has one of those."

"But does everybody in the Flying Corps have a brother named Edgar?" asked Cordelia softly.

Will gave a stunned shake of his head – and then became animated, angry, as if realising that a grave injustice had been done to him. "Miss Walker, what have you got me mixed up in?"

"It wasn't us – we were minding our own business – but the Wind Witch—"

"You dragged me into this mess! I was on a mission, trying to turn the tide at Picardy, and all of a sudden I've abandoned my commanding officers and come to read about myself in some elaborate game played by American children?! *It's not right!*"

Children? Cordelia thought. *I'm almost as old as he is!*

And probably a lot smarter. Brendan put a hand on the pilot's back to calm him down. Will took a deep breath to continue yelling – and coughed. Blood sprayed across the kitchen table.

"Oh my God—" Eleanor said.

Will's eyes rolled back in his head. He collapsed into the pillows behind him. Cordelia gulped and stared at his shoulder.

"Nell, take those pillows away. Bren, get the kitchen scissors, a candle and some matches. We're operating on him. *Now.*"

23

The only candles Brendan could find were a bunch of scented ones, so the kitchen filled with the aroma of Truffle White Cocoa as the Walkers prepared to do home surgery on Will. The smell tickled Brendan's nose as he dipped the kitchen scissors in the spilled whisky from Will's flask. They had to sterilise the blades.

Cordelia knew she had one chance to get the arrow out of Will's shoulder. It was strange; before he'd collapsed, she'd had a million different thoughts in her head: *Where did he come from? Could he help us find our parents?* Now she had only one: *What's the quickest way to get that arrow out?*

Or, she corrected, *what's the safest way?* Because the first rule of being a doctor was 'do no harm', and there were plenty of ways to harm a person when you started digging into them with kitchen scissors. Like germs. She heated the scissor blades in the candle flame. She wondered if 'do no harm' had been invented to keep doctors from feeling guilty.

"How can I help?" Eleanor asked.

"Go upstairs and get Mum's sewing kit," Cordelia answered.

"Seriously?" said Brendan.

"And some Tylenol. Or ibuprofen. Any headache stuff you can find in the medicine cabinet. He's going to need it."

"I'm not allowed in the medicine cabinet."

"You are now."

"But I don't want to miss what you're doing!"

"Yeah, you do. Trust me."

Eleanor went up the spiral stairs with her sister's serious tone echoing in her head. Maybe it *was* better to be the youngest.

Cordelia inched the scissors slightly open, towards Will's wound, then hesitated.

"What are you waiting for?" Brendan asked.

"*Shh!* I'm trying to pretend Dad is here, guiding me!"

"That's just gonna make you feel pressure—"

But Cordelia had already tuned him out, remembering what her father had told her: hands were tools. The body was a machine. Sometimes you had to get in and fix it just like you had to fix a dishwasher. *Just dig in. One quick tug, like a plaster, and it'll be over.*

On television Cordelia knew dramatic music would be playing while she did this. In real life the house stayed horribly quiet. She heard the crackle of the burning candle wick. She heard her breath. As the hot scissor blades approached Will's skin, she heard the tiny hiss of hairs curling back on themselves... and smelled them. Truffle White Cocoa was no match for Eau de Singed Hair. Cordelia lost her nerve and pulled back.

"Maybe you should think of it like a video game," Brendan suggested.

"Like a game where you *operate* on people?"

"Yeah, pretend they just came out with this high-tech version of Operation. Just imagine getting points if you pull the arrow out right."

"And if I don't?"

"Duh. Game over."

Cordelia cleared her head and decided to try. Advancing on Will a second time, she pictured a counter above his shoulder starting at 0 points. With every inch she brought her hand closer, it ticked up: 10 points, 20, 30… She pressed the tips of the scissors into Will's flesh: 40, 50… The singed hair didn't bother her, nor did the sizzle of skin, because – 60, 70 – *she was doing it*. She dug in, gritting her teeth, going for the arrowhead. Will's body twitched, but he stayed unconscious.

"Awesome, you've almost got it!"

Upstairs, Eleanor jumped off the bathroom sink with a bottle of painkillers and entered the master bedroom to grab her mother's sewing kit. She wondered what colour Cordelia would want to sew Will shut with. *Black will make him look like a scarecrow. Maybe pink.* She took the kit, which was in a wicker basket, and headed out, moving too quickly to notice the *RW* trunk in the middle of the room.

Downstairs, Cordelia felt the tips of the scissors hit the arrowhead: 80 points… She pinched and pulled straight up: 90… The blood-soaked shaft inched out of Will's body…

"Almost!" Brendan said, and then Eleanor shrieked upstairs. Cordelia flinched – "Nell?" – and jerked the arrow up too fast.

It came out, but so did blood, like a fountain.

Brendan bolted for the spiral staircase – he didn't know what had happened to Eleanor, but Kristoff House had given them lots to fear. Cordelia dropped the scissors and scrambled for a tea towel. She figured she must have hit an artery, because blood was pulsing out of Will with the rhythm of a heartbeat. It slid into his armpits, down his sides… Cordelia was suddenly filled with guilt and regret. How could she have been so stupid? How could she possibly have thought she was smart enough to pull this off? Now she was going to have a dead guy on her hands, and a cute one at that. Maybe the first rule of being a doctor should be 'don't try'.

"Bren! Get back here!" Cordelia screamed. The blood spread beneath the excised arrow on the floor. She held the tea towel to Will's shoulder. Brendan and Eleanor barrelled in.

"Sorry, I bashed into that stupid trunk upstairs!" said Eleanor, before turning away in shock. "Oh no! What happened?"

"He's dying!" Cordelia said, pressing on the reddening towel. Will twitched. "And waking up!"

"He can't be doing both." Brendan tossed the sewing kit on the table next to Will. He wiped the tea towel over the wound and threw it down. "We've just got to stop the blood."

Will moaned as Brendan showed Cordelia the wound: "Look how small it really is." With the blood wiped away, the tear was smaller than a coin, but the problem was that the blood kept coming back.

"Tie it off!" Cordelia opened the sewing kit and began to thread a needle, but her hands were shaking too badly. All she had to do was get the tiny tip through the hole, but she couldn't stop trembling. She made herself stop. She had done this before. She could do it now.

Brendan ransacked the sewing kit for something to tie off the wound. He found a reel of thread and bit a length off with his teeth, then looped it around Will's shoulder. As he did, he got a sudden flash of the veins and arteries in the Wind Witch's face during the attack. *She's behind this,* he thought, *and we have no idea why.* It was easier, in a twisted way, to focus on the looming evil that hung over them than on the situation at hand.

Brendan drew the yarn so tight – *thwip!* – that he thought

it would break. Instantly the blood flow lessened.

Cordelia finally threaded the needle, knotted it and moved towards Will's shoulder.

"Here!" Eleanor yelled, pouring a tray of melted ice cubes over the wound to douse it clean.

Cordelia jabbed the needle in. No turning back now. She pulled Will's skin together – *one stitch, two, three, four* – and then knotted the end of the thread (it was pink, the colour Eleanor had hoped for) and stepped back.

It was done. The stitches held. The wound was closed. But Eleanor had an idea for one more thing that might be helpful.

She dumped candle wax all over it.

"Nell!" Cordelia exclaimed. The wax hit Will's skin and quickly cooled into a hard white shell.

"Isn't that good?" Eleanor rapped her knuckles against it. "Like a big scab."

"I guess it can't hurt," said Brendan.

"And it smells nice," Eleanor said. Will moaned beneath them.

"Is he dead?" Eleanor asked.

"Yeah, maybe the candle finished him off," said Brendan.

"Shut up; he's breathing," said Cordelia.

"Well, he *should* be dead." Brendan grabbed a roll of paper towels. "I don't even know how we did that. Good job, guys." He started to wipe up the blood. It didn't look red on the floor; it looked black. In all the excitement the sun had gone down, and the Walkers found themselves facing one another in a kitchen full of moonlight.

"Here's medicine, Deal." Eleanor handed her sister the painkillers.

"I hope they're extra strength," chuckled Brendan.

Cordelia put the bottle next to Will's head. "We'll give them to him when he wakes up. We have to keep an eye on him tonight. If we move him, we risk reopening the wound."

"I'm not staying down here," Brendan said. "If anyone or anything comes through the front door, I want to be upstairs."

"Yeah, can't we just go up and go to sleep? I'm so *tired*," Eleanor declared, and it was like casting a spell; they all suddenly realised how tired they were. "Let's wake him up and carry him. Then we can sleep in Mum and Dad's big bed."

"I'm not sleeping in the same bed as you two," said

Brendan, "but we should move him. Will! Wake up!"

"That's not going to work! It's too bad we don't have smelling salts," Cordelia said.

"Wait, doesn't he have a gun?" asked Brendan.

"He keeps it on his left side," Cordelia said. Brendan reached for the gun—

"*Bren!* Are you crazy? What are you doing?"

"I was going to fire some shots to wake him up."

"You can't just use a gun!"

"Why not?"

"Listen." Cordelia stared at her brother intensely. "Just because we've been magically sent inside a book doesn't mean you can ignore common sense. You have no idea how to use a gun. If you tried, you'd probably get us all killed."

"Hey, guess what? If I had a gun, maybe none of this would've happened in the first place! Maybe I could've shot the Wind Witch before she sent us here! Did that ever occur to you?"

"Don't be ridiculous. I'm the oldest. I'm in charge. No gun."

Brendan paused, letting his anger build. "Who needs you anyway? *Any* of you! I was doing just fine by myself!

I could have been at my friend Drew's house and missed the whole thing! It's not like you'd miss me! You don't ever care about me – and I don't care about *you*!"

Before Cordelia and Eleanor could respond, Will moaned on the table and opened his eyes. "What's going on? What is that woman screaming about?"

24

"That wasn't a woman," said Cordelia. "That was my brother. Having a tantrum."

"He thought you were a girl!" said Eleanor, laughing hysterically. "At least you woke him up."

"It wasn't a tantrum," an embarrassed Brendan argued, trying to lower his voice a few octaves. Will shook the cobwebs out of his head and stared at his shoulder.

"What have you done to me?"

Even in the dark blue light, Will could see that he hadn't been the recipient of the most expert medical care. He sniffed his shoulder. "And what's that smell?"

"Truffle," said Eleanor. "You can pick that off."

Will started to, but then held off. "It actually makes a nice bandage. But *crikey*, it hurts. Do you have anything for the pain?"

Cordelia handed him two tablets.

"What is this, ingestible morphine?"

"Sure."

Will took the pills dry and checked that he still had his gun on his hip. Brendan looked at it enviously.

"Can you walk upstairs?" Cordelia said. "We really need to get some sleep."

"I suppose so, given a bit of help."

Cordelia put *The Fighting Ace* under her arm so she would have something to read. Then she and Brendan got under Will's shoulders (Cordelia took the injured one) and eased him off the kitchen table. Will groaned and complained, but he could walk. Eleanor ran ahead to make sure there was nothing on the floor that would trip him. As they all mounted the spiral stairs, Brendan's sneakers stuck to each step, their bottoms soaked with blood from the kitchen floor.

"Thank you," Will said quietly. It was all he said before he entered the master bedroom and declared: "Now that's what I call a bed!"

The king-size mattress with plush sheets and extra pillows did look very inviting, even though it was on the floor and the bed frame was broken around it. "Since I'm injured, I'll take it," said Will.

"Hey, hold on, we can all fit in that bed," said Cordelia.

"Out of the question. Unseemly."

"Where do you expect us to sleep, on the floor?"

"I've got an idea!" Eleanor scampered away and returned with the mattress from her bedroom and a fluffy Hello Kitty sleeping bag. "Will can take the mattress and Brendan can have the sleeping bag."

They were too tired to argue. Will lay on Eleanor's mattress at the foot of the bed. Brendan climbed into the too-small sleeping bag. Cordelia and Eleanor used the last of their energy to go through the upstairs rooms and open all the shutters, just in case the house travelled somewhere else at night and they had to get their bearings again in the morning. Then they got the big mattress, but not before Eleanor aimed a kick at the *RW* trunk: "That's for tripping me before."

"Don't do that..." managed Cordelia. "Not the trunk's fault... We actually need to open that. Tomorrow... for sure..." Her head sank into the pillow. She was asleep before the air seeped out of it.

It would be tempting to say that night passed quietly in the primeval forest of Denver Kristoff's fiction. In truth it was only the extreme fatigue of the Walkers and Will that prevented them from being woken up every five minutes from the sound of a giant unknown beast howling or an oversize dragonfly buzzing by the window. They all had dreams, although only Cordelia remembered hers – tunnelling nightmares where the Wind Witch blew her down a corridor as blood sprayed from the walls. When she awoke in terror, grey dawn light sifted through the windows.

Cordelia hated waking up too early. She could never go back to sleep. It had happened to her at a sleepover last year. She'd had a bad dream and woken up in a sleeping bag in a room full of five girls, not daring to go to the bathroom or get a book because the others would ask her why she was up so early. And then one of them would say, "Why are you so *weird?*"

Luckily Cordelia had *The Fighting Ace*. She opened it and started reading – fast. She could speed-read with the best, and she had the added motivation of really wanting to know what happened to Will Draper. She read about aerial dogfights and backroom army dealings, but most disturbingly, she read about a woman named Penelope Hope. A woman who was older, more beautiful, and more mysterious than she.

As Cordelia neared the end of the book, she heard, "You've been busy this morning."

She turned. Will was smiling at her.

"How'd you know I was up?"

"I've been listening to you turn pages for an hour. Woke up early. Can't get any kip in here. What are you reading?"

"Nothing." Cordelia hid *The Fighting Ace*. She didn't want Will to know she'd been reading about him. But thanks to the book she knew that *kip* meant 'sleep'. "How's your shoulder?"

"Feels like a tiny man built a campfire on me. But you did a wonderful job, Miss Walker."

"Call me Cordelia."

"From *King Lear*…"

"*Buffy*, actually. My mother loves it."

Will draped a hand off his mattress, inches from Cordelia's. "Have you ever read *King Lear*?"

"No, actually. I've read most Shakespeare, but not that."

"American education. Tragic."

Cordelia was glad her siblings weren't awake to see her turn beetroot red. Getting called out on a lack of literary knowledge was the worst – and besides, what was Will doing with his hand? Was he just going to leave it there as if she hadn't noticed? She totally noticed.

"Cordelia," Will declared, "was King Lear's youngest daughter. At the start of the play, when the king asks his less fit daughters what they think of him, they give flowery speeches. But Cordelia tells the truth and gets banished."

"I actually think I remember that—"

"You're a lot like her. I can see it in your eyes."

He took Cordelia's hand so smoothly that she found it hard to pinpoint when it happened.

"You're controlled by your emotions. Ruled by your heart."

"Actually, I like to think I'm ruled by logic," Cordelia said, pulling her hand away.

"Then why is your heart beating so fast?"

Cordelia glanced at Will's fingers. He'd been taking her pulse. She rolled over on her side, holding her hand close to her face, and felt the sharp shape of *The Fighting Ace* under her pillow. Will was brave in the book. And bold. And he had a lot of girlfriends.

"You know, all of a sudden, I am actually tired," Cordelia said. "I'm going to try and get some sleep before everybody wakes up."

"I understand. By the way, what's a Buffy?"

They had Lunchables for breakfast. It wasn't anyone's first choice (except maybe Eleanor's), but it was the last edible thing in the fridge; Slayne and his men had been alarmed by the bold packaging and had chosen to ignore it. Cordelia and Brendan pooled the snacks on a plate and arranged them into a passable spread of cold cuts and processed cheese. Will looked on with disdain. "What is this, wartime rations?"

"Nope, they're for school," Eleanor said, expertly constructing a cracker sandwich.

Will pulled out a twenty-five-centimetre knife and stuck it into a piece of sausage.

Eleanor gasped, "That's huge!"

"Just ignore it," Cordelia said, rolling her eyes. "It's his Sheffield bowie knife. He takes it with him everywhere."

"How do you know that?" Will asked.

"Can I see it?" said Brendan.

"No," Will and Cordelia said together. Then Cordelia explained to Will, "I saw your knife before." Of course that was a lie; she had read about it in *The Fighting Ace.*

"So when will you be helping me get back home?" Will asked. "I have a war to return to."

"As we explained yesterday," Cordelia said, "you're a character in a book. So the war you have to get back to isn't real."

"Not real? It's just as real as I am! Just as real as these... Lunchables!" Will nibbled sausage off his knife.

"It's only real to you because it was written by Denver Kristoff," Brendan said. "I hate to say it, but Cordelia's right."

"Listen here!" Will said. "If I'm a poncey character in a book, I demand to see the book! Are you hiding it somewhere? I have a right to know what happens to me... what if I die at the end?!"

"I don't know where it is," Cordelia said, lying again: the book was upstairs under her pillow. She didn't want to give it to Will until she herself read if he lived or died. Which she planned to do as soon as breakfast was over.

Will sheathed his knife and approached her. "You're lying. Men of the Royal Flying Corps don't like being lied to. Where is it?"

"Hey! Hold on!" Brendan got between Will and his sister. "Are you threatening a woman? I expected more of someone who fought in the Great War."

Will looked for a moment like he might punch Brendan – but then he stepped back, impressed with the compliment. Brendan knew that people who fought in World War One never called it World War One.

"Anyway, Will, it doesn't matter *how* the book ends," Brendan continued, "because you came here and met us. So now you have a different destiny."

"I don't want a different destiny. I want to go back."

"I understand, but look. You saved our lives. We owe you. If you help us get home, we can… I dunno… take you with us! You can play *Red Dead Redemption* on a real TV instead of a little screen. I guarantee you it's better than what you did for fun in pre-war England."

"Tormented sheep, mostly," Will admitted.

"Thing is, we don't have any idea how to *get* back," Cordelia said.

"Maybe I can help," said Will, "but I just want to make sure: where you come from, there's still an *England*, yes?"

"Oh yeah," said Cordelia.

"And you can take me there?"

"Sure. Coach tickets, deportation… we'll find a way."

"Excuse me?" Eleanor asked. "I'm sorry, but can you move, Will? The garbage is behind you."

Will stepped aside. Eleanor opened the cabinet under the sink and threw the Lunchables packaging away. "I just want to tell you guys: except for the fighting and the giant knife, that was an awesome breakfast."

The Walkers and Will had a moment to appreciate Eleanor's words, and the fact that they were safe and warm and they didn't have to go to school or war, but the moment didn't last long.

A thunderous crack sounded outside the house.

It sounded like a tree splitting in two. And then, sure enough, there was a lengthy, groaning creak – Brendan tried to picture how long it would take one of those trees to reach the ground – and then a crash. A mass of branches and fernlike leaves slammed down outside the kitchen window. The tree bounced before settling, shaking all of Kristoff House.

"Who knocked that over?" asked a terrified Eleanor.

"I have no idea," Will said, "but let's find out, shall we?"

26

The last time the Walkers went outside, Brendan had made sure they had weapons. This time Will seemed weapon enough. He made quick, staggered movements down the front hallway, holding his arm at his side. He couldn't move it freely yet, but Cordelia was just impressed that he was alive and awake. *Dad would be proud.*

A second tree landed outside with a thud, shaking the house.

"What's *doing* that?" Eleanor said. "Another plane?"

"Pray it's not a German Zeppelin," said Will.

Another crack. Another long, creaking groan, this one from a tree that sounded like it was about to make the house cave in. Instead it landed just outside the utterly busted front door.

"I'm not scared of any zeppoles," Eleanor said firmly. She pulled the door aside and stepped out over Cordelia's protests: "No! Stop! What are you—"

"Come and *look*, guys!"

Brendan, Cordelia and Will followed Eleanor out. Three enormous trees lay in front of Kristoff House. Brendan remembered the three pines that stood on the lawn back in San Francisco... but these were jungle trees, ramrod straight all the way to the top, with bristly, primitive leaves.

"Odd," Cordelia said. "None of them have any roots."

Brendan walked to the base of one. It was snapped on a diagonal, like a blade of grass someone had ripped up.

"What could have done this?" Cordelia asked.

"I don't know..." said Will. Another crack sounded to the right. They turned to look, but immediately snapped their heads at another crack to the left. Then at another, hundreds of metres in front of them. And another behind them.

Suddenly, four enormous, snapped-off trees floated upwards, dozens of metres in the air. The Walkers and Will squinted in disbelief as the trees began to spin, their branches dipping under their trunks and up again, until they were whirling like Catherine wheels, performing a surrealistic air ballet, blowing down air that pushed everyone's hair away from their faces.

"Not what I expected!" yelled a stunned Will – and then the trees began to drop.

"*Run!*" screamed Cordelia. They all sprinted forward as the trees crashed around them. Each time one hit the ground, it produced a shock wave that blew them over; they had to scramble up to avoid the next massive, plummeting trunk. The final tree crashed directly in front of Eleanor, missing her by centimetres.

"Raining trees. This is a first!" said Brendan.

"What's doing it?" asked Cordelia.

"Magic!" Brendan said. They huddled by one of the fallen trees.

"But we haven't seen any magic. Not like that. The only person who can do things like that is—"

"Don't say her name!" said Eleanor, but now the tree trunks were moving again. The furthest one, by the open door to Kristoff House, rose as if pulled by a string attached to its top. Once it was at a forty-five-degree angle to the ground, it stopped and stood there impossibly, like an optical illusion, before a second tree rose to mirror it, forming an arch that dwarfed the house. Soon enough, all the trees rose to form a majestic tunnel, with the house at one end and the Walkers and Will at the other.

Striding towards them under the unbelievable timber formation, in a fine purple robe, was the Wind Witch.

"Heck of a way to make an entrance," said Brendan.

27

The Wind Witch walked barefoot on the flattened undergrowth. She held her arms out to her sides, clearly unashamed of her missing right hand. She had a beatific smile on her face. She was still bald, and her skin was still wrinkled and mottled, but her gold and silver necklaces gave her a royal appearance. She seemed more comfortable here than in San Francisco.

"My friends!" she announced. "Congratulations on still being alive!"

Will drew his gun. "Stop. No further. Who are you? What do you want?"

"Such a brave young man," said the Wind Witch, "pointing a gun at an unarmed woman."

"Unarmed? You tried to drop a bloody forest on us! It's not my fault you've got bad aim—"

"Will, remember we told you about the Wind Witch?" whispered Cordelia. "That's her. You might not want to upset—"

"*You're* the one with bad aim, Mr Draper," said the Wind Witch. "You can't even hit someone from five metres."

Will snarled. He couldn't abide lies about his marksmanship. He squeezed the trigger twice: *BLAM! BLAM!*

The Wind Witch kept walking forward.

"Look at that. Missed. And what a temper you have! Cordelia, do you really have a crush on him?"

Cordelia blushed, but held her tongue. She didn't know how the Wind Witch had got in her head. Will checked his gun to make sure it was loaded and shrank back, terrified.

Now the Wind Witch was close enough for them all to smell her: the same sulphur smell that she had emitted during her first attack, augmented by the compost odour that came from her mouth.

Brendan stood tall. "You want to kill us? Give it your best shot, jock breath. But you tried once and failed. We're a lot tougher than you think!"

"You're right. You're as resilient as I'd hoped," the Wind

Witch said. "If I'd wanted to kill you, I would've done so. I sent you here to test your mettle. And you Walkers have done brilliantly!"

"What do you mean?" Cordelia asked, joining her brother.

"The world you've been flung into is not a kind one."

"You think?" said Eleanor.

"You survived the attack of Slayne. You avoided getting eaten by the more… active wildlife. You have even begun to theorise where you are. You have succeeded where many others have failed."

"It's not a theory," protested Cordelia. "We know we're trapped in your father's books."

"Yeah, and what about our parents?" shouted Eleanor, mimicking the defiant stances of her brother and sister. "Where'd you put 'em?"

"Oh, they're safe, little one," said the Wind Witch.

"I want to see them *now*!" cried Eleanor. "Where are they?"

"Patience," said the Wind Witch. "Soon I will reunite you with them, so long as you follow my instructions."

The Wind Witch waved her hand in a small arc in front

of her. The air shimmered and spun where her fingers passed through it, and out of the disturbance came a book.

It wasn't a real book; it flickered and twinkled, with a burgundy cover and no title. A hologram.

"Is that another Denver Kristoff book?" Cordelia asked.

"Not quite," said the Wind Witch, waving her hand again. Now a symbol began to burn into the holographic book's cover. It started in the middle, like fire running along an oil-filled trough, and traced two half-circles: a bigger one that curved down like a rainbow over a smaller one that curved up like a smile. Between the two, an iris…

"That's what Dad carved in that guy's stomach!" Eleanor blurted.

"The eye of God, used by the ancients to signify great power." The Wind Witch smiled. "Your father carved it because this book was calling to your family. It wanted to be found. And when this book wants something, it gets it. It's the most seductive, most powerful book in human history. Do you know its name?"

They all shook their heads.

"*The Book of Doom and Desire*."

"That was on my summer reading list," Brendan said,

"but I read *Jaws* instead. What's this one about?"

The Wind Witch didn't appreciate his humour, answering in a hushed snarl, "It's not 'about' anything. If you were to open the pages, you would find them blank. But this book possesses a power that was only meant for gods. My father once owned it, but was too weak for it. He hid the book – and I want it back."

"What kind of power does the book have?" asked Brendan.

"That's not for you to know!" The Wind Witch spasmed as if she were going to sprout wings again. "I have searched for the book since before you brats were hatched. I cannot find it, because my father, in his misguided desire to 'protect' me, put a curse on it. Any time I get too close to it, it disappears. So I need you to find it for me."

"Why us?" Cordelia asked.

"Because you're Walkers," said the Wind Witch, "and the Walkers and the Kristoffs have a strong connection to the book."

"Hold on a second: you sent us into your dad's creepy old stories to find one stupid book?" said Brendan.

The Wind Witch nodded.

"But that could take years!" said Cordelia.

"Don't worry, children. To find the book, just follow your hearts, your wishes and most importantly… your selfish desires."

"Follow our selfish desires? What does that mean?" asked Cordelia.

"Do something that isn't in the best interest of your family. Something for your own… hedonistic fulfilment. The book responds to that. Reveals itself to those who are consumed by ego. Seeks readers who seek power."

"Sounds like you, baldy," said Brendan.

Will spoke up: "You reprehensible old troll. Making these poor innocent children do your dirty work? You're bent as a nine-bob note!"

"I'm pure as a silver crown, Mr Draper," said the Wind Witch. "*The Book of Doom and Desire* belongs to me and was taken away from me by deceit and dark magic. I deserve to have it back."

"And what about all that stuff you were saying before, back in our house?" Brendan said. "Who is Dr Hayes?"

"And if our parents are safe, can we at least see them?" pressed Cordelia. "That's what kidnappers do. They show a picture or play a video so—"

"*Silence!*" the Wind Witch snapped. "Find the book. Then I will send you home and reunite you with your parents. Not a moment sooner. You have my word. And if you find yourself in a real bind, a situation you can't get out of… call for me. Perhaps I'll help."

"We'll never ask you for help!" said Cordelia.

"So you say. But it can be hard to see the future."

"Say! Miss Witch! Where do I fit into all of this?" asked Will.

The Wind Witch scoffed. "What does it matter, you preening puppet? You're nothing but a storybook character! One of my father's more paper-thin and forgettable protagonists, I might add."

Will's face fell. Cordelia glared at the Wind Witch. "Was that really necessary?"

"Yeah, the guy's still in shock from finding out he's not a real person," said Brendan. "No offence, Will."

"None taken," said the pilot. "I may have originated from a novel, I may not be considered 'real' in the traditional sense, but my feelings of hatred and disgust for this bald creature are very real, as is my duty to protect you three children! I owe you a life debt."

"Then stay with the Walkers, Mr Draper. Help them find the book, and I will send you back with them. But betray me… and all of you will be obliterated."

"Excuse me?" Brendan asked. "Can you define 'obliterated'?"

The Wind Witch growled at this, but Brendan was on a roll: "Like… does 'obliterated' mean that you're gonna set us on fire and burn us alive? Or does it mean that you're gonna blow us up in this big explosion that will turn us into tiny dust particles? Or will you just obliterate us by sending us into outer space—"

"*Enough!* I will obliterate you in the most horribly painful way possible!"

"OK. Good. Thanks. Just curious—"

The Wind Witch raised her arms above her head. She clasped the stump of her right hand with her left hand and began to spin in a circle, faster and faster, like a top, becoming a purple blur as she rose off the ground… and then she was gone.

"The woman may be a monster, but she certainly has a flair for the dramatic exit," said Will.

Though its conjuror had departed, the vision of *The Book of Doom and Desire* remained, hovering, turning back and forth as if it were on the Home Shopping Network. Cordelia approached it.

"So in order to get our parents back, to do what's right, we have to do what's wrong?"

"Deal? What are you doing?"

Cordelia reached forward. Her hand went through the book. It vanished in an instant – along with the rest of the Wind Witch's enchantments. The trees lost their resistance to gravity and crashed to the ground. The Walkers and Will dived back to avoid being crushed, landing face down in dirt and, in Brendan's case, centimetres from a huge slug.

"Deal! You've gotta not *touch* things!" Brendan yelled as they stood up and brushed themselves off. The birds and bugs were bringing the forest back to life. "What do we do now?"

Something selfish, thought Cordelia. *Hedonistic. Impulsive. Against the best interest of your family.* She knew that she shouldn't believe the Wind Witch's promises, but she respected the way the woman spoke – the way she had a plan. Maybe if they did what she said, things *would* go back to normal. After all, what reason did the Wind Witch have to double-cross them? She wasn't a madwoman; she just wanted a book. Cordelia could relate.

She turned to Will and looked him square in the eyes. Will smiled, but the intensity of Cordelia's gaze made him uncomfortable. "Cordelia. Why are you looking at me like—"

She reached up, grabbed Will's face with both hands, and planted a deep, long kiss on his lips.

They all stood frozen for a few seconds. Cordelia kissed Will with every bit of hedonism she could muster (which wasn't much, considering it was her first kiss) as his eyes went wide in total panic. Brendan and Eleanor were gape-mouthed and frozen: Eleanor with glee, Brendan with disgust.

"*Gross!* Stop! Guys—"

But he didn't need to pull them apart. Cordelia pushed Will away suddenly.

"What was *that?*" Will asked, holding his palm to his lips and checking his hand for lipstick. There was none.

"Sorry," Cordelia said. She faced the forest, her face blazing red. "I just thought that if I did something crazy… impulsive… we could find the book and get our parents back."

"So you've been wanting to kiss Will this whole time," said Brendan.

"Oh no. Of course not," said Cordelia.

"Liar! You liked Will from the beginning!" Eleanor grinned. "Cor*delia* has a *boy*friend!"

"Nell, be quiet! That's not it at all. I was just—"

"Just being selfish. Morally weak. Hedonistic," said Will.

"Exactly. I'm sorry. I was confused and…" Cordelia started to tremble, tears filling her eyes.

"*Shh,*" said Will. "It only lasted a few seconds. Not long enough to be considered amoral. Which is probably why the book didn't appear. I actually thought it was sweet."

Ugh, Cordelia thought. *Now he's speaking to me as if I were a child. Maybe another tree will fall and put me out of my misery.*

That wasn't all. Cordelia was scared. When she'd kissed Will, she hadn't been in control of herself. She'd been thinking about *The Book of Doom and Desire* and how to find it. It was almost as if the book, and not Will, had been the target of her lips.

They all started walking back to Kristoff House, lost in thought. Eleanor asked, "So… are we gonna find Mum and Dad and go home now?"

"We're gonna try," said Cordelia.

"How?"

Cordelia shrugged: "Do what the Wind Witch said."

"No way," Brendan said. "I don't believe a thing that old hag says. Act selfish and you'll get what you want? What an obvious trap! Besides, you tried to do it and it didn't work!"

"Maybe *you* have to do it. Or maybe we all do. She seemed like she was being logical, at least. We should try."

"She's setting us up. I say we find another way back."

"I have to side with Brendan on this one," said Will. "It's nothing personal. I just don't trust women with mouldy teeth."

"And he's from England," said Brendan.

"I say we listen to her, at least until we find the book, and then maybe double-cross her," said Cordelia.

"No way, Deal. It's too dangerous—"

"You're scared!"

"I'm not scared—"

"Are you aware that your family argues an exceptional amount?" asked Will.

Eleanor stomped her foot: "*No more fighting!*"

They all winced. Eleanor could be super-loud when she wanted.

"We don't know who to trust because we don't know *anything*! We don't know which book we're in, we don't know why the Wind Witch picked us, and we don't know if those horse-killing warriors are coming back! Until we find that out, there's no point doing *anything*!"

"How do you suppose we find the answers?" Brendan asked. "Do you see Wikipedia around here?"

"We can read," suggested Cordelia.

"Read what?" asked Brendan.

"Kristoff's novels," said Cordelia. "*All* of them."

"Say, that's a good idea," said Will. "That will show us which books we're trapped in."

"We already know some of the stuff here is from *Savage Warriors*," said Cordelia, "and Will's from *The Fighting Ace*, but is there more we need to find?"

"Sounds cool," said Eleanor. "Like a scavenger hunt!"

"Exactly," said Cordelia. "But first… Will, can you stand guard at the door? If Slayne and his warriors show up—"

"Or baldy butt breath," added Brendan.

"*Or* that giant wolf that almost bit my head off," added Eleanor.

"Right, if *anybody* shows up, call us, and shoot them," Cordelia said. "Not necessarily in that order."

Will saluted. "Happy to do my duty."

"I'm going upstairs to get that *RW* trunk open," said Cordelia. "That might be a clue too."

"*I* want to open the trunk," Eleanor started, but then she caught herself. "Right. I mean, no fighting."

Eleanor and Brendan went to the library. With the sun just reaching the top of the sky there was plenty of light to search the books. Eleanor had already separated Denver Kristoff's novels from the rest, so she felt like a bit of an expert, at least enough to boss her brother around.

Brendan didn't mind. He started reading a Kristoff book called *Gladius Rex*. He got twenty pages in before he decided it wasn't one of the ones they were trapped in. (He was glad, too, because it was full of people getting eaten by lions.) He looked at Eleanor. She was trying to read *Savage Warriors*.

"How far are you?" he asked.

Eleanor scrunched her mouth. "Page thirty."

Brendan could tell she was lying. "That's great, Nell, but here, why don't we switch?" Brendan knew that reading *Savage Warriors* might be the difference between life and death. He handed her *Gladius Rex*. "I think there might be some good stuff in here." Eleanor accepted the trade and Brendan got into *Savage Warriors* quickly.

It wasn't only about Slayne and his men. It was also about their boss, an evil queen named Daphne, who lived in a castle called Castle Corroway. Brendan recognised those names from his run-in with Slayne. But there was another side to *Savage Warriors*: the Resistance, a group of freedom fighters who were trying to stop Queen Daphne. They were common townspeople who secretly had jobs as spies and archers and weapon makers. They were led by a general, but more interesting to Brendan was the general's daughter, this heroic girl named Celene.

Celene had purple eyes. She was smart and pretty and she wasn't scared of anybody and she believed in something. Precisely the sort of girl who Brendan never came close to meeting in his school, where the only thing the girls were into talking about was each other. Brendan thought Celene was awesome.

He kept reading, getting scared when he came to a part of the book that featured a creature thousands of times more powerful than Slayne, when Eleanor called, "Bren! This book you gave me isn't helpful! It's all Ancient Rome stuff!"

"Uh, is it?"

"Don't play dumb with me! You gave me some book you know we're not trapped in to keep me busy, because I don't read fast enough!"

"Nell, that's not true—"

"And now you're lying! I'm going to help, whether you believe in me or not." Eleanor put down *Gladius Rex* and picked up *The Heart and the Helm*, a book about pirates. "Maybe we're trapped in this one too."

Brendan gave her a hug. "You are helping, Nell. You are."

Meanwhile, upstairs, Cordelia was secretly nearing the end of *The Fighting Ace*, but the book had a horrifying conclusion. No matter how hard she tried, she couldn't finish it. *You're being ridiculous*, she thought. *He's just some stupid boy. He's not even out of high school.* (*The Fighting Ace* had revealed that Will had lied about his age to get into the

Royal Flying Corps. He was seventeen.) But no matter how she denied it, Cordelia cared about his fate.

She put the book down and went to the *RW* trunk. The heavy padlock was impossible to deal with, so she tried to smash the latch with a hammer. Unfortunately, the only one she could find was a tiny ball-peen hammer that she got from downstairs under the sink. The hammer didn't work and she put it back.

She tried to pick the lock. Hanger… hairgrip… the rusty sword from one of Brendan's old Civil War toy soldiers that had been blown into the bedroom during the attack… nothing worked.

"Will!" Cordelia called downstairs. "I need help!"

Within moments Will reached the second-floor bedroom. Cordelia explained: "I can't open the trunk. Do you have any ideas on how I—"

BLAM!

Will smiled and held up his revolver. A whiff of gunpowder slid past his face. The lock lay splayed open on the floor.

"Unnecessary machismo," commented Cordelia.

Will shrugged. Brendan and Eleanor rushed into the

room. "Cool," Brendan said, looking at the shot-open trunk. "Will, do you think you could teach me how to use your gun?"

Will stashed his weapon. "It's not a gun. It's a Webley Mark Six revolving pistol. And it isn't a toy. I don't want you going near it, Brendan."

"Fine," said Brendan as Cordelia yanked open the trunk. It was a superbly made vessel, suffused with a pleasant tang of oak and brass, but all she cared about was what was inside.

"Yes!" she yelled. "Finally we might be on to something!"

Brendan didn't understand what Cordelia was so excited about. The trunk was full of brown accordion folders packed with stacks of yellowed papers.

"Documents? What are we gonna do with these?"

"Don't you see the name?" Cordelia said. "Bren, you were right!" She handed him one of the accordion folders. A stamp on top said RUTHERFORD WALKER, MD.

"Our great-great-grandfather…" Brendan said, trailing off as he turned the folder around in his hands. He thought back to the pictures of the Kristoff family in the hallway. *Time really does make things important,* he decided. *Once these were just ordinary papers. Now they're history. My history.* He was almost afraid to look. He thought about his parents and how they were still missing, how he was missing too. *There are probably news broadcasts about the disappearance of the Walker children. What if my history ends with me?*

"What kind of documents are they?" asked Eleanor.

"They appear to be medical records," said Will.

"Correct," said Cordelia, examining a folder on her lap. "Dr Walker's records for each patient. Let's see… 'Mrs Mary Worcester of Duboce Avenue, San Francisco. Date of first visit: March the sixteenth, 1899. Complaint: nervous distress. Treatment: one vitality tonic.' Huh."

"What's a vitality tonic? Like a Red Bull?" Eleanor asked.

"I don't think so. More like—"

"Quackery," interrupted Will.

"Excuse me?" said Brendan.

"It's quite clear. Your great-great-grandfather was a flimflam man."

"A what?"

"Bamboozler. Con artist. Sham druggist."

"Druggist? No. He was a doctor! *MD*, hello?" Brendan said.

"That may be, but he prescribed panaceas that—"

"Pana-*what?* Isn't that a piece of land surrounded by water on three sides?" asked Eleanor.

"That's a peninsula," said Cordelia.

"A panacea is a medicine that people wrongly expect will cure all sorts of ills," said Will. "Look at the rest of this list. Mrs Worcester was given a new 'vitality tonic' every two weeks at the cost of forty cents, for 'mercurial eruptions' and 'neuralgia', and she kept coming back for a year, at which point her husband probably told her to stop seeing that Walker quack—"

"That's our family you're talking about!"

"Calm down. I'm not *blaming* the man. You Yanks are wild for your 'elixirs' and 'supplements' and 'Coca-Cola'. Put a healthy label on something and you can make a fortune in America!"

"He has a point," Cordelia said. "Like acai berries. But anyway, maybe there's a connection in these records between Rutherford Walker and Denver Kristoff."

For the next ten minutes, the Walkers searched their great-great-grandfather's records. None of them liked to think of the man as being a sham, any more than they liked to think of their father and 'the incident', but they found no evidence to the contrary. Other than the vitality tonics, people who visited Rutherford Walker were prescribed "catarrh snuff", "Oxien", and "Indian root pills".

"Look at this. He was officially a snake-oil salesman," said Cordelia, finding a prescription for Stanley's Snake Oil Liniment.

"This is depressing," said Brendan. "I don't wanna read any more." He reached his hands into the trunk – by now they were almost at the bottom – and flung the remaining folders aside, ready to storm out—

But he stopped. He was staring at a book. Right there at the bottom of the trunk. *The Book of Doom and Desire.*

"No way," Brendan said. "It was that easy?"

The book's cover had the eye that the Wind Witch had shown them. Brendan reached down – but Cordelia was faster, snatching it.

"Stop!" Eleanor called. "That's not safe!"

"Relax," Cordelia said. "This isn't *the* book. It's just the same symbol. See? It's black, not burgundy. And the symbol isn't burned in; it's drawn with a pen."

"Looks like a journal," said Will, peering over Cordelia's shoulder.

"I don't think we should open it," said Eleanor. "Could be a trap."

"We have to open it," said Cordelia. With a deep breath

she turned to page 1, which was filled with the same script as the patient records. "Rutherford Walker's handwriting! We found his diary!"

"Journal," Will corrected. "Men don't keep diaries."

"Whatever – start reading!" said Eleanor.

They all sat around Cordelia, as if she were sharing a campfire story, while she began.

"'April the tenth, 1906. Dear Diary.'" Cordelia shot Will a look; he rolled his eyes. "'Today I awoke with my head still spinning, thanks to the lecture I witnessed last night, delivered by the astounding Dr Aldrich Hayes.'"

"Dr Hayes! The Wind Witch mentioned that dude!" said Brendan.

"'The lecture was entitled "Mythology and Magical Lore of the Californias". It more than lived up to its name. In previous months, I had heard rumours of this secret talk in salons and seances about town. The lecture was to be delivered at the Bohemian Club, where my less-than-spectacular aristocratic standing made it impossible for me to get in. I feared I would never see Dr Hayes, who is both a lauded Yale professor and the rumoured leader of the Lorekeepers.'"

"Lorekeepers? Who are *they*?" Eleanor asked.

"Doesn't say," answered Cordelia. "Now where was I...?"

"There," said Will, pointing to her place on the page. He had been reading along. Cordelia smiled and continued.

"'When it seemed all hope was lost, I was called upon by my dear friend, a man who was never short of ideas: Denver Kristoff.'"

"Kristoff!" Brendan exclaimed. "You were right, Deal! Our great-great-grandfather did know him!"

"Keep reading!" urged Eleanor.

"'Kristoff, like myself, was obsessed with matters of the occult. He felt it would be criminal to miss Dr Hayes's lecture. So he concocted an equally criminal plan: the two of us would sneak into the Bohemian Club. Surreptitiously, we smashed a basement window at six twenty-four Taylor Street and wiggled in like worms. We made our way to the lecture hall and heard Dr Hayes's amazing speech.

"'He spoke of many things that more "level-headed" men deny: the untapped powers of the human mind, the existence of spirits, and the haunted places of California. But most shocking was the moment when he spoke of a haunted place in our own backyard: Goat Island.'"

"We have a goat island in our backyard?" asked Eleanor.

"He wasn't being literal," said Brendan. "By 'our own backyard' he means the city. Fortunately, I know a lot about San Francisco's history."

"Ugh, Bren, we know," said Eleanor as Cordelia rolled her eyes.

"Goat Island is called Yerba Buena Island now. When you go over the Bay Bridge and you see signs for Treasure Island? That's connected to Yerba Buena."

Cordelia kept reading: "'According to Hayes, Goat Island once housed the Tuchayune people, a native tribe, who buried their leaders sitting up.'"

"Creep-ola," said Eleanor.

"'The Tuchayunes believed the island was a soft spot in the barrier between the human world and the spirit world, where powerful forces could sneak on to earth and wreak havoc. They buried their leaders sitting up under a carved stone shaped like an eagle to scare off any spirits who did slide through.

"'Kristoff and I couldn't resist this. We decided that we would travel to Goat Island, find the Tuchayune graves, and dig until we found the skeletons!'"

Cordelia closed the book. "That's it?" Eleanor asked.

"That's the end of this entry," said Cordelia.

"Cool. Our great-great-grandfather and Denver Kristoff were ghost hunters!" said Eleanor.

"More like grave robbers," said Will, "without a shred of respect for the dead! Imagine. Digging up some poor man who never did them a bit of harm."

"You're not thinking about the environment he was in," said Brendan. "San Francisco has always been a place for freaks and weirdos. Seances and ghost hunting were huge back when this was written. Mediums were like rock stars."

"Like what?" asked Will.

"The next entry is dated two weeks later," said Cordelia, reopening the book.

"'April the twenty-fourth, 1906. Dear Diary: The tragedy that has befallen our city is too large and awful to comprehend, and too fresh to write about… so I will return to the story of Goat Island, and perhaps the part I played in the overwhelming calamity of our time!'"

"What's he talking about?" asked Eleanor.

"I know," said Brendan. "It's the—"

But Cordelia continued.

"'Kristoff and I made our journey on April the seventeenth. We left in the dead of night. Kristoff had to do everything in the most impractical and exciting manner, so we stole down to the Embarcadero and unfastened a rowboat bobbing in the waves. Given my skill at seamanship I was not troubled by the currents. The moonlight shone clear as day. Taking turns rowing, we reached Goat Island without incident.

"'I opened a map I had purchased from a Chinatown souvenir shop, showing the location of the eagle stone. With shovels on our backs we hiked for two hours until we found it. The stone was crowned with an intricately eroded tip, and the moonlight that shone through created a most curious shadow on the ground. I feel no need to describe this shadow, Diary, for I have sketched it on your cover, so that some future explorer might be similarly affected by its odd manner.'"

Cordelia flipped the book around so everyone could see: the eye.

"'We began digging. After an hour we had got only a metre down, but then my shovel jabbed through the ground and registered no resistance, as if it were sticking into thin air! Kristoff felt a similar phenomenon, and then the ground gave way beneath us!

"'Kristoff and I landed on a dirt floor. With only a few minor bruises and scrapes, we lit our lanterns, revealing a chamber around us. It was a rough sphere with a two-metre diameter, hewn out of the earth as if by a giant insect. It was cool and dry… and in the centre was a seated skeleton!

"'The man had been a leader, no question. Beside him were a bird-bone whistle and a saw made from a coyote's hip. But the most fantastic thing about him was what he held in his hands. A book. The skeleton was reading! His elbows rested on his knees. It almost looked as if he were surprised at the book's contents! Kristoff approached the book. The cover bore the same symbol as the ground above.'"

Cordelia stopped.

"What? What happened next?" Eleanor asked.

"That's it. The last entry." Cordelia showed them how the rest of Rutherford Walker's diary was blank.

"Are you kidding?" Brendan said.

"Infuriating!" Will snorted.

"It was *The Book of Doom and Desire*," Cordelia said in a small voice. "Rutherford Walker and Denver Kristoff found it, together. A couple of amateur occult nerds digging up a Native American grave."

"And that's not all," said Brendan. "All that stuff happened on the night of April the seventeenth, 1906. You know what happened on April the eighteenth?"

They all shook their heads.

"The Great San Francisco Earthquake."

"Of course!" Will slapped his forehead. "Even I've heard of that one."

"Biggest natural disaster in California history. Whole city was flattened. Three thousand people died. I did a report on it."

"The day after Walker and Kristoff found the book…" said Cordelia.

"Not just the day after. At five a.m. So if the diary's right, it might've happened *literally* as they were taking the book."

"Who says they took it?"

"How do you think it ended up with Denver Kristoff? I'll bet he and Gramps stole the book, which angered the spirits, who got their revenge by causing the quake. That's what Rutherford felt guilty about."

"Our great-great-grandfather caused the San Francisco Earthquake?" Eleanor asked.

"I don't think he purposely meant to—"

Brendan was interrupted when the room suddenly went dark. The Walkers and Will looked at the windows. A huge shape completely blocked their view.

"What is that?" Eleanor shrieked. "A dinosaur?"

"I hope not," said Brendan. "I always wanted to see a real dinosaur, but not so much any more." Cordelia rushed to one of the bedroom windows.

"It looks like... a *wall*," she said. They all nodded: it appeared that someone had placed a slightly concave wall that stretched up, blocking the sun, two metres from Kristoff House. The wall looked textured and tan, almost as if it were made of sandpaper. And while it hadn't been there a minute before, it appeared perfectly still, as if it had been there forever.

"Wait a minute," Brendan said, "that looks like... no way."

"Like what?" Cordelia asked.

"I was reading *Savage Warriors*, and the warriors run into big problems when—"

"Follow me," Will interrupted. "Let's get out of here. You three saved my life. It's my duty to keep you safe."

Will led the Walkers out of the master bedroom. As they came to the stairs, they looked out of another window: the wall was there too. It was the same size and colour – but the texture looked different. The wall was still covered with fine, grooved lines, but the lines here were different from the ones outside the bedroom.

The wall quivered.

"*Ah!*" Brendan pointed. "Look!"

As he spoke, the wall disappeared, shooting up from the window.

"Where'd it go?" Eleanor asked. They heard a huge crunch outside. "Is that the Wind Witch again?" They heard more crunching sounds, each fainter than the last, before the birds and bugs started up again.

"What *was* that?" Cordelia asked Brendan.

"I'm scared to say," he said, "and I could be wrong. I'm going to keep reading *Savage Warriors* to learn more." He bolted back towards the library. Cordelia had never seen her brother run to read a book.

"I'm going to keep reading *The Heart and the Helm*!" said Eleanor, following.

"What's that about?" asked Cordelia.

"Pirates."

Cordelia smiled: "Go for it, Nell." It seemed pretty clear that they wouldn't be encountering any pirates in the forest.

Day crept into afternoon. Will took on guard duty at the front door as Cordelia joined her siblings in the library. Brendan read *Savage Warriors*, while Cordelia skimmed as many Kristoff books as she could – *Gemstone Mine*, *The Great Snake* – looking for characters or situations that matched the world they were in.

"You know what?" Brendan said. "During the Wind Witch's attack, there was this moment when these three books were hovering in front of my face, and then they started to grow bigger and bigger. I bet *those* are the books we got sent to."

"And one is *Savage Warriors*, and one is *The Fighting Ace*," said Eleanor, "so we're just looking for the third."

"That's right!" said Cordelia. "That makes sense!" When they weren't fighting, it was amazing what the

Walkers could accomplish. "The problem is we have like fifty more books to go through. But at least we know we're trapped in a world that fuses books."

"Like a Denver Kristoff mash-up," said Brendan.

They went back to reading, but after five minutes Brendan couldn't take it any more. "Deal, can you take over *Savage Warriors*? It's getting terrifying, and I need a break." Now that he had done it once and hadn't spontaneously combusted, he was more comfortable admitting to his sisters when he was scared.

Cordelia took the book. She knew how important it was to know it from front to back. Every sentence could potentially hold the secret to the Walkers surviving, or even getting home. When Cordelia looked up, Brendan was gone.

Meanwhile, at the front door, Will watched the shadows of the trees lengthen. He had to stay focused on every snap and rustle in the woods, every smell and sound. Guarding was hard work.

"Will!" shouted Brendan. "Can I relieve you?"

"Absolutely not," said Will. "You just want to get your hands on my gun."

"That's not true. I want to get my hands on your Webley Mark Six."

Will sighed. "Why are you so eager for one of these, Brendan? You think it's a toy like your little technological games?"

"What you call a toy, I call a simulator."

Will shook his head. "There's no simulation for firing a gun. It bites back. Cuts into your hand. It's hot and nasty… and that's if you *miss* your mark. Think what happens if you hit."

"What?"

Will leaned close. "People don't flash and disappear. They lie on the ground and bleed."

"C'mon! I thought you were my friend!"

Will smiled. "I appreciate that. Since I found out I'm only a character in a book, I've been wondering if any of my old acquaintances – Frank Quigley, Thorny Thompson – even count as friends. But you still can't have the gun."

Brendan sighed. "What about the knife?"

Will scrunched his lips. "I don't think so—"

"Come on. I use a knife when I eat dinner!"

"That is true—"

"And I don't need a licence for a knife."

"You do not."

"So what's the big deal?"

"Here, then." Will handed Brendan his Sheffield bowie knife. "Take guard, and treat this *very* carefully. Understand? I'll just take a small break."

"Thanks, Will!" Brendan couldn't believe his good fortune. But then he realised something: "Let's say we got attacked by someone really big. Then the knife wouldn't be much help."

"Possibly… How big are you talking about?"

"Say, two hundred and fifty metres tall?"

Will laughed. "If we get attacked by something that big, nothing will help."

"I agree. But your grenade might."

"My grenade? How do you know about that?"

"I know pilots in the Great War sometimes carried grenades. I don't want to get you worried, but I read some stuff… and I have a feeling that we're being hunted by something that's pretty freakin' big, something only a grenade might be able to stop."

"Very well," Will said, pulling an oval-shaped hunk of

metal out of his jacket. Brendan's mouth dropped open.

"Seriously?"

"Yes. Pull the pin, count to three and throw. I assume you can throw?"

"Four years of Little League, starting shortstop!" said Brendan. In response to Will's blank expression, he added, "Baseball?"

"Just keep safe, Brendan. And if you see anything out of the ordinary, *call me.*"

Brendan gave Will his knife back and left, tossing the grenade up and down in his palm.

31

Will went inside to find Cordelia and Eleanor. They had moved from the library to the living room, following the sun so that they could keep reading Kristoff's books. "Your brother has taken over guard duty," Will told them.

Cordelia closed *Savage Warriors*. From the moment Will had entered, she'd seen him with her peripheral vision, but she wanted to make it clear that he was less important to her than her book. "You trust my brother with our lives?"

"For a little while anyway. Have you found any clues?"

Eleanor explained their theory about being in a mash-up of three Kristoff books and showed her progress with *The Heart and the Helm* – she had made it to page 50.

"Wow!" Will said. "You've got very far!"

"Well," Eleanor said, embarrassed, "I'm not reading

everything. Reading is hard for me. So I just read a little on each page and skip ahead."

"But she's doing great," said Cordelia.

"Not that great," said Eleanor, "because nothing in this book can help us."

"Then take a break," said Will. "We need to stay sharp."

"Good idea," said Cordelia.

"Yeah!" Eleanor jumped up. "I'm going to play with my American Girl dolls in the dumbwaiter!"

"Wait, Nell, don't climb in—" Cordelia started, but her sister was already out of the room, leaving the book flipped over on the couch. Cordelia sighed, smoothed out the pages, and replaced the dust jacket. "We have to be respectful," she explained to Will. "These are rare books, and obviously very powerful. If we're trapped in them, maybe one wrong crumpled page could cause a typhoon. Or an earthquake."

"Have you finished the book about me?" Will asked.

Cordelia looked away. "I did," she admitted.

"Well, then… shouldn't *I* be permitted to read it?"

"No. That would be like meeting yourself in a time-travel movie," Cordelia said. "Besides, we think your fate has changed now."

Will gave a slight smile: "In other words… I die at the end."

Cordelia stayed stone-faced.

"And do I fall in love?"

Cordelia stammered, refusing to answer. She didn't want to tell Will about Penelope Hope. *If his fate really has changed, then this is a good test.* Eventually she said, "You do a lot of heroic things."

"Like fight? That's not so heroic," said Will. "It's the war. Everyone fights. D'you mind if I sit?"

"Absolutely – I mean, no, please do."

Will sat next to her on the couch, but not too close. He left enough space between them for a phantom person to occupy. He surveyed the room. It was still full of rubble. The coffee table lay splintered in a pile of glass next to the piano. On the wall was a dark stain: Mrs Walker's blood.

"I imagine this was once a beautiful room," Will said.

"It was. And my family just moved in too! We didn't even get a chance to really live here." Cordelia thought of how gorgeous Kristoff House had been when she'd first stepped inside it.

"Shall we clean up the mess?"

"Right now?"

Will nodded.

"I don't know if I have the energy… I mean, we can leave it for a while…"

"I see," said Will. "If the room remains in tatters, you can pretend this is all just a bad dream that you're waiting to wake up from. But if it's back to normal—"

"It reminds me of my parents," finished Cordelia. "And if I think too much about them—"

"It makes you weak. You worry that you may not be strong enough to go on."

"It's impressive how well you can read people."

"Have you ever heard the expression 'You learn a lot by listening'?"

"Sounds like something from a self-help book. Did you read that somewhere?"

"No. I heard it from Frank Quigley."

"Who?"

"RFC captain. One of the aces of Squadron Seventy. Canadian, too, so I wasn't inclined to listen to him, but he had real presence. During mealtimes, even though he was a popular chap, he never uttered a word. Once I asked him why, and he told me an expression that he said had helped him immensely: 'You learn a lot by listening.' So I try to do that with you Walkers. And I've learned that *you*, Cordelia, bear the burden of responsibility."

Cordelia nodded, transfixed.

"Your siblings look to you. They respect you. And that puts pressure on you. To lead, to find the answers… to get their *lives* back. That sort of pressure can be overwhelming."

Cordelia sighed. "All true."

"Well, I've been in the Great War. Sometimes you *can't* get your life back. Sometimes you have to *take* it back."

Will stood and offered his hand. Cordelia took it.

"The fact is," Will said, "we may be stuck in this house for a long time. It's all we have. There's no point in letting it fester around us. We're going to have to start catching our own food, washing our own clothes, getting regular exercise…"

"And cleaning this room," Cordelia said.

"I'll start with the heavier items," Will said, indicating the legless piano. "You take care of the broken bits of wood."

They began to clean up, Cordelia glancing every now and then at Will, unable not to. The few times she caught his eye, his smile was an expression of comfort, something a father or teacher would offer a youngster. *He still thinks I'm a kid. Maybe it'd be better if he didn't think anything at all…*

Meanwhile, outside, Brendan hadn't detected any suspicious activity to guard against, but he had become slightly obsessed with the grenade. He wanted to blow something up. *It's crazy,* he thought. *I've seen so many explosions in movies and games, but I've never set one off in real life. And besides, I've been through a lot today. I even almost died a couple of times. I deserve to have some fun.*

He left his post at the door. The forest was feeling a little safer now; he hadn't seen the wolf or any nasty dragonflies or heard any hoofbeats. He headed into the woods past the downed trees that the Wind Witch had left. He wasn't going far. Just far enough.

As he walked, Brendan wondered how he had ever been scared of the forest. It was a beautiful day full of bright air and fresh smells… *like being in a shampoo commercial,* he thought. He came to a small cliff, a seven-metre rock face that rose out of the forest floor to meet the top of a slight hill. There were trees above the cliff and beside it, but nothing on its grey surface.

"Perfect," Brendan said. He remembered, years ago, being fascinated on a family trip to Colorado as his dad drove along a treacherous mountain road. Their car had been centimetres away from a cliff! Brendan had asked his father, "How'd they put the road *through* here?" And his dad had said, "See those little hollowed-out cylinders in the rock? That's where they put the dynamite."

Now Brendan was ready to do some dynamiting of his own.

He pulled the pin on the grenade. He threw it at the cliff. He spun behind a tree, shut his eyes tight, put his hands over his ears—

BOOM! Even through his flesh, his eardrums felt almost pierced.

Inside the house, Cordelia and Will abruptly stopped cleaning when they heard the sound.

"What was that?" asked Cordelia.

"Uh-oh," said Will, dashing out of the room, "I knew I shouldn't have given him the grenade."

"*You gave Brendan a grenade?*" shouted Cordelia, running

after Will. "*Are you completely insane?*"

Outside, Brendan slowly opened his eyes and peeked at his handiwork. He had a blown a hole in the bottom of the cliff. Shards of stone were scattered around as if pointing to it. The hole didn't go deep – it was about the size of a fireplace – but as the smoke cleared, Brendan saw something inside.

A book.

No way, he thought, but as he approached, it came into focus: *The Book of Doom and Desire*. Sitting right there in the hole.

Because I did something for myself. Because I listened to my own selfish desires.

Brendan remembered that he had warned Cordelia about this book, that finding it for the Wind Witch was an obvious trap… but none of that mattered now. It was right there. Just one look at it told him it was magical, more magical than anything he had seen in his life. It wasn't its shape or its size; it was something he couldn't put into words. *Power* was the closest word.

What's inside? If it's blank, then what in there is so powerful?

Brendan ran to the book. Grabbed it. The ground

around his hands was hot and smoking. He was about to open it—

When he heard a thundering crunch in the forest. Very big, very close.

"Oh no…" Brendan looked at the book as he thought of his sisters. All of a sudden he knew he'd made a big mistake. His desire to open the book was too strong, too *weird*. Leaving his post at the door, coming out here to blow up a cliff… he'd left his sisters vulnerable – *abandoned his duty*, as Will would say. And now something was coming.

Brendan flung the book down. "You stay away from me," he said. "You're totally evil." He ran back to Kristoff House.

Cordelia and Will burst through the front door and stopped dead, trying to process what they were seeing. Two enormous, crusty, bare feet were planted in the clearing in front of them. Each foot was nearly as big as Kristoff House itself. The legs that came up from them were redwood-sized and just as naked.

"A giant," Will said.

"Bigger," said Cordelia. "A colossus."

Cordelia was terrified to look up and see *more* naked parts, but when she did, she saw that the colossus was wearing a loincloth, tied under him like a nappy – and he was even taller than the trees. Cordelia couldn't see past the loincloth.

Brendan suddenly appeared, racing out of the forest. He looked up at the colossus, saw Will and Cordelia on the front porch, and didn't stop running. He knew the monster could stamp him flat with one step – but he couldn't risk getting separated from his family.

"*Rrrrrrr?*" he heard from above, a huge sound like machinery, as the colossus picked up one foot—

But Brendan was already on the front porch, dashing inside with Cordelia and Will.

"Bren! Where were you?"

PTOOSH! The foot hit the ground outside the door.

"I'm sorry!" Brendan said. "I got distracted with that grenade—"

"*Distracted? You set it off!*" Will shouted, as the colossus thudded its huge hand into the ground outside, shadowing the hallway.

"Sorry," Brendan said. "It was something I've always wanted to do—"

"Please tell me you used it for something that will help us?" said Will.

"Not exactly," said an embarrassed Brendan. "I wanted to see how big a hole I could blow in the side of a cliff."

"You wasted a perfectly good grenade because you wanted to see something explode?!"

"Kind of, yeah."

"*Bren!*" Cordelia said. "Maybe that grenade could've stopped the colossus!"

Before Brendan could tell them the part about seeing *The Book of Doom and Desire*, a rumbling threw them all off balance. It was like an earthquake – the whole ground shook – and then the floor of Kristoff House tilted upwards. Brendan, Cordelia and Will tried to keep their footing, but it was as if the house were on a seesaw and something heavy were in the kitchen.

"What's happening?" Will yelled. He and Cordelia grabbed the wall to steady themselves as Brendan tumbled down the hall.

"It's the colossus from *Savage Warriors*! And he's lifting the house from that corner!" Brendan said, pointing as broken tables and vases and books slid past him.

"Nell!" Cordelia called. "If you're in the dumbwaiter… get out!"

Eleanor didn't answer – and suddenly Cordelia grabbed Will as the floor's angle got too steep and they all began to slide towards the kitchen. Brendan was terrified that the floor was going to go vertical and make them fall, like in that old video game *Castlevania*, but all of a sudden it became level again. Everyone paused to take a breath – and then the floor began to tilt in the opposite direction!

"I gotta see what's going on!" Brendan called. He felt horribly guilty – more guilty than scared – and that guilt pushed him back to the front door.

"Bren! It's not safe!" Cordelia warned, but her brother stumbled out – and he wasn't in the forest any more.

Brendan stood where the welcome mat would be if Kristoff House had one. In front of him, instead of downed trees, he saw the hand of the colossus. Its fingers were pressed together to make the leathery, springy wall they had seen before.

Brendan ran and jump-kicked the hand.

"Stop!" Cordelia cried, watching from the doorway with Will – but Brendan bounced off, hitting the colossus's palm.

"I'm trying to get him to put us down!" he explained. Behind him, as if they had felt the kick, the colossus's fingers separated.

Cordelia gasped. Through the fingers was blue, clear sky. Brendan inched forward, peered down—

And saw the forest canopy. *Below him.*

"**H**ey! Up here!" a voice called. Brendan, Cordelia and Will turned to see Eleanor leaning out of one of the second-storey windows. "Do you guys realise there's this big, ugly, hairy guy carrying us around?"

"Yes!" they all said at once. Then Cordelia spoke. "Nell, are you OK?"

"I'm fine."

Brendan asked, "How do you know he's hairy?"

"I can *see* him from up here! He looks like that really skinny British guy on the cover of Dad's old CDs…That guy who sings about not getting enough satisfaction?"

"Mick Jagger?" Brendan asked.

"Yeah! He looks like Mick Jagger if Mick Jagger ate a whole truckful of Snickers."

They rushed inside, went upstairs, and lurched down the second-floor hall, sometimes powering forward as the house tilted up, sometimes scrambling for something to hold on to as it tilted down. They were relieved when they made it to Eleanor's room and found her staring out of the window. "Look!"

From the second storey they could see much better. Four of the colossus's jumbo fingers made up the wall, over which they could barely glimpse the sky. The house sat in the colossus's immense palm.

"He's carrying us through the forest like a giant Domino's pizza!"

"Nell," Cordelia said, "you can't be enjoying this."

"Why not? Maybe he's taking us home!"

"How do you know he's a he?"

"I guess he could be a lady with a beard," shrugged Eleanor, "but come and see for yourself."

She led them across the hall to the master bedroom. There they beheld the colossus in all his glory.

The view started with the base of his palm, which stuck out underneath the house like a limestone outcrop. Leading down from it, impossibly huge, was his foreshortened, tanned right arm. Brendan started calculating: in order to hold Kristoff House, the colossus had to have a hand that was twenty metres by twenty metres, and your arm was about six times as long as your palm, so…

"His arm's the size of a thirty-storey building!"

"Yeah, he's like a mountain man who's as big as an actual mountain," said Eleanor.

The colossus's flowing black hair draped over his bare shoulders, each of which was the size of a lorry. He didn't look like he was going bald any time soon. (With a direct view of the top of his head they would've seen a carousel-sized bald spot.) Large white specks like giant snowflakes dotted his hair.

"Yeccchhhh! He's got dandruff!" Brendan said, frowning. "With pieces as big as my head!"

The colossus's voluminous hair obscured most of his face, but he definitely had black eyebrows, a wide, perfectly triangular nose, and crazy huge lips. He really did resemble a mammoth Mick Jagger.

"What's that horrible smell?" asked Cordelia, placing her hand over her nose and mouth.

"He has body odour," explained Eleanor.

"Smells like Mr Benjamin, my third-grade science

teacher," said Brendan. "The guy was allergic to showers."

The colossus took no notice of his passengers, forging ahead with his face just above the treetops, using his left hand to snap the trees aside as he traversed the sea of green. His movements were so Himalayan that he almost looked as if he were operating in slow motion. Cordelia felt dizzy. She wondered how his heart could pump blood to his entire body – *maybe it's as big as Kristoff House and only beats once a minute.*

"I think we should ride it out," Cordelia said, "and hope he's taking us somewhere with food."

"Unless he's taking us somewhere where *we're* the food," said Brendan.

"If you look at this with the proper perspective, it could be a tremendous opportunity," said Will. "We've been trying to figure out where we are by reading books. Here's a chance for direct observation."

Will poked his body out of the window, leaning so far that Cordelia grabbed him to keep him from falling. He held his palm over his eyes and swivelled his head 180 degrees to gaze as far as he could... but saw only the oppressive green trees.

"Forget it," Will said as he slid back. "No sign of civilisation. Maybe we *should* just 'ride it out', as Cordelia suggests."

Brendan rolled his eyes. His sister beamed.

"Can I see again?" asked Eleanor. She loved being up so high; it beat sitting around in the forest waiting for wolves. Taking Will's place at the window, she stared down at the colossus, who she'd come to think of as her friend Fat Jagger – after all, he hadn't done anything really bad, not yet. But then the house shuddered and became still.

"What's happening?" Cordelia asked.

"I'm not sure…"

Fat Jagger had stopped. He moved his left hand to his face. There was something wiggling between his giant finger and thumb. Eleanor saw it squirm, heard it buzz, and yelled, "*Ew, it's a dragonfly!*" just before the colossus popped it in his mouth and chomped down. The insect squelched, squirting its juices across the treetops.

"He's not vegan! He's a meat eater!" Eleanor jumped back from the window. "Bren was right! He's taking us somewhere to *eat us*! Guys, if he likes bugs, how much better are *we* gonna taste?"

"Like juicy pineapple wrapped in bacon!" said Brendan. "We gotta do something."

"Too bad we don't have that grenade," Cordelia said pointedly to Brendan, but Eleanor was already running down to the kitchen. When she came back, she had a hunk of limp meat wrapped in plastic.

Brendan asked, "Nell, what is that?"

"Pork tenderloin. From the freezer."

"That freezer hasn't worked for two days! That's rotten!"

"He just ate a *dragonfly*!"

Eleanor went to the window and unwrapped the tenderloin. An unpleasant, sweet odour wafted into the room as she yelled, "*Hey! Mr Colossus! Look up!*"

The giant turned to her. For the first time the Walkers and Will saw his face. More than anything he looked like the homeless war vets they'd seen in downtown San Francisco, with sad, bloodshot eyes bordered by deep creases.

"Try this! From the Walkers!"

Eleanor dropped the tenderloin. It snaked through the air – and landed in Fat Jagger's open mouth.

"Nice job!" Eleanor called. "D'ya want more?"

The colossus nodded, wobbling his arm (and the house).

Eleanor tore out of the room. "I'm getting more!"

"Nell, wait, this isn't a good idea – like you know how you're not supposed to feed bears?" Brendan said, but his sister came back with a box of formerly frozen fish. She leaned out of the window and let the yellow patties fall into Fat Jagger's waiting maw.

"This is from the Walkers! Wa-lkers, remember? We're your friends!" She kept saying the nicest things to him – and then she froze. "Uh-oh. Guys? You might want to see this."

They all crowded around the window. Fat Jagger wasn't eating any more. He was making a huge fist in front of his face. His immense knuckles cracked in succession. He stared dead ahead—

At another colossus striding through the forest. Coming right for them.

"Do you think he wants our colossus's food?" Eleanor asked.

"I think he wants his *head*," said Brendan.

The new colossus didn't have the kind face that Fat Jagger did. He looked like an all-out bruiser, with a bald, acne-spotted skull, sharp red eyebrows, and a goatee like the devil's tail. His face was twisted in a furious scowl, and he was snorting, sounding like a wild boar filtered through concert speakers. He used one hand to push the trees aside, while the other bounced a huge boulder in his palm. And he was even bigger than Fat Jagger.

"He's like a colossus on steroids," Brendan said.

"Maybe it'll be OK," Cordelia said. "Maybe they'll just talk."

"Talk? Look at his face! He's madder than Uncle Pete

after two six-packs!"

Eleanor called out of the window to the advancing giant: "Mr Colossus! We don't mean you any harm! We're the Walkers! Wa-lkers!"

The bald colossus didn't react – but Fat Jagger looked up.

"Fat Jagger!" Eleanor yelled.

"A touch rude, don't you think?" asked Will.

"What?"

"The fat bit."

"Oh, right," said Eleanor. "Jagger! Sorry about calling you fat. You're not really fat; you're just a little… husky. That means 'muscular' at Target. But you can hear us, right? So listen, this other colossus guy—"

"Let me try," Brendan said, pushing Eleanor out of the way. "Jagger! This bald dude who needs a Clearasil shampoo? He looks like he wants to mess you up, and we're kind of in the middle of it, so before you start wailing on each other, could you put us down?"

"*Rrrrr?*" Fat Jagger said. There was just enough intelligence in his eyes to register frustration and fear.

"It's no use," Brendan said. "I think he's got a learning disability."

"You just don't know how to talk to him!" Eleanor shouted, shoving her brother. "Jagger! If you put the house down, I promise that next time we see each other, I'll give you *more* food… *cooked* food… *better, tastier* food! Please?!"

Fat Jagger raised an eyebrow.

"*Please?!*" Eleanor pleaded. Jagger nodded… and began to lower the house! The Walkers and Will felt themselves descending as if in the world's largest lift.

"He's doing it! He likes me!" Eleanor said, but then her eyes went wide as she saw a huge blur race towards Fat Jagger's head.

"Jagger! Duck! The mean giant is throwing the boulder!"

Fat Jagger turned in time to see a boulder speeding towards him like a major-league fastball. He kicked his massive skull to the side. It almost looked like a dance move, and Eleanor cheered, but although the boulder missed his face, it hit him in the shoulder, producing a thunderous meaty snap.

With a roar Fat Jagger grabbed his new injury – and then Eleanor's view went screwy. All of a sudden instead of peering outside she was looking up at the ceiling as she skidded across the floor. It took her a second to realise that

Kristoff House was *turning around in mid-air…* because Fat Jagger had dropped it.

The house fell with sickening speed. Eleanor's stomach rocketed into her neck as she grabbed the bed. Brendan hugged the Hello Kitty sleeping bag. Cordelia put her head between her knees in the aeroplane crash position. Will protectively wrapped his arms around her.

And then, suddenly, the house stopped.

It sat smoothly just above the tree canopy. No crash. Only Fat Jagger's immense eye in the window.

"*You caught us!*" Eleanor yelled. She turned to the others. "He caught us with his other hand! He saved us, even though he was hurt!"

"Thank you!" Cordelia said, standing up with Will and Brendan. In response Fat Jagger winked. The folds of his eyelids were so huge that they made a wet click. He gave a wide, sweet smile. His rotting, crooked teeth were the colour of mouldy candy corn.

"Awww. He's kinda cute," Eleanor said.

The others looked at her with incredulous expressions.

"In a smelly Muppet kinda way," explained Eleanor.

Brendan grinned and approached Fat Jagger to ask him

to put them all the way down, but he stopped as a curious shadow (it almost looked like the peaks of giant knuckles) fell across the giant's head. Jagger's smile disappeared as Brendan said, "Guys! Look out—"

But he didn't have time to explain. The bald colossus was punching Fat Jagger. His immense fist knocked Jagger's head back with the force of a TNT blast. And like any good punch, it didn't stop at the point of contact. It followed through… right into Kristoff House.

The bedroom wall buckled but held as the fist hit it. Plaster rained down. The window shattered. Brendan bounced across the room like a rag doll – and suddenly the house was spinning back into the air!

"Bren!" Cordelia screamed. She tried to go to him, but she might as well have been going to the moon. The room – the floor – all of Kristoff House was whirling out of control. Within its walls, up and down didn't mean much any more. Cordelia could only watch her brother's body crumple into a corner and hope he was still alive… but then she wondered, as the house entered the slow embrace of freefall: *What's the point? He won't be for much longer!*

35

Whenever Cordelia saw movies and television re-enactments where dying people's lives flashed before their eyes, she wondered: *Is it really that easy?* Life was long and complicated – even hers, already – and remembering it in sequence seemed like a serious task. Instead she yelled for her sister: "*Nell!*"

"*C'mon!*" Eleanor said, running towards Cordelia as blue sky streaked past the windows. "*We're getting in the wardrobe – hurry!*"

Cordelia saw that Will had dragged Brendan into the master-bedroom wardrobe and grabbed all the pillows, sleeping bags and duvets. Now the enclosed space was like a cocoon. She lurched in with Eleanor, slamming the door – just as Kristoff House hit the tree canopy.

It sounded like a crashing wave: a *ksssshhh* of displaced

mass as the house reduced the crown of one of the forest's mighty trees to a falling collection of splinters. Cordelia bounced against the hastily padded walls of the wardrobe, letting out muffled screams, until bark squealed against cladding and the house came to a stop. She found herself clutching a handful of hangers.

"I say, we've landed," said Will, inching open the door.

The bedroom looked like it had been shaken inside a snow globe: the *RW* trunk was upside down; the bedside tables were totally busted; the mattress was peeking out of the broken window. *If I'd been out there*, Cordelia thought, *I'd have been impaled.*

"We appear to be resting on a very large limb," said Will, seeing the cross-hatching of branches outside the windows.

"I always wanted a tree house," said Cordelia morbidly.

Wood cracked and strained below them. The floor tilted to the side. "I don't expect you'll have one much longer," said Will.

They all held their breath as the branch they were sitting on groaned and bent, snapping in many tiny places. Every time it seemed to settle and bear the weight of the house, another piece of furniture somewhere slid aside with a thunk, causing the house to pitch over more, causing the wood to rupture more…

"We have to go!" said Cordelia. "Bren! Are you awake?"

"*Uggggggh…*" Brendan was bruised and groggy. He looked like he should have cartoon stars circling his face.

"*Brendan! Wake up! You're late for school!*" Eleanor screamed in his ear, and all of a sudden he was alert.

"Hey!" He turned to Eleanor. "Not fair. Where are we?"

"In a tree," Cordelia said. "We've got to climb down 'cause the branches won't hold."

"A *tree*?" Brendan poked his head into the bedroom. He saw the leaves outside and realised what a ticking-time-bomb situation he was in. *It's gonna fall and smash! And I'll end up trapped in the rubble like a victim from one of those horrible 8.0-magnitude earthquakes.* His mouth started running: "Oh man – I gotta get outta here!"

"Not so fast, Bren – calm down—"

But he bolted from the wardrobe. *Get to the window. Get outside. Outside, you'll be safe.* He tripped, fell and rolled over the debris-filled floor. He landed with the accumulating broken furniture at the opposite wall. He had a second to look at the others and realise his mistake as his weight added to the pile—

And the branch under Kristoff House snapped.

The home and its inhabitants dropped.

This freefall wasn't so free – it was more like being in the centre of a roaring avalanche. Kristoff House crashed through limbs and scattered branches on its way down, shearing off one entire side of the mighty tree.

"I love you guys!" Brendan called unexpectedly. Eleanor hugged Cordelia. Cordelia closed her eyes. Will kept his chin up. They all braced for impact in their small, bewildered ways—

And then Kristoff House hit the ground.

And kept going.

Cordelia couldn't figure it out – was she in some kind of afterlife? Hitting the earth should have turned off the power button, but she could still see a now-brownish blur outside the canted windows and hear a rolling, crunching rumble. It felt like they were sliding down a hill. Brendan whooped, "The barrels!"

"*What?*" Will asked.

Cordelia got it: "The earthquake barrels! There's dozens

of them strapped to the foundations, and we're rolling on them!"

Indeed, if they had been outside Kristoff House, they would have seen an awesome sight: a three-storey, landmarked Victorian home literally barrelling down a steep, rugged incline like an out-of-control shopping trolley, devastating everything in its path. Ferns, logs, anthills, some of the barrels themselves and various shell-shocked rodents were sent flying. Inside the home, it was like being on a sleigh ride, and as with so many things that the Walkers and Will had experienced in the past forty-eight hours, it would have been amazingly fun if not for the element of death.

"Go, Denver Kristoff!" Brendan yelled, clambering back into the wardrobe.

"What are you on about?" asked Will.

"Kristoff designed this place to float away on barrels if there was a really bad earthquake, and now we're rolling down a hill on those barrels!"

"Into *what*?" Will asked.

"…Uh-oh," Brendan said. "We didn't get a look at what was on the other side of the house, did we, Will?"

The rocky slope came to an end – and Kristoff House flew off it, soaring into open air.

The Walkers and Will knew what to do. They were scared, of course – but at this point they were beyond scared. They all shut the door to the padded wardrobe. Cordelia heard the barrels; they were whistling. She grabbed her siblings' hands. Eleanor and Brendan grabbed Will's.

"Whatever happens, I hope it's quick!" yelled Eleanor bravely. "This up-and-down stuff is driving me cra—"

With a deafening, shuddering slap, the house hit the ocean.

36

Seawater spouted up and fell away. The Walkers and Will stayed in the wardrobe for a long minute, letting their adrenalin levels return to something like normal. Then they left the wardrobe, stared out of the window and breathed. *Breathing is really amazing,* Brendan thought before he asked, "Are we sinking?"

"Not yet," said Cordelia.

"So we're floating."

"It would seem that way."

Kristoff House was in the middle of a vast bay, bobbing in rocky waves. Behind it, the forest stretched as far as the eye could see, ending in a steep incline with a brown scar where the house had gouged out its path. Ahead of it, the sun was sinking behind snow-capped mountains. The perspective seemed wrong: the Walkers were so far from the mountains that the base of each one began below the horizon, yet the peaks of each one reached into the clouds.

"Are we sure this isn't San Francisco? And we aren't sailing towards Marin?" Eleanor asked.

"There's no mountains like that in Marin," said Cordelia. "These look bigger than Everest."

"Oh, right. So maybe we'll float somewhere with food! I'm hungry. And thirsty. Like, really bad."

"Don't count on it," said Brendan. "Some colossuses will probably wade out here and grab us first."

"Coloss*i*," corrected Cordelia.

"Will you stop it? Who cares? If the stupid giants don't get us, we'll drown!"

"Drown?" asked a frightened Eleanor.

"Did you hear those barrels getting snapped off when we rolled down the hill?" Brendan said. "There's probably only a couple of 'em still strapped to the house. It's only a matter of time before we sink."

"I miss Mum and Dad," said Eleanor in a quiet voice. She wiped a tear off her cheek. "And I want juice. And I'm scared."

"C'mere." Cordelia wrapped an arm around her.

"The scary part's over. Now we just have to deal with Brendan." She smiled – and despite himself, Brendan did too. *Still breathing*, he thought. *Isn't that crazy?* They all stood together as the last rays of sunlight disappeared behind the mountains, wondering how they'd make it through a night at sea.

"Do you hear that?" asked Will. They listened. At first, all they could register was the soft smack of waves against the house, but then Cordelia heard it. Sinister like the noise of fluorescent lights in a school toilet.

"Hissing," she said.

"Exactly. Soft but consistent. Let's go and check on it."

Will offered his hand to Cordelia, who offered hers to Eleanor. Brendan took up the rear. They went forward as a human chain down to the kitchen. The sky was filling with glittering stars, more than the Walkers had ever seen, but even in the surprisingly bright starlight, they had to tread carefully to avoid the debris on the floor. Kristoff House was such a mess that it was tough to imagine it had ever been a decent human habitation.

In the kitchen, Brendan went to the basement door.

"Look," he said, opening it and peering down the

steps, "we're flooded!"

"Let me see." Cordelia sighed when she saw that the water came up to the top step. It had been easy to be hopeful upstairs – it was harder when confronted with her own reflection in dark seawater. "Oh no. We've got about thirty centimetres before the entire first floor gets soaked!"

"It doesn't look like it's getting higher," said Eleanor. "Maybe it'll stop there."

"Look," said Will, pointing to a disturbance in the water. A pod of bubbles burbled towards the back of the stairwell.

"Air from one of the ruptured barrels," said Cordelia. "We're losing buoyancy."

"You mean *sinking*?" asked Eleanor.

"Exactly," said Cordelia, plopping down on the kitchen floor.

"Deal, c'mon, why are you sitting?" Brendan asked.

"Why should I not sit? You were right. This house is gonna sink and we're gonna be swimming to land in the middle of the night trying not to get eaten by sharks or colossi," Cordelia said in a monotone.

"You are such a downer," said Eleanor. "I thought it was Bren we had to worry about."

"Yeah, well, hate to break it to you, but I don't have any more answers," Cordelia said. "I don't know how a bunch of kids lost at sea can possibly escape a sinking house."

"We could build a boat," Brendan said, "and sail away, like that song, y'know?" He started singing the Styx classic "Come Sail Away", trying to get his sister to laugh, but she wasn't having it.

"The three of us don't know how to build a boat. Do you, Will?"

Will shook his head. He was stone-faced, betraying no reaction.

"See? Even a pilot can't save you when you're lost at sea." Cordelia looked down. Brendan and Eleanor looked at each other. Eleanor's stomach rumbled so loudly they all heard it. "Plus there's that," Cordelia said. "We haven't eaten since breakfast Lunchables."

"It hurts…" Eleanor moaned, holding her stomach. "I didn't want to tell you guys, but it hurts like something sharp and empty. And all I can think about is food."

"Well, you won't have to worry much longer," Cordelia declared, but before she could say another depressing thing, Will stood over her and she got quiet.

"I was wrong about you," he said.

"Oh?"

"You're not like Cordelia in *King Lear* at all. You're a coward."

"Excuse me?"

"A snivelling, weak little coward!" said Will. "I thought you were mature. Thought you had backbone. But now, when things get a little rough, you're ready to toss it all in and pull the rest of us down with you! Well, I won't have it. I refuse to give up!"

He grabbed Cordelia and pulled her to her feet.

"Do you know what my boss, Lieutenant-Colonel Reginald Rathbone the Third, told me on my first day in the RFC? He said we're only here because someone, somewhere, didn't give up! The Spanish navy tried to rule the seas, but the British didn't give up! Napoleon tried to take over Europe, but his brave enemies didn't give up! Your father asked your mother out on a date once, and *he* didn't give up! The people who give up never write history! And you're *giving up*!"

"But we've got no options," Cordelia said.

"No options? We haven't even explored the house!"

"Uh, yeah, we have," said Brendan. "It used to be just books and expensive furniture, and now it's just books and junk."

"What about that hissing?"

Will gave them all a moment to be silent so they could hear it. It was still there – an insistent high whine.

Will strode into the hallway and pressed his ear against the wall. "I'll tell you what *I* think, before any of you catch a nasty case of cowardice from Cordelia. I think it's another barrel, and it's been punctured, just like the one underwater in the basement. This barrel is somewhere under this house releasing air, and the reason we can hear it everywhere" – he rapped his knuckles against the wall – "is because the walls are hollow."

"Hollow?" asked Cordelia.

Will knocked again. Sure enough, the sound echoed as if reverberating through a hidden chamber. Cordelia placed her ear against it and tried herself.

"He's right," she said. "There's space back there."

"See?" Will said. "'No options.' Piffle! There are always options."

"One question, Will," said Brendan. "I'm all for trying

to stay positive and upbeat when we're about to face a pretty nasty death, but exactly how do hissing barrels and hollow walls give us options?"

"Hollow walls mean passageways. Passageways mean other rooms, hidden chambers. And hidden chambers mean…"

"Food!" said Eleanor, clutching her stomach. "I hope."

"Hope," said Will, "is the most important thing." His eyes burned straight through Cordelia.

37

The Walkers and Will set about finding a way into the hollow walls. They lit some scented candles and placed them on the floor, secured in makeshift aluminium-foil candleholders, which Eleanor chided was very dangerous. ("Then you're in charge," Brendan told her. "I'm making you official fire-safety officer.") Will pressed his ear against the wall, moving to different spots and rapping with his knuckles as if listening for the house's heartbeat. Cordelia, embarrassed by her previous fit of hopelessness – and by the way Will had called her out on it – tried to help, imitating Will's movements.

"Please stop," Will told her, "I'm trying to concentrate."

"Excuse me? You told me not to lose hope; here I am, not losing hope. Why the attitude?"

Brendan and Eleanor grimaced at each other: *Here they go.*

"I do appreciate you pitching in," said Will, "but I'm trying to determine where to break into the hollow wall, and I can't if you're mucking about making a racket."

"I'm *helping* you!"

"You're distracting me."

"Maybe *I'll* be the one to find a way in; did you ever think of that?"

Will smiled and shook his head. "My dear, that's not possible. The male brain is far more refined than the female brain when it comes to visualising physical space."

"Really?" Cordelia asked, turning red with anger.

"It's a scientific fact, and I won't hear any arguments to the contrary."

Cordelia didn't intend to respond with an argument. She was looking for something to throw. Fortunately for her, the metal foot from the suit of armour lay right beside her. She flung it at Will.

"Crikey!" Will threw up his hands to protect his face. The hunk of metal bounced off his forearm, nearly hitting his still-injured shoulder, and smashed through a hall window; Cordelia heard it plop into the ocean outside. The window curtain swept out, pulled by the breeze, and billowed over the waves.

"You unbelievable harridan!" Will rubbed his arm. "How dare—"

"I'm not going to be lectured by someone whose view of women is stuck in 1910s Britain!" Cordelia exclaimed. "Especially when our house is *sinking*! I'm going to *do* something about it!"

"I doubt that," Will replied.

Cordelia turned on her heels and strode towards the kitchen: "You'll see. My less-refined female brain has *somehow* come up with an idea!"

Eleanor went after Cordelia.

"Where are you going?" Brendan asked.

"Us sisters have to stick together!"

Eleanor climbed the spiral stairs with Cordelia. "How do you live with them?" Will asked Brendan. "Must be maddening."

"I play a lot of video games," Brendan said.

Will turned back to the wall. As he tapped on it and listened, Brendan took notice of the wall-mounted lamps all around. He had an idea about them… but just as he was about to share it, Will pulled his ear away and declared,

"There. That's the spot. The wall's weak point. Can you fetch me a hammer and pencil, mate?"

Brendan went to the kitchen and found a pencil and the small ball-peen hammer that Cordelia had tried on the *RW* trunk. When he presented the items, Will baulked at the hammer. "What's this? I'm not trying to break into a doll's house!"

"It's all we've got. But you know what? I might have a better solution," said Brendan.

"What's that?"

With supreme confidence Brendan grabbed one of the wall-mounted lamps – and yanked down with two hands. The lamp snapped off, leaving an ugly wire sticking out and plaster crumbling on to Brendan's face.

"Have you lost the plot?" asked Will.

Brendan got mad: "Listen, buddy, you might be a hotshot when it comes to flying planes and making my sister angry, but you're looking at a veteran of hundreds of hours of *New Adventures of Scooby-Doo,* and when Scooby and the gang need to get into a hidden passageway, they always do the same thing – pull on a lamp!"

"Scooby *who*?" Will asked.

"Scooby-Doo – he's a talking dog who happens to be a detective." Brendan grabbed the next lamp and pulled. Once again, the lamp snapped off. Will burst out laughing.

"OK… so maybe Denver Kristoff didn't rig the lamps," said a frustrated Brendan, picking plaster chunks out of his hair.

Suddenly a splash of water on Will's neck made him spin around. "Bombs away!" he heard from upstairs.

He poked his head out of the broken window and saw part of a desk drifting in the sea. The moon had risen, and its luminescence made the waves look as if they were laced with crystal.

"Watch out!" Cordelia yelled from above. "Wouldn't want to hurt your massive male brain!" Will pulled back – just before a broken chair fell from the second-storey window and hit the water, sending another burst of sea spray at him.

"Are you mad?" he called up.

"We're lightening the load on the ship!" Cordelia shouted. "'Jettisoning the ballast', as your naval colleagues might say!"

"That – that—" Will sputtered; Brendan was sure he

was going to unleash an insult. "That is a *fantastic idea*! Bloody good thinking! Keep it up!"

"You're too kind!" Cordelia replied with a healthy dose of sarcasm before tossing a frayed wicker hamper into the water. Eleanor was feeding her an endless supply of ruined items from the master bedroom.

"See?" Will turned to Brendan. "Now your sisters are actually helping, and all you're doing is pulling on lamps. Stay out of my way and don't cause trouble."

"What do you want me to do?" asked Brendan.

"Just bugger off until I break through this wall," said Will.

Brendan grumbled and kicked a lamp as Will marked an *X* on the wall with the pencil and began hitting it with the ball-peen hammer, trying to focus while an alarm clock – and a shoe tree, and a vacuum cleaner – hit the ocean behind him. Brendan walked to the living room and plopped down on the now-legless piano. Resting on the floor was *Savage Warriors,* the book Cordelia had been reading that she had flipped over on the couch – and that reminded Brendan of something important.

"Deal! Nell!" Brendan rushed into the upstairs hall.

Cordelia and Eleanor couldn't keep from smiling as they threw magazines and bookends and paperweights that had migrated into the hall out of the window.

"Bren, see how it's working?" Cordelia said. "We're lighter!"

"Yeah, that's great, but I forgot to tell you guys," Brendan said. "I saw *The Book of Doom and Desire*."

"What? Where?"

"Before the colossus thing. When I sneaked into the woods to set off the grenade. Inside the cliff where the explosion happened."

"How did it get *there*?" asked Eleanor.

"I don't think the book exists in just one place. I think it can jump around. Like if we follow our selfish desires, it'll show up. And we'll be tempted to open it. But that's my point: *don't*."

"Why?" Cordelia asked. "Did *you* open it?"

"No! I was going to, but – it would've been wrong. That book is pure evil."

"How can you know that?"

"Because it…" Brendan searched for the right words. "As I got closer to the book, it started to have this incredible hold over me. It was an amazing, really kinda awesome feeling. Like I could do anything, like I was stronger and more powerful than anybody. It was like what they talk about at those special assemblies at school, where they teach us about the dangers of drugs? And how you become so obsessed with them they can take over your life and ruin everything? The book was like that. When I was holding it, I didn't care about anything else. And worst of all… I didn't care about any of *you*. And that's when I knew… I had to do everything in my power to keep from opening it, and throw it away. Because if I had opened it… I'm pretty sure I'd still be in that forest. Alone." Brendan gulped. "And I don't want to be alone. OK?"

Eleanor gave him a hug. She couldn't remember a time when her brother had admitted to needing anyone in his family. Cordelia watched and nodded… but she thought, *Maybe the book scared Bren because he's not the one who's supposed to open it. Maybe I am.*

"Now… do you want my help?" Brendan asked. "Should we chuck these?" He pointed to the pictures of Denver Kristoff's family. The frames were splintered on the floor.

"It doesn't seem right to throw away somebody's

memories," said Cordelia, looking at the portraits in the moonlight, especially the ones of baby Dahlia. "It's weird," she said. "She was such an adorable baby, so cute and happy—"

"But she grew up to be the Wind Witch," said Brendan.

"Yeah. There's no indication whatsoever. Rousseau says that we're all born as a blank slate, that we learn evil as we get older."

"*Pff*, no way," said Eleanor. "There's kids in my grade who are already evil. There's this one, David Seamer, who attacked his brother with a sledgehammer."

"That's ridiculous," Brendan said. "What eight-year-old would be able to lift a… Hold on…"

Brendan suddenly ran back down the stairs. "See you soon!"

Cordelia and Eleanor looked at each other: "What got into him?"

Downstairs in the kitchen, Brendan searched through the detritus on the floor. Will approached, hearing the commotion. He hadn't made much progress with the ball-peen hammer.

"What in blazes are you looking for?"

Brendan was too possessed by his latest idea to answer. He grabbed a cluster of plastic shopping bags, a stack of clear disposable cups, and the roll of duct tape. He put two of the cups over his eyes and attached them to his head with rough circles of tape.

"What are you *doing*?"

"Making water goggles. Now help me blow up these plastic bags." Brendan demonstrated, inflating a bag like a balloon and tying it off. Air leaked out, but it kept its basic filled-up shape. Will followed, impressed by Brendan's pluck. Soon they had five bags full of air. Brendan opened the door to the basement.

"You're going down there?"

"I'm *diving* down there," Brendan said. Without further explanation he stripped down to his boxers and handed Will the high-powered Maglite. "Just shine this towards the water."

With plastic bags looped around his fingers and makeshift goggles on his head, Brendan waded into the flooded basement.

The beam of light cut through the murky water, but the goggles didn't work as well as Brendan had planned. They immediately filled with briny liquid that made everything fuzzy. He squinted and tried to navigate, seeing only shapes in the gloom: the eerie old mannequin, the BlackoutReady generator... the cans!

Brendan had forgotten about the stack of cans. They were still on the floor – and the Walkers and Will still hadn't eaten since breakfast Lunchables. Brendan needed to get those cans; it didn't matter what was inside. He scooped five of them up in one arm and kept looking for the thing he had come for. He knew that it would be on the floor too – it was too heavy to float. His lungs burned as he felt along the wood grain until he reached...

The sledgehammer.

Working quickly, with ripping pain brewing in his chest, Brendan slipped the now buoyant shopping bags over the handle of the hammer. Then he pushed off the bottom with his last bit of strength, swam up, and burst out of the water in front of Will.

"I got it!" he shouted. "A real hammer! And *these*!" He passed the cans to the pilot.

"Cordelia! Eleanor!" Will called. "*Food!*"

The Walker sisters arrived in the kitchen almost before

Will had finished shouting. They quickly dug up a can opener and got into the Green Giant sweetcorn Brendan had salvaged. It might've been cold and soggy, but sweetcorn had never tasted so good.

"*Mm*, how much of this do we have?" Cordelia asked.

"Lots," said Brendan. "I can keep diving down to get them whenever we're hungry."

"Are there canned peaches, too, for dessert?" Eleanor asked. Everybody laughed. But Eleanor kept talking: "Or bottled water?"

No one laughed at that. They were all terribly thirsty, and there wasn't any fresh water in the house; all they had to drink was canned sweetcorn juice.

"Sorry, Nell," said Brendan. "Maybe when we bust open the wall we'll find some water."

"Let's get to it," Will said, lugging the sledgehammer into the hallway. "Sweetcorn gives me strength!"

The Walkers followed. Will lined the sledgehammer up with the *X* and looked over his shoulder. "I must ask you ladies to stand back."

"Excuse me?" asked Cordelia. "Have you decided to become sexist again?"

"This isn't women's work," Will said, and before Cordelia could fire off a comeback, Eleanor interrupted—

"What about your shoulder? You'll break your stitches!"

"Nonsense," Will said, even though the pain in his shoulder was intense and he knew he'd have only one chance to do this. Gritting his teeth, he swung the sledgehammer back—

And smashed it through the wall!

It was one clean hit, direct at the *X*, and given what happened next, even Cordelia had to be impressed with Will's engineering precision. From the crater in the wall, a single crack sprang up to the ceiling, zigging and zagging as it rained down paint chips, and then two chunks of plaster fell inward in one clean motion.

The Walkers and Will were staring at a large hole in the wall, coughing on dust that hadn't been disturbed in nearly a century.

As the cloud cleared, a passageway was revealed behind the hole, black and foreboding, with a row of unlit torches mounted at eye level. It disappeared into the darkness in both directions.

38

Cordelia grabbed a candle from the floor and touched it to the nearest torch. With a thick whoosh the torch burst into flame; the hallway was illuminated in flickering orange. In one direction it stretched towards the living room; in the other it went towards the kitchen; but in both ways the corridor seemed to turn at the last minute, leading to points unknown. Aside from the rows of torches it was bare.

"Shall we?" Will asked, moving inside.

"Only if I get to hold the flashlight," said Eleanor. "I don't trust torches."

Cordelia handed it to her as they entered single file. "Which way?" she asked. Eleanor insisted on doing eeny-meeny-miny-moe to determine that they would head towards the kitchen.

Will took the first torch off the wall and used it to light the others. Each torch lit made the passageway a little brighter and less intimidating for Eleanor. Checking over her shoulder to see the way back, she said, "It's like Hansel and Gretel with the breadcrumbs."

"Didn't they wind up getting eaten?" Brendan asked.

"*Shhh*," scolded Cordelia, but Eleanor had already smacked her brother, sending his hair dangerously close to open flame.

Around the first bend, the corridor widened into a three-metre chamber. Against the wall was a pale bookshelf – but instead of rushing up to investigate it, Cordelia recoiled.

"It's made of bones!" she said. Indeed, it looked as if the bookshelf were constructed from a bleached human skeleton, with twisting, knobby femurs for legs, and tibiae for shelves, on which the books sat crookedly. Brendan looked closer, tapping his fingers against it.

"It's just wood, Deal."

Cordelia's vision snapped back into place: the bookshelf was made of white driftwood held together with brass screws. The dancing, mocking light of the torches was playing tricks on her.

"Sorry," she said.

"What are these books?" asked Will. "More Denver Kristoff trash? He was quite the prolific egomaniac."

"These look different," said Eleanor.

Cordelia pulled a book off and opened its worn leather cover to find a title page in French with a wood-block print of Adam and Eve in the Garden of Eden… except Adam's head was split into four sections with brains spilling over the edges and Eve had a withered third leg protruding from her torso. Cordelia shuddered and turned the page to see an etched print of a skull with four eye sockets – and then a rosy-cheeked baby with stunted flippers instead of arms—

"*Ugghh!* It's like an ancient book of medical curiosities," she said, closing the volume and returning it to the shelf.

"Cool! Let me see!" Brendan exclaimed, but the moment he opened the book, it only took him one glance to close it. "Not really cool."

Will grabbed a second book. This one appeared to be a Spanish encyclopedia. But the topics…

"Human sacrifice," Will said, showing Cordelia and Brendan a print of a feather-crowned Aztec priest ripping a beating heart from the chest of a terrified victim. Will held the book away from Eleanor to prevent her from seeing the grotesque image.

"This Kristoff dude was into some sick stuff," said Brendan, opening something called *The Gods of Peg na,* one of the few volumes that was in English: "'Before there stood gods upon Olympus, or ever Allah was Allah, had wrought and rested Mana-Yood-Sushai.'"

"A god of sushi? What's that about?" asked Eleanor.

"That's a rare work by Lord Dunsany: a compendium of invented deities," said Cordelia. "May I see?"

Brendan handed it over and opened something called *The Redolent Garden.* Cordelia looked at *The Gods of Peg na* before she and Will checked out the other books. It was tough to determine the subject matter, because they were in so many languages – French, Arabic, German – but they seemed to cover indigenous fertility practices, herb cultivation, potion making, witchcraft, and demonology, complete with pictures of howling spirits and the fires of hell. The books even *smelled* evil – the yellowing pages mixed with the old ink produced a sharp tang.

"Smells like rotting flesh," said Cordelia.

"Oh," remarked Will, "and when have you smelled rotting flesh?"

"Well, never, really… but I, um… I've read a lot of detective stories, and they always say that rotting flesh smells like five-month-old luncheon meat or red snapper that's been sitting in the sun for too long," said Cordelia.

"Rotting flesh smells nothing like this book," said Will. "And trust me, once you've smelt it, you will never forget it."

Cordelia stopped herself from asking exactly where Will had been when he'd smelled rotting flesh and went back to paging through a book called *The Apocrypha Bestiary*. She stopped looking after seeing enough flashes of human misery – men pulled apart on the rack, babies torn from their mothers by woolly beasts, corpses feasted on by ghouls – to give her a week's worth of nightmares. Eleanor calmly looked down the hallway the whole time. She wasn't worried about what was in the books; she was worried about what was in the house.

"Let's move on," said Cordelia, snatching *The Redolent Garden* out of Brendan's hands.

"Hey! I was just getting to 'Painting the Female Body for Ritualistic Sacrifice'."

"You hate reading."

"Not stuff like *that*!"

"We've got to stay on course and see where this hallway leads. These books are giving me the creeps."

The Walkers and Will continued into the bowels of the house, lighting torches as they went. The passageway twisted back and forth, but didn't branch – until they reached a thick, rusted steel door on the left side. The door looked as if it would have a very strong lock, but it stood partially open, tempting them.

"A little too easy," said Brendan. "Who wants to go first?"

No answer.

"Will?" asked Brendan.

"Why me?"

"Because you're the oldest."

"Not by bloody much."

"Because you have a gun," Eleanor suggested.

"That won't help against whatever spirits are down here!"

"Because we trust you," Cordelia finally said. Will couldn't back down from that remark. He slowly pushed the door open with his Webley to reveal—

"A wine cellar! Now *these* are my kind of spirits!"

The room was twice as big as the chamber that held the bookshelf. It was lined with unlit torches – and dominated by a wooden rack cradling countless bottles of wine. Will stepped in.

"1899! A very good year," he grinned, holding up a bottle.

"Put that back," said Eleanor. "Isn't there any Coke?"

"They don't keep fizzy drinks in wine cellars," said Will. "There's no corkscrew?"

"She's right, Will. Put the wine back," said Cordelia. "Why don't you and Bren keep exploring the passageway while Eleanor and I look in here?"

"Look for *what*, exactly?"

"Water!" Eleanor snapped. "Wine doesn't count!"

"Fine," said Will.

The two boys stepped out, but not before Brendan warned his sisters, "Careful you don't lock yourselves in. Looks like this room locks from the inside." He pointed to a metal bar that could slide into place across the door.

"Thanks, Bren." Cordelia fired up the Maglite and

began to search the wine cellar with Eleanor. The light flashed against a gorgeous antique vanity by the door. The mirror was streaked with dust; its edges were cracked with age.

"I'll bet Denver Kristoff's wife spent a lot of time in here," Eleanor said. "This looks like girl stuff."

"I think Denver was a vain person. Most writers are," said Cordelia. "He probably sat here and trimmed his beard and waxed his moustache before hitting the town with our great-great-grandfather." To prove her point, she opened one of the vanity drawers and pulled out a rusted straight razor. "See? Clearly for a man."

"Then… he wore make-up too?" Eleanor asked, holding up a velvet pouch of beige powder.

"That's actually strange; I didn't think men still wore make-up in Kristoff's time."

Eleanor opened another drawer containing a tin of cream, a book of matches and an old, yellowed photo, which she handed to her sister. Cordelia examined the photo and saw an inscription on the back.

"'The Lorekeepers, 1912. The Bohemian Club.'"

The picture showed a group of men standing on a grand

spiral staircase in an ornate hall, with tiny gargoyles carved into the posts of the banisters. The men wore black robes and huge powdered wigs that rose a foot above their heads.

"This is the club that Rutherford Walker wrote about!" said Cordelia.

"And those are the Lorekeeper guys he talked about," said Eleanor.

"What a ridiculous sense of fashion. I mean, powdered wigs were retro even in 1912!" Cordelia began scanning the faces in the picture; there were about forty men. "There! Denver Kristoff."

She pointed to a man with a stern face and a perfectly manicured beard – the same face they had seen in the photo upstairs. The man had eyes that both stared at Cordelia and seemed to gaze unfocused into empty space, as if looking out at horrors only they had seen.

"See our great-great-grandfather anywhere?" asked Eleanor.

"I'm not sure. Try and find someone who looks like Dad," said Cordelia, but no matter how hard they looked, they couldn't find anyone. After a while the faces began to look the same.

"It's useless! I hate it!" Eleanor yelped, grabbing the

picture to rip it up – but Cordelia stopped her.

"Nell, no. It's another piece of the puzzle. We can't let our emotions get the better of us. Think. Denver Kristoff and Rutherford Walker were best friends in 1906, but by the time this picture was taken, six years later, it looks like Walker's nowhere to be seen. So what came between them?"

While Cordelia and Eleanor pondered that question, Brendan and Will arrived at another door in the hallway. This one wasn't metal; it was made of decaying wood. Will held one of the torches from the wall for light; the torchlight played off the grain.

"This time, you go first," suggested Will.

"Only if I get your gun," said Brendan.

"Nice try. I'll cover you."

Brendan stepped forward nervously, turning the doorknob and pushing in. The door wouldn't budge.

"D'oh," he said, "I guess it opens out." He pulled the door open – and collapsed back with a shriek as a skeleton fell on top of him!

Will almost shot the skeleton, but he quickly realised that it wasn't a threat, even though it was covering Brendan

with clacking bones. Brendan scrambled away. "What the
– *what*?"

The open door revealed an empty cupboard; the only
thing inside had been the skeleton, whose bones were
kept together by screws or glue. It lay on the floor now,
splayed out as if it had belly-flopped there, the toothy face
staring at Brendan. Just above the left eye was a chip in the
skull.

"Calm down," said Will, picking the skeleton up by its
head. The bones draped limply. "Looks like an old medical
prop. Haven't you ever heard of a skeleton in the cupboard?"

"Not funny," Brendan said. "That used to be a real
human being."

Will shrugged and pushed the skeleton back in as
Cordelia and Eleanor came running down the hallway to
find out what their brother was screaming about.

"Tell them we saw a spider or something," Brendan
whispered to Will. "If Eleanor sees that skeleton, she'll
need like twenty years of therapy."

"What happened?" Cordelia asked.

"No worries. Brendan opened this cupboard. There was
a spider inside," said Will.

"How big?" asked Eleanor.

"Huge," said Brendan. "Probably a tarantula."

"A *tarantula*?" exclaimed Eleanor. "I've never seen a real live *tarantula*!"

She whisked open the cupboard before Will or Brendan could stop her.

Once again, the skeleton fell out, this time directly on top of Eleanor, covering her like a bony blanket. Eleanor shrieked and grabbed it to get it off, but the jumble of fingers, bones and teeth got caught in her hair and clothing. She tried to shake it away, but as she twisted and turned, it only got more tangled up with her. For a moment, it looked as if the two were doing a high-speed Cirque du Soleil routine – before Eleanor took off running back down the hallway, screaming her head off, with the skeleton still attached.

39

"Come back!" called Brendan, but Eleanor wasn't listening. She didn't stop running until the Walkers and Will caught up with her by the driftwood bookshelf.

"Nell! Stop moving! You're just gonna get more tangled up!" Cordelia said.

"It's *alive*!" Eleanor screeched. "It's trying to strangle me!"

"You're imagining things." Cordelia knelt in front of her sister just like Mrs Walker always did. "Relax. Everything will be fine."

Cordelia slowly began extricating the clingy skeleton from Eleanor, first removing the fingers from her shoulders and then untangling the arms and legs. Within moments the fearsome hanger-on was reduced to a jumble of bones on the floor.

"He left bone marks on my *clothes*, see?" Eleanor said. She was breathing in gasps, with tears streaming down her face.

"I see," said Cordelia, licking her thumb to rub clean the imaginary spots Eleanor insisted were on her outfit. "All gone, see?"

"And there's something here…" said Eleanor, plucking a very *un*imaginary skeleton's tooth from her ear and handing it to Cordelia.

"Ew," said Brendan, watching with Will. Cordelia gave Eleanor a hug as she dropped the tooth and motioned for the pilot to take care of the bones. Will picked up the skeleton and carried it down the hall. Only the tooth was left winking on the floor.

"Sorry, Nell," Brendan said as he hugged his sister. "I made up the part about the tarantula because I didn't want you seeing that thing."

"I'll take a million tarantulas over a dead skeleton!" said Eleanor. "From now on just tell me the truth. I'm old enough to handle it."

Brendan nodded and took his sister's hand. Cordelia

took the other… and a few minutes later the three Walkers stepped out of the hole in the secret hallway and back into the "normal" side of Kristoff House – to the extent that any part of it could be considered normal. Will followed, extinguishing torches.

"Did you lock the cupboard?" Eleanor asked.

"Unfortunately, there's no lock, but that skeleton's not going anywhere. He's dead as a doornail."

"In this house? I wouldn't count on anything staying dead," said Brendan.

"That's why I'm sleeping between you guys tonight," said Eleanor.

"It *is* bedtime," said Cordelia. "We've had a long day."

"And I'm *so* thirsty," said Eleanor. "I hate even saying it, because it's making my lips feel extra dry. It's like my body is shrivelling up inside."

"Eleanor's right," said Will. "We need to drink something. Dehydration kills. We've used up all the melted ice?"

Cordelia nodded.

"And obviously there isn't anything coming out of the sinks… what about the loo?"

"Gross," said Brendan. "I'm going to pretend you didn't even say that."

"So the toilets still have fresh water?" Will asked.

"Not fresh water, hello?! *Toilet* water!" said Brendan.

"Better than seawater," said Will. "And didn't you just move into this place? It's not as if the toilets have seen much use." He started walking to the downstairs bathroom. "You coming?"

The Walkers followed. Sure enough, the toilet bowl was full of clear water. Will dipped his hand in and drank a mouthful.

"Fine," he said. He drank a second helping. "Tastes like diamonds."

Brendan's mouth watered as he watched, but he was still queasy about the concept. "I can't do it," he said. "As thirsty as I am, I can't drink water from a toilet bowl."

"Just think of it as a punch bowl," said Will.

"I don't pee in a punch bowl," said Brendan.

"What about from here?" Cordelia said, pulling the cover off the tank behind the bowl. Inside was crystal-clear water. "Something seems less gross about drinking from here."

"I agree," said Eleanor, who took a deep breath and drank from the tank. Cordelia joined in, followed by Brendan… and in a moment all the Walkers were gulping water out of the toilet tank like it was the only H_2O in the house – because it was. Brendan had never tasted water like this before. It seemed to heal him as it went down his throat, and soon – too soon – his belly felt full and he felt sleepy.

"That should get us through the night," Will said. "Tomorrow we'll keep searching the hallway for fresh water… and eat whatever we can find in cans in the basement."

"Do we have to brush our teeth before bed?" Eleanor said.

"Absolutely not," said Cordelia. Eleanor pumped her fist before they all went upstairs to the master bedroom, hearing the waves lapping outside.

Conditions had deteriorated considerably from the previous night. Instead of a bed and some mattresses on the floor, there was now only the king-size mattress, which they had to pull out of the broken window. (The other mattress had apparently bounced out of the same window after the colossus punched the house; it was nowhere to be seen.) They could only all fit on the king-size mattress if they lay like sardines. The boys got the outside and the girls got the middle.

"I call not-outside tomorrow night," said Brendan.

"Why?" asked Cordelia.

"Because there's *glass* on the floor, hello? What if I roll over? I'll wake up with glass sticking out of my face!"

"You're such a baby!" teased Eleanor.

"And a wimp," said Cordelia.

"And a right proper weasel!" said Will, laughing.

"I hate you guys," said Brendan, yawning. But as everyone's chuckles quietened in the hushed night, he looked out of the window at the moon… and it occurred to him that inside this house, no matter what, even if his stomach was full of toilet water, he had a warm family and a friend. Outside was a cold moon and colder ocean. No contest.

"I take it back," said Brendan. "I don't hate you. I wouldn't wanna be trapped inside a floating house with anybody else."

Eleanor was the first to nod off, holding her sister's arm. As Brendan closed his eyes, he heard Will whisper to

Cordelia: "The way you took care of your sister back there, quite touching. Reminded me of someone who took care of me once… my older brother Edgar."

"I remind you of your *brother*?" Cordelia asked, offended.

"No, no, you're much prettier!" Will corrected himself. "Edgar, wonderful bloke, but rather lacking in the beauty department."

Brendan opened his eyes so he could roll them properly. *Guess those two are back on good terms,* he thought as he turned over, making sure he didn't fall off the bed on to any glass shards. He listened until he heard the steady breathing of Will, Cordelia and Eleanor… but he couldn't sleep.

Brendan was certainly tired; his body was bruised and worn like he'd just played three lacrosse games in a row. The little things were keeping him awake – the hard slap of a big wave, the splash of a fish outside the house (*or is that some other, nastier creature?*); that continuous hiss of the barrel somewhere in the walls. He was afraid to go downstairs, so he stayed in bed in a kind of half-sleep, tossing and turning in the tiny space he was allotted on the mattress.

And then he heard someone enter the room.

Brendan kept his eyes shut. *It's my mind playing tricks on me. As long as I keep my eyes closed, it'll go away.* He used to play these games when he was younger: he would imagine that Shiva, the Hindu destroyer god, was inside his room, standing over his bed, and would kill him if he got scared enough to open his eyes. (He'd read about Shiva in an encyclopedia, and frankly, it had turned him off ever opening an encyclopedia again.)

The sound of footsteps got closer. The whatever-it-was rustled and clacked as it moved. Brendan stayed absolutely still, absolutely terrified. *Don't look, don't look,* he willed himself, trying to get a grip on his brain, but then he thought, *You have to look – don't you want to see the thing that* kills *you?* He snapped his eyes open—

To see the skeleton from downstairs standing above him.

It stared at Brendan, and although its eyes were just empty hollows, it had a keen gaze. It also had a chip above its eye. The bones at the top of its cheek scraped against each other as it stretched its jaws into a grin, revealing a missing tooth. Then it raised its hand to its face, extended a bony finger over what used to be its lips, and uttered a tiny sound…

"Shhhhh."

B rendan liked to think he was a manly person, but with the skeleton above him, he made a noise – *"Ah, ih, ah"* – that didn't sound like any man. It sounded like he was choking on a Dorito.

The skeleton unfolded an arm and reached towards Brendan's neck. Brendan tried to back away, but his muscles had turned to jelly; he tried to scream, but he had forgotten how to breathe. He knew the fingers were going to wrap around his throat—

But instead the skeleton touched the bottom of his chin and lifted it to face the ceiling. With its other hand it pointed upstairs. Towards the attic.

Brendan shoved the skeleton away and screamed louder than he had in his life. He sounded like a three-hundred-kilogram bovine being slammed with a bulldozer.

"Bren! What is *wrong* with you?" groaned Cordelia.

Brendan blinked – and the skeleton was gone. He was sitting straight up on the mattress with sweat on his forehead and his hands tapping his face and chest, making sure he was still there.

"No way," he said. "Seriously? A *dream*?"

"Apparently," said Cordelia, turning over on her stomach. "Unless you were practising your fire-alarm impersonation."

"Guys, be nice. He had a nightmare!" said Eleanor. "Are you OK, Bren?"

"I guess so… I'm sorry I woke you guys up…"

"You probably woke up some *fish*," grumbled Will.

"What was the dream about?" Eleanor asked. "Drowning?"

"It wasn't…" Brendan shook his head. "I was *awake*. And that skeleton from the cupboard downstairs… I *saw* it. It was missing a tooth, it had the same chip above its eye… and it was *right here*."

"I knew that thing was pure evil," said Eleanor.

"Stop it, Bren," Cordelia said. "You're scaring your sister, and the rest of us need to sleep! Keep your dreams to yourself."

"I *wasn't* dreaming! And I bet the skeleton's still in the room—"

"Where?"

They all looked around. No sign.

"Remember last month?" Cordelia asked Brendan. "You dreamed about that old Mickey Mouse wizard cartoon, and you started crying '*Mummy! Mummy!*'"

"OK, whatever," said Brendan, glancing quickly at Will. "Go back to sleep for all I care."

Cordelia and Will both mumbled and did so. But Eleanor reached her hand out to Brendan's. "I believe you."

Brendan squeezed Eleanor's fingers as she dozed off, her breathing slowly becoming regular. Once he was certain she was asleep, he gently laid her hand at her side and slipped out of bed.

Brendan grabbed the Maglite, tiptoed to the opposite side of the bed and extended his hand towards Will's holster. He wasn't going to go on this mission without being armed. He remembered Will's warning about the seriousness of guns, and how things had gone wrong with the grenade, but he would be more cautious this time. It wasn't a matter of breaking the rules. It was a matter of survival.

Brendan removed the Webley exceedingly carefully, making sure not to wake the pilot. Then he inched out of the bedroom and down the spiral stairs, flashlight in one hand, trembling gun in the other, thinking about, of all things, the astronomer Galileo.

Galileo was one of Brendan's historical heroes. When the guy was brought to the Inquisition for making too much trouble about the earth moving around the sun, he supposedly put his head down, apologised, and then, under his breath, said, "And yet it moves!"

Later historians concluded the entire incident was an urban legend, but Brendan didn't buy that. Galileo was too smart, too brave, too *manly* to just sit back and let other people tell him how things worked when he knew the real deal. Brendan sometimes wondered what that would be like: to be in a room full of people who believed the wrong thing and *know* that you were right. Now, walking alone through Kristoff House to the secret hallway, he did. *They can say whatever they want about that skeleton – but it moved! And it told me something important…*

It belongs in the attic.

The journey through the hallway was easier this time.

Brendan had been down the path before; that made all the difference. He went to the cupboard where Will had re-stashed the skeleton and opened the door with the Webley drawn, nervous finger on the trigger, surprised at the weight of the weapon.

"Come out with your hands up!"

The skeleton crumpled at Brendan's feet.

"So what was that all about?" he asked, pointing the gun at the bones. "Why do you want to go up to the attic?"

The skeleton lay still. Silent.

"Was it some kind of sign? Some kind of clue?"

No answer from the bones.

"Fine. Make me do this the hard way."

Brendan heaved the skeleton over his shoulder and carried it down the hall, wincing as its bony appendages poked and pinched his skin. He stopped when something glinted on the floor: the tooth Eleanor had pulled out of her ear.

"You'll be needing that," Brendan said, leaning down to pocket the tooth. He found that talking to his passenger kept him from being scared: "I knew I wasn't dreaming about you, Skeletor, so I figured you had to be a vision.

And I thought, If you're a vision, you've gotta be telling me something. And maybe you're like that bat skeleton… maybe if I take you up to the attic, you'll come back to life. Maybe that's a special power that this house has in this world. And maybe you're Denver Kristoff, or Rutherford Walker, or somebody else who can help us get outta here!"

Brendan went upstairs, bypassing the master bedroom for the attic. Slayne's men had turned what had once been the attic steps into a gaping hole. Brendan tossed the bones up and piled debris into a makeshift stepladder, grunting as he worked. Finally he managed to hoist himself into the attic, collapsing next to the skeleton. He turned off the Maglite and pointed Will's gun at the grinning skull.

"So you and me, we're just gonna stay here like this… all night. And at some point, if you feel like coming back to life, or just getting up and telling me what's going on, I'll be ready to listen."

The skeleton's chipped head seemed almost to hear him. As Brendan peered at it, he started to drift off – and then he remembered.

"Your tooth! Right, sorry. If you do speak, I don't want

you talking with a lisp. I want to understand everything you say."

He inserted the tooth into the skeleton's mouth, smiling at the smile he'd recreated, and then laid his head down and found the wood floor softer than any pillow. The sense he'd had earlier of not being able to sleep was reversed; now, with his strange mission completed, he could have slept through a fireworks display… and then, suddenly, the attic was lit up by the morning sun.

Brendan awoke, turned over, and gasped.

Overnight the skeleton had come back to life. But it hadn't turned into Denver Kristoff or Rutherford Walker. It was now a pale, terrified-looking and very naked redhead.

"Uh…" Brendan said. "Who are you? Are you OK?"

The redhead snapped her eyes open, covered herself, kicked Brendan with her bare feet, and screamed even louder than he had the night before. "*Helllllp!*"

41

In the master bedroom, Will snapped up. "Cordelia! Eleanor!"

"What?" they asked, rubbing their eyes. Then they heard the shrieking upstairs, as if a very angry young woman were defending herself with a high-decibel assault... and with small household objects, which bounced off the walls. Brendan shouted in pain.

"That's Bren!" Cordelia said. "Sounds like he's in trouble."

"But who's the girl?" asked Eleanor.

"Hopefully not that blasted Wind Witch!" said Will as he leaped off the mattress. "Follow me!" He reached for his gun – and suddenly got very angry. "*Brendan!*"

Upstairs, Brendan was backed into a corner, trying to swat away ornaments and busted bureau pieces that the reanimated redhead threw at him. She was turned sideways, going for anything she could grab with one hand and covering her body with the other.

"Stop ogling me, you debased child!"

"Stop throwing stuff at me and I won't have to – *ow!*"

"What have you done with my clothes? Where is Mr Kristoff?!"

"Dead! *Ow!* I'll ask my sister for clothes! What's your *name?*"

"I'm asking questions, not you!" The redhead picked up the Maglite—

"*Stop!*" Brendan ordered, his voice cracking. "That's our only one!" Hands shaking, he pointed the gun at the woman—

BLAM.

Brendan had no idea how it had happened. His fingers must have slipped. As soon as he heard the shot, he knew it had been wrong to steal the gun. It kicked back with a fearsome snap, like an angry little animal.

The shot went into the ceiling; Brendan had no idea how to aim. The bullet hit a hanging light – a metal globe on a chain – and the light fell on the red-haired woman.

The glass had already been shattered by the colossus attack, but the frame made her slump to the floor.

"No!" Brendan yelled, tossing aside the gun (it was hot) and running over. "I'm so sorry – please, wake up – I didn't mean to – I shouldn't have taken that gun – I don't even – *Errr*!"

The woman kicked him in the groin.

In imitation of Will, Brendan managed a single "*Crikey!*" before crumpling to the floor. The woman stood over him, lifting the dented light fixture. A trickle of blood ran down her forehead, but that wasn't going to stop her from slamming the fixture into Brendan's face—

"*Stop!*" Will ordered.

He had climbed into the attic with Eleanor and Cordelia. The woman looked at him, dropped the light, and covered herself.

"*Leave me alone!*" the woman screamed, dabbing her fingertips in the trickle of blood on her head. "*He tried to kill me!*"

"Calm down," said Will, stepping forward cautiously. He covered the woman in his bomber jacket and pressed a handkerchief against her head to staunch the blood flow.

Cordelia watched, fascinated; she thought she recognised the woman's red hair and olive-green eyes.

"Who are you?" she asked.

The woman didn't answer.

"Brendan!" Will ordered. "Give me my Webley, you thief!"

Scared and ashamed, Brendan handed the gun to Will.

"I specifically told you not to touch my gun," said the pilot. "Why would you do something so ridiculously irresponsible?!"

"I just… I wanted to be safe," Brendan said.

"*Safe?*" asked an incredulous Will. "By stealing my gun you put yourself and the rest of us in danger!"

"I was on an important mission. I wanted a man's weapon."

"A gun doesn't make you a man. You can't steal manhood. Do you understand?"

"Yes, Will," said Brendan, mortified.

"Very well." Will holstered the gun. "Now, miss," he said to the woman, "my name is Draper. Wing Commander Will Draper. Royal Flying Corps, Squadron Seventy. These are my travelling companions Brendan, Cordelia and Eleanor. Who might you be?"

Cordelia scowled, remembering: *That was the same way Will introduced himself to me in the forest.*

"First you had better control that little lunatic!" the redhead said, defiantly blowing a hair away from her face. "If he had decent aim, he would've killed me. Plus I don't like the way he's looking at me."

"Hey, Pippi Longstocking, I'm *not* looking at you. I have no interest in redheads with freckles on their—"

"That's quite enough!" Will said.

Brendan clammed up. "Miss," Will continued, "I completely understand your discomfort and embarrassment. Plus you've been injured. Cordelia, can you fetch the young lady some clothes?"

"Fetch?" Cordelia asked. "I'm not a dog. And I know her name. It's Penelope Hope."

The woman gave Cordelia a shocked look. "You know my name?"

"I read it in a book by Denver Kristoff," Cordelia said. "You're Penelope Hope, a nurse living in Frimley during World War One."

"No…" Penelope said, utterly bewildered. "I don't even know what a Frimley is. My name is Penelope Hope, yes, but I'm a maid. Here. At Kristoff House. And I would really like some clothes."

"We'll get you something," Cordelia said, climbing down from the attic with Eleanor. She thought about how twisted this situation had become: in the book *The Fighting Ace*, Penelope Hope was the woman Will Draper fell in love with.

Back in the attic, Will and Brendan kept their distance

from Penelope. She stared out of the window at the shingled waves, wrapped in Will's bomber jacket. The sun was up and shimmering.

"Are we floating on the sea? How is that possible?"

"First, please tell us where you come from," said Will.

"The cupboard," said Brendan.

"What?" asked Will.

"Last night she was the skeleton from the cupboard. This morning she was… *her*."

"You're confusing me," Penelope said. "I was a *skeleton*?"

"Please, allow me." Will eased Brendan aside. "Penelope, do you know what year it is?"

"1913."

"Afraid not. According to my companions, it's *2013*."

"That's ridiculous."

"Have you ever seen one of these?" Will reached into his pocket and handed Penelope something that took Brendan by surprise.

"My PSP! Where'd you get that?"

"You steal my gun; I steal your games. Miss Hope? Any idea?"

"Not a clue," Penelope said, turning the device around.

"Allow me to demonstrate."

Will turned it on. Penelope's mouth hung open. "It's like a photograph… in colour?! And it's *moving*?!? *How?!*"

For the next ten minutes, Brendan and Will filled Penelope in on their adventures – and Brendan related a century of world history. It was a long, involved conversation with lots of smiles and jokes, and by the end of it, Brendan had forgiven Penelope for waking up scared and kicking him. Then the Walker sisters returned, bringing a dress for Penelope: purple and green, with a crocheted collar and hulking shoulder pads. They all left the attic so she could change.

"That's the nasty dress Grandma gave you for Christmas!" Brendan told Cordelia. "Why couldn't you get her something prettier?"

"Brendan's got a crush on the new girl!" teased Eleanor.

Brendan was ready to defend himself, but he got help from Will: "So? Penelope's intelligent, well-spoken – especially for a maid – and quite beautiful. Your brother could do a lot worse."

Brendan gave Will a horrified look.

"You two," said Cordelia, "don't get enchanted by this

woman. There's a character in Denver Kristoff's book *The Fighting Ace* named Penelope Hope, and I'll bet this maid was the inspiration for her. Unless you want to have a crush on the same girl as Kristoff…"

"I don't have a crush on anybody!" Brendan said.

"And I'm a free man; I can do as I please," said Will.

Cordelia looked crestfallen. Will sighed, put a hand on her shoulder, and tried to be as understanding as possible, searching for the proper words.

"Cordelia," he said, "I'm too old for you."

"Too old?" Cordelia was suddenly livid. Will's words had exactly the opposite effect than he had intended. "You're only seventeen! Two years older than me!"

"What? But how—"

"You lied about how old you were to join the airforce."

"You knew that?"

"I know everything about you from reading *The Fighting Ace*—"

"Wait, Will's a kid, like us?" asked Eleanor. "Cool. Now it won't be so creepy if we get back and he goes to the prom with Deal—"

"I'm dressed!" Penelope called from the attic.

They all went up, with the tension between Cordelia and Will very much unresolved.

Penelope Hope looked graceful even in the awful dress. As she sat in the window and told her story, Will darted his eyes around the room so he wouldn't stare at her. Brendan stared. Eleanor thought she was pretty. Cordelia thought she was OK.

Penelope began: "I started working at Kristoff House as a laundry maid, above stairs, two years ago – er, I mean, in 1911. Of course, when I took the job, I knew that Mr Kristoff was an odd one. Even when he stopped by to shake my hand during the interview, there was something dark behind his eyes. I assumed he was thinking about his stories. After I was hired I learned that he didn't eat or sleep when he was working on one."

"With your limited education," Cordelia said, "it might be difficult to understand the work habits of a genius."

"I don't mean that he worked hard," said Penelope, annoyed at Cordelia's dig. "I mean that he literally did *not* sleep or eat." Her voice got quiet. "Things got much darker when Kristoff became obsessed with something he called his 'greatest work'."

"His greatest work?" asked Cordelia. "What was it?"

"At first, I assumed he was writing another novel," said Penelope. "But he was no longer working in his study. He started in the attic for several months, and then moved somewhere more private to work, somewhere hidden. He would disappear for days. And when he returned, his eyes were deep red, bloodshot. There was always a mad grin on his face. At this point, he started to develop an affection for me. It was all rather disturbing, but I played along because I was frightened of him. I would talk with him, listen to his problems, worries. Sometimes he just rambled incoherently. Once, when I asked about his 'great work', he became quite furious. Slapped me. Told me it wasn't meant for simple-minded people like me. The great book was meant for someone with extreme intelligence and power, someone very gifted. Someone like him."

"He *slapped* you?" said Eleanor. "That's horrible!"

"Not the worst thing that's happened to me," said Penelope, staring at the waves.

"Well, I can assure you it won't be happening any more," said Will. "You're with us now, and I'll make sure you're protected."

"Thank you," Penelope said, moving on. "I tried to put Kristoff and his great book out of my mind. But nearly a year later I discovered the hidden side of Kristoff House."

"You found the secret hallway?" Brendan asked.

"Hall*way*, as in one? There isn't just one!" Penelope laughed. "This is a house of secrets. I don't think even Kristoff knows them all."

"How did you discover them?" asked Will.

"I was dusting the library and bumped into a wall lamp. I reached up and attempted to adjust it. But when I moved it—"

"A door slid open," said Brendan.

"How did you know?" asked Penelope.

"Scooby-Doo," said Will.

"Who?"

"A talking canine who – never mind."

Penelope continued: "I went inside and found a passageway with torches and ghastly books. Past a wine cellar and a cupboard, I found another passage, and another… it was endless. Every night, I sneaked back in, discovering new hidden corridors and chambers. The house was so much bigger than it appeared from outside. Then, just a few hours ago – I can't believe it was a century ago – I ventured so deep that I heard drips of water that sounded as if they echoed from caverns… and that's when I found Kristoff."

"What was he doing?" Cordelia asked.

"He was inside… it's difficult to say. I'd describe it as a cave of delights."

"A cave of delights?"

"A hollowed-out cavern," continued Penelope, "filled with everything a man could want. Beautiful gems, treasure, women, wine, servants. Kristoff was dancing, singing… he looked mad, raving with joy. It was like heaven, or hell. Like something from a dream. But definitely real—"

"Absolutely fascinating," Will said. He had given up trying not to look at Penelope. It felt as if he'd known her for a long time. "You're a wonderful storyteller."

"I could listen to her for hours," agreed Brendan.

"Then shush and let her finish!" said Cordelia.

"Thank you," Penelope said. "In the centre of the cavern, on a pedestal as if it were a beautiful statue, was a book."

"I bet I know which one," said Brendan.

"I assumed that this was the great book Mr Kristoff was

working on, of course. It had no title, just a picture on the cover—"

"Let me guess: like an eye?" Brendan asked.

"That's right!"

"Look at that. Pop quiz winner, right here."

Penelope ignored him. In fact, she aimed her story at Cordelia, who despite her prickliness seemed to be the most serious listener. "When I saw the book, I had this overwhelming urge to touch it. I wanted to immediately open it and see what was inside. It was obvious from the book's position that it was the key to everything. I stepped out of the shadows towards the book... and that's when Kristoff saw me."

"Uh-oh," said Eleanor.

"He demanded to know how I'd found his private place. But more importantly, he was concerned about his daughter."

"The Wind Witch?" Eleanor asked, confused.

"No... your brother told me about this 'Wind Witch', but as I knew her, Kristoff's daughter was a sweet girl named Dahlia. Mr Kristoff adored her. She was the only thing he cared about more than his writing! Even though

Kristoff would disappear for days to work, whenever he was with Dahlia, he was the perfect example of a doting father. And when he was with Dahlia, he never had that crazy, bloodshot look in his eyes. Or that mad grin."

"So what happened?" Brendan asked.

"Mr Kristoff became incandescent with rage. He called me horrible names, said that because of my carelessness, Dahlia could have followed me. And this was a place that Dahlia could never see! And a state she could never see him in. I promised Kristoff it wouldn't happen again. I begged him to believe me… and he suddenly became very, very calm and told me not to move, to stay perfectly still. He turned around and went to the book. He stood in front of it for a few moments, writing something. I'll never know what he wrote, because when he turned around, he was holding a mace, and it was on fire."

"A flaming mace?" Brendan said. "Awesome."

"Oh no, this mace didn't inspire any awe in me," Penelope said. "It was terrifying. Like a weapon for Satan himself. Even though it was made of black metal, it burned as if it were made of wood, and the flames didn't even make Kristoff flinch. I didn't understand what I was seeing.

And when I looked at Kristoff…" Penelope trailed off as if it hurt to remember.

"What about him?" Cordelia asked.

"His face was… twisted. He had this hideous grin on one half and this horrible frown on the other, almost as if his mouth were too wide for his face. He said to me, '*You have angered the Storm King.*' Then he raised the mace over his head and swung it towards me – and I woke up in this attic."

43

"The Storm King?" repeated Eleanor.

"Yeah, like the Wind Witch," said Brendan.

"Denver Kristoff and his daughter must have both fallen under the spell of the book," said Cordelia. "This explains a lot—"

"Like that scar on your skeleton!" Brendan said to Penelope. She stared at him in confusion, so he went on, "When we found your bones, you had this dent above your eye, like a big chip taken outta your skull, which must've been where the mace whacked you—"

"Stop it! Don't remind me! Denver Kristoff killed me in *cold blood*!" shouted a very upset Penelope.

"There, there. Don't," said Will, patting her back.

"Yeah, look on the bright side," Brendan said, nervously trying to correct himself. "The attic healed you perfectly.

You look fine. I mean, not *fine* fine. Decent. You know."

"Thank you, I suppose," said Penelope, sniffling.

"Penelope—" Eleanor started.

"Hold on, Nell," said Cordelia. "Penelope, it's horrible what you went through, but I have another question: did Denver Kristoff ever mention someone named Rutherford Walker?"

"You mean your ancestor?" asked Penelope. Cordelia looked at her with suspicion. She explained, "Brendan told me his last name, and I assumed there must be a connection. I'm sorry to say it, but Kristoff hates Walker. If Walker ever came near the house, we were supposed to report him to the police. Isn't he some sort of charlatan physician?"

"He *was* our great-great-grandfather," said Cordelia, "and we really don't need to hear any more awful things about him."

"But what about—" Eleanor started, and this time Will spoke over her.

"Dr Walker was a flimflam man who prescribed all sorts of absurd concoctions and tonics, but we should let bygones be—"

"*Stop talking!*" Eleanor yelled suddenly. "All of you keep

interrupting me, and I'm trying to say something important! It doesn't *matter* if Kristoff hated Walker or Walker hated Kristoff! What matters is *finding our parents* and *going home*! *Don't you care about that any more?*"

Everyone kept quiet as Eleanor took deep breaths.

"Of course," said Cordelia, "but we're trying to solve the mystery—"

"*Your* mystery! *My* mystery is when I'm gonna get to eat Chinese food with Mum and Dad again! Or go to Golden Gate Park! Or see my friends! Maybe I should just go off by myself and find that stupid cave with the book!"

Eleanor ran towards the hole in the attic floor and jumped down.

"Nell! Wait!" her siblings called, but by the time they reached the hole, she was running down the hall.

Cordelia turned to Will: "We've got to stop her. She's not behaving rationally." She waited for Will to move. "You coming? We should probably stick together."

"Uh…" Will looked at Penelope and said quietly, "Do you want to go with the Walkers?"

Penelope shook her head.

"I'll stay here and protect Penelope," Will announced.

"What are you two, joined at the hip?" Cordelia asked. "What are you scared of?"

"Mr Kristoff may be downstairs," said Penelope. "If he sees that I'm alive, he may try to kill me again."

"Kristoff's dead!" said Brendan.

"So was I."

"She has a point," Will said, giving Penelope a quick smile. "This Kristoff git may return for her – and if he does, I'd like to go a few rounds with him, whether he calls himself the Storm King or the king of France. We have unfinished business."

"You knew Kristoff?" asked Penelope.

"Not exactly," explained Will. "But he knew me. Messed with my head good and proper when I found out I was merely one of his creations. Made me question everything about myself."

"What do you mean 'one of his creations'?" asked Penelope.

"I was a character in one of Kristoff's novels," said Will. "Let me tell you all about it. I was flying a mission over…"

Cordelia scoffed and hopped down into the upstairs hallway. Brendan followed. As they went to the spiral stairs, calling for Eleanor, Cordelia vented: "I can't believe him. 'Protect', my butt. He's got one thing on his mind. I saw that look in his eyes, the way he's turning on that British charm—"

"Don't worry," said Brendan. "He also has British teeth."

Cordelia laughed and hugged her brother. She truly appreciated him sometimes. *Who needs Will anyway?*

They hustled down the stairs and saw Eleanor sitting on the bottom step, crying, with a half-eaten can of sweetcorn beside her. Cordelia went to comfort her sister—

When a huge boom sounded outside the house.

It was an explosion the Walkers had heard before, somewhere in the movies or on TV. They all looked up. Before they could figure out what it was—

A cannonball crashed through the wall in front of them.

The iron ball – smaller than a bowling ball, but a whole lot faster – whistled into the kitchen and hit the stove with a *gong*. The appliance puckered in on itself as if it were made of paper. The Walkers stared open-mouthed as the ball rolled out and hit the floor, which was now covered with a centimetre of sloshing water. As if the cannonball weren't enough, the house *was* sinking slowly.

"Please tell me that did not just happen," said Cordelia.

Brendan and Eleanor didn't answer – they were too busy rushing to the hole created by the cannonball. The hole was surrounded by jagged splinters of wood and torn electrical wires. Eleanor had to stand on her tiptoes to look through.

Outside was a real-life pirate ship.

Fifty metres away, with its sails flapping harshly as it bore down on them, the ship was a huge and terrifying sight. It had three masts; the centre one flew a black flag with a skeleton clutching an hourglass. It had wheat-coloured wood down to the waterline, where its hull was plated in copper so that it glowed beneath the waves. It had twelve square holes spaced evenly along its side, like windows – but instead of glass they housed cannons, and the cannon at the front was smoking. The bow of the great ship had a spear of wood protruding forward with a carved grey serpent wrapped around it.

"It's the *Moray*!" Eleanor shouted.

"The what?"

"The *Moray*! The pirate ship in *The Heart and the Helm*."

"*What's that?*"

"The book I was reading! The one about pirates!" Eleanor was much more animated than she had been a minute before.

"I thought you were only skimming that book," Cordelia said.

"I skimmed to page fifty! That's enough to know what the front of the ship looks like! And that it has this awful captain, Captain Sangray, who has a terrible laugh and who likes to do these horrible experiments—"

"It must be the third book we're trapped in," said Cordelia to Brendan. "Remember? Three books grew in front of you. *Savage Warriors* with Slayne and the colossus, *The Fighting Ace* with Will, and now *The Heart and the Helm.*"

"Guys!" shouted Eleanor. "Look at them! They're all staring at our house!"

Eleanor pointed to the pirates gathering on the deck of the ship. The sun had leathered their skins to a nut-brown colour. They were dressed in a variety of felt hats, scarves, and bandannas. Their faces sported thick scars, elaborate earrings, and a gold tooth for every missing tooth – except on the ones who opted for the toothless, maniacal-grin look. Over their shoulders were pistols slung in sashes; in their hands were cutlasses and axes.

"Weird," said Cordelia. "None of 'em are as cute as Johnny Depp."

The pirates spat and barked as they neared Kristoff House; every word that reached the Walkers' ears was a profanity of notable colour and conviction.

"*Hey! Who's that?*" A pirate on the deck pointed at the

cannonball hole. He wore an eye patch – but apparently that didn't stop him from having very good eyesight. "*I see you in there!*"

Brendan pushed Cordelia aside. Now that they'd been spotted, Brendan thought honesty might be the best policy.

"*We're kids and we need help!*" he yelled back. "*We're sinking!*"

The pirate with the eye patch smiled and nodded to the front of the ship.

Another boom sounded.

The Walkers scrambled up the spiral stairs, just managing to avoid the next cannonball. It smashed through the kitchen and the wall at the far side of it; Brendan glanced down in terror.

"*Occupants of this floating house!*" called a voice outside. It wasn't the pirate with the eye patch; this voice was booming and theatrical. "*You have been spotted by my first mate, Tranquebar! You have strayed into my territory! Prepare to be boarded!*"

A shadow fell over the two holes in the wall as the ship pulled up to the house.

"Oh no," said Eleanor. "They're here!"

Scraping noises sounded from above, followed by whoops

of glee, a host of snarled curses and the thud of heavy boots.

"They're on the roof!" Brendan said. "*They're going to get Will and Penelope!*"

The Walkers dashed into the upstairs hall. Cordelia was the first to reach the entrance to the attic. She was about to pull herself up when she heard a window smash – and Brendan tugged her into Eleanor's tiny bedroom.

"They're already inside! C'mere!"

"*No!* We can't leave Will and Penelope up there!"

"We don't have a choice! Will has a gun! He'll protect himself!"

Brendan gathered his sisters and heard the crack of gunfire upstairs, followed by Penelope screaming and Will yelling: "*Let her go! Don't touch me! Who the hell are you?*"

"*Don't move!*" interrupted the thunderous voice they'd heard before. "*Drop your pistol, runt! Try anything funny and I'll hack up the lady and toss her to the sharks – except, of course, for the bits I keep to myself!*"

The voice laughed: a high, squealing laugh two octaves up.

"That's Captain Sangray," Eleanor said.

"You call that a terrible laugh?" Brendan said. "He

sounds like a four-year-old on nitrous oxide."

Something hit the attic floor with a clank. "Will's Webley," said Cordelia in disbelief. They all knew how the pilot guarded his gun.

"We have to go up there!" whispered Eleanor.

"It's too late," said Cordelia. "They must be surrounded."

"But Captain Sangray's going do experiments on them! You don't understand: in the book, he wanted to be a doctor, but he got kicked out of medical school for killing his professor. So now, as a pirate captain, he studies the human body by cutting people open while they're still alive!"

"Don't say any more," Cordelia said. "It's too horrible." She hung her head. She knew she had left the attic to help Eleanor – but she wished her last words to Will had been kinder. Now they might be the last words she ever said to him. *And Penelope! Did we raise her from the dead just so she could get tortured by an evil pirate?*

Powerless to act, the Walkers were forced to stay quiet and listen to what was happening upstairs.

"*Ow!*" Penelope cried. "*That's too tight! You'll break my wrists!*"

"*Good!*" said Captain Sangray. "*Broken wrists can't untie ropes.*" He let out another laugh before asking: "Where are the others?"

"There's no one else here," said Will. "Just the two of us."

"*Liar!*" screamed the captain. "*There was some scrawny, ugly little boy talking to us from down below!*"

Brendan's face turned red and almost looked like it was starting to swell. Nobody called him names and got away with it. From above, Will continued to deny the existence of the Walkers.

"I don't know what you're talking about. I haven't seen anyone else in the house."

The captain cursed, and shouted to his men: "*Phenny, Frowd, Ogle, take these two back to my quarters!*"

"What about the rest of the house, Cap'n?" asked a pirate with a froggy voice.

"Have at it, Stump! You boys are entitled to every trinket you can find, and be on the lookout for more valuable treasure, for it's not every day one finds a floating house. I suspect enchantment. And when you see that little ankle biter and his friends, shoot to wound." Captain Sangray's voice got almost philosophical, and Eleanor could picture him tapping his chin (she had an idea of what he looked like from the book): "A nose, a kneecap… be creative. I want them permanently disfigured."

"Aye aye, Cap'n!"

There was a clamour of boots and weapons as the pirates moved towards the hole in the attic floor.

"Let's get outta here," Brendan said. "How am I gonna talk to girls with no *nose*?"

"But what about Will and Penelope?" Cordelia asked.

"We'll hide in the wine cellar – it locks, remember? And then we'll come up with a plan to get them free. It's the only way. If we get killed, they're really done for."

Brendan pulled his sisters towards the bedroom door, but stopped when he spotted something through the crack between the hinges. One pirate had already dropped onto the hall and drawn his sword.

Brendan guessed this was Stump. He was a little over five feet tall, with a squat, muscular physique and two eyes veering off in different directions.

"Hallway's been compromised," Brendan said, but before he could form a new plan, the door snapped open and Stump was right there, grinning.

"*Cap'n Sangray! Found 'em!*"

Stump grabbed a gun slung across his chest. Brendan quickly turned to Eleanor: "Nell, you went to swimming camp last year?"

"What – yes – *what?*"

Brendan scooped her up.

"Hey! Stop!" shouted Stump as he tried to get his gun to work.

"Bren? What are you—?" Cordelia yelled.

"Follow me!" Brendan said. Holding Eleanor tightly in his arms, he smashed through the window shoulder-first.

Brendan and Eleanor plunged towards the ocean. The ship was in front of them and the house was behind them and there were enemies on both sides – but they were moving too fast and they'd done something too crazy. Brendan pointed to his toes and shouted, *"Pencil dive!"*

Pirates on the *Moray* shot at the falling pair, but the ocean spray made some of their pistols click harmlessly. Others shot wide. Brendan and Eleanor hit the water, and the world turned freezing.

Brendan opened his eyes – the salt burned, and he wished he had those makeshift goggles from before. A column of bubbles next to him dispersed to reveal Eleanor, kicking for the surface. Brendan grabbed her ankle and shook his head, pointing to the underside of Kristoff House.

There were the earthquake barrels, strapped to the foundations, with ropes trailing off them in the water… and streams of bubbles escaping from their seams. Eleanor nodded; they both swam towards them.

Back inside, Cordelia was face to face with stumpy Stump. He came after her with his cutlass, but Cordelia was too fast, diving gracefully out of the broken window, slicing into the water fingertips-first.

She surfaced, calling, *"Bren! Nell!"* – and realised that the only answer she was going to get was from the pirates above. She dived as they opened fire, anticipating the burn of a shot any second—

But it never came. In the slow world beneath the waves, the bullets missed her by centimetres. Through their watery, zipping paths she saw the silhouettes of her brother and sister. They were at the Kristoff House barrels – for a horrible moment, she thought they were dead, but then she saw that they were moving, pushing their faces into the roiling bubbles that poured from the barrels' sides.

Cordelia swam to them and held her face against a flow of air, her lungs burning. She got a mouthful of seawater that made her cough and heave. Brendan silently showed her how to press her lips against the barrel cracks, drawing out precious air while sealing off water. Her first pull of oxygen was so wonderful that she almost swallowed it. She gave her brother and sister a thumbs up and raised her eyebrows: *What now?*

Brendan pointed to a spot under the house where there was a breach in the foundations. He puffed out his cheeks, miming a deep breath, and jammed his face against the barrel to fill his lungs. Then he held up his fingers – *three, two, one* – and broke off with his sisters behind him.

They swam through the breach into a different part of the Kristoff House basement, a part they hadn't seen before. It was totally bare with dark walls. They saw light coming through a hole above and swam towards it…

And the world turned noisy again as they flopped back on to a solid floor. They looked around. The surrounding walls were dimly lit and familiar.

"The secret hallway!" Cordelia said, seeing the torches above her.

"Did I come up with a brilliant plan or what?" Brendan said. "I gotta get a little credit for that!"

"How'd you know we were gonna be able to breathe

underwater?" asked Eleanor.

"It's like in classic *Sonic*, in the Scrap Brain Zone, when… hello? No? Forget it."

"Brendan, look!" Cordelia said. "The flooding's a lot worse!"

Indeed, forty-five centimetres of water now filled the hallway, pouring in from the hole the Walkers had swum through. Brendan looked at the wall and saw a cannonball hole right around the waterline.

"The second cannonball! It came in here from the kitchen, angled down and hit the floor, and got water rushing in. This place is going to sink even faster!"

Even as the Walkers spoke, the water was rising. To their left they saw the entrance that Will had made with the sledgehammer. Light seeped in, giving the hallway a bluish tinge that was just enough to make out shapes and larger details. A book floated past – the book of medical curiosities that had freaked Cordelia out earlier.

"*Pff,*" she said.

"What?" Brendan asked.

"Just thinking: even the scariest book is better than being shot at."

"*Gilliam hears yez!*" a voice called.

The Walkers turned to see a pirate sticking his head through the sledgehammered section of wall. He was enormous and bald with hunks of ivory hanging down from both ears and one side of his face was covered with a dolphin tattoo.

"And Gilliam's gonna *get* yez!" he concluded.

Brendan, having just saved his sisters with a brilliant scheme, was feeling particularly bold: "I'd like to see you try!"

"Bren! Don't taunt the pirates," Cordelia warned – but Gilliam had already pulled his pistol and fired.

The Walkers dived; Brendan hit the water and thought he was safe in the split second before the pain travelled from his left ear to his head.

He screamed with his mouth closed and covered his earlobe. Blood ribboned in front of him. Over half a metre of water filled the hallway now, enough to float in, and his sisters were swimming away. Brendan had to fight the pain as he followed, doing the breaststroke as the light grew dimmer. The Walkers heard Gilliam order them to stop each time they came up for air – until they entered the wine cellar.

"*I've been shot!!*" screamed Brendan, clutching the bottom of his ear. Blood poured down the side of his face.

"Lemme see," said Cordelia. She gently moved Brendan's hand, barely able to look at the damage. The bullet had sheared off the tip of his left earlobe.

"It's a flesh wound, OK? It's just causing a lot of bleeding. You don't have to freak out—"

"*I'm freaking out!*" yelled Brendan. "*I'm dying! This time I'm really dying!*"

"No, you're gonna be fine!" said Cordelia. "Dad always said that getting hit anywhere in the head causes a lot of bleeding, but it isn't necessarily fatal."

"Isn't fatal?!" screamed Brendan. "The head's where you shoot when you *want* it to be fatal!"

"You were grazed!" said Cordelia. "You can barely tell there's anything missing!"

"There's something *missing*? What's missing?"

"A tiny, minuscule part of the tip of your earlobe."

"The tip? That was my favourite part!"

"Get a hold of yourself, Bren!" shouted Eleanor. "You don't even wear earrings! We gotta do something!"

"You're right," said Brendan. The pain was intense –

a huge red buzz that filled his head – but fighting against it was a surge of adrenalin way more powerful than anything from lacrosse. He grabbed the wine cellar's heavy metal door. It wouldn't budge, but when Cordelia and Eleanor pitched in, pressing their feet against the wall and shoving, it swung closed through the water. The Walkers slid the bar and locked it as Gilliam banged on the other side.

"If yez come out now, ye'll get to join Gilliam, aye! It'll be adventure on the high seas for all of ye!"

"Adventure?" screamed Brendan. "You shot my ear off, dude!"

"Sorry, matey," said Gilliam. "If it's any consolation, I lost one of me butt cheeks last year!"

"Good!"

The dressing table where Cordelia had found the picture of the Lorekeepers floated by. Cordelia had an idea, opening one of the drawers (which now came out vertically instead of horizontally) to salvage a book of matches she had seen before. She lit the torches around the room, illuminating the scared faces of her siblings.

"So are yez gonna come out?" asked Gilliam.

"Never!" said Eleanor.

"So be it," Gilliam said. "Cap'n Sangray may want yez alive, but he can't account fer nothing that happens in the heat of battle. Son, I'd cover your other ear if ye want to leave a halfway decent-looking corpse!"

Brendan, Cordelia and Eleanor exchanged a stunned look, right before they heard Gilliam call out, "Boys?"

The Walkers realised that the sloshing they were hearing outside wasn't just *one* pirate. A bunch of others barked "*Aye!*" before they all opened fire on the door.

46

The Walkers dived – the water in the room was getting cloudy with Brendan's blood – but they didn't need to. The door held. Countless bullet indentations scattered the door's surface, popping out like instant metallic acne.

"Good thing these pirates have outdated technology," said Brendan. "The morons are shooting balls of lead at a steel door. *Nice try, guys! Too bad Denver Kristoff made you historically accurate!*"

"When I gets in there, I'lls be chewing off the rest o' that ear!" promised Gilliam.

"I'm not afraid of you," said Brendan. "How can I be scared of someone with one butt cheek and a dolphin tattoo on his face?"

"Bren! Stop!" Cordelia said. "We need to find a way out

of here so we can rescue Will and Penelope, remember?"

Outside the door, Gilliam looked at his fellow pirates, who were now studying his dolphin tattoo. He turned back quickly and said to Brendan, "What, may I ask, is yer problem with my tattoo?"

"It's lame," said Brendan from the other side of the door. Cordelia shook her head and started looking for a second exit. *We have to get to Will and Penelope. They've probably been taken to the pirate ship by now!*

"Lame?" Gilliam growled.

"Especially for a pirate. I would expect something scary, tough… maybe a snake or a spider, even a scorpion. But a dolphin? That's so *tween!*"

"I'll have yez know," said a furious Gilliam, "that a dolphin's the fiercest, meanest creature in the ocean! I been told! A dolphin'll tear a man's flesh from his bones in seconds!"

"You idiot! You're confusing a dolphin with a shark," said Brendan.

Eleanor whispered angrily: "Bren! Stop arguing! It's not helping!"

"I am not confusing anything! Dolphins are man-eaters! Killers!

Predators!" screamed Gilliam. But all the other pirates were now looking at one another and mumbling and raising their eyebrows.

"What are yez lookin' at?" Gilliam demanded. One of the pirates cleared his throat. "We've been meanin' to tell ya, Gilliam."

"What, Scurve?"

"Dolphins are sweet, good-natured, intelligent-like creatures. It was a trick Kit and Phenny played on you, to give you that instead of a shark—"

Gilliam interrupted Scurve's explanation by punching him in the nose. Scurve kicked Gilliam's torso – and in a moment the two were in a heated, clumsy fistfight.

On the other side of the door, Brendan grinned in triumph. "See? All part of the plan."

"That wasn't a plan!" Cordelia said. "Help us find another way out!"

Brendan started swimming with his sisters, looking for a back door to the wine cellar – but they all stopped when they heard the familiar, booming voice of Captain Sangray. "*What's going on? What's all this fighting?*"

"Scurve called my tattoo a trick, Cap'n!" said Gilliam.

"It *was* a trick, you mindless gnat. I've half a mind to maroon you for falling for such an idiotic prank! We want to strike fear into the hearts of our enemies – that tattoo makes us look ridiculous!"

"Oh," said a dejected Gilliam. "I understand, Cap'n. I'll have it changed into a proper shark—"

"You may not need to. Perhaps I'll simply remove it for you." The Walkers heard the *shink* of a knife being drawn. "But now's not the time! Here I am wading through a hallway like a lungfish to find men of the *Moray* fighting with each other and wasting gunshots on a magic door! Did I not tell you this house was enchanted?"

"Well… but… what do yez like us to do, Cap'n?" asked Gilliam. "The ankle biters are in there!"

"Then we shall blow the door with black powder," Captain Sangray said.

The pirates murmured in a agreement, except Gilliam: "But howzat gonna work, Cap'n? If'n it's a magic door?"

"Nothing can resist black powder!" snapped the captain. "Fetch it, before I decide to take off your tattoo right now!"

Gilliam and a few other pirates splashed away on the far side of the door as the Walkers gathered by the wine rack.

"What *is* black powder?" Cordelia asked.

"Gunpowder," said Brendan. "Like a whole barrelful."

"But that won't break the door, right?"

Brendan didn't answer.

"*Right?*"

"I have no idea," Brendan said, taking off his shirt and tying it around his head to stop the bleeding, "but it'd probably be better if we weren't here to find out."

"Little whelplings! I can hear you in there!" Captain Sangray called. "So far your floating wreck has provided little of interest for me and my men, so I do hope you're guarding something of value!" His high-pitched laughter pealed against the door, making them wince.

"Hey, Captain!" said Brendan. "Your laugh's even more girly than Gilliam's tattoo!"

"*Girly?*" said the captain.

"Yeah," said Brendan. "You and Dolphin Boy should open up a nail salon!"

"Brendan," whispered Cordelia. "Enough."

"Son," said a furious Captain Sangray, "are you familiar with the practice of live human vivisection?"

"No…"

"Oh no!" Eleanor said. "Bren, this is what I was talking about. He's—"

"When I get through this door, I am going to take you apart piece by piece. I am going to use a saw for your bones. And I am going to take hours, *days*, just so I can hear your 'girly' screams of agony."

"At least if he's threatening us, he's not *doing* any of that stuff to Will and Penelope," Eleanor said.

"What if he's already killed them?" asked a worried Cordelia. "We have to find another way out of here!"

"Here!" said Eleanor, swimming behind the wine rack.

Brendan and Cordelia joined her, but all they saw were three brick walls covered in faded tapestries illustrating scenes of ancient wine making. One had half-naked, buxom women smashing grapes with bare feet; one had men in elaborate costumes gulping wine from wooden barrels…

"*Where* is the exit, exactly?" Brendan asked.

"I don't know *exactly*, but it's here," said Eleanor. "It's gotta be. Press against walls and stuff. Or maybe it's under one of the rugs."

The bottom of the tapestries trailed in the salt water, so it was easy to pull them aside and look under them.

There was nothing there.

"Hurry now, before the water gets too high," said Captain Sangray. The Walkers heard the pirates push something against the door outside. Something wooden. Something big.

"They're about to blow the door!" yelled Cordelia. Sure enough, splashes echoed down the hall as the pirates retreated from the wine cellar, leaving the hiss of a burning fuse.

"We're goners!" said Brendan. "What do we do?"

Wait, Eleanor thought. *That's what we do. Don't freak out. Wait. Think.*

Eleanor knew that the idea she had must be right. There was something missing, though. The hiss of the fuse got louder in her head as she looked up and saw a small track against one of the walls, mounted in the brick, like the tracks in the Kristoff library that the ladders went on. It ran from the wine rack to a tapestry with a huge drooping grapevine…

Eleanor grabbed the tapestry and yanked it down.

At water level, where she was, there was nothing. But a metre up, above where the track ran? There was a tiny metal door.

The dumbwaiter.

"*Guys! Look!* I knew it was here! This is where Kristoff must have passed his bottles up to the kitchen! There was a ladder, see, but now it's gone—"

"No time, Nell! Great work!" Brendan leaped out of the water and hit the dumbwaiter door with the side of his fist. It swung open like a cat flap and fell into the water, damaged from Kristoff House's many adventures. Brendan hooked his fingers on the brick below it and pulled himself into the shaft.

The dumbwaiter box lay crumpled at the bottom. Above Brendan the shaft went straight up, like a chimney, with light shining down. It was going to be a tight fit, but he could do it. Cordelia was next, grabbing Brendan's hand. He pulled her into the dumbwaiter shaft. It was too close for comfort – as in her face was pressed against his bloody head – so she climbed over him, pressing her hands against the shaft like Spider-Man. Brendan knelt down to grab Eleanor.

She leaped out of the water, reached up – and just missed his hand. She splashed back down.

"Try again!" Brendan yelled.

Eleanor's breath came in fast, panicked gasps. She was alone now, the only one treading water in the room. It was terrible to think that the door would blow open and Captain Sangray would get her – but it was even worse to think that she would lose Bren and Deal. *I can't. I won't.*

Eleanor jumped again, held Brendan's hand for a moment… then slipped and splashed back in the water.

"Come on, Nell! I'm not letting my sister get vivisected!"

Eleanor pumped the fear from her stomach into her legs as she propelled herself out of the water—

And this time Brendan grabbed her wrists. And held. Eleanor screamed in triumph, her feet still dangling – but it became a different kind of scream as a deafening blast rocked the wine cellar and a spray of burning ash exploded on to her legs.

47

Eleanor was convinced that her legs had been burned to flaky ashes like the inside of her dad's barbecue. She'd be forced to spend the rest of her life in a wheelchair! But then she remembered: *There aren't any wheelchairs in Kristoff House! You're going straight to Captain Sangray's to get vivified!*

Before Eleanor could imagine the scenario in more detail, a wave of water rushed into the dumbwaiter shaft, propelled by the blast outside the metal door. Eleanor sputtered and spat, touching her calves... and the ash was gone.

"Are you OK?" Brendan asked.

"Yes!" She had tiny red splotches on her skin, and it felt like she'd been playing too close to a campfire, but she didn't need a wheelchair.

"Then climb!" ordered Brendan. "Will and Penelope, here we come!"

Eleanor winced and clambered over Brendan's shoulders. As she wormed her way up the shaft, the pirates swarmed into the room.

"Eh, then! What's this, a room full o' wine?"

"We've gone to heaven, mate!"

"Who's got the corkscrew, then?"

"Who needs one? Just bite the top off!"

"This is pinot noir! I'll not be ruinin' it with little bits and bobs of glass particles! No, we need a proper corkscrew!"

"I'm chewin' off the top! Now leggo – *ow!*"

Brendan paused in his climb and smiled as the pirates degenerated into wine-crazed beasts, fighting and splashing and cursing.

"Look here, what's this, then? 1899?" asked the pirate named Scurve. "This is grog wot's from the *future!*"

"Yez be lyin'!" said dolphin-faced Gilliam. "It says nothing o' the sort!"

"How would you know, Gilliam? You can't read!"

"*Quiet, all of you!*" ordered Captain Sangray. The wine cellar went completely silent. Brendan froze inside the dumbwaiter shaft. "Scurve is right! These vintages are labelled with dates that haven't happened yet! What'd I tell you about witchcraft? This entire house is cursed! You aren't to open a single bottle, understand?"

The pirates looked at one another, waiting for someone to respond. Gilliam did.

"But Cap'n Sangray, begging your pardon, yez told us we could take any provisions we found on this vessel."

"Did I? Gilliam, your memory is so astute! Can you remember anything else I told you today?"

Brendan grimaced. He could hear the menace in Captain Sangray's voice, but apparently Gilliam couldn't.

"Yez said to shoot the ankle biters to wound, Cap'n…"

"That's right… anything else? Do you recall anything about a dolphin tattoo?"

"Oh! Right! I's to have it covered up… no, wait, yez are gonna remove it… wait, Captain! No! Not now, oh no, at least let me drink some wi-*iiiiiii*—"

Brendan climbed the shaft as fast as he could while Gilliam's voice became a high-pitched scream. The only thing higher was Captain Sangray's hysterical laughter.

"Move, guys!" Brendan hissed when he ran into his

sisters. "Sangray's doing something horrible down there!"

Cordelia and Eleanor were perched at the entrance to the upstairs hall. "We can't," whispered Cordelia. "Stump!"

Brendan saw the diminutive pirate guarding the hall. "So? He's like four and a half feet tall! We can take him!"

"No way. He's got a gun. He's cleaning it."

"That's perfect! Now's the time!"

Brendan shoved his head into Eleanor's backside, which really hurt his injured ear. Eleanor yelped and pushed Cordelia, who tumbled out of the dumbwaiter shaft on to the hall.

"*Ankle biter!*" yelled Stump.

He fired at Cordelia, who leaped to the side. The bullet streaked into the dumbwaiter shaft, burying itself in the bricks above Eleanor, raining down dust. Brendan had to hold his breath, bite his tongue, use every bit of his inner strength to keep from sneezing.

"*Cap'n Sangray! I got one of 'em!*" Stump called. He pointed another gun at Cordelia's head. She backed against the wall and raised her hands.

"Where are your friends, missy?"

"Behind you," Cordelia said. She wasn't kidding:

Eleanor was creeping out of the shaft right behind Stump.

"You think I'm gonna fall for that?"

"You're right," said Cordelia. "How silly of me."

Eleanor eased herself to the floor. She was looking for a weapon – but the only thing she saw was a souvenir paperweight from her father's hospital. It was a black hexagonal lump about half the size of a Coke can. Eleanor reached for it as Cordelia kept Stump distracted: "In fact, I bet you never fell for a stupid trick like that in your entire pirate career. Obviously you're very intelligent…"

Stump scrunched his eyebrows. He'd been called many things in his life, but *intelligent* wasn't one of them. Suddenly he didn't trust Cordelia. He turned his head slightly – and saw Eleanor!

Cordelia screamed. Eleanor slid the paperweight across the floor between Stump's legs. Stump fired at Eleanor, but the shot went high, cleaving her hair. Cordelia grabbed the paperweight and raised it above her head. Stump cursed and drew his cutlass to finish off Eleanor—

And his chin shot up as Cordelia struck the top of his skull.

Stump crumpled to the floor. Cordelia dropped the

paperweight. Eleanor caught her breath. Brendan climbed out of the dumbwaiter shaft.

"Are you OK? Do you need help? Oh."

"You're a little late," said Cordelia.

"Wow, you were awesome! I mean, girl power, right?"

"Shut up, Bren!" Cordelia shoved him. "You almost got us killed!"

"I'm sorry," Brendan said, "but I knew you'd handle yourselves."

"Should we keep his gun?" Eleanor asked, nodding to one of Stump's pistols. The pirate was out cold.

"Wouldn't be much use," said Brendan. "I saw this Discovery Channel thing about pirates. The guns they used were single-shot flintlocks. You have to reload them between each shot, and they mess up if there's moisture in the air. That's why they carry so many."

"What about his sword?" Eleanor asked.

"*That* we can use to help Will and Penelope," Brendan said. "We're gonna need something to save them from the pirate ship." He reached for the cutlass – but Stump's body started to stir.

The Walkers took off down the hall. By the time Stump

groggily got to his feet, they were in the attic, staring out of the window, trying to figure out how to get to the *Moray*.

48

The mighty ship was towing Kristoff House with huge ropes. The ropes were attached to the house's roof on one side and the ship's stern on the other. At the stern, the Walkers saw the *Moray*'s rear cabin, with stained-glass windows featuring goats and howling men.

"Sangray must be taking us somewhere horrible," Eleanor said.

"Not if we rescue Will and get him back his Webley," said Brendan. "He could take out these pirates no problem." Brendan sounded confident, but his face quickly went from hopeful to terrified as he heard the pirates themselves downstairs.

They were charging towards the attic: "*Shoot to disfigure!*"

"That was Captain Sangray," Eleanor said. "We *can't* let him get us!"

"What are we going to do, go back in the water?" Brendan asked.

"Maybe we don't have to," said Cordelia. She stepped on to the windowsill as the pirates' rough hands appeared around the hole in the attic floor:

"*This way!*"

"*Aye!*"

"*Arrrgh!*"

Cordelia grabbed the moulding that ran above the window. She pressed her feet against the inside of the frame, swung her legs over the top, and pulled herself on to the shingled roof. She didn't make it look easy, exactly, but even she was impressed at what adrenalin could make you do.

"How do you expect me to—" Eleanor started, but Brendan grabbed her and leaned out of the window while holding her. Cordelia took her wrists and pulled her up. Then Brendan hoisted himself on to the roof, his butt disappearing over the top of the window just as the pirates fanned out across the attic.

"*Where'd they go?*"

"*Out of the window, Cap'n!*"

The Walkers scrambled to the peak of the roof, squinting in the punishing sun, their feet slipping and sliding on the shingles. They were desperate for a place to hide, trying to stay low so none of the pirates on the *Moray* could spot them. Cordelia spotted a large, six-sided cone of shingles at the corner of Kristoff House. It was the ornamental peak that crowned the bay window in the upstairs hall.

"We can hide behind that."

"What?" Brendan asked. "There's nowhere to stand! We'll fall—"

"Ringrose, pull me up!" called a pirate below them, and Brendan reconsidered. He and his siblings slid down the roof, stopped themselves on the gutter that hung over the sparkling waves, and shuffled their feet sideways to edge to the cone of shingles.

They pressed their backs against three of its six sections and held on as the wind tugged their clothes. Brendan's bloody shirt, still wrapped around his head as a bandage, whipped into Cordelia's face.

"Bren! Would you control that thing?"

"I'm trying not to fall in the ocean—"

"Hold on," Cordelia said, "I have an idea." She ripped

the shirt off Brendan and let the wind sling it out to sea.

"I need that!"

"No, you don't! You stopped bleeding!"

"Why'd you throw it in the water—?"

"I've got a plan. When the—" began Cordelia.

"*Shhhh!*" hissed Eleanor. "Pirates!"

The pirates had reached the top of the roof. Brendan peeked. He first saw Tranquebar, the pirate with the eye patch who had spotted him before. Tranquebar was old, with a pockmarked face. Next to him, casting a long shadow, was a man who had to be Captain Sangray.

Brendan stifled a gasp. Sangray looked like a wrestler, but not one of the new ones who were all body-shaved and clean-cut: one of the crazy retro ones like the Undertaker. He was six feet six, with one strong leg perched on either side of the roof's peak; he wore leather breeches and a gold-fringed waistcoat… and he sported the wildest beard Brendan had ever seen. It extended down thirty centimetres from his chin, jet black and tapered to two points, but it didn't really end there, because the points were woven in with two leather straps that reached his belt and attached to crescent-shaped blades.

"Holy… Captain Sangray's got knives attached to his *beard*!" Brendan said.

Eleanor inched forward for a look.

"Guys, careful, we're gonna get caught…" warned Cordelia.

But it was too late. Next to Captain Sangray, sharp-eyed Tranquebar pointed to the cone the Walkers were hiding behind.

"Look at that, Cap'n! Three of them."

Brendan gritted his teeth and tried to imagine how he would fight Captain Sangray – he didn't think he stood a chance against those razor-sharp beard blades. But instead of rushing down the roof to catch the Walkers, Sangray asked, "What are you talking about, Tranquebar?"

"Sharks!" said the first mate. "Three fins whipping around in the water, tearing at something!"

Cordelia looked. Far behind the house, the ocean frothed around a trio of sleek, blue-grey predators that were fighting over…

"Your shirt, Bren! They're going after the blood!" Cordelia said. "My plan worked!"

"What plan?"

"*Shh*. Listen."

Tranquebar pulled out a spyglass and held it up. After getting a good look at the sharks he rose on the balls of his feet to whisper in his captain's ear. "Cap'n, the sharks have the ankle biter's shirt!"

"Are you certain?" asked Sangray curiously.

"Has mine eye ever let you down, Cap'n? It's the shirt that brat was wearing."

Sangray considered this, then mumbled: "Bet the shirt's all that's left of them." His beard was shaped by oil, which glinted in the sun. His calculating eyes darted from the ocean to his men, who were fumbling around on the roof, complaining that they weren't allowed to drink the wine, asking one another how it was that they'd been given the slip by a bunch of children…

"Men, the spoon-fed brats are *dead*!" declared Sangray. "Shark food, as I suspected. Back inside – and to celebrate, *let's all have a bottle of enchanted wine!*"

The pirates responded with a roar. "San-*gray*! San-*gray*! Long live the Cap'n!"

Sangray smiled; he knew how fragile his position could be. "To you, my men! To *you*!" He trilled a laugh – but, as the pirates climbed back into the attic, cut it off and pulled Tranquebar aside.

"If you've made a liar of me, old friend, I'll cut out your good eye, chew it up, and spit it back into the socket under that patch, understand?"

Tranquebar nodded. "Wouldn't be the *Moray* without threats like that, my captain."

The Walkers waited until Sangray and Tranquebar were gone before they crept out from behind their hiding place. They flopped on to the roof, totally exhausted.

"Guys, we need to keep moving…" said Cordelia. "Let's get to the chimney. It's safer. See?"

The Kristoff House chimney offered some shade, plus it had a flat platform surrounding it. Using the last of their strength, the Walkers got to their feet and climbed.

"Wait," said Eleanor. "Won't the pirates on the *Moray* see us?"

"We'll keep our heads down," said Brendan, "and besides, I think most of the pirates are in our house." Sure enough, as if in answer, a window shattered below. Eleanor looked down to see a pirate calling, "Ho, mates! Time to use the privy!"

Before Eleanor could look away, the pirate urinated into

the sea as he swigged from a wine bottle.

"*Arrrrrr!*" he called, impressed with his arc.

"Gross! What are you waiting for? Go!" Eleanor said, completely freaked out.

The Walkers reached the chimney and curled around it. Eleanor was nearly hyperventilating at the disgusting sight she had just seen.

"Guys, we need to get out of here," she said. "Can't one of us just do something selfish? Something greedy? Then the book will show up and the Wind Witch will send us home."

"We can't abandon Will and Penelope," Cordelia said.

"We don't stand a chance against those pirates," argued Eleanor. "We need to think about ourselves."

"Nell—" began Brendan.

"Yes! I know," interrupted Eleanor. "I know it's a horrible thing to say – and I know worse stuff than you, because of the story; I know what Sangray *does* – but Will is just a character from a book. And Penelope, she was brought back to life by magic. But I'm a kid with a real life ahead of her. And I don't want to die here!"

"Nell, Will is very real to us," said Cordelia. "You know

how much I love books, but I've never felt this way about a character I've read about—"

"Me too," said Brendan. Since everyone else was saying what they were really feeling, he decided to chime in. "Penelope feels very real to me."

"And we're the only ones who can help them," Cordelia said. "We have to try. But we'll never get past those pirates in the daylight. We have to wait up here until it's dark."

Eleanor didn't answer. She just laid her head down with her siblings and thought, *They don't understand anything.*

Something jabbed Cordelia's side. "My phone," she said, removing the dripping device from her pocket. "Dead from seawater."

"And you don't even have insurance," yawned Brendan.

"What good is insurance gonna do me out here?"

"It was a *joke* – jeez. Maybe you should let it dry out; sometimes they work again."

Cordelia placed the phone beside her, letting it cook in the sun, as the Walkers fell into a fitful state of unconsciousness beside the chimney. They awoke every few minutes with the sun baking them, shifting positions to stay in the shade… and to keep from falling into the sea. Eleanor was still angry and didn't want to sleep, but when the human body is completely spent, it can recharge anywhere.

Eleanor woke up under the stars.

Her brother and sister were still asleep. The air temperature had dropped dramatically; she hugged herself in the cold. The wind whistled across the chimney. The moon was nearly full, rising over the horizon. The *Moray* sailed through the water at a steady clip, towing the house. The pirates had made their way back to the ship and were having a raucous party. A screeching *whiz* produced a firework that exploded in the air like a giant dandelion. Pirates cheered as sparks drifted down. Someone on deck was playing a fiddle; someone else was tap-dancing (or maybe it was the same, very talented person).

Am I dreaming? Eleanor wondered, and then it all came back to her: the ship, the attack, her situation. She wasn't dreaming at all, and she wasn't close to going home.

Unless I do something selfish. Something against the best interest of my family. Something only for me.

Eleanor eyed her brother and sister, curled around the chimney as if it were a perfectly normal place to sleep.

Soon they're gonna wake up, and they're gonna want me to go on that pirate ship to rescue Will and Penelope, which is impossible. But with one little push…

Eleanor stood behind Cordelia. In a moment of crisis, her brain had its own twisted logic. *If I push her off the edge, I'll be doing something really selfish. That book will appear. And then I can give it to the Wind Witch and we can all go home. I'll be a hero!*

Of course Eleanor knew it was a terrible idea – but a voice inside her head told her that Cordelia wouldn't be in the ocean for long. She was a great swimmer, and she would only need to tread water for a few minutes, and then… Chinese food! Golden Gate Park! Mum and Dad.

Eleanor reached out and gently placed her hands on Cordelia's back, about to push her off the edge – when she saw something out of the corner of her eye.

The Book of Doom and Desire.

It sat at the peak of the roof, balanced perfectly, teetering as the house moved through the water. *Wow!* Eleanor thought. *I didn't even have to push her off! I just had to think about it!*

Eleanor moved away from Cordelia and crawled towards the book. As she got close, two shapes began to materialise on either side of it. At first, they were just streaks of curling purple light, but as Eleanor watched in disbelief, the light took shape and substance, becoming a leg, an arm, a face…

She was looking at her parents.

"Mum! Dad!"

Dr and Mrs Walker nodded. They were dressed in the same clothes Eleanor had last seen them in, when they were all eating pizza before the Wind Witch attack. They looked calm.

"Is this a dream?"

Eleanor's parents shook their heads and stared at the book. Eleanor crawled closer. *They want me to open it. It makes sense. That's what the Wind Witch wants too.*

She put her hands on the book – and remembered her brother and sister. She turned: "What about them?"

Her parents didn't answer.

"They'll come home too, right?"

Her mother shook her head.

"But they have to! I can't go back *alone*!"

Her mother whispered: "You have to. Only one person can go home at a time. You need to be the first. You're our baby."

Eleanor scowled. "But I can't leave them behind—"

"Of course you can. They'll get home. Eventually."

"I don't know…"

"Just open the book, Eleanor. You'll be home within seconds, just like the Wind Witch promised. We'll order dim sum and chocolate sundaes and we'll take you and your friends to the new Pixar movie and then you can all come back to the house for a sleepover and I'll make French toast for breakfast…"

Warmth seeped through the book's leather cover as Eleanor started to open it.

"That's it… good girl," her father and mother said, now speaking in perfect unison. Their voices cracked ever so slightly.

"What's wrong with you guys? You sound weird," said Eleanor, holding the book's cover halfway open.

"Just open the book," her parents said.

"You don't sound like my parents," said Eleanor, starting to close it.

"Of course we are," they said in perfect stereo. "*Just open the damn book!*"

But that made Eleanor even more wary. "My parents

would never swear around me. Who are you?"

And then her parents snapped.

"*I said open it! What are you doing? You always were a stubborn little fool!*"

And with that Eleanor saw that her parents' teeth were turning yellow – and she knew where she'd heard that voice before. She slammed the book shut. In front of her, her parents roared, and now they were twisting and changing, surrounded by purple light, their skin cracking and ageing, their hair falling out like in a horrible time-lapse video. They rose from the roof and, in the night sky, melted their bodies together to become the Wind Witch.

She wasn't the real Wind Witch; she shimmered and shook – a conjured vision, a hologram like the book the Walkers had seen back in the forest. But she was just as scary as the real thing.

"*Open the book!*" screamed the Wind Witch.

"No! I'm not opening this! Ever!"

"*Then you'll never get home!* Don't you understand? Your brother and sister don't *want* to leave. They *don't* love your mother and father the way you do! And they don't love *you*, either!"

With a screech the Wind Witch illusion shot up like a comet and disappeared into the night sky. The book slipped out of Eleanor's hands, slid down the roof, and fell into the ocean – but when it hit the waves, instead of splashing, it vanished without a sound. Eleanor screamed.

"What's happening?" Cordelia asked.

Cordelia and Brendan rushed to their sister. Eleanor was shaking, terrified by the nightmare vision she'd just had.

"I... I..." Eleanor almost lied and said she'd been dreaming. "I saw the book. The book was here."

"*The* book? *The Book of D and D?*" Brendan asked.

"Yeah. And Mum and Dad were here too, telling me to open it... but they weren't really Mum and Dad. They were just some fake hologram made up by the Wind Witch, trying to convince me to leave you two behind—"

"But you didn't," Cordelia said. "You beat her, Nell."

"We're so proud of you," said Brendan, hugging his sister.

"I don't know if I could do it again," said Eleanor. "She promised me all my favourite foods. She knew how to get into my head—"

"It won't be you next time," said Brendan.

"What do you mean?"

"Well, the book tried to tempt me," said Brendan. "Then you. And with you it was worse because you saw an image of the Wind Witch too." He shook his head. "That book's bad news. I'd rather read a biography of Barbie."

"Hey!" complained Eleanor.

"Next time she'll probably go after Deal. Hopefully she's as strong as us—"

"Ha, I have better willpower than both of you," said Cordelia, but there was an uncertain tone in her voice. She immediately changed the subject. "It's night. We need to get to that ship and save Will and Penelope."

"How are we gonna do that? Climb across those?" Brendan pointed to the ropes that connected Kristoff House to the *Moray*. He had woken up freezing, much colder than his sisters because his shirt was gone, pieces of it scattered inside the bellies of three sharks. He felt his chin and found a throbbing pimple growing there. As if this adventure weren't difficult enough.

"I think so," said Cordelia. "It's not like we have a choice; we're really sinking now." She nodded to the side of the roof. The water was much closer than it had been when they'd fallen asleep. "The first storey's totally flooded by now."

"So where do you think Captain Sangray was taking Will and Penelope?"

"Probably his quarters," Eleanor said, pointing to the rear cabin of the *Moray*, the one with the stained glass. Through the glass the Walkers could see a large table with coils of heavy chain on it, surrounded by masks mounted on the walls. The three kept watching as the pirates partied on deck, singing inappropriate songs and setting off more fireworks. Soon enough, three silhouettes entered the cabin.

The first was hulking; it had to be Captain Sangray. The other two were limp bodies he carried over his shoulders. Cordelia recognised Will (with his lanky frame) and Penelope (with her massive shoulder pads).

"It's them! Are they *dead*?"

"I don't think so," said Brendan. In silhouette, as if he were part of a grotesque puppet play, Sangray heaved Will and Penelope on to the table and chained up their wrists and ankles.

"What's he doing with them?"

"He's gonna do his horrible experiments," said Eleanor, stifling a gulp.

"Live human vivisection," intoned Brendan, remembering the words Sangray had used to threaten him.

In his cabin, the captain stepped away from the bodies and took a mask with a long tapered nose off the wall. He strapped it to his face and kicked his head back. The Walkers heard his laughter over the waves.

"Oh no," said a frightened Eleanor. "It's just like it was in the book. And that was the grossest, sickest thing I've ever read in my—"

"Let's go," interrupted Cordelia, stepping towards the ropes and almost tripping over her phone. It was right where she'd left it, dried out.

"Try it," Brendan said. Cordelia turned it on. The screen lit up. Brendan gave her a look like, *Who's the man?*

"Don't get too excited; still no bars." Cordelia pocketed the phone. "Follow me, guys. Maybe we can cause a distraction and get Will and Penelope out of there."

The Walkers approached the thick ropes that were towing Kristoff House. They stretched high over the water to the stern of the *Moray*, taut – they looked like they could slice skin open on contact.

Cordelia took a breath and slowly reached for a rope, but Brendan said, "Let me."

He took one in his fist. It felt strong, secure. A lifeline.

"We can do this," Brendan said in his best pep-talk voice. "Between us we have like nine hundred years on these guys." He slung himself under the rope and started across the waves, hand over fist, hanging upside down. Cordelia smiled. *Sometimes my little brother really does seem grown-up.*

"Not looking down," Eleanor said, following Brendan, trying to ignore the wind lashing at her clothes. Cordelia brought up the rear. Soon the Walkers were five metres from the *Moray*, then three, then two... Then a pirate appeared.

The Walkers went absolutely still. "Nobody move," whispered Cordelia. The pirate was totally wasted, clutching a bottle of "enchanted" wine, stumbling along the deck, singing a sea shanty whose lyrics spoke of unmentionable horrific acts in contrast to its cheery tune. He turned back towards the front of the ship.

"Sweet," said Brendan. "He's leaving. We made it—"

The pirate tripped. The wine bottle flew out of his hand, flipped through the air, and fell into the sea. He swore and ran to the ship's stern: "Yesh took m'drink! Yesh greedy ocean!"

The pirate broke down and started crying into the waves. The Walkers felt their hands cramping and collectively willed him to go away... but before he did, he saw them.

"Issh... ish the ankle biters!" He pointed his gun at the Walkers. "Come aboard – and if ye try anything, I'll blasht ye inter the sea!"

Eleanor's brain spun. "I know who that is!" she whispered to her siblings. "One of the pirates in the book: Ishmael Hynde."

"What do you remember about him?" asked Cordelia.

"He's from England... He's a 'womaniser', but I don't know what that is," she said, trying to remember. "He's good with a bow and arrow, superstitious, believes in all sorts of supernatural stuff..."

"That's good," said Cordelia, who had a plan. "Start making sounds. Like this: *woooo*-oooh."

"What, like we're at a party?" Brendan said.

"*Silence! Come for'ard—*"

"Like we're in a graveyard! Like we just climbed out of maggoty old coffins. C'mon!"

Eleanor understood. She let out an eerie cry as Cordelia called to the pirate on the ship: "*We're spirits of the dead!*"

"No, ye aren't. Yer just the ankle biters, and ye somehow got away from them sharks! How'd ye manage that?"

"We're *ghossstss-sss*!" Cordelia insisted.

"Yez think I'm gonna fall for that, jesh because I had a few dips of the grape? Ghosts *float*!"

"*Ooooo-eeee*," Brendan said. "Everyone knows ghosts can't float over water, *chuuuump*—"

Cordelia cut him off. "Aren't you Ishmael Hynde?" she asked.

"What?" the pirate blurted. "How'd ye know my—"

"Father!" Cordelia called.

"I ain't yer daddy," said Hynde.

"We are the ghosts of your unborn children," said Cordelia.

"My *unborn* children?!"

"Why have you abandoned us, Father? Why have you left us alone, to fend for ourselves, in all the corners of the world?"

"Naw, ye can't be. I got no children—"

"Were you ever in Barcelona?" asked Cordelia.

"Yes," said Hynde, smiling. "Spent five glorious days there!"

"And I am the fruit of those days!"

"Yer a liar!"

"And the boy here?" said Cordelia, pointing at Brendan. "He's from Monaco!"

"But I only spent three hours in Monaco!"

"And for those hours he will haunt you forever" – as Cordelia spoke, she reached for her phone – "for being a deadbeat dad. I mean for abandoning us—" Her fingers slipped!

Cordelia's phone fell. She let go of the rope and grabbed it in a desperate swoop, hanging by her legs with her ankles wrapped around each other.

"Deal! Are you – I mean, *ooooo-oooo*!" Brendan called to Hynde.

"Yer not me children!" the pirate screamed, taking aim. "What kinder ghosht has ta keep itself from *falling*?"

In answer, Cordelia put the phone under her chin and lifted her head. The bright screen transformed her face into something truly ghostly – especially if you were a sailor with a preschool education who'd never seen an Apple logo. Lit in blue from below, Cordelia's nose and cheeks cast a shadow over her eyes, turning them into black pits above her shining mouth. She looked like a turquoise-faced zombie from the bowels of the *Titanic*.

"*Why have you done this to us, Fatherrrr!*" Eleanor screamed.

"*My babies!*" Hynde shrieked. He reached out, tears spurting from his eyes. "*Please forgive me!*"

He ran towards the Walkers and leaped over the edge of the ship, stretching his arms out, trying to embrace his "children" – and fell into the ocean. He managed to fight the sea for a few moments, popping above the waves to shout: "*Forgive meeee!*"

Within moments Hynde was surrounded by sharks. He started to scream as they tore at his body and dragged him underwater.

"Ugh, that could've been us," Brendan said in a small voice before leading the Walkers the rest of the way to the *Moray*'s stern. When he was close enough to touch the wood, he dropped his feet, held the rope with his hands, and started swinging back and forth.

"What are you doing?" Eleanor asked. "You'll shake us off!"

"Hang tight, pun intended," said Brendan.

He gathered momentum and went airborne, pointing his legs at a circular window to the left of Sangray's cabin. He smashed through the glass with both feet. He had sort of planned ahead, enough to bend his knees to catch himself on the edge of the window – but he hadn't counted on his head swinging back to *whap* against the side of the *Moray*.

"*Ow!*"

For a moment, as he hung upside down, Brendan saw stars: literal ones and those of the cartoon variety. Then he tensed his stomach, dug deep for the kind of strength he always needed to do the last sit-up in lacrosse practice, and pulled himself up to peer into the cabin on the other side of the window.

Brendan gasped.

"What?" said Cordelia.

"It's… just… forget it. Nothing!" Brendan climbed inside the cabin, steadied himself, and stretched back for Eleanor.

"I'm cool," she said, waving him off. She had grabbed

the thick, rusted bolts that held together the *Moray*'s sides and used them to climb down. She came inside with Brendan – and froze just as he had.

"Whoa."

"What?" Cordelia started, climbing in last.

It was a small cabin, two and a half metres by two and a half metres.

And the floors, walls and ceiling were covered with human bones.

51

The floor was tiled with leg bones. Tibiae and fibulae interlocked so that there was little space between them. The bones weren't set in anything, so when the Walkers shifted their feet, the floor moved, clicked and snapped.

"What is this place?" Cordelia asked. The walls were covered with thinner radii and humeri – arm bones – which also didn't appear to be mounted in anything. "How are those *sticking to the wall?*"

"Magic," said a stunned Eleanor.

"Let's get outta here," Brendan said. "They're only bones; they're not gonna hurt us. And check this…"

Brendan pointed to a cutlass mounted on the wall. A spear hung beside it along with a load of other weapons. They were the only things in the room that weren't made of bone. Brendan reached for the cutlass and spear—

"Wait, Bren!"

But it was too late. When he pulled them off the wall, he triggered something.

The room started coming alive.

It began at Brendan's feet. The bones jittered and shook, each activating the one next to it, spreading like a wave until…

Brendan froze. Years ago he had seen a nature documentary, and he recalled a vivid scene set in a cave filled with bats, where the floor was so filled with bat poo (*guano*, they called it, but really it was bat poo) that it became a living carpet of mealworms and beetles. You glanced at the guano and it looked like a normal floor, but if you focused for a moment, it wriggled and swarmed. It was one of the freakiest things Brendan had ever seen, and now the floor of bones was doing the same thing.

A femur stood up in the middle of the room. "Duck!" Brendan yelled to his sisters. Cordelia and Eleanor just managed to comply as a humerus zipped past their heads.

"What's happening?" Eleanor asked.

The bones clicked and clacked and stood and flew, like

an explosion played in reverse. Many somersaulted through the air, while others shot forward like arrows. The weapons that were still mounted on the wall went with them. Every bone seemed to have a purpose, flying towards the centre of the room, right next to Brendan. He buried his head in his elbow, certain he was about to get hit, and peeked out as the bones and weapons started interlocking. Triquetrals snapped in place with cuboids; scaphoids met calcanei; hunks of skull and teeth sailed down from the ceiling. For a minute, the Walkers thought some kind of horrible super-skeleton monster was being constructed… but then, as suddenly as it began, it was over.

The room was now a simple wooden ship's cabin.

And the bones had formed a rectangular dining table.

"You OK?" Cordelia asked Brendan.

"Um, *impressed*, actually." Brendan tapped his fist against the table. It didn't wobble; the bones had fused together perfectly. And on it were actual place settings!

The plates were made of shoulder blades. Upside-down skulls formed goblets (mounted on tripods of ribs). Finger bones, with toe bones for tines, served as forks. Knives were made of ribs and teeth.

"All that's missing is food!" Brendan said. He looked up: "Please, God, could we get some food in here?"

"I don't think God made that table come together," said Eleanor. "Besides, aren't those human bones? You can't eat off human bones!"

"Hey, I'm hungry. Right now I'd split an ice cream sandwich with the Wind Witch," said Brendan.

Cordelia laughed, but Eleanor held her stomach. "I actually feel sick thinking about it," she said.

"Are you OK?" Brendan asked.

Eleanor shook her head. "I think I'm gonna throw up."

"You're getting seasick," Cordelia said. "The ship is moving more than the house did. Go to the window for fresh air."

Eleanor did – but it was too late. Spit was flooding her mouth. She got on her tiptoes and tried to aim out the window… but nothing came out. She was dry heaving.

"Ick!" she said, wiping stringy spit from her mouth. "I haven't eaten in so long I can't even *throw up*!" She started crying—

And suddenly three sizzling porterhouse steaks appeared on the bone plates, along with hand-cut French fries and creamed spinach.

"Whoa," Brendan said.

Root beer rose inside each skull goblet until fizzy bubbles popped out. Brendan lurched towards the table—

"Don't do it." Eleanor grabbed him. "I haven't eaten anything but sweetcorn for the last two days, but even I know it's not right to eat that stuff. There was something in *The Heart and The Helm* about it… it's some kind of test the pirates set up to protect them from their enemies."

"It can't be that big a deal, right?" asked Brendan.

"Probably not," said Cordelia.

Cheese appeared on the fries. Dripping, creamy, orange cheese.

Brendan shoved Eleanor aside, grabbed a fork, and constructed a bite of steak, fries, and cheese that filled his mouth with 100 per cent pleasure – which became 200 per cent when he washed it down with a swig of root beer. Brendan didn't even realise it, but he closed his eyes as he ate, and when he opened them, he was looking at Cordelia, who was having just as good a time, slicing off her second strip of meat.

"Cordelia!" screamed Eleanor. "You're supposed to be the logical one!"

"I *doummppphht*" – Cordelia chewed quickly, swallowed, and continued when she could properly articulate her response – "I doubt that I'm gonna die from this food after all the other insanely dangerous stuff we had to go through."

"You guys are *idiots*!" Eleanor said. "I'm happy that I'm seasick!" She headed for the door—

As Brendan slumped on the floor. Unconscious.

"Bren!"

Cordelia and Eleanor rushed to him. His head was twisted back, and his tongue stuck out. "I told you!" Eleanor said—

And Brendan sat up and laughed.

"*You*—" Cordelia shrieked, smacking her brother as she showed off some of the new vocabulary she'd learned from Captain Sangray's men.

"Lighten up!" said Brendan. "Can't we have a little fun?"

"Not like that! We thought you were *dead*!"

"Whatever." Brendan returned to his plate. Cordelia joined him. When the two siblings finished, taking care not to eat so much that they would get sleepy, they picked up the cutlass and spear that Brendan had pulled off the wall.

"Why are you staring at me?" Cordelia asked Eleanor.

"I'm waiting for you to shrink to the size of an ant or get super-fat like in *Alice in Wonderland*."

"Very funny." The Walkers left the cabin and stepped into the lower decks of the *Moray*, holding the cutlass and spear.

Taking care to move carefully so as not to arouse the interest of any pirates who weren't partying above, they walked a metre… to what had to be Captain Sangray's cabin.

Hanging on the door was a stuffed goat's head with emerald eyes. Muffled screams came from inside.

Brendan put his hand on the doorknob – but then it started to turn on its own. The Walkers scrambled behind a barrel as the door swung open and Tranquebar, the first mate, stepped out of the room.

"Captain's starting to really lose it," Tranquebar mumbled to himself, scratching absently at his eye patch as he walked down the hall.

"Can we do this?" Brendan asked when Tranquebar was gone. He put his hand back on the doorknob. The Walkers looked at each other. Brendan had the cutlass; Cordelia had the spear; Brendan still didn't have a shirt on. They were covered with dirt and cuts and bruises; Brendan had lost the tip of his ear. They almost looked like pirates.

"Let's do it," said Cordelia.

Brendan opened the door.

Captain Sangray's cabin resembled a witch doctor's den. It had Polynesian masks on the walls, many small candles on the floor and two huge black cauldrons next to the door, seated on coals, filled with bubbling black fluid.

In the centre of the room was the table, made of grey stone.

On it were Will and Penelope.

They were chained to the table, covered in thick black tar; it looked like they'd been fished out of a bog. They struggled desperately against their chains... and they screamed through the gags around their mouths, which were two slimy, thick, dead eels.

Captain Sangray stood over them, wearing the mask the Walkers had seen through the stained glass: a rat mask with a giddy, toothy face and a long nose that ended in walrus whiskers. He held a wavy dagger over Penelope's chest.

"My friends!" His voice boomed through the mask's too-white teeth: "Welcome! You'll make a fine addition to my bone collection!"

52

The Walkers' hearts and mouths and hands froze. If Captain Sangray hadn't been masked, and he hadn't made Will and Penelope into pitch-dark golems, and his cabin didn't look like a place where children got turned into newts… then they might have charged him and taken him out. But hesitation breeds hesitation. Sangray smiled behind his rat teeth.

"Oh, so you came to watch? Then let the vivisection *begin!*"

"*Nuh!*" Penelope Hope begged underneath him.

Sangray unleashed a high-pitched laugh. *He* sounds *like a rat,* thought Brendan in some far-off corner of his brain. Penelope twisted back and forth on the table, trying to bite through the eel that gagged her—

But Captain Sangray sank the knife into her chest.

"*Nnnngggggggggeeee!*"

Penelope's gag couldn't muffle her scream. "First," Sangray said, "we open up the chest cav—"

"*No!*" Brendan shouted, charging with his cutlass.

Brendan's jab pierced Sangray's hand. The captain cried out and dropped the knife. Cordelia threw her spear but missed; it clattered off the stained-glass window behind Sangray.

"Split up!" Cordelia yelled.

She and Eleanor ran for opposite corners of the room. Sangray tore off his mask to inspect his wound. "You cut a hole in me," he mused, rotating his bloody hand in front of his face, staring at Brendan through the slice in his palm. Then he charged.

Brendan backed against the cabin door. Sangray jerked his chin up – left, then right – to draw out the curved razor-sharp daggers that were attached by straps to his beard. As he ran towards Brendan, he whirled his head in circles, spinning the knives like helicopter blades. The daggers spun so fast that Brendan could only see flashes of chrome. Brendan held up his cutlass, trying to sever the straps—

But one of the whirling blades slammed into Brendan's sword. He dropped it.

"*Help!*" Brendan called, knowing that the electric tremor in his arm was the last thing he'd ever feel. "He's gonna chop me into tuna tartare!"

At that moment, Eleanor pushed over one of the bubbling cauldrons. The tar inside hissed as it hit the wood of the cabin, causing Sangray to turn his head. His spinning daggers were inches from Brendan's face.

Brendan took the opportunity to kick Sangray in the groin. Penelope had taught him well.

The captain fell, his beard blades clattering to the floor as his injured hand landed in steaming tar.

"*Rraaaggh!*" He shot to his feet and turned to Eleanor, spiralling his beard. "*I'll kill you all!*"

The sound of the rotating blades was the worst part, like an industrial fan in a wind tunnel. Eleanor dived – but one of the blades caught her shoulder, slicing deeply. She screamed as she landed next to Cordelia, who was unchaining Will from the table, and then she gritted her teeth and started crawling towards Cordelia's spear.

Cordelia had already freed Will's ankles; she was working

on his wrists, unwilling to touch the smelly eel wrapped around his mouth.

"*Guh thuh uv muh!*" Will said.

Cordelia closed her eyes and grabbed the eel from behind Will's neck, yanking down, causing the creature to burst into two slimy pieces that fell away from his face.

"*That's* more like it!" the pilot exclaimed, spitting out some bits of eel guts, as Cordelia freed his wrists. Sangray turned, his head still spinning the deadly blades, and moved towards Will. The pilot rolled off the table and hit the floor. Sangray's blades struck the stone, shooting out sparks that hit his greased beard—

And turned into flames that licked up his face!

The captain cursed and stopped in his tracks, patting out the fire with his good hand. Eleanor retrieved the spear and handed it to Cordelia – and Cordelia thrust it into Sangray's chest, holding on to the shaft as if to drive it through his heart.

The captain was too strong for that. Even as his beard filled the room with the smell of singed hair, he grabbed the spear's shaft and turned it, wrenching Cordelia's arm aside. She cried out as her elbow twisted the wrong way. She let go of the spear. Sangray ripped it out of his chest. Will crept along the floor towards a wooden chest in the corner.

Captain Sangray opened a wall cabinet and removed a brass pistol inlaid with niello. It was a beautiful gun, and he admired it for a moment as Eleanor sneaked behind him, opened her mouth, and bit down hard on his ankle.

"*Ankle biter!*" Sangray cried. Eleanor bit through the skin, drawing blood, and then scampered up the captain's back and climbed onto his shoulders.

"*Come here!*" Sangray roared, trying to grab her. Eleanor gripped the two straps that hung from his beard and flipped over the top of his head like a parkour expert, taking hold of the leather just above the beard blades. She hit the floor and sank them into the pile of cooling tar. The blades stuck fast. Sangray tried to pull away, but he was trapped like a cockroach in maple syrup.

"*You—*" he screamed at Eleanor, letting out a string of curses.

"I know you are, but what am I!"

Eleanor scampered away. Sangray wanted terribly to shoot her, but he was stuck, so he aimed his gun at Will, lying by the trunk—

But Will had already got what he wanted out of that trunk.

His own gun.

BLAM!

The bullet from the Webley Mark Six hit Captain Sangray's weapon, sending off a cascade of sparks...

And when the sparks hit the tar, it erupted in flames...

Completely engulfing the captain.

"*Aiieeeeee!*" Sangray screamed. He was suddenly flailing, his entire body sheathed in orange flame, trying to release himself from the fiery tar, trapped by the stuck daggers.

"Put him out!" Cordelia yelled. "He's going to set the whole ship on fire!" Brendan started looking for something he could use to douse the captain, but just then the flames ate through the straps that connected Sangray's beard to the blades. Sangray was free.

He lurched forward, grabbing for his enemies in a rage like the Cyclops in *The Odyssey*, his face a grotesque melting roar, his eyes dark pits behind fire—

And then he crashed through the window and fell!

Everyone ran to the edge of the cabin. For a shining second, Captain Sangray was a meteor, screaming and smoking, his arms cartwheeling—

And then he hit the ocean with a *kssssssssssh*.

For a moment, the Walkers had nothing to say. Then Brendan said, "Tonight those sharks are getting barbecue."

"Help me with Penelope!" Will yelled behind him. He had found a cask of water and used it to put out the burning tar; now he was standing over the maid, who was still chained to the table.

"Is she OK?" Cordelia asked. Penelope's condition made them all forget their moment of triumph. They rushed to Will.

The pilot, who had tar flaking off his RFC uniform, pulled Sangray's dagger out of Penelope. Her chest was a sunken pool of blood and tar. He scraped her neck clean and felt for a pulse with trembling fingers.

"She's alive!" he said. "We can save her!"

The Walkers looked at one another. Penelope Hope wasn't breathing or moving. When Brendan felt her arm, it was ice cold.

"Wake up!" Will said, clutching Penelope's shoulders. "I promised I'd take care of you!"

"Will? I think you gotta let her go," said Brendan. He was afraid to be near Penelope, but he swallowed his fear and closed her eyes. Her upper and lower eyelashes met with a tiny click.

"No! Why? She's alive! Feel!"

Will guided Brendan's hand to Penelope's neck, but the only thing Brendan could feel was the pilot's uncontrollable shaking.

"She's gone, Will," said Cordelia. "There's nothing you can do."

"But it's my fault," Will said. "I should have protected her. I'm in the RFC, and she's a civilian! What kind of man does that make me?"

"A brave man. One who did everything he could," said Cordelia.

"But it wasn't enough. And I doubt if I'll ever meet anyone quite like Penelope again."

Cordelia quickly drew back and turned away, stung by Will's words. But then she felt guilty for putting her feelings ahead of the harsh reality facing them all: a woman had just been murdered. Everything else seemed small.

"Is something wrong, Cordelia?" Will asked.

"No, nothing," she said, continuing to look away. "I just feel… I feel so bad for Penelope."

"And she feels bad that you liked Penelope better than her," said Eleanor.

"Shut up, Nell!" shouted Cordelia. "That's not true—"

"Have some respect for the dead!" Will ordered. "No fighting!"

Everyone went quiet. They all looked at Penelope's lifeless body. Cordelia took a sheet from Sangray's bunk. She gently covered Penelope with it. They observed a moment of silence, but really it was one moment in many, because they stayed silent as they set about bandaging their wounds. Eleanor's shoulder was cut badly, but she could move her arm. Cordelia's arm hurt from being twisted by Sangray – but there was nothing she could do about that. Brendan found a new shirt. It was much too large for him, but he stuffed it in his trousers and decided to make the best of it.

"Now what?" Eleanor asked.

"We should bury Penelope," Will said, "but not at sea. We'll wait until we get ashore."

"And how do we stay alive until then?" Brendan asked.

"Simple," Will said. "Declare me captain of the *Moray*."

"Excuse me?" Cordelia asked. "Why do you get to be captain?"

"Because we killed the old captain, and I'm the oldest. Plus I possess the English heritage these sailors will be looking for."

"Can't the four of us be captain together?" Brendan asked.

"It doesn't work that way," said Will, approaching Sangray's wooden chest, "but it's not as if I'm cutting you three out. You'll all be my mates. And you're entitled to any treasure we find, split equally among the four of us. One of the first things one does as a new pirate captain is take possession of all treasure aboard the ship."

Will opened the chest. Inside was a pile of gold doubloons, a cloth bag filled with emeralds, an ornate crown that looked as if it came from a South Sea island… and several rolled-up pieces of yellowed parchment.

"There are some impressive coins and gems in here," Will said.

"Unless they can buy us a ticket back to San Francisco, they're pretty useless," said Brendan.

"And what are these?" asked Will.

He unfurled one of the parchment rolls. It was a scroll, with line after line of dense text.

"Latin," said Will.

"I remember reading about these in the book," said Eleanor. "These are secret spell scrolls, written by ancient warlocks, discovered on an island by Captain Sangray."

"How do they work?" asked Cordelia.

"I didn't get to that part," said Eleanor. "Sorry."

"Lucky for us, I studied Latin in the first form," said Will.

He read the top of the scroll, where the text was biggest.

"*Terra ipsa fenerat viribus!*"

A stone wall appeared in front of them.

It was as wide as the room, reaching from the floor to the ceiling. It was made of huge grey blocks sandwiched together. It looked like it would take a bulldozer to get through.

"Holy—" Cordelia started, and she used some of that pirate vocabulary again.

"*It works!*" said Eleanor.

"So all you have to do to make the spell work is read the title?" Brendan asked.

"It appears so."

"Sort of like instant-oatmeal spells," said Eleanor.

"That's *amazing*," said Cordelia. "What do the other spells do?"

"Yeah, and why didn't Sangray use these on us?" Brendan asked.

"Perhaps he couldn't understand Latin. But me… *Terra ipsa fenerat viribus* means 'The land itself lends strength'." Will unfurled a few more scrolls. "This one turns frogs into cows… This spell makes hair grow on your head…"

"Anything in there that removes zits?" asked Brendan, touching the growing pimple on his chin.

"Not yet," said Will, unfurling more spells. "Hmmm, this could be useful… This creates some sort of fireball—"

"How are you going to make this wall go away?" Eleanor said. "We're trapped in here now."

"There must be a way to reverse the spell," Will said, reading the smaller letters on the appropriate scroll. "Here we go…" He went to the wall and uttered the spell in reverse: "*Viribus fenerat ipsa terra!*"

The wall disappeared.

Brendan moved to the treasure chest, pocketed some doubloons (*you never know when those are going to come in handy*), and started to pick up some of the scrolls. Will grabbed his hand to stop him.

"What are you doing?" Brendan asked.

"I'll be taking these," said Will.

"But you said we could split the treasure," said Eleanor.

"The spell scrolls aren't treasure," said Will. "And what would be the point? None of you can read Latin." He picked up all the scrolls and clutched them in his arms.

"Will," Cordelia said, "you're starting to go on a serious

power trip. I mean… I know that Penelope's death hurts you, and maybe you feel like you've gotta take control to make up for it, but – you haven't even thanked us for freeing you!"

"Thank you," said Will, overpowering a hitch in his throat. "I owe you my life again. I'm only taking these scrolls so I can protect you. So I won't let you down… like I did her."

A bang sounded at the door.

"Who is that?" Will asked.

"Maybe it's that first mate, Tranquebar, come to check what the heck is going on," said Cordelia.

"Very well," Will said, putting the scrolls back in the chest and giving the Walkers a look: *Don't touch them.* He picked up the cutlass to answer the door. "Ahoy!" he called. "Fellow sailor mate! I welcome you into the service of Captain Wat—"

But Will didn't get to finish, because when he opened the door, he wasn't looking at Tranquebar. He was face to face with a skeleton, standing on two feet, with a sword pointed right at him.

54

"*G*ah!*" Will shrieked, dropping the cutlass in a very un-captain-like manner. He slammed the door shut in terror, but it went *thunk* without latching, as if someone had wedged a broomstick in the frame to keep it open. Will saw the skeleton's arm protruding from the doorway's crack, holding a sword, wildly slashing up and down.

"Can someone please explain this?" Will asked, pressing his back against the door. Although the skeleton could easily have cut him, it appeared to be aiming for someone else, making arcing swoops towards the centre of the quarters.

"It must've come from the bone room!" said Eleanor.

"*Bone room?* What in bloody blazes is a bone room?"

"Don't worry! I got this," Brendan said. He took a deep

breath, charged the door, shoulder-barged it like he was in a lacrosse game—

And snapped the skeleton's arm clean off.

"Nice work," said Will as the arm and sword hit the floor with a calcified clatter. He went back to the chest and started looking through the scrolls for one that could hurt skeletons…

But the clatter never stopped. The skeleton's arm twitched… raised a finger experimentally… and started feeling around for its sword.

"No *way*," said Eleanor. "That's not even fair!"

"Neither is this," said Brendan, kicking the arm across the room. "Let's see how you handle that, manorexia."

The skeletal arm landed in a corner and began crawling back towards the sword, pulling itself forward with four fingers at once.

"Persistent," said Will. "There must be a spell in here that can stop that – they're all mixed up—"

"The door!" Cordelia yelled.

Will and Brendan turned. The doorknob was twisting. Brendan grabbed it and tried to hold it still, but the grip on the other side was surprisingly powerful. "Help!" Brendan yelled. His sisters and Will joined him, but the knob inched anticlockwise. They all heard the scraping creaks of finger joints with no cartilage trying to open the door.

"Sounds like there's a lot of skeletons out there!" Cordelia said.

"They're the bones from earlier!" said Eleanor.

"What bones?" asked Will.

"The ones that formed into a table," said Eleanor.

"You're totally confusing me."

"They re-formed!" Eleanor told her siblings. "Now I remember! That was the part I skimmed over in the book. If you eat food from the cursed bone table, the skeletons come back for revenge—"

"*Now* you remember?!" screamed Brendan.

"I tried to warn you—"

"And they're all coming after us?!"

"They're just coming for you and Deal," said Eleanor. "Not me or Will. We didn't eat the food."

"A lock!" Cordelia interrupted, seeing a rusty metal chain near the top of the door. "I'll get it! Just keep the door closed!"

Cordelia let go of the doorknob to reach for the chain,

but without her adding to the group effort the skeletons prevailed, turning the knob all the way and shoving the door open, knocking everyone to the floor. With a rustle of bony legs they flooded the room.

Will and the Walkers stared in awe. There were two dozen skeletons, moving in fits and starts like predatory dinosaurs. They were armed with cutlasses, sabres and spears. They all waited, seeming to sniff the air even though they lacked the necessary equipment. The armless skeleton walked to the corner of the room and picked up its severed limb, pressing it against its elbow…

And with a dry sucking sound it reattached.

"Oh, *great*," said Brendan.

55

The skeleton grinned. Its bony face, like the faces of the other skeletons, was strangely capable of conveying emotion.

"Hold on," Brendan said. "I have an idea—"

"Me too." Cordelia stood to face the skeletons. They flinched in surprise. It almost looked like they blinked.

"Ah, sirs and/or madams? We don't mean you any harm, and we're sorry that we ate that food in the bone room. I mean, it was really delicious, and you have to understand, the only food we have right now is cold canned sweetcorn…"

The ex-armless skeleton, who appeared to be the leader, approached Cordelia. The others followed. The skeleton nonchalantly kicked Eleanor out of its way. The others handled Will, lifting him and tossing him towards the stained-glass window as he continued to rifle through spell scrolls, still trying to find the right one.

"Wait – hold on – can't we negotiate?" Cordelia asked the skeletons.

"Negotiate *what*?" Brendan whispered to his sister. "*This* was your big plan?"

"It was all I could think of!"

The skeletons surrounded Cordelia and Brendan and raised their weapons. Cordelia couldn't believe it: after everything she'd been through, was she really going to get killed by these stupid dead things?

"C'mon!" she snapped. "If we hadn't eaten that food, we'd have ended up looking like *you*—"

"Maybe you shouldn't insult their appearance," said Brendan.

The skeletons extended their weapons towards Brendan and Cordelia's faces. Both Walkers gasped as they saw the circular gathering of blades around their heads.

"They're going to give us a three-hundred-and-sixty-degree skewering!" shouted Brendan.

"We're sorry – *please don't*!" Cordelia screamed, shutting her eyes as the blade tips got closer. The skeleton leader's only reply was to click its teeth, a behaviour quickly mimicked by its followers, who snapped their jaws faster and faster, as if anticipating the moment when they would simultaneously stab the two siblings. Brendan and Cordelia thought of their eyes rupturing and dribbling down their cheeks, their brains being penetrated from every conceivable angle, blood and brain matter oozing everywhere...

"Duck!" Will yelled. Brendan and Cordelia did. Then they heard the pilot call, "*Inter cinis crescere fortissimi flammis!*"

A tremendous fireball roared out of the back of the room and slammed into the skeletons.

It was as big as a small car: a whirling sphere of orange flame, which scalded the Walkers' arms and singed the backs of their shirts as they planted their faces on the ground. The fireball knocked the skeletons over like a set of bowling pins – but when it hit the wall at the opposite end of the room, it disappeared, leaving only a charred crater in the wood.

For one quiet second, the skeletons were scattered across the room, just piles of bones with smoke coming off. Then they started stirring and grabbing their weapons.

Will pocketed a few of the spell scrolls, grabbed the cutlass and led the Walkers to the cabin's broken window.

"It's us they want, because we ate the food!" Cordelia said. "You go. We'll handle them!"

"No," said Will. "If I'm to be captain, I must take care of my mates." He peeked out of the window and saw a small ledge that a person could stand on. He showed it to Cordelia. "Ladies first."

Cordelia stepped out. The ocean spray made her draw in her breath. The sound of the waves under her and the cawing of seabirds made her dizzy for a moment. It was still dark, and she was terrified. But she stayed calm and looked at the stern of the *Moray*. The thick beam that she stood on ran the length of it. She could escape by turning her feet sideways and clinging to the back of the ship as she shimmied along the beam.

Cordelia went for it; Brendan followed, and then Eleanor. Will brought up the rear, carrying the cutlass in case any skeletons followed.

"What do we do?" asked Eleanor.

"I really did have a plan, guys," said Brendan, nodding to the ropes that connected the *Moray* to Kristoff House. "But to make it work, we have to get across those and back to the house before dawn."

Cordelia glanced at the horizon. A faint pinkish blue bled into the sky. She couldn't believe it. It was rising like on every normal, boring day: the sun.

"I thought I'd never see daylight again!" Cordelia told Brendan as they moved carefully along the beam.

"Might be the last time," he said, pointing back. The skeletons were climbing out of the window, following. One moved too fast, slipped, and fell into the sea. The rest learned from their cohort's mistake and moved with creeping persistence, holding their weapons in their teeth.

"Take a rope!" said Brendan. They had reached the ropes that led back to Kristoff House.

Cordelia shook her head. "My arm! I could barely hold a pencil."

"Just use one hand; I'll help," said Brendan. As Cordelia gripped the rope with her good arm, Brendan lifted his sister's feet while clinging to a metal bolt on the side of the ship. Cordelia laughed as she started to move towards Kristoff House – there was no other response to the pain of struggling with one arm and two feet to climb across a rope.

Brendan waited for Eleanor next. Behind her was Will,

and behind him, the skeletons were closing in.

"I can't!" Eleanor pointed to the rope and nodded to her bandaged shoulder.

"I know," said Brendan. He took the rope and offered Eleanor his back. "All aboard?"

Eleanor wrapped her good arm around Brendan's neck and locked her legs around his stomach. Brendan dipped out over the sea just ahead of Will, who had to struggle against the pain in his recently operated-on shoulder to grab the rope and start moving. Seconds later the lead skeleton, which now had a blackened skull, buried its sword into the side of the ship where Will had been standing.

Eleanor closed her eyes, clinging to Brendan like a baby koala. The two of them followed Cordelia. The rope sagged towards the waves.

"Keep moving!" Will ordered from behind. The lead skeleton was climbing on to the rope now, wrapping its bony phalanges around it. The others were watching. Learning.

Will and the Walkers reached Kristoff House without a moment to spare. They collapsed on the roof and hurriedly scrambled into the attic window. They heard the spidery sound of the lead skeleton landing outside.

"OK," Cordelia said, staring out of the window. The water had flooded the second floor; now the attic was the only thing above sea level. "T minus fifteen seconds. What's your plan, Bren?"

"'mon." Brendan pulled everyone across the attic to a far corner, then panicked. "Where's the rollaway mattress? It was here before—"

"The pirates probably took it," said Cordelia.

A rattle came from the window. The lead skeleton was climbing into Kristoff House, bending its bony limbs at angles that were slightly too sharp for living humans to muster.

"This way!" Cordelia said, nodding to the hole in the attic floor, under which water now filled the upstairs hallway.

"Not without the mattress!" Brendan said. "That's the plan—"

"There!" Eleanor pointed. The mattress was perched on one of the rafter beams. "It must've flown up there when Fat Jagger dropped us!"

The lead skeleton was halfway across the room now, sword out. Its brethren were making their way through the window two at a time. In a flash, Brendan grabbed Will's cutlass – "*Hey, now!*" – and tossed it at the mattress.

The mattress wobbled and fell off the beam, landing with a thump directly in front of the lead skeleton. The skeleton clicked its teeth angrily before walking across it, heading straight for Brendan.

Brendan leaned down, grabbed hold of the mattress and pulled hard. The mattress zipped out from under the skeleton, causing the creature to flip in the air and slam into a pair of its bony followers. The three skeletons fell, and their limbs became hopelessly intertwined – but Brendan knew it wouldn't be long before they were back on their feet. He dragged the mattress to the edge of the attic hole and jumped into the water below.

"Come on, guys!" he yelled, bobbing up, sputtering seawater. "Get down here! Will… you go last and close the hole with the mattress!"

"A mattress isn't going to stop these knobby numskulls!"

"It won't have to stop them for long—" Brendan started to argue, but the skeletons provided a more convincing argument by slashing at Cordelia. She jumped down next to Brendan in the flooded second-storey hallway. Eleanor followed; Will came last with his cutlass, tossing his spell scrolls to the floor of the attic so they wouldn't get wet. (He figured the skeletons couldn't read, let alone read Latin.) He pulled the mattress over the hole above him.

"OK, now everybody grab hold!" shouted Brendan. "Keep it in place!"

They all tore a hand into the underside of the mattress, securing it over the hole, sealing themselves off from the skeletons.

"Now what?" Eleanor asked.

For a second, everything was quiet. The Walkers and Will trod water in the hallway as their hands clasped springs in the bottom of the mattress. But they found it extremely difficult to tread water using only one arm each – and in Will, Cordelia and Eleanor's cases, their arms were injured anyway. As if that weren't enough, there was only thirty centimetres of space between the water's surface and the ceiling. And the water...

"The water's rising!" said Eleanor. "How are we—"

Suddenly a sword slashed through the mattress, directly

in front of Eleanor's nose. This was followed by a spear, piercing swiftly down, just missing Will's shoulder.

"They're turning this thing into a pincushion!" Cordelia yelled.

And that wasn't all: the mattress had started to move, inching to the side as the skeletons began to push it away from the hole.

"Hold steady!" Brendan said. "And watch out!"

The skeletons sent more swords, spears and daggers plunging through the mattress. Many of the blades got stuck, trembling as the skeletons tried to pull them out again. The Walkers ducked and dodged the avalanche of weapons…

And the water continued to rise.

Now it was less than fifteen centimetres from the ceiling. "I can't bloody breathe!" Will yelled. "We're running out of air!"

"Only a few more seconds!" Brendan said. "Until the sun comes up!"

"Then what?"

A sword slashed down directly in front of Brendan's chin, popping his zit.

"*Owwwwww!*" He grabbed his chin. "Then they turn into something we can kill."

"That's so gross on your face!" said Eleanor. "But I get it. You think the sun is going to change the skeletons back into people, like with the bat. And Penelope."

"Exactly."

"And who's going to kill the blighters once they become human?" Will asked. "You?"

"Uh… sure," Brendan said, dodging more weapons coming through the mattress.

"And you're prepared to do that?" Cordelia asked.

Brendan hesitated. He wanted to be brave. "Look, not all of us get to be in a history-changing war like Will. But if I was born in a different place, in a different time, I might already be out having big-time adventures, fighting Nazis, hunting wild animals… being a man! So once those skeletons get turned back into normal pirates? Yeah! I'm gonna be the first one through that hole, and I'm gonna kick every one of their flabby butts! Now, are you with me or not?"

Everyone stayed quiet. Unbeknownst to them, the sun had come up.

"What?" Brendan said.

"Either the skeletons were enthralled by your rousing speech, or something else happened, because they're not moving," said Cordelia.

It was true: the hollow rattling sound of bones was gone from the attic. No more weapons slashed through the mattress.

"Does that mean it worked?" Eleanor asked.

"Not a moment too soon," said Will, spitting out seawater. "My arm has just about had it. Besides, I don't know what's worse, the fishy taste of this water or the smell of you three."

"Ironic," Cordelia said. "An Englishman complaining about hygiene. Don't you guys only bathe on Sundays?"

"And Wednesdays!" protested Will.

Brendan moved the mattress aside, re-exposing the attic. "I'm going up."

"No. I'll go first," said Will. "You may think you're a killer, but I don't believe you have the guts for it. And you haven't a single weapon on you."

Brendan responded by snatching the sword from Will's hand.

"Hey!"

Brendan quickly hoisted himself into the attic, the sword dripping wet between his teeth. Cordelia was worried he'd be cut down—

But Brendan said, "Come up, guys! You're going to want to see this!"

Cordelia, Eleanor and Will climbed back into the attic of Kristoff House. Two dozen people stood there, attempting to cover themselves, shouting in anger and confusion.

"What's all this madness?" asked a pale, fat man.

"My dress! My petticoat!" said a hysterical, black-haired woman. "I'm exposed for all the world to see!"

The crowd – mostly men – appeared to hail from all over the world. Some of the gruffer ones had already picked up weapons.

"What's goin' on here, boy?" asked one, snarling at Brendan. He appeared to have come from a Polynesian island, complete with tattoos that had re-formed on his flesh. He held a sword in one hand and covered himself with the other.

"Y-y-you… all of you have been brought back from the dead," Brendan said.

"This don't look like heaven!" laughed the pale, fat man. He didn't seem worried about exposing himself – a paunch hid his groin.

"People this savage and disgusting only exist on the third level of Hades!" said the black-haired woman.

"No, you're still on earth," said Brendan. "I mean, not earth, exactly, but—"

"Shut yer mouth!" the tattooed man warned. "This is some sort of magic trick. Last thing I remember, Captain Sangray had me chained to a table in his quarters, preparing to vivisect me—"

"That happened to me too!" said the woman.

"And me!" said the pale man. "Although I was on the floor; he said I was too big for the table—"

"I say these four are in league with Sangray. I say we cut their throats from ear to ear in exchange for Sangray's treachery!" said the tattooed man, shaking his sword at Brendan.

"*Quiet!*" ordered Will. "I am Captain Will Draper! And these are my trusted mates: Cordelia, Brendan and Eleanor."

"Power trip, here we come," Cordelia whispered to her brother.

"You seem a little young to be a captain," said the pale, fat man.

"Yeah, captain o' *what?*" asked the tattooed one.

"Of the *Kristoff*, the vessel on which you stand," said Will. He grabbed the cutlass back from Brendan and paced with it, cutting quite a figure. "Your memories do not deceive you, my friends. All of you were victims of Captain Sangray, and after your deaths you walked the earth in skeletal form. But the *Kristoff* is a magic ship shaped like a house, and using this attic that you stand in, which is activated by sunlight in this magical realm, we have restored your lives. We have also slain Captain Sangray. Now all we ask is for your help in taking back his ship, the *Moray!*"

The ex-skeletons looked at one another. The tattooed one asked, "Wait, we were dead and you brought us back to life?"

"Correct," said Will.

"Well…" He turned to the others: "We can all support that, can't we?"

The ex-skeletons nodded and shrugged. "Long live Captain Draper!"

"To Captain Draper!"

"Huzzah!"

"Um, would any of you like clothes?" Brendan asked.

"Yes!"

"Of course!"

"Oh, please!"

"Long live Captain Draper!"

"I'll get them," Brendan said, headed towards the hole in the floor. "There's plenty in Mum and Dad's wardrobe. They'll be wet and salty, but at least it's something."

Brendan took a deep breath, jumped into the water and breaststroked through the flooded hallway, surfacing in the master bedroom. He took a quick breath in the bubble of air that lined the ceiling and began grabbing things from his parents' wardrobe.

Meanwhile, back in the attic, the pale fat man held up one of the spell scrolls that Will had tossed on the floor. "What is this… Latin?"

"Give me that!" Will ordered, grabbing it. "None of you are to touch these scrolls. They contain confidential captain's orders!"

Will hurriedly picked up the rest of the scrolls from the floor.

When Brendan returned with a bundle of sopping wet clothes, the ex-skeletons hurriedly got dressed, completely ignoring the gender of the clothing they were putting on. This resulted in some men wearing Mrs Walker's silk blouses or skirts – and some women stuffing themselves into Dr Walker's sports coats and chequered golf trousers.

"Is there any food, perchance?" asked the pale, fat man, who now wore Dr Walker's pyjama bottoms and his novelty Bermuda shirt.

"There's canned sweetcorn if you wanna swim for it," said Brendan.

"There's no fresh food here on the *Kristoff*," said Will. "But back on the *Moray* there are plenty of things to eat. All we need to do is take the ship from Captain Sangray's men."

Will gave a knife to the black-haired woman, who now sported a pair of Dr Walker's slacks and one of his Izod shirts.

"What am I supposed to do with this?" she asked.

"Kill pirates," said Will.

"I beg pardon, Captain Draper, but I'm an importer's wife from Philadelphia. I've never held a dagger in my life. And I've certainly never killed anyone."

"Well, you did just fine when you were a skeleton!" Brendan snapped.

"Look," Will told the crowd, "you all took a long road to get here. Some of you were merchants, some sailors, some—"

"I was a pharmacist!" called a wizened old man in one of Mrs Walker's dresses.

"Exactly. A pharmacist. But now you're a crew. *My* crew. And you have to be strong, and brave, and quick. Captain Sangray is dead, but his bloodthirsty pirates live on! Don't you want to take revenge on the men who let your insides be torn out?"

A resounding cheer and several cries of "*Yes!*" went up.

"Then follow me!" Will went to the attic window—

Where Cordelia stopped him. "I hope you know what you're doing," she whispered.

"This house is still sinking," Will answered. "Either we take over the *Moray* or we go in the drink. Do you have a better idea?"

Cordelia tried to come up with one – but Will's solution was all she could think of. She stepped aside and let the pilot climb out of the window. The ex-skeletons followed. Brendan and Eleanor brought up the rear... and stopped when they saw their sister. She was almost crying.

"What's wrong, Deal?" asked Brendan.

"It looks like the *Moray*'s going to be our new home," Cordelia said. "I'm going to miss this place."

"Why?" Brendan asked. "Think of everything it's put us through! Kristoff House sucks!"

"True," said Cordelia, "but when the going got tough, Kristoff House really stuck together."

"Like us," said Eleanor.

"And... being here," Cordelia, said, her voice cracking, "it feels like we're closer to Mum and Dad."

"But we're only gonna see Mum and Dad if we move on," said Brendan.

Silence held the trio for a moment. Then they clasped hands and climbed out on to the roof.

The tears that had been welling in Cordelia's eyes were instantly blasted away by the wind. The Walkers could feel salt spray on their cheeks. Will was leading the ex-skeletons across the rope to the *Moray*, hanging underneath it, toughing out the pain in his shoulder. A dozen men and women trailed after him and the next dozen waited their turn. The ex-skeletons looked a lot less intimidating now that they weren't made of bone – and that some of the men were dressed in ladies' clothes.

Suddenly a pirate called from the *Moray*'s stern: "*Eh! What in blazes is this?*"

Will tried to sound tough: "*I am Captain Draper and I order you to stand down! I sent Sangray straight to hell and I'll do the same to you!*"

"*Bah,* you're nothing but a boy with a bunch o' funny-dressed prancers at your back," said the pirate, aiming a gun at Will. "Killed Captain Sangray – a likely story!"

The pirate cocked his pistol, seconds from putting a bullet into Will's skull—

But a spinning knife thumped into his shoulder. The pirate lost his balance and went tumbling into the sea. Will whipped around and saw the tattooed man grinning as he clung to the rope. He might have been wearing a blue dress, but he was deadly with a blade.

More pirates gathered at the *Moray*'s stern: "What's them on the rope?"

"Basil's gone over!"

"Shoot 'em!"

The pirates took aim. The black-haired woman couldn't stand it; she let go of the rope and plopped into the sea, screaming as she was carried away by a current. The pirates watched her with amusement, giving Will a chance to bargain. He began, *"I am Captain Draper—"*

"No," said a pirate from behind his gun, "you are fish food."

"Please!"

"No!"

"You can't!" yelled the Walkers, back on the roof. They were in absolute terror. They knew they couldn't survive without Will. And he was their friend. They couldn't imagine him dropped into the water as a lifeless hunk of flesh—

"Stop!" a voice called.

Tranquebar stood on the deck of the *Moray* with his chin up and his good eye glinting.

"Stay your weapons!" Tranquebar ordered. "You're all to let them on board."

Grumbling, the pirates stowed their guns. Will opened his eyes; he had shut them tightly in anticipation of his death, although he would never admit that to anyone.

"Who are you, sir?" Will asked. "To whom do we owe our lives?"

"The name's Tranquebar," said the pirate. "First mate on this vessel. I served Captain Sangray – and now, it appears, I serve you."

58

In short order, under Tranquebar's direction Will, the Walkers and the ex-skeletons were brought aboard the *Moray*. Tranquebar took "Captain Draper" and his mates into his quarters and explained the situation from his point of view.

"I've had a very eventful morning. Not five minutes ago I was going to speak with the captain, to deliver my daily report, when I found him missing and his quarters completely destroyed. But what caught my attention most of all… was a huge burned spot on the wall. And I found that very strange."

"Why's that?" asked Will.

"There wasn't a single piece of ash on the floor," said Tranquebar. "How could that happen? I suspected magic. Then I heard shouting, and I saw all of you, climbing across the ropes with your… crew." He looked at Will: "Do you really think you're captain material?"

"I do," said Will. "I defeated the last captain, with my mates here. And being the oldest of them and the most experienced, I deserve the honour of commanding this ship."

Cordelia rolled her eyes. Will's ego was growing by the minute.

"The ancient laws of the sea say you're correct," said Tranquebar. "He who kills a captain takes the captain's place."

"Brilliant," said Will.

"Pending a vote," added Tranquebar.

"A vote?"

"Just a formality. All you need to do is make a speech: promise the men a lifetime supply of rum, treasure and women. Then they'll swear undying loyalty to you. But before I can allow that to happen… explain something to me."

"Yes?"

"How *did* you burn that wall without starting a fire? Magic?"

"Uh…" Will hesitated.

"Yes," Cordelia said. "*Captain Draper* possesses magical spell scrolls. He used one of them to create a fireball that burned the wall."

Will glared at her angrily: "I don't know what she's on about—"

"The scrolls from Captain Sangray's trunk?" pressed Tranquebar.

"How do you know about those?" Will asked quickly, before realising he'd revealed himself.

"Captain Draper," Tranquebar said with a knowing smile, "I know everything about this ship. I was here before Sangray… and I expect I'll be here after you. Sangray stole those scrolls years ago, on a raid in the East; luckily he never learned to read them. I made sure of that. Any time he started talking about learning to read the scrolls, I'd distract him with whisky or women."

"Why is that?" asked Will.

"Sangray was an evil, sadistic man," said Tranquebar. "He was horrible enough with his hatred for failing medical school, his twisted hobbies, and his vivisection… he didn't need to learn magic as well. I did it for the safety of our crew."

"You're an honourable fellow," said Will.

"I'm a survivor," said Tranquebar. "Now, Captain Draper… I'd like you to hand over the scrolls."

"I'd rather not," said Will. "They could be of use to us."

"Captain…" Tranquebar lowered his voice. "Don't take me for a fool. Just because I followed Sangray and obeyed his orders does not mean that he was in charge of this ship. The most powerful people are often the ones you see whispering in others' ears. Because I've always protected them, the men on this ship listen only to me. They only take orders from me. And with one word I can have you all thrown overboard."

Will exchanged a concerned look with the Walkers.

"I suggest that you give me the scrolls," said Tranquebar, "and I'll place them back in Sangray's chest, where they'll be safe and sound. Then we can move forward with the vote to make you captain."

Will paused, considering his other options.

"I think that beats the heck out of being thrown overboard," whispered Brendan. "Just sayin'."

Will silently handed over the spell scrolls.

"Excellent. Now let's get you cleaned up, Captain Draper. You too, children."

The Walkers were sceptical, looking at Tranquebar with narrowed eyes.

"Oh, please," Tranquebar said. "If I wanted to kill you, you'd already be dead. Relax. You're safe. Don't you think we're all happy to see Sangray gone?"

As Tranquebar finished speaking, Gilliam, the pirate who had the dolphin tattoo, entered his chambers. Instead of a tattoo he now had bandages wrapped around his head like a mummy. "Thank yez fer takin' care o' that horrible captain," he said. "Would yez like some food?"

The Walkers could hardly believe their ears. Soon they were given a meal of salt pork and warm biscuits that tasted better than anything they had ever eaten (with the exception, for Brendan and Cordelia, of the enchanted skeleton food – but they knew that shouldn't count). Eleanor got seasick, but Tranquebar showed her how she could beat it by going on deck and keeping her eyes trained on the horizon. In a sombre moment, they moved Penelope's body into the ship's storage room to keep her safe until they got to shore to bury her. Then they went to a room on the ship, a sort of pirate lost-and-found, where they picked out new, very cool pirate clothes. They even got a chance to bathe in the *Moray*'s precious fresh water – although they weren't allowed to drain the tub between uses. (They did rock-paper-scissors to determine the order; Brendan, who was supposed to go last, decided not to bathe at all.)

But as the day went on, a strange idea began to bloom in Cordelia's mind. She wasn't sure where it came from, only that it started small, like something she happened to chance upon, and grew every hour into something she couldn't find a reason not to do.

She wanted to try out a spell scroll for herself.

Partly it was to show Will that he wasn't anything special. Partly it was to find out if the scrolls would work for her. Cordelia had kept her mouth shut about it back in Sangray's chambers, but she'd taken Latin since freshman year, and she'd got straight As. She could probably translate most, maybe all of the scrolls. *And if I can read the Latin from the scrolls, I can perform real magic… I can create something out of nothing. If Will could conjure up a fireball, I can make something even cooler. Maybe I can make it snow or hail; maybe I can make myself look completely different… and then I can make the spell disappear by simply reading it backwards. Just like that. Just for fun. Just for me. Not a big deal at all.*

59

At sunset, following a short speech by Tranquebar, the pirates unanimously voted for Will as captain. Then they threw another party, less drunken than the night before. The butcher in the hold slaughtered some chickens, and the meat was cooked on deck, under the stars. When the Walkers, pirates, and ex-skeletons dug in, it was tough to tell them apart: they were all sailors on the *Moray* now.

"To Captain Draper! May he lead us well!" said Scurve.

"Ay, and may 'e be a helluva lot kinder than Sangray!" called Gilliam.

"Please, enough accolades," Will said. "You're all very kind. But I prefer to do my job in a quiet, humble manner."

The pirates nodded and went back to their chicken. After a few moments of silence Will looked around.

"Well, now… I wasn't bloody serious! Come now, no one else has a compliment for me?"

"Ahmmmm," said Scurve, who was gaunt like Ichabod Crane. "Ye got a sweet face. Very kissable."

The other pirates turned, all staring at Scurve.

"What are yez lookin' at? Have any of yeh ever seen a woman or man with eyes so deep blue?"

The pirates all looked at Will, and shrugged. They couldn't disagree.

"Anyone else?" asked Will, looking around for more compliments.

"Your hair," said one of the women. "It's like spun silk."

"And your jaw," said another man. "You could carve the pietà with it."

"That's better," chuckled Will, pretending to know what the pietà was. The pirates laughed with him.

Cordelia turned to Brendan: "I can't watch this. He's becoming as power-mad as the Wind Witch."

"Maybe it'll pass after he's been captain for a while. Are you gonna eat that?"

Cordelia huffed – and then realised that now, with everyone distracted by food and drink, was the perfect time to enact her plan.

"No, Bren, take it. I'll be right back." She handed Brendan her chicken and went below decks. Will watched her with suspicion.

I'll just pick one scroll. I'll just do one spell. That's all. Cordelia walked the corridors of the ship. *Because… because nothing. Because I want to.*

Inside Captain Sangray's chambers, the table was still dark with Penelope's blood. The chains that had held her and Will were draped across the floor, secured to the table with iron rings. The trunk was undisturbed and unlocked. Cordelia opened it. Inside were the gold coins and gems, but Cordelia only had eyes for the spell scrolls. She pulled all of them out and began to unfurl one—

When she noticed something else in the trunk.

The Book of Doom and Desire.

Cordelia dropped the scroll she was holding. As soon as she saw the book, she felt only one thing: *need.* The need to see what was inside. To have the power that had driven Denver Kristoff mad. The future didn't matter. The past didn't matter. The only thing that mattered was the book.

With her lips parted slightly, Cordelia picked up the

book and held it in front of her face. She didn't realise it, but her head and hands were in the same position as that Tuchayune skeleton's had been back on Goat Island. She was ready to dive in and flood her mind with secrets – *I'm going to find out, I'm going to find out,* she thought in an endless, mindless loop—

And she opened to page 1.

At first, there was no writing. A blank page lay before Cordelia. She was ready to throw the book away... but then the letters came. They floated up from behind the page, or *inside* it, like little animals rising to the surface of a pond, tiny black shapes that twisted and connected as they went from a scattered mass to something maddeningly close to English, sharpening, becoming words that were clear and beautiful, that made Cordelia feel perfect just by looking at them, even though they didn't make sense yet—

"*Stop!*" Cordelia heard behind her. "*What are you doing?*"

Will rushed into the room and grabbed Cordelia's shoulders, whirling her around. "Cordelia, your *face!*"

It had started as soon as she'd opened the book. Cordelia's skin was fading, as if the pages were sucking the lustre out of her and leaving a maggot-white husk. She stared down in a trance while the colour streamed out of her chin in a spectral streak that connected to the book. Her eyes were turning grey. Her veins were horribly visible, branching over her cheeks like the veins on the Wind Witch—

"*Close the book!*"

Cordelia didn't respond. Her skin was tightening now, hardening to stone. She looked like she was made of marble.

Will slammed the book shut. "Cordelia! Can you hear me?"

The colour and life returned to her face. The veins disappeared. Her skin reacquired its natural softness. Even a few splotches of acne came back. But she was incensed.

"*Give it back!*" Cordelia snarled, grabbing for the book.

"No!" Will tossed the book into a corner of the room. Then he looked at it. There was something oddly compelling about it. Some reason why he might want to open it himself. Perhaps, as a man, he would be able to handle its contents better than Cordelia, but he shook the thought away.

"You're not even supposed to be here, Cordelia. This is the captain's chamber—"

"Out of my way!"

Cordelia pushed Will aside and scrambled for the book. If she could get to it, open it… she would find the answers. But Will grabbed her, lifting her off her feet. She kicked at his shins: "*Put me down!*"

"Cordelia Walker, I'm sorry, but this is for your own good," he said. "Don't you remember Penelope's story? This is the book that drove Kristoff to sixes and sevens! And I just saw all the life draining out of your face as you opened it. You need to stay away from this book. You need to stay somewhere safe tonight, somewhere secure."

"What?! Like where?"

"A prison cell," said Will.

Clang! An iron gate shut behind Cordelia as Will tossed her into a barred chamber below decks. She landed face down in a dense pile of straw. Cordelia pushed herself up, spat out a mouthful of hay and whirled around.

"This isn't fair!" she sputtered. "Will Draper! You... you're a pathetic excuse for a man, even a fictional one!"

Will fought the urge to respond. Tranquebar had accompanied him, to secure the lock, and Will didn't want to get into his personal history with the first mate. If Tranquebar discovered that Will wasn't a real person, that could be grounds to have him removed as captain.

"Hold your tongue," Will told Cordelia. "Not another word!"

"And be happy you're not sharing your cell with a gaggle

of smelly swine," Tranquebar added.

"Excuse me?" Cordelia twisted her nose. She suddenly realised that her pen smelled of something besides hay.

"Like any decent ship, the *Moray* set sail with two dozen pigs," Tranquebar said. "They were kept here, and each week one was sent off to be butchered for crew dinners – but now it's a right proper place for you to be kept until you show proper respect to your captain."

"He's not a *captain*!" Cordelia screamed, grabbing the bars. She held them so tight that Will thought her bones were going to pop through her knuckles. "He's not *anything*! He's just a pilot from a pulp fantasy novel. And you know what? He's not even a good pilot!"

Tranquebar turned to Will: "What does that mean?"

"She means… uh… that I used to pilot a different sort of craft, and that I learned my skills from a book," Will said quickly. "Come now, enough of this nonsense. Let's leave this mad girl alone."

Tranquebar nodded, and they headed down the hall. Will looked back at Cordelia, trying to give her a glance that said *I'm sorry*, but she glared at him with such fury that he flinched.

"She seems quite insane," said Tranquebar. "I'm glad you made the decision to lock her up. And what about the book?"

"It's still in the quarters, and that's where it's staying," said Will. "I won't tell her brother and sister about it. That whole family is a little crazy about that book."

"I must ask," Tranquebar said, "what did she mean about you being 'fictional'?"

"She… ah… she didn't say 'fictional'; she said 'frictional'. As in I cause a lot of friction. Because… uh… well, the girl has become rather obsessed with me."

"*Really?*" said Tranquebar.

"Yes," said Will. "It's embarrassing. She has this massive schoolgirl crush. Anyway. As captain of this vessel, I have more pressing matters to discuss. For example, where is this ship headed?"

Tranquebar smirked. "I forget that you yourself are so young and naive, Cap'n. It's almost as if you haven't spent much time in the real world." He paused. "The *Moray* is bound for the port of Tinz, to meet with Captain Sangray's trading partners. These are very shrewd men who have travelled months across many continents for the sole purpose of meeting Captain Sangray. It's a straightforward transaction. They want to trade gold for our spices and cocoa leaves – and who knows, maybe they'll be interested in purchasing a house that can bring skeletons back to life. There's no telling what *that* might command on the black market."

"When do we meet these traders?" Will asked.

"Tomorrow afternoon."

"And then?"

"Then you're free to do what you like! Maybe a shore leave? I know of this tropical isle occupied by only women: stunning, beautiful goddesses who wear nothing but the shells of—"

"Perhaps, Tranquebar. But for now my wish is to retire to my chambers and have a peaceful night's sleep."

"Of course," Tranquebar said. They had reached Captain Sangray's chambers. "But… here? You can't sleep *here*, Captain."

"Why not?"

"The whole place is destroyed!" Tranquebar gestured to the room. "The stained glass must be repaired; the tar must be cleaned out; the torture paraphernalia must be removed. And that nasty book is here. I have a much better room prepared for you."

"But I *want* to sleep here," Will said, looking at *The Book of Doom and Desire*. There it was! On the floor! Just waiting for him!

"Captain. In these early days of your command, the men of the ship will be looking to see if you can take the counsel of your first mate. If not, they may become suspicious that you're too headstrong. Too ruled by emotion. Too proud to lead."

Tranquebar closed the door to Captain Sangray's quarters and locked it with one of his many keys. As he led Will further down the hall, Will wondered who *really* had the power on the *Moray*.

Meanwhile, Cordelia was searching for some sort of structural weakness in her jail cell. It wasn't looking good. Under the hay was a simple wooden floor with no trapdoors. A nasty smell emanated from one corner, where the wood was discoloured and warped. The window wouldn't work, because there *was* no window. And when Cordelia went searching for a key amid the hay, she found only one disturbing item… a severed pig's snout.

It's not even humane to keep a pig in here! Cordelia thought. As half her brain tried to plot an escape, the other half started thinking about all the ways she could get back at Will – and her siblings. How could Bren and Nell not have noticed she was missing? They were probably eating and playing dice and toasting their new captain up on deck. If Cordelia got hold of them, the first thing she would do was lock them *and* Will in this cell. Then she'd forbid them to talk to one another. Then she'd—

She thought she spotted a weakness. The cell's heavy lock was close enough to the bars for Cordelia to sneak her fingers past them and get her nails into the keyhole. She tried to pick the lock (without having any idea how) and managed to get her fingernail deep inside… but then she moved too quickly. *CRACCCKKK!* – she snapped off her fingernail against the metal mechanism.

"*Aaaagh!*" Cordelia inspected her hand. It was a bad break – not only was her fingernail reduced to a jagged stump, but her fingertip was bleeding. The pain reduced her to a child: "*Please! Help! Somebody! Anybody!*"

No one answered. In frustration, she threw her mobile phone against the wall. *Nobody in my address book is going to help me.* The phone bounced and landed in straw. And then she remembered one person who could help.

One person with real magic.

"Dahlia!" she called. "*Wind Witch!* I'm lost, and I need your guidance! Please, please, *please*, come and get me out of here, and I'll bring you to *The Book of Doom and Desire*, I promise!"

Cordelia had hardly finished when she heard a rustling sound. The hay on the floor began to rise and pirouette in the air, along with her mobile phone. The straw swirled faster and faster, turning into a mini hay storm, whirling like an egg-shaped cocoon…

And the Wind Witch appeared in front of Cordelia, exploding the hay across the chamber. She was unmistakable – bald head, fierce blue eyes, purple robe – but something was different about her this time. At first, Cordelia couldn't figure it out. Then she saw.

The Wind Witch had a big smile on her face.

62

"Cordelia, my dear," the Wind Witch said, eyeing the shabby surroundings, "this doesn't seem like the proper room for someone of your stature."

Cordelia didn't realise it, but she was on her knees, her head bowed low. She had sunk in terror when the hay had come to life… and now that the Wind Witch was in front of her, she felt it was appropriate to stay on the floor.

"I agree," said Cordelia, "but I had no choice in the matter. Will locked me in here."

"Well, it's obvious what he thinks of you as," said the Wind Witch. "A pig to be kept in a pen."

Hearing those words aloud made Cordelia wonder if Will could be that cruel. She rose to his defence: "Will's not a truly bad person. He just doesn't understand—"

"He understands perfectly well! The world has always been difficult for women like us, Cordelia. Do you think that's by chance?"

"Well, I never really—"

"Of course not. We're a threat. And all men know it. Originally, they were better at hunting, so we let them take charge. We needed their strong arms to operate bows and arrows. We needed their fast legs to chase wild animals. But times have changed – in my lifetime and yours. Hunting has become a routine trip to the supermarket. Defending the home has become something we can do ourselves. We don't need men any more, and they know it. So they'll do anything – lies, tricks, *murder* – to see that we don't rise up against them."

"*We?*" Cordelia asked.

"People like you and me," said the Wind Witch. "The world's brilliant women."

Cordelia smiled. It had been a long time since anyone had called her brilliant. Her father was so stressed out about not having a job – and before that, about the job that he *had* – that he hardly found time to praise her. Her mother said she was smart… but that was what mothers were *supposed* to say. Her teachers at school took notice, but there was nothing worse than having a teacher give you a compliment. A teacher's compliment only meant something if you were in college and your teacher had a PhD.

"And as brilliant women," said the Wind Witch, "we have a right to use this powerful book."

"When did you first learn of it?" asked Cordelia.

The Wind Witch sighed. "Do you really want to hear the story? It won't bore you, coming from an old woman like me?"

"Of course not," said Cordelia. "Please, tell me."

"I was eight years old," said the Wind Witch. "I sneaked out of bed one evening, followed my father, and watched him use the book. As you can imagine, I was enthralled by what he was able to conjure… but he was upset that I had found him. He screamed at me. I started to cry. To calm me down, he did something with the book – and a new stuffed animal appeared for me. I understood that, somehow, *the book made wishes real*. First it was the stuffed animal… then a doll's house… chocolate… it was a young girl's dream. But he made me promise *never* to open the book myself. It was a promise I kept for a few years. Until I was thirteen."

"What happened?" asked Cordelia.

"I started to have issues with some classmates at school," continued the Wind Witch, "There was one girl, Charlotte LeVernais, who was particularly cruel. She made fun of the way I spoke, the way I dressed."

"You were bullied?"

"That's what they call it now," said the Wind Witch. "Back then it was just called being young. It got so bad, so hurtful… that the only thing I could think to do was sneak into my father's hidden chamber and use the book to grant a wish. To make Charlotte stop."

"I can understand that," said Cordelia. "I'd probably wish for something like that too, if some awful kid was messing with me, and I was only thirteen—"

"I wished for Charlotte to lose her voice," explained the Wind Witch. "For her vocal cords to evaporate, so she would never speak again, never hurt another person for the rest of her life."

"Wow," said Cordelia. "That's a bit extreme."

"But it worked," said the Wind Witch. "And as a result, I started using the book for more wishes. I wished for popularity. I wished for the most handsome boyfriends.

I was suddenly happy. It could have lasted forever, if not for my father's interference."

Cordelia just stared at her, waiting for her to go on.

"He was weak," said the Wind Witch. "Worried that using the book would turn me into someone different, the way he became the Storm King."

"And how exactly did that work?" asked Cordelia.

"He believed that removing the book from its original location had somehow been responsible for the Great San Francisco Earthquake," said the Wind Witch. "And that gave him an idea: what if he had the ability to control weather? To create natural disasters? That would be the ultimate power. The power of a god. He began to conjure storms, each one more turbulent than the one before. His last was so treacherous it caused the deaths of thirteen people."

"That's horrible," Cordelia said. "Why would you want a book that let you do that?"

The Wind Witch didn't answer. Cordelia wasn't surprised. Deep in her heart, she knew the answer: power.

"We had a creepy old gardener who was always staring at me," said the Wind Witch. "This made me feel uneasy.

So I used the book and blinded the man. When my father confronted me, I admitted to him what had happened. He was furious. He forced me to restore the gardener's eyesight, and then hid the book from me. He met with Aldrich Hayes of the Lorekeepers. It was Hayes who taught my father the magic that enabled him to hide the book in the world of his novels. But before he got the chance, I transformed myself into the Wind Witch. I wanted to convince my father to *share* the power. To make him realise that *together* we could rule over anything… any city, any country."

"I assume he did not react well," said Cordelia.

"He was livid. At that point he was far more powerful than I, so he banished me from our home. He thought he could keep me from the book. But I was smarter than that."

"What did you do?"

"I disguised myself as a man," said the Wind Witch, "and became a member of the Lorekeepers. They taught me strong magic, and soon I learned ancient spells that enabled me to enter the world of my father's novels. I began my search for the book…"

"But when your father discovered this," Cordelia said, "he put a curse on the book so you could never go near it."

"Exactly. But now I have you. And why should you not use the book? Unlike your siblings, you had the courage to open it."

"I don't know if I should have. It felt good at the time… but Will told me it was hurting me. Changing my face."

"What does he know? Your siblings and Will don't deserve the book. They aren't as clever as you. They're holding you back."

"That's not true," said Cordelia. "Even though we fight and disagree about almost everything, my brother and sister love me, care about me."

"Stop fooling yourself," the Wind Witch said – and she took Cordelia's hand.

Cordelia had never felt the woman's skin before. It was papery and dry, rough and old – but *electric*, charged with a force that surged into her.

Cordelia's arm hairs stood up like fibre-optic cables. Her fingertips tingled like they were dipped in mint. The Wind Witch's grip grew tighter. Cordelia stood to attention, trying to hold herself together despite the spider-crawl pinpricks blooming in her spine – and then something snapped, and she stood outside herself, seeing a vision of her own mind.

It was blue and etched with fine lines. Within it she could see her memories. Each one was like an old movie reel, a ribbon of images recording something that had stuck with her, that she cared about. Some of the longest and most important ones had to do with her siblings. There was the time she saved Eleanor from playing in the dryer in their old house; the time she and Brendan got caught making potions in the bathroom. The time they went to Disneyland; the time Brendan caught a ball at a Giants game and he talked about it for a month. She saw these memories twist into a small bundle—

And then they disappeared. And with them her love for Brendan and Eleanor. It was replaced by the pure, true knowledge the Wind Witch provided: her siblings were really just average kids who'd never cared about her, never really loved her. Her parents were failed protectors who were too weak. And Will? He was a pale imitation of a real pilot, a real fighter.

Only one thing in Cordelia's life mattered now: *The Book of Doom and Desire*.

"Is it all becoming clear?" asked the Wind Witch.

"Very," said Cordelia, snapping back to reality in a

docile state, the Wind Witch's hand still clutching hers.

"Good. And without those others in your life you are free to concentrate on your own dreams."

"The book," said Cordelia.

"It wants you. *Needs* you. It's your destiny."

"Yes," said Cordelia, as a creepy, otherworldly smile covered her face. Her eyes were dead.

"And I promise: if you take me to the book, we'll both be free."

Cordelia stood, suddenly eager. "I can take you. But you have to get me out of here. You're powerful enough to blast away these bars—"

The Wind Witch shook her head. "We don't want anyone to hear us."

"Of course…" said Cordelia. Every second that the Witch held her, her mind drifted more into a fog.

Her fingers suddenly got very cold. The intense chill moved through her arms, chest and face. Her legs started to freeze. She noticed that her hands were losing their colour and hardening into something transparent and shimmering.

"What are you doing?" she asked the Wind Witch.

"Getting us out of here." The Wind Witch's body had also begun to transform. Cordelia couldn't decide what was more fascinating: watching her skin solidify into something translucent and cold, or seeing the Wind Witch's do the same. In minutes, although they could still move and speak, they were both completely transfigured from flesh into—

"*Ice!*" said Cordelia. "You turned us into *ice*! Why?"

"Come," the Wind Witch said, pulling Cordelia towards the bars of the cell. "The pain only lasts a moment."

"Pain?"

But it was too late. The Wind Witch and an unwilling Cordelia were running together, hand in hand, straight for the metal bars – and when they slammed into them, their icy bodies shattered into a million pieces.

The shards flew past the bars, landing in a pile in the hall. Cordelia, who somehow maintained consciousness, realised: *I'm mixed in with the Wind Witch now. I'm part of her.*

The ice pieces sprang to life, skittering towards one another, connecting. Piece by piece the Wind Witch and Cordelia turned back into ice-sculpture versions of themselves. Then the ice warmed and coloured to flesh, and they were human again, although Cordelia still felt a bit of coldness inside her, somewhere in her chest, that she couldn't quite place.

"That wasn't so bad, was it?" asked the Wind Witch.

"Not so bad? It felt like a billion parts of my skin were being stung by jellyfish. Like that time in Florida with Mum and Dad and Bren and Nell, when—" Cordelia paused as the old memory returned. The Wind Witch quickly noticed and grabbed her hand, transporting her back into a state of mental mishmash that only permitted one feeling: selfish desire.

"Now, my dear. Show me the way."

Cordelia led the Wind Witch down the hall, knowing just where to go – she could almost taste the book. In a few minutes, they reached Sangray's chambers. But someone was there.

Her sister.

"Deal!" Eleanor said. "I was worried about you; I came – *why are you holding hands with the Wind Witch?*"

Cordelia surged forward. It was an instinct deep inside her; her memories of Eleanor weren't as buried as they'd seemed. She looked at the Wind Witch: "Why are you scaring my sis—"

The Wind Witch clutched her hand so tightly that all the blood drained from it. Cordelia was back under her spell.

"Don't let her stop you. Open the door!"

Cordelia tried, but it was locked.

"Deal! *Stop!*" Eleanor cried.

The Wind Witch waved her stump – and a sudden gust of wind knocked Eleanor over. She waved it again – and a bolt of lightning blew the lock off the door.

"Cordelia!" Eleanor screamed, lying on the floor. "You have to listen to me. Whatever this old lady is shoving in your head, it's not true, and you have to *fight*—"

"Shut her up," said the Wind Witch.

"Yes." Cordelia put her feet on either side of Eleanor's small body, raised her free hand, and made a fist.

Although her brain was given over to the Wind Witch, Cordelia still had her intelligence, and her intelligence had a cruel streak. She realised that hitting Eleanor would be far less effective than getting her where it really hurt.

"Did you even skim *The Heart and the Helm*?" she asked. "Or did you just pretend while you got Brendan to read it for you?"

"What?" Eleanor asked. "You know I read it! You were in the same room as me!"

"I think you were faking," said Cordelia. "Because we all know you can hardly read at all. You couldn't even get the address of Kristoff House right. Sometimes I don't think you're dyslexic; I think you're just *dumb*."

Eleanor burst into tears. The Wind Witch purred as she

clutched Cordelia's hand: "*Good*. Now I can't get close to the book, because of the curse my father put on it. So I need you to take this" – the Wind Witch gave a slip of paper to Cordelia – "and put it inside the book. Can you do that?"

"Yes…" Cordelia answered. "But why? What's on the paper?"

"That's not for you to know. Just do as I say, and you'll learn the book's true power."

The Wind Witch let go of Cordelia's hand… but Cordelia remained under her spell. It was as if the tiny piece of the Wind Witch that was inside her were exercising its power. She entered Sangray's chamber with her sister wailing in the background. She moved towards the book, a blank look on her face—

But suddenly she heard a thud behind her, and when she turned around, the Wind Witch was sitting dazed against the hallway wall.

In her place stood Will, looking like he'd just shoulder-barged a rugby player. Behind him was Brendan.

"What's happening?" Cordelia asked, lucid again.

"We heard Eleanor call for help," said Will, "and I—"

"*Maggots!*" the Wind Witch yelled.

She got to her feet and shot out her bad arm. A cone of air howled from her stump, spiralling across the chamber. Will hit the deck, avoiding the powerful blast, but Brendan was right in its path. He was lifted off his feet like a doll and blown across the room towards the opposite wall.

SNAPPPP! Brendan's head hit the ceiling. His neck bent forward at an odd angle, and he dropped to the floor in a heap.

"No!" Cordelia said, charging for him.

Will grabbed her ankles: "Be still!"

Eleanor knelt in front of Brendan's unconscious body.

"Children have such short memories," the Wind Witch said, panting as the veins in her head pulsed.

"Keep her talking," whispered Will to Cordelia; he started crawling backwards across the floor.

"A few moments ago you agreed that your family was useless. Now you defend them?" the Wind Witch continued.

"You better believe it," said Cordelia.

"Don't you still want the book?"

"Not in a million years. That wasn't me. That was you, messing with my head… you tricked me. Changed all the good memories I had about the people in my life into dark feelings."

"Those dark feelings were your own," said the Wind Witch. "No one can be tricked into hatred. Some part of you might even be happy to see your brother lying on the floor right now, possibly with a broken neck… possibly never to walk again."

The Wind Witch beamed with horrible pride — but like most proud, narcissistic people, she had a tendency to overlook details. In this case, the detail of Will opening Sangray's trunk to get the spell scrolls. By the time she noticed, he had unrolled his favourite ones—

"*Inter cinis crescere fortissimi flammis!*"

The ball of fire whooshed towards the Wind Witch like a comet; Cordelia dived. The Wind Witch shrieked, waving her disfigured arm at the flaming orb—

And a rainstorm suddenly slashed through the room, dissipating the fireball and pushing everyone towards the broken stained-glass window.

"Who do you think you are now? A wizard?" the Wind Witch yelled.

"He's a better wizard than your father! At least he's not

crazy!" said Cordelia.

"*Don't speak of my father!*" The Wind Witch sliced her arms through the air in strange motions. The rain pounded harder. The wind blew faster. Eleanor clutched Brendan's limp body as she and Cordelia leaned into the indoor storm, as if they were trying to walk in a hurricane, but the Wind Witch's anger caused it to reach an intensely violent level. They were ripped into the air with Will and blown towards the sea—

"*Terra ipsa fenerat viribus!*" Will read.

The stone wall materialised behind him.

Will and the Walkers hit it and fell to the floor.

The Wind Witch was not pleased. She didn't have words for this indignity, just a high-pitched keening that she let ring through the chamber. She stepped forward, put her good hand on the stone table and raised her disfigured one. Lightning started crackling out of the gnarled skin at the end. Cordelia knew a bolt was coming.

She spotted the metal chain that was draped on the floor. She snatched one end and tossed it in the air as the lightning darted towards her. It forked down and hit the chain. *CRACCKKKK!* The bolt travelled back along the length of the metal and down to the iron ring… which was resting beside the Wind Witch's good hand.

The Wind Witch didn't have time to scream. The bolt zapped her with a fierce white crackle that made everyone shield their faces—

And when they had the courage to peek again, the Wind Witch was *gone*.

Only a puff of smoke remained.

For a moment, no one spoke.

"Did we… kill her?" Eleanor finally asked.

"Doubtful," said Will, standing and patting the stone wall. "She's too clever. I think she took evasive action because Cordelia outsmarted her."

"Who cares?" Cordelia said, rushing over to her brother. "None of it matters if Brendan's hurt!" She knelt down and cradled him. He had a pulse; he was breathing. But he was out cold.

Cordelia hung her head. Something about this fight was worse than the ones before. She felt hollow inside: no excitement, no joy at staying alive. She heard sniffling and turned around to see Eleanor crying. Will had a hand on her shoulder.

"Help Bren," Cordelia said to Will as she knelt in front of Eleanor. A tear hit her arm. It was hot. Cordelia said, "I'm sorry I was so mean... about you not being able to read... I was wrong. What I know is, you are a good reader, who will some day be a great reader."

Eleanor nodded.

"Do you believe me?"

"I don't know what to believe."

"Believe *me*."

Cordelia hugged her. *We have to get off this ship or we're going to lose it. We're going to lose everything.*

"Ahemmm." Will interrupted the sisters. "Brendan's OK. He took a rough knock, but I've seen worse."

"Still my fault," said Cordelia. "You should put me back in that pigpen."

"Nonsense. You did what you did because of this." Will picked up *The Book of Doom and Desire*. He meant to get rid of it, but when he held it in his hands, he suddenly thought, *Maybe I'll just peek*—

"Will! What are you doing?" Cordelia asked.

"Nothing!" Will said, realising he was still holding the book. "I'll just throw this in the ocean."

"Except you created a magical stone wall between us and the ocean."

"Oh yes. *Viribus fenerat ipsa terra!*" The wall collapsed into thin air, and the stained-glass window became visible again. Outside, Kristoff House was still being towed by the *Moray*, bathed in moonlight, but now the water had covered the roof, and only the chimney was visible.

Will tossed the book out of the window.

Cordelia was amazed at how simple it was. All that trouble, all that fighting – and it could be stopped by throwing it away, as if the book were an old Starbucks cup or an empty tuna-fish can. The book opened while it sailed through the sky, its pages flapping… but then the wind underneath caught it, lifted it a little, and dropped it into the chimney of Kristoff House. It fell out of sight.

"*Bah,*" said Will.

"That's crazy!" Eleanor said. "Right down the chimney? You couldn't do that again if you were LeBron James!"

"The book's not gone," said Cordelia, shaking her head. "It's caught somewhere in there, high and dry, waiting to be found. Now that I've opened it, it doesn't want to leave."

"You opened it?" Eleanor asked. "What happened?"

"I don't really remember," said Cordelia. "I remember it was dreamy, and beautiful, but the contents are a blank."

"What happened was her face started changing," said Will, "and not for the better."

"What are you holding in your hand, Deal?" Eleanor asked.

Cordelia looked at the piece of paper the Wind Witch had given her. She unfolded it and read, "'Dahlia Kristoff will be able to open *The Book of Doom and Desire*.' That's it."

"That's all it says?" Will asked. "What is that, a wish?"

"Maybe that's the power of the book," said Cordelia. "Maybe if you open it up and put a wish in…"

"*It comes true*," said Eleanor.

For a minute, Cordelia, Eleanor and Will thought about it. *A book that could make real anything put between its pages.* It would be the most powerful book ever made. It would turn people into gods.

"Forget it," said Will. "We're not going to find out if that works, because no one is to go near the Kristoff House chimney. When we reach land tomorrow, we'll have the whole house dismantled and the book burned. Now… I'm going to look for some smelling salts to rouse poor Brendan." Will started to leave the chamber, but stopped and looked back. "And Cordelia…"

She stared at him. His eyes were filled with warmth and true kindness. "I never should have locked you up. I'm sorry."

"I accept your apology," said Cordelia, "and promise not to get all weird again."

Soon after, Brendan was roused by the truly heinous smelling salts on the *Moray*, which Tranquebar said could raise the dead (a turn of phrase that Cordelia, Eleanor and Will found amusing, considering their experience in that area). When Brendan tried to sit up, everyone yelled for him to stop, worried that his neck might be broken, but he leaped to his feet.

"I'm fine, guys," he said. "Yeah, I slammed into that ceiling pretty hard, but I've been hit a lot worse in lacrosse." And to prove his point, Brendan did a few impromptu dance moves, including a pretty decent moonwalk that he had picked up from seeing all those Michael Jackson memorial specials on TV.

An hour later they were all in bed – or what passed for bed at sea. Will started out in the quarters Tranquebar had arranged for him, but when a rat crawled on to his cheek, paused, and started to nibble at the hairs inside his nostril, he switched rooms. He ended up on a camp bed next to Cordelia, Brendan and Eleanor. The last thing he did before going to sleep was identify whose breathing was whose.

The next morning, Cordelia woke up last. It was rare

for her – she was an early riser – but the constant battering and exhaustion that had been her life for the last few days had made her sleep almost until noon. She rubbed her eyes (she missed brushing her teeth) and went up to the deck. The ocean air woke her more than the coffee she sneaked in before school every morning. Will, Brendan and Eleanor were standing at the side of the *Moray*.

"What are you doing?" Cordelia asked.

"Looking for Tinz," Brendan said. "We should be able to see it somewhere on that land over there—"

"*Land?*" Cordelia said. Sure enough, a sliver of grey stretched out in the distance. "Oh my God! Land!"

"I know, right?" Eleanor said. "I forgot what land *feels* like!"

"Tranquebar spotted it at dawn," said Will, nodding to the first mate, who stood in the crow's nest at the top of the mainmast. "He'll be the first to spot Tinz too. But one of us can be second."

"Aye aye, Cap'n!" said Cordelia. "But what do we do when we get to Tinz?"

"I've got a trading meeting set up," said Will. "But before we arrive… there's something I need to discuss with you."

"What's that?" asked Brendan.

"I have an idea, about how you can see your parents," said Will, slipping away from the edge of the deck.

The Walkers all exchanged looks of intense hope, overcome with excitement.

"When?" asked Cordelia.

"Soon," said Will. "Maybe immediately."

"Well, go on, tell us – how, how?" asked Brendan.

"First, you need to ask yourselves one question," said Will.

"What's that?" asked Eleanor.

"Are you prepared for the consequences?"

"What do you mean?" asked Eleanor. "Like if they're *dead*? I could never be prepared for that!" Her voice trembled.

"Me neither," said Cordelia. The thought of her parents being dead erased any emotional maturity that she had over her sister. "But if we can know… we should."

"I'm with you," said Brendan.

"Me too, I guess," said Eleanor, mustering all her courage.

"Very well," said Will. "Wait here."

Will went below decks as the Walkers tried to see the first sign of Tinz; they imagined it would be a glint of glass, spiky ships' masts, or the flutter of a flag. When Will came back, he held a spell scroll with trembling fingers. He slowly unfurled it. The Walkers crowded around him, trying to read the Latin.

"Hold on," said Cordelia. "I can translate this one… In Latin, it says, 'Show me the ones who brought me the world.'"

"Very impressive," said Will. He paused and looked at the Walkers. "Shall we give it a shot?"

On the deck of the *Moray*, Will instructed the Walkers to read the spell in Latin. Together.

"Ostende mihi isti qui, introduxisti me terrarum," said all of the Walkers in perfect unison.

A small ball of light appeared in front of them. Will used his body to shield it from the pirates. The light grew to the size of a basketball. The Walkers looked inside the glowing orb – and what they saw sent them into a state of shock.

It was Kristoff House – but not the Kristoff House being towed behind the ship. This was Kristoff House as they had left it in San Francisco: destroyed by the Wind Witch. Eleanor gasped.

It was an aerial view, far above 128 Sea Cliff Avenue. It looked like the house had been ripped open by a tornado.

Wooden beams splayed out from the first floor in a wide, flat heap. There was no second floor. All of the furniture had been blasted to bits and was strewn across the lawn.

"I don't understand…" Brendan said. "What are we looking at? How can that be Kristoff House? Kristoff House is right there, underwater!"

"There must be two versions," Cordelia said. "The house that was transported here by the Wind Witch, and the one that stayed behind in San Francisco… the one that still exists in reality."

"So this is reality?" Will asked, pointing at the ball of light.

"For us, yes," said Brendan.

"Wait… stop," Cordelia ordered, suddenly realising what she was about to see.

"*Terrarum me introduxisti, qui isti mihi ostende!*" said Will, shouting the spell in reverse.

But the ball of light did not disappear. The spell continued.

"What's going on?" asked Cordelia. "Why can't you make it stop?"

"Obviously the spell can't be stopped in progress!" said Will.

Inside the bubble-like ball of light, the house grew larger, as if an aerial camera were zooming in. Now the Walkers and Will could see yellow police tape around the house. There were grey placards marking evidence locations. And there, in stark white against the splintered wood—

Two chalk outlines of bodies.

"*No!*" Eleanor said. "*No! Make it stop!*"

It was clear that the Wind Witch's attack had killed the Walker parents.

"*No!*" Eleanor disintegrated into tears and hugged Brendan.

Brendan tried to stay strong – "*Nell, it's OK*" – but once he felt his sister literally shake his body with sobs, he broke down too.

"*It's not OK!*" Eleanor screamed. "*It'll never be OK again!*"

Cordelia hugged them both and stared at the magical bubble Will had created, at the simple and final accessories of death that pervaded the real world: tape, chalk and wreckage.

"Try again, Will!" Cordelia yelled. "We don't need to see any more!"

Will again said the spell in reverse, and this time the

bubble disappeared. The Walkers sat on the deck, staring at the ocean.

"Will," Cordelia said quietly, "maybe you should leave us."

Will nodded, but he had something to say. "I just…" He made his voice quiet. "I wanted to try the spell on myself too. To see my own mum and dad. I don't know if they're alive or dead. I don't know anything."

Cordelia was going to say no, but then she reconsidered, wiping away one of the tears that was streaming out of her eyes. She would take any excuse to see something different from what she had just witnessed. "You do that, Will. Try it out."

Will said the spell again; the ball of light reappeared. But this time there was nothing inside. Nothing but light.

"I don't understand," said Will. "Does it mean my parents are dead?"

"I don't think so," said Cordelia solemnly. "I think it means that you don't have parents."

"Excuse me?"

"Kristoff never wrote any parents for you. They don't exist."

Will suddenly got angry, despite how heartbroken and grieving the Walkers were in front of him. "That's rubbish! I can picture 'em! I remember crystal-clear!"

"Are you sure?" Brendan asked.

"Well, Pa had a… he was bald, wasn't he? No, he had grey hair… or was it auburn? And Mum had… blue eyes… no, wait…"

Will tried to look tough, but he was crumbling inside. It was true. The place where his parents were supposed to be in his mind, where he'd *seen* them before, or thought he had – because who doesn't have *parents*? – that place was blurry and slithering.

"Well, who needs 'em anyway?" Will yelled. But then he saw the Walkers: they did. They needed their parents more than anything. And they were never getting them back.

He sat down with them. They all stayed in this position for a long time. They stayed quiet as Tranquebar announced the first sight of Tinz, which turned out to be a golden dome on its biggest church. They stayed quiet as they watched the town grow – at a rate so slow that it almost felt like they were travelling backwards – from a tiny speck into a busy port that filled their vision. They stayed quiet as they saw the wooden homes, taverns, marketplaces and docks. The smoke rising from chimneys. The horses blocking lines of sight along narrow streets.

As they made their final approach, the pirates furled the sails and discussed which adult establishments they would hit first. The Walkers and Will watched them drop anchor, pile into smaller boats and row ashore, whooping and hollering. Then Cordelia finally said, "We should go. The fact that our parents are gone doesn't change what they would want from us. They would want us to live. To succeed. To—"

"To get revenge against the Wind Witch," Brendan said in a cool, calm voice. His sisters had never heard him sound so determined.

66

Eleanor couldn't believe she had made it to land. Even after she got off the *Moray* and into the small rowing boat that ferried them to a dock under Tranquebar's supervision, and after she got off that dock and on to the beach, it still felt like the ground beneath her feet was moving with the push and pull of the waves. It was almost a different kind of seasickness. She lay down.

"What are you doing?" Brendan asked.

"Making a sand angel," Eleanor said. "Remember? Dad used to show us how to do this on beach holidays."

Brendan smiled – and a minute later he was on the ground with Eleanor, making sand angels and acquiring sand bogeys. Every time he laughed, he thought about how he was fighting the Wind Witch. Maybe she had killed his parents, but she hadn't killed him. Not yet.

Meanwhile, Tranquebar was hanging around. He had covered for Will when the captain and his mates were in obvious distress on the *Moray* and he stayed close now. "The trading partners will be here in two hours, Captain," he told Will. "They'll want to meet you… if you're feeling up to it."

"I am," Will said flatly.

"And what about you, Mate Cordelia? Do you want to go to town?" Tranquebar gestured to the thrumming town of Tinz. Greasy smoke came out of the buildings.

"I'll stay with Will," Cordelia said, drawing close to him. She wanted to be close to anyone right now. Anyone who understood what she was going through.

For ten minutes, the Walkers and Will stayed on the picturesque beach, trapped in beautiful weather and dark thoughts. Then Brendan got restless.

"I can't sit around all day thinking about what we just learned," he announced. "I'm going exploring in the town."

"Me too!" said Eleanor.

"We shouldn't split up," said Cordelia. "That town could be dangerous."

"Oh, come on, Deal… when has that ever stopped us?"

Eleanor said. Then she stopped and yelled, "*Horse!*"

The Walkers all looked. In the distance, a horse with a man on its back traipsed past the beach – a beautiful palomino with sheer, slick muscles.

Eleanor took off running: "Hey! Wait! Sir! Hold on! Can I see your horse?"

"I'll keep an eye on her!" Brendan yelled back to Cordelia.

Will put his hand on Cordelia's. "Let them go. We're the oldest. We've got to stay here and take care of this trading-partner business so we can keep moving. If it's revenge you want."

It is. And I'll never be satisfied until I have it.

Brendan caught up with Eleanor in town, next to a bakery, as she stared up at the horse. It was ridden by a tall man who looked down at Eleanor with concern.

"Miss, are you all right?"

"Oh yes," said Eleanor. "Your horse… she's beautiful! I always wanted a horse like that! Do you think I can ride her?"

"Have you ever been on a horse, little one?"

"Once," said Eleanor. "At a carnival. No, wait… I think

that was a pony. But it doesn't matter; I'm not afraid. Not if I ride with you."

The man smiled. "How can I say no? Do you know how to climb on?"

"Hold on a minute, dude—" Brendan said, but the man was already leaning down and offering Eleanor one of his long arms. She got on the horse behind him.

"Nell, are you sure this is a good idea? You don't know—"

"I'm Jacqui," the horse rider said proudly, "and this is Majesty. I'm her trainer. I raised her."

"I'm Brendan, and if you try to hurt my sister, I'll come after you," Brendan said, narrowing his eyes.

Something in Jacqui's face changed. "Wait… are you… are you from the *Moray*?"

"That's right," said Eleanor. "We've just been on a journey full of horrors."

"Please," Jacqui said, bowing his head to Brendan, "do not harm me, powerful brother. I will take good care of your sister, give her a riding lesson, and return her to you and your leader, Shaman Tranquebar."

"*Shaman* Tranquebar?" Brendan laughed. "He's not a

shaman. He's a first mate—"

"Our town has known Shaman Tranquebar for many years, Master Brendan. We have known him and loved him. Now if you'll excuse me." And Jacqui was off, with Eleanor whooping behind him, into the winding lanes that threaded the town.

Weird, Brendan thought, *but it's nice being called Master.*

Brendan kept walking, eager to see what the town had to offer, trying not to think about his dead parents. He was careful to avoid the pirates from the *Moray*, who clogged any street where a tavern was located, laughing and vomiting matter-of-factly in the gutter.

Brendan came across a sweet shop. The windows were stacked with ridiculously oversize, mouth-watering toffee apples. Brendan hurriedly went inside and approached the elderly shopkeeper.

"Excuse me, sir, do you think I could trade something – maybe one of these gold doubloons – for one of those apples in the window?"

"Are you from the *Moray*?" asked the suddenly frightened man.

"Well, yes—"

"And you're friends with Shaman Tranquebar?"

Brendan shrugged: "I guess you could call us acquaintances—"

"Any friend of Shaman Tranquebar is entitled to all the apples in my store! Take as many as you like, son! Free of charge!"

"OK… sure," Brendan said, "but one will be just fine." He grabbed the biggest apple he could find. "Thanks, Mister."

Two minutes later Brendan munched the apple suspiciously as he approached a shop. The front window was filled with amazing weapons of all varieties: gigantic axes, obscenely sharp knives and swords that would make the characters in *The Hobbit* drool. Brendan was about to enter… but on seeing him, *this* shopkeeper locked the door and scuttled beneath the counter like a squirrel. Every now and then, the shopkeeper's head would peer above the countertop.

"I can see you!" Brendan said. Then he turned and walked away, throwing his apple into the gutter. It had tasted perfect… *maybe too perfect*. Brendan suddenly thought the people in this town were under an enchantment spell, or they knew something they weren't telling. He knew how fast secrets spread at school, how if you opened your ears, you could literally hear them zinging through the halls. It felt like that here, like Brendan was the last one to know what the deal was...

And then he got to an open-air market and forgot all about it.

Because he saw her.

Celene. The girl Brendan had read about in *Savage Warriors*. That seemed like ages ago, but it had to be Celene; she fitted the description perfectly. She was about Brendan's height, with short brown hair and a tiny nose that poked up, but not like a pig – like she was curious. She had smart, sparkling eyes that were purple, just like the book said, and Brendan got a good look at them – because from the stall where she was picking out fruit, Celene was staring right at him.

Brendan didn't hesitate. He felt like he already knew her. *And besides,* he thought, *what's the worst that can happen? My parents are dead, I'm trapped in a mystical world... what is she gonna do? Not laugh at my jokes? Big deal!*

"Hey," Brendan said as he approached Celene.

"Hello," Celene responded. She kept picking up fruit as she spoke to him, looking at it closely and putting it back in front of the merchant, who watched her and Brendan with wary eyes. Not a single fruit was put in her canvas bag.

"None of them seem up to your standards. What's your criteria?" Brendan asked, happy for once to use one of Cordelia's words.

"Physical perfection," Celene said, holding up an orange and putting it back.

Brendan looked at himself. He didn't exactly scream "physical perfection", but he refused to be psyched out. *If I think I look bad, who's going to think I look good?*

"I'm Brendan Walker," he said as confidently as he could.

"Celene," the girl answered. "And I know who you are, Brendan."

"You do?" *Wait a minute… I'm supposed to know who she is. I do know who she is! What's going on?*

Celene came to a lemon that she actually seemed to like. She gave it to the merchant, who put it on a hanging scale… but as Brendan watched, the merchant slipped a folded note on to the scale at the same time.

Brendan stared at the merchant – and realised that he was a little too well built, with too-good posture, to *just* be a merchant. This man must be part of the secret group that Brendan had read about in *Savage Warriors*…

The Resistance. An army of freedom fighters who opposed the evil queen that Slayne served, Queen Daphne. Celene was part of the Resistance – one of the secret fighters, with a hard look on her face. As she paid for the lemon with copper coins, she pocketed the note. Brendan figured he'd better not mention the Resistance immediately.

"A lot of people in this town seem to know me," he managed. "Why is that? They've never met me."

"Your reputation precedes you," Celene said.

"That's probably a good thing, right? Unless it's a bad reputation. I don't feel like I've done enough bad stuff to have a bad reputation. I mean, once I taped together all the silly straws in the kitchen cabinets to make a minipipe that took water from the sink to my sister's room, and I kind of flooded the house and destroyed her laptop, but—" *Stop, Bren; what're you doing?* "But that was like, years ago, and I'm a lot more mature now."

"How many years ago?" Celene asked.

"Mmmmm… one," Brendan admitted. They were walking together now. Celene laughed. Her smile showed all her teeth. Brendan remembered from *Savage Warriors* that one of her top teeth was crooked, and sure enough, there it was. He had to make her really smile to see it.

Celene came to a stall that sold fish and octopus. Brendan saw the tentacled creatures stretched out on boards with their arms pressed together like they were wearing skirts. The smell was horrible, and as he gagged, he almost didn't notice: Celene slipped the note out of her pocket and gave it to the fishmonger. He had the same look as the first merchant, like he was just doing his job while he had something much more important on his mind.

Another Resistance freedom fighter. And she's passing messages for them, just like the book said.

"So why do people here know me?" Brendan asked.

"Because you're from the *Moray*," said Celene. "The *Moray* always docks in our town, to trade."

Brendan tried to put it together. The *Moray* was from a totally different book than Celene – it was from *The Heart and the Helm* – but now that the books had got mashed up, the *Moray* obviously had made some visits here. The reality of each book was quickly becoming entangled with the others. Maybe Will's squadron would soon show up and rescue all of them.

"Who does the ship trade with?" Brendan asked.

"Why should I tell you?" Celene responded. "Haven't you read about it already, like you read about me?"

"Hold on," Brendan said. *Who* is *she? Does she* know *she's trapped in a book?* "I'm not good with riddles. Please. Tell me what's going on. I've been through too much to get blindsided by another stupid spell or secret."

"But don't you know all the spells and secrets? Aren't you from outside?"

She does know, Brendan realised. *She's just as smart as she was in the book.* All he could say aloud was, "Maybe."

Celene grabbed his arm: "There is a prophecy that you will free us. That when one comes who is not of this world, we will finally be able to throw off the yoke of Queen Daphne and be free. You have to help us. Me and my father."

"Yes, fine, I'll help," Brendan said. He knew from the book that Celene's father, a general, expected a lot of her. "But how?"

"You should know in your heart," Celene said. "It is your fate to help. To be a hero."

"Is that why everyone in this town treats me so strangely? Why are they giving me free food and running away from me?"

"Because they're scared, Brendan. Of the powerful men on the *Moray*. Tranquebar. Captain Sangray."

"Sangray's dead."

"Dead?" That surprised Celene. "Who killed him? A man like Sangray doesn't die unless he's killed."

"My friend Will did it. The new captain of the *Moray*."

"That means trouble for all of you when Sangray's brother finds out."

"Sangray has a *brother*?"

"Of course. He's the one who trades with the *Moray*. He's here with his men today, probably down on the beach—"

"Who is he?" said Brendan, a terrible realisation sinking in.

Celene whispered a name in Brendan's ear.

Brendan bolted.

Celene was left standing in the market, confused, as he dashed past the fruit stall, past the weapons store, past the place where he'd got the toffee apple, through the narrow dirt streets filled with donkeys and horses and pirates, all the way down to the beach where he had started. The whole time, his chest was heaving, his breath straining through his mouth like something sharp. *I have to get there before it's too late. I have to tell them. I have to—*

When he reached the beach, the first thing he saw was Kristoff House, still at sea, sunk in the water with just its chimney sticking up. On the sand a few dozen metres in front of it were Cordelia and Will…

Tied up and gagged.

Next to them was Eleanor, similarly secured. Jacqui the horse trainer was riding away on Majesty, looking very relieved and guilty.

"Hey!" Brendan yelled. "What did you do to my sis—"

But he stopped talking as men stepped towards him.

One was Tranquebar. The rest wore shining full-plate armour. They had gruff faces, swords and axes. One had a red beard… and one had a fresh scar from a barbecue fork on his cheek.

"Slayne," said Brendan – and then the Savage Warriors grabbed him.

"There's nothing quite so satisfying as having all one's enemies in one place," said Slayne, looking down at Brendan, Cordelia, Eleanor and Will. They were under one of his chain-link nets on the beach, trapped as they had been back in the forest. Slayne's men, who'd been terrified and fleeing on horses when the Walkers had last seen them, were now taking turns kicking sand in their faces.

"Careful, we need them unspoiled for the queen!" Slayne warned.

"Right, sir, sorry," Krom said.

"What queen?" asked Eleanor.

"Queen Daphne," Brendan said. He started to explain about the cruel ruler he had read about in *Savage Warriors*, whose existence Celene had confirmed.

"Silence!" Slayne ordered. He knelt in front of Eleanor and turned his face so that the scar on his cheek was directly under her nose. "Remember what you did to me?"

"I think it's an improvement," said Eleanor.

"I'll have my revenge," growled Slayne. "I'll cut off your fingers, one by one. And then, as you're watching, I'll coat them in boar batter and deep-fry them. That's Queen Daphne's favourite appetiser: fried kiddie fingers dipped in chocolate sauce!"

That freaked Eleanor out. "No!" she screamed. "*Let me go!*" She shook against the metal net, trying to break free and hurt Slayne with anything – her teeth, her toenails – but her hands and feet were tied, and she couldn't do much except flop around like a flounder.

"My little warrior," said Slayne, "I'm impressed by your spirit. I'd wager you could put up a good fight against Krom here. But sadly, we've no time for games. There are more pressing matters at hand."

Slayne raised the net and pulled Will out by the ankles.

"Let go, you grotty blighter! You crusty brute! And *you!*" Will spat at Tranquebar: "You deceitful old gasbag!"

"I told you not to take me for a fool, Captain Draper,"

said Tranquebar. "I suspected quickly after you dispatched Sangray that you and your companions were keeping secrets. My friend Slayne here tells me you're a warlock protecting a coven of dangerous witchlings. And so... I get a hefty reward; you go with him. Can you really blame me for being a smart businessman?"

"Saving us, then sending us to our deaths? You deceitful beast!" Will yelled. "You'll rot in hell!"

Slayne dragged Will away from the net, leaving a trail in the sand that reminded Brendan of the angels he had made with Eleanor.

"I want a fair fight!" Will demanded. Slayne let him flop on to the sand. He tried to stand but, with ropes securing his hands and feet, could only manage a defiant kneel. "Cut me free and give me a sword! Or aren't you man enough?"

Slayne just glared at Will.

"I thought so," said Will. "You're afraid I'll send you to the bottom of the sea!"

"Like you did my brother?" Slayne asked quietly.

Will paused. "Your brother? What in blazes are you—"

Slayne pulled a sword and darted it under Will's chin, raising Will's face.

"Captain… Sangray," Slayne said slowly.

"Ohhhh…" said Will. The Savage Warriors and the Walkers were all staring at him, but no one was more terrified than Cordelia. She saw how close the blade was to Will's throat. She knew a quick flick of Slayne's wrist would send him slumping over to darken the sand. She'd already lost her parents. She couldn't lose him. *Apologise, stupid! Apologise and beg for mercy!*

"I should have known," Will said with a smirk.

Oh no, Cordelia thought. "Be *quiet*, Will!" she called.

But Will said: "Same freakish body, same foul face that only a mother could love…"

"*Stop!*" Cordelia screamed.

But Will grinned at Slayne: "Oh, that's right. You must never have known your mum. I bet she worked in a—"

Slayne pressed his sword into the triangle of flesh under Will's jaw. Drops of blood patted the sand.

"*Mmm!*" Will said, keeping his mouth shut so he wouldn't open his chin. He'd been looking at this all wrong. Having frightened these Savage Warriors off with bullets before, he wasn't really scared of them. But the clarity of pain made him re-evaluate the situation.

"Did you ever pull apart spiders when you were a boy?" Slayne asked.

Will shook his head just the tiniest bit, even though it cut him more.

"I did. Big hairy wolf spiders. And with each one, there was a moment I loved most of all: when I held the spider's first leg… right… here."

Slayne pinched the air. It was the perfect time for Will to lunge aside – but doing that would tear his throat open.

"When I made that first pinch, I always heard a voice in my head: 'You don't have to hurt this spider. What did he ever to do you?' It was a test of strength. I had to ignore that voice and" – Slayne *yanked* with his finger and thumb – "pull the leg off. Soon I wasn't killing spiders. I was killing the voice of weakness."

"Please! Let him go!" Cordelia said.

Slayne nodded to Krom. Krom aimed a precise kick at Cordelia's chest. She went down under the net with the wind knocked out of her.

"My queen requested that I deliver your friends alive," Slayne said, "but she has no orders regarding you, Mr Draper. And *you* killed my kin."

Will's mind was in overdrive, jumping backwards through his life. He saw Penelope Hope – Cordelia – the war – his mates – the training field – but then his memories went grey. *Do I even count?* he thought. *I've no mum, no dad… if I die, who's going to care?*

But then he realised… there were three people who *would* care. One perhaps most of all. He glanced to his left and locked eyes with Cordelia.

"Satisfy your bloodlust," Will said. "As long as you let my friends live through the day. I promised to protect them."

Slayne smiled, and pulled his sword away from Will's throat. He made as if to sheathe it—

But then, with a quick move, he stabbed it into Will's back.

Will stumbled and hit the ground.

"*Will!*" Cordelia cried from under the net.

Slayne wiped his blade clean on the pilot's trousers. Then he stepped away and left Will bleeding on the sand.

T he Walkers didn't stop screaming for a long time. Not until Slayne had tossed Will's body into the ocean. Not until Tranquebar had been paid with a wheelbarrow full of gold bars. The first mate put the word out to the pirates that they were setting sail again; by nightfall the *Moray* was being outfitted for a new journey.

Meanwhile, Krom and a few warriors came forward with a cart.

"What is that?" Eleanor asked. "Is that for us?"

The cart was ancient and full of dirty hay, with flies. The warriors rested it on the dock, lifted the net from the Walkers, and dumped them in one by one.

"Help!" Brendan yelled.

"Let us go!" Eleanor screamed.

But Cordelia did nothing. She kept seeing Will die. Kept

hearing the silence of that moment. She knew there had been a sound… but she couldn't hear it any more, and she couldn't speak.

"Tie 'em up so it hurts!" Krom ordered.

The warriors did, binding the Walkers together as if they were entering the world's cruellest six-legged race. Their ankles and wrists were fastened in spirals of rope.

Krom swung a metal cage over the cart, trapping the Walkers inside, before he and the other warriors pulled them down the dock. Slayne and Tranquebar parted ways with the group, going to the *Moray*. Inside the cart, Brendan called to Krom: "Hey, how long are we gonna be locked in here?"

"Until we arrive at Castle Corroway and you meet Queen Daphne. Two days."

"Two *days*?" asked a worried Eleanor. "How are we supposed to use the bathroom?"

"That's what the hay's for!" cackled Krom. The other warriors laughed with him.

"No way am I peeing in front of my brother," said Eleanor. "I'll hold it."

"Suit yourself," said Krom. "Bad for the kidneys."

"What about food?" asked Brendan.

"We'll be slaughtering goats along the way," said Krom. "We'll be cookin' the meaty parts for us. You lot can feast on the kidneys, intestines and all the other wet, dangly bits."

At the end of the dock, the Savage Warriors put the cart down and attached it to a horse. Then they mounted their own steeds. Within minutes the group was off.

It was a sight to silence the peaceful town of Tinz. Krom and his companions' shining weapons discouraged onlookers from coming to the rescue of the kids in the cart, who clearly were being held against their will. At first, Brendan and Eleanor called for help (Cordelia was still in shock), but after Krom gave them a few smacks with the butt end of his axe they were silent.

"What do we do?" Eleanor whispered. She couldn't see her brother, because their backs were facing, but his angry breathing gave her hope.

"Roll over," Brendan said. "I need to get a good look out of this thing."

Eleanor turned into the hay, yelping as stalks went up her nose. Cordelia did the same, but stayed quiet. With his two sisters face down Brendan could see through the cart's bars, and just in time… because they were passing through the market.

"Where are you, where are you?" Brendan muttered to himself.

"Who?" Cordelia finally asked.

"Deal! You're talking again!" Eleanor said.

"I want to know who Brendan's looking for," Cordelia said.

"Honestly? It's this girl I met."

"A girl?" said a surprised Eleanor. "You like a girl?"

"Well…" Brendan said. "I'm more interested in making sure she saves us. Cordelia, you remember Celene from *Savage Warriors*?"

"Sure – she's brave and smart," Cordelia said. "Let's try not to get her killed too."

"*Shut yer traps!*" Krom yelled from the front of the cart.

Celene was standing in the market, staring at the hay cart in as much disbelief as all the other townspeople, many of whom had the hard look of Resistance fighters. She got even more surprised when she recognised Brendan, and when he mouthed, with all the desperation he could convey in silence, *Help us!*

69

Two days later the Walkers looked a lot worse than they had at the start of their journey. Hard travel through a pine forest under the cruel eye of Krom (not to mention a steady diet of goat parts that wouldn't make it into a sausage) had given them a sunken, bloodless appearance. They rarely spoke, and when they did, it was to share hopeless insights like, "Bren, I guess your girlfriend from Tinz isn't going to save us."

"She's not my girlfriend, Deal."

"And we're probably going to die in this cart."

"No, we're probably going to die once we meet Queen Daphne…"

But then they saw Castle Corroway – and went silent.

It sprang up from the forest like a massive stone tree, made of grey limestone that resembled birch bark. The far side of it was perched on a bluff overlooking a gorge, which held the river that Krom and the warriors had been following on their journey. The near side had an enormous black gate, topped with rows of sharp metal spikes, set up to impale anyone who attempted to charge it. And the castle had four circular towers, but instead of ending in a parapet each one split into four smaller towers. These narrow towers rose high above the trees like clustered smokestacks, with a purple flag atop each.

"Have you ever seen anything like that?" Brendan asked.

"It's Sixteen Flags, the archduke's castle in *The Fighting Ace*," Cordelia said. "Will would recognise it. He *bombs* it. But of course…"

"Quiet! Don't make me beat you before we meet the queen!" Krom ordered. He didn't need to. Cordelia was already trailing off, thinking about Will and how there was no way his knowledge could help them now.

As the cart arrived at the gate, Castle Corroway loomed larger for the Walkers; if they tilted their heads back, two of the four towers marked the left and right limits of their vision, with blue sky in between. They had to roll around to glimpse the awe-inspiring sight, because they were still cruelly tied together – indeed their proximity over the past two days had made them familiar with one another in ways they would *never* mention again.

"All hail Queen Daphne!" Krom called at the gate. "Krom of Slayne's Savage Warriors, here with prisoners for the queen!"

"Password?" prompted a guard.

Krom cleared his throat… and then he started making horrible retching noises, like a cat trying to bring up a hairball.

"Is *that* the password?" Eleanor asked, but then Krom said—

"Sorry, sir! A bit of goat went down the wrong way. The password is… 'Panama-Pacific'!"

The gate ratcheted open.

"Weird password," Brendan murmured. He had heard it before, but he couldn't remember where.

After the gate came a courtyard, where the Walkers were surprised to find signs of life. Flocks of chickens ran around *bwak*ing. Women with dirty faces had lively conversations as they hung up laundry. Fires were burning; meat sizzled on grills. Men in canvas booths shouted out:

"Sword sharpening!" "Archery lessons!"

"It's like a village from *Game of Thrones*," said Eleanor.

"You're not supposed to be watching that!" said Cordelia.

"Brendan lets me," said Eleanor, "when Mum and Dad go out on date night—"

She went silent. There wasn't going to be any more date night.

"*Help!*" Brendan called to the women hanging laundry. They didn't move. They didn't react in any way. They stayed focused on their clothes as one of the warriors slapped Brendan with a spear blade.

"*Ow.* Lot of help they were," Brendan whispered, wiping his cheek against straw (which also didn't help).

"Maybe they're too scared to do anything," Cordelia said. She was scared herself as the cart rolled into a dark structure that she recognised as the castle keep. The warriors stopped and pulled the Walkers out, cutting their bonds, giving them a few moments of blessed relief before forcing them to march up steps on jellied legs, past guards who snapped, "*All hail Queen Daphne!*"

In a few minutes, the Walkers were in a throne room

with bright windows and intricate, lush tapestries on the walls. The guards there repeated, "*Hail Queen Daphne!*"

But far across the room, sitting on a throne constructed from bone and amethyst, the Walkers didn't see any Queen Daphne.

They saw a ghastly bald woman in a sumptuous purple robe.

"The Wind Witch!" Eleanor exclaimed.

"That's it!" Brendan said. "Panama-Pacific was what they called the old San Francisco world's fair!"

Dahlia Kristoff smiled on her throne and looked at the Walkers one after another – as if to see who would snap first. Cordelia obliged.

"You killed our parents!" she yelled, surging forward – but the warriors shoved her to the ground and pushed her with her siblings to the Wind Witch's feet.

"Hello to you too," Dahlia Kristoff said. She had two stumps for hands now – the arm that had been zapped by lightning was cut off at the wrist. But on each stump she sported a diamond-studded false hand.

"Tacky," Eleanor said.

"Yeah," said Brendan, "you think you can hide from us

by changing your name and getting some bling?"

"I'm known by many names in many places, children. More than you can imagine. When you've spent as long as I have travelling through the worlds of Father's imagination, you can't help but get a little bored. I enjoy being Queen Daphne, because she has a certain classic imperiousness. Like Maleficent. But when I travel to Ancient Rome, I'm known as Paculla Annia."

"We're gonna make you pay for Mum and Dad," Brendan said.

"Collateral damage. It's not my fault adults are less easy than children to manipulate. We've taken some strange turns along the way, Walkers, but you've brought me what I asked you for, and I don't know that your parents would have. I'm truly sorry that to do it I had to destroy them, and your home—"

"And Will!" Cordelia screamed.

"I didn't kill Will," the Wind Witch said. "That was your friend Slayne."

She clucked her tongue. (She couldn't very well snap her fingers.) Slayne entered the throne room, wheeling a rectangular stone casket on a wooden trolley. The Wind

Witch warned him: "Keep it at least three metres from me! If you bring it close, my father's curse will make it disappear."

The throne-room guards tensed as Slayne lifted the lid from the casket.

Inside was *The Book of Doom and Desire.*

"Slayne and Tranquebar brought it up the river for me," the Wind Witch said, shaking with anticipation. "Now it's time for one of you to open the book… and slip this inside."

She held up a slip of paper in one of her diamond-studded prostheses. The Walkers stayed quiet.

"Which child will have the honour?"

No one answered.

"Cordelia? Since you went the furthest with the book? Brendan? Since you don't like books? Eleanor? Since you can barely read?"

"None of us," Eleanor spat.

"Yeah, we're not giving you the satisfaction, you bald bat," said Brendan.

"Very well. I'll have one of my men open it," said the Wind Witch. She turned to one of her largest guards. "*You!* Open the book!"

The guard's face went pale. He started to tremble with fear.

"I order you to open the book!" shouted the Wind Witch.

The terrified guard nodded and stepped forward. He reached for the book. His hands were shaking. He touched its cover… started to open it… and his hand burst into flames. The guard screamed and ran to a far corner of the room, where he buried his fiery hand in a fountain. A loud hiss and a cloud of steam rose from the water.

The Walkers stared in horror. "You'll be *fine*," the Wind Witch told the guard, and then she turned back: "Your move, Dahlia – I mean Cordelia."

"Don't you dare call me your horrid name!" said Cordelia.

"But you remind me of myself. So smart, so driven, so perceptive. Such a little – what's the word? – *nerd*! Come, now. How many more innocent guards need to burn their hands until you give me what I want?"

Cordelia had no response.

"You understand that if you open the book, I'll owe you something?" said the Wind Witch. "I've got plenty of my own desires I want to slip between its covers, but I can make room for yours. I can give you anything you want. I can make the impossible possible. All you have to do is—"

"No," Cordelia said. Then, quietly: "I'd rather die."

"Really?" asked the Wind Witch. "Slayne!"

Slayne stepped towards the Walkers.

"Start with the youngest!"

Slayne grabbed Eleanor's little finger and pressed it against the floor.

"*No!*" Eleanor screamed. She had hoped that, somewhere along the way, these people had forgotten their promise to cut off her fingers and have them deep-fried in boar batter. She began hyperventilating, shaking… and then she seemed to float above herself and see Eleanor Walker in front of the throne, a soon-to-be victim of the kind of torture that was only supposed to happen in faraway places.

"*Stop!*" Cordelia yelled.

"*Let her go!*" Brendan screamed.

But the Wind Witch shook her head. "You've made your decision. After I've tasted that first finger maybe you'll have a change of heart."

Slayne raised his sword. But as he was about to bring it down—

A huge bang, and then a slow creak, sounded outside the throne room. The Walkers heard shouting! Screams! Guards yelling "*To arms!*" Weapons clanging!

"What in the—?" asked the Wind Witch. "The *gate?*"

A flaming arrow crashed through a window of the throne room. It pierced a tapestry on the opposite wall. Flames leaped up—

But no one was looking at that. They were all looking out of the broken window at something impossible: a giant, hairy chest that towered over the keep like another castle.

Eleanor said, "Fat Jagger?"

70

"What is *that*?" the Wind Witch gasped, staring out of the broken window at the colossus's gigantic gut and flowing dark hair.

"A… colossus," said a dumbstruck Slayne.

"I know *that*! How did it get in my castle?"

"I suspect it ripped the gate—"

"*Take your men and kill it!*"

Slayne nodded grumpily and left the throne room with his sword drawn. The rest of the Savage Warriors followed suit. "Not you!" the Wind Witch barked at Krom. "You stay here and watch the whelps."

Krom looked longingly at Slayne – the two had been killing together since they were kids – but Slayne just shrugged: *Better listen to her.* Krom stayed.

The Wind Witch turned to the still-flaming tapestry on

the wall. She pointed her diamond-studded arms at it. A blast of water shot out and immediately extinguished the fire. It wasn't like the rain the Wind Witch had conjured before; this was like a fire hose.

"She's even *more* powerful with *two* messed-up hands?" Brendan said. "That's really not fair."

"The hardest steel is tempered in the hottest forge," said the Wind Witch, looking at her sparkling fake hands. Then a flash of motion outside got her attention; she turned to see Fat Jagger tossing a Savage Warrior over his shoulder like a pebble. The man's screams were drowned out by the tumult of battle in the courtyard.

"I believe I'm needed," said the Wind Witch. "Guards! Take the book down to the ship!"

Two guards quickly grabbed the stone casket that held *The Book of Doom and Desire*, closed it, and wheeled it out of the back of the room. Meanwhile, the Wind Witch bent back, cracked her spine in that horrible way the Walkers had seen before, and unfolded her dirty, greasy wings to whip up a column of air. Her veins and arteries pulsed in her face. Cackling, she flew out of the broken window to confront the colossus.

"What's she gonna do to Fat Jagger?" Eleanor pleaded. "He *came* for us. He knew we were in trouble, and he must have walked across the whole ocean—"

"Look!" Cordelia called.

Three grappling hooks had flipped into the broken window and caught against the stone inside.

"Intruders!" Krom called. "Get them!"

As Krom and two guards tried to get in position to defend the throne room, three fighters in black cloaks jumped down. (Outside, the Wind Witch flew at Fat Jagger; he bellowed and swatted at her as if she were a gnat.) In a flash, the cloaked figures landed in crouches, whipped out crossbows, and – *thwip thwip thwip* – shot Krom and the guards!

Brendan cheered; Krom and the guards were wearing armour, but the cloaked figures had buried the crossbow darts right in their faces. Krom was twisting on the ground, screaming, trying to pull one out of his eye. He finally managed to extract it, but his eyeball came out along with it; seeing his eye attached to the top of the dart like a martini olive made him scream at a higher pitch than anyone would have thought possible.

"Who are *you*?" Eleanor asked the intruders.

Brendan could hardly speak, but he managed to say, "Celene."

The cloaked figures pushed back their hoods – and sure enough, it was Celene from Tinz and the two men she had been ferrying messages for in the marketplace. The Resistance fighters.

"Of course. The Resistance against Queen Daphne," said Cordelia.

The Resistance fighters strode towards the Walkers. The other guards in the room ran for the stairs, not wanting to end up on the floor with crossbow-dart piercings.

"Brendan? Are you all right?" Celene asked.

Brendan lurched forward and hugged her. "You saved us! *Thanks!*"

"You're welcome, but we—"

"These are my sisters: Cordelia and Eleanor."

"Nice to meet you, but we need to move fast," said Celene. "I've got to get back to the rest of my team; they're out there fighting the castle guards."

"How did you find us?"

"I had guessed where you were going when I saw you

in the cart, and then" – Celene pointed her thumb behind her – "the big guy showed up."

Outside, the colossus was stomping and roaring. The Wind Witch was nowhere to be found. "His name's Jagger," said Eleanor.

"Then I'll have you know that yesterday, Jagger waded out of the sea into Tinz. And the only word he said was 'Wa-lker'."

"I knew he came for us!" Eleanor said. "I fed him well."

Celene nodded in a way that made it clear she had no idea what Eleanor was talking about. "The Resistance decided it was time to strike, since the ultimate weapon was here to help us. After we win we're going to elect a new leader and never live under the tyranny of Queen Daphne again. But" – she grabbed Brendan's arm – "you need to get to the top of one of the towers, *now*. That way Jagger can see you and carry you away. This battle isn't getting any stablerer." She frowned. "I think that's a word."

Outside the window, Fat Jagger caterwauled; the Wind Witch was flapping her wings and shooting bolts of lightning at him. One of Jagger's eyebrows was singed off. His nostril hairs were on fire.

"I'm rejoining the battle," said Celene. "The big guy needs all the help he can get."

"But…" Brendan said, suddenly tongue-tied as he looked at Celene's flushed face. "Will I see you again?"

"And are you my brother's girlfriend?" Eleanor said.

"Nell!"

Cordelia laughed. Brendan suddenly looked about seven years old.

"I don't know about girlfriend, but I think your brother's very brave," Celene said to Eleanor. She pulled Brendan close.

Afterwards, Brendan would tell his sisters that they hugged. Celene would tell her Resistance compatriots that Brendan kissed her on the cheek. What really happened was that she went for his cheek, but he awkwardly turned his head, so they just bumped their cheekbones together. "*Ow!*"

Celene whispered, "Maybe we'll see each other again some day. In your world."

"I've been meaning to ask you. How do you know about—"

"Another time," Celene said. She stepped back and looked at the Walkers: "*Go!* Take weapons!"

Brendan went to the dead guards, picked up their swords, and gave them to his sisters. He took Krom's axe for himself. Krom was still staring in shock at his eyeball-on-a-stick.

"Wait!" pleaded Krom, pointing to the axe in Brendan's hand. "Kill me. Please. Put me out of me misery."

"Don't be such a wimp," said Brendan. "Get an eye patch!"

The Walkers tore out of the throne room, ran down the stairs, and entered the courtyard.

It was sheer chaos. Castle Corroway's black gate had been ripped clean off; it lay in two pieces on the ground. The castle guards were engaged in hand-to-hand combat with Resistance forces. Towering over it all was Fat Jagger, who grunted and groaned as he pushed against a blistering column of icy air that the Wind Witch blew at his face. She was holding her position like a harpy in front of him, trying to knock Jagger into the gorge that was next to the castle.

Eleanor recognised fear in the colossus's eyes even as she stood in his shadow. "*Jagger!*" Fat Jagger looked down. Eleanor pointed at the tower behind her and made a gesture indicating she was going up. Jagger gave a tiny nod (which of course was huge) before a flying icicle pierced his ankle. The Wind Witch was shooting icicles at his feet! As several more missiles pierced his flesh, Jagger cried out and lifted his foot, nearly toppling into the gorge. He quickly regained his balance and grabbed for the Wind Witch.

"C'mon! He sees where we're going!" Eleanor said.

Brendan and Cordelia followed Eleanor into the tower, slicing at any guards who got too close. Inside, they climbed past frightened horses and pigs, past even more frightened servants, through bedchambers, past stacked oak barrels, through a nightmare room with gigantic hunks of salted mystery meat hanging from hooks… They climbed the tower until they were dizzy from turning up the next flight of steps. Then they came to a landing with four spiral staircases.

"This is where the tower splits into four," said Brendan. "Which one do we go up?"

At the bottom of one of the staircases lay a dead guard. "Look," Cordelia said, "his armour's all battered. Maybe he got killed upstairs and rolled down."

"So?" Brendan said.

"So maybe there are Resistance forces up there."

"Good thinking." The Walkers started up.

This tower was tiny. The spiral staircase walls were peppered with rectangular slit windows for archers. The windows only faced in one direction, so as the Walkers ascended, they glimpsed the same view of Jagger from higher and higher up.

"See how the stairs go anticlockwise?" panted Brendan. "They built them this way because it would put an attacking swordsman at a disadvantage."

"Why?" Eleanor asked.

"Most soldiers are right-handed. So the soldiers defending the castle would swing with their right arms, but if any attackers tried, they'd hit the wall. Wikipedia."

The Walkers neared the top of the tower; they could make out Jagger's face and wave at him. He was burned, bloodied and bruised from the Wind Witch's assaults.

"We're almost there, Jagger!" Eleanor called.

The colossus nodded – but suddenly the Walkers heard a roar from above. They stopped in their tracks as, with the momentum of a roller coaster coming down the first big hill, Slayne the Savage Warrior attacked them.

His sword was swinging, his black eyes were flashing and the scars on his face looked extra angry. "When will you brats *learn*?"

Brendan instinctively held up his axe; Slayne's sword rang off it. The axe flew out of Brendan's hand, hit the wall, and landed on the stairs.

"That's Krom's axe!" Slayne said in disbelief.

"Why are you hiding up here?" asked Cordelia.

"I'm not *hiding*!" Slayne yelled, slashing. Cordelia had to roll down a few steps to avoid him. "I'm waiting for the proper moment to strike!"

"You're lying," accused Eleanor. "You're a coward. The only thing you're not afraid of is little kids!"

"*Die!*"

Slayne cleaved down with his blade; Eleanor scrambled back to join Cordelia. Brendan gulped. He was the only one standing between Slayne and his sisters. *It's one thing to call this guy a coward and another to beat him in a fight.*

"Wait!" Brendan yelled, picking up Krom's axe. "Don't you wanna know what happened to your buddy Krom?"

Slayne paused, staring at the weapon.

"If you kill me, you'll never know," said Brendan. "If you listen, I'll take you to him."

"Where is he?" Slayne finally ventured. "Is he alive?"

"Let's just say he won't be seeing any 3-D movies in the near future."

"Huh?" grunted a confused Slayne.

Brendan dived forward. He knew from lacrosse: when you committed to a move, you had to stick with it. You couldn't turn a hip-barge into a shoulder-barge, or you'd get no follow-through.

He brought the axe down on Slayne's boot-clad foot.

He hit the steps, kicking his legs back to do a somersault *up.*

He felt Slayne's sword leave a burning tear in his side—

And then he was above Slayne on the steps. Still holding the axe.

"You're bleeding," Slayne said triumphantly. Behind him, Cordelia got ready to attack, but Brendan shook his head: *I got this.*

"You're right-handed," Brendan said.

"So?"

"So *block*!"

Brendan tossed the axe at Slayne's head. It sang through the air in a tight spiral. Slayne tried to slash at it – but the wall blocked his arm! His sword sparked, and the axe hit him in the forehead—

Unfortunately, handle first.

The axe clattered as it fell down the spiral stairs. Slayne smiled and flipped his sword to his left hand.

"I'm ambidextrous."

He stepped towards Brendan with a glint in his eyes. Brendan wanted to say it was unfamiliar, but it actually looked a lot like the expressions that some rabid lacrosse dads had when their sons injured the visiting team—

And then Slayne slipped to the side.

Cordelia had grabbed his foot from behind.

"That's for *Will*!" she yelled as she yanked him over – and he fell towards the centre of the spiral stairs.

He hit the steps below. *Clang!* Brendan looked at Cordelia. She had that same glimmer in her eyes: the death glint. Slayne screamed as he hit more steps. *Clang!* The sound echoed as he ricocheted down the tower. *Clang!* Scream. *Clang!* Scream. Until there were no more screams.

"Bren! Are you hurt?" Eleanor rushed to her brother. Brendan held his side, where blood was sticking to his oversize top.

"I'll be OK," he said. "Cordelia, how do you feel?"

"Like I avenged Will." Cordelia wiped her forehead. Far below, Slayne's body hit the bottom of the tower. *Clang!*

"Let's go," Brendan said.

The Walkers continued up – but at the next window, when they looked for Fat Jagger, his giant eye filled their view with terror.

"*Rrrrr!*"

"What's wrong? Did the Wind Witch hurt you?" Eleanor asked.

"*Rrrrr!* Wa-lker! *Rrrrrrrrr!*"

"Where is she, Jagger? Where—"

A howl silenced Eleanor. A wind-tunnel blast was coming up the tower. Cordelia's hair was blown up from her face, standing vertical. The Walkers backed against the wall as Slayne's body – eyes open, trailing blood – whirled past them and shot towards the top. Below him, flying up the steps like a banshee, flapping her wings and screaming like one too, was a very angry Dahlia Kristoff.

"She's coming!" Eleanor shouted. "What do we d—"

And then things happened fast enough to be slow motion.

The tower cracked and crumbled as Fat Jagger's giant hand wrapped around it. Blocks of stone rained down on the Walkers, who hugged the wall to avoid them; below, the Wind Witch blew the stones away with a cackle. A brittle snap of cracked mortar shook the tower—

And the top of it was *gone*. The Walkers were staring at Fat Jagger's face, backlit by sky.

"*Rrrrr!*" Jagger ordered, holding out his palm. The top of the tower hit the courtyard with a *kssshoom*.

"C'mon!" said Eleanor, jumping on the colossus's hand. Her siblings followed; in seconds, Jagger was whisking them all away from the topless tower.

They clung to his skin and looked down at the ruined courtyard and the gorge next to the castle. Far down there, floating in blue-green water, was the *Moray*, attached by ropes to a tiny sliver of roof and chimney. The pirates were ant-like specks running away from it.

"Look! Kristoff House!" Brendan said. "Part of it still hasn't sunk!"

The Walkers didn't have much time to appreciate the view. The Wind Witch flew out of the broken tower in a rage, screaming, *"That giant cretin won't help you now!"*

"That's bullying!" Eleanor yelled from Jagger's palm, not sure what a cretin was, but certain the comment was mean-spirited.

Suddenly the Wind Witch flew directly in front of them, beating her wings to maintain her position, and pointed her diamond fake hands at the river below. The river came to life, bubbling and thrashing, and a curling spout of water began to move upwards, snaking towards the witch's arms. Jagger, distracted, watched as the water met her hands… and shot back down, instantly transformed into blasts of ice!

The ice jets hit Jagger's feet like comets, wrapping around his ankles, hardening and clinking as they connected. Within seconds Jagger was handcuffed – or footcuffed – by frozen manacles, which left him dangerously off balance.

"*No! Jagger! Don't fall!*" Eleanor pleaded, but it was too late. The colossus's centre of gravity was somewhere outside the castle. He resembled the Leaning Tower of Pisa. He was going down.

Jagger closed his fingers around the Walkers, trying to protect them. The world went dark in his palm. As Jagger fell, the Walkers were thrown against the inside of his knuckles, feeling the earth-shaking crash of his body hitting the Castle Corroway wall—

And then they kept going. Down, down, down. Until something splashed around them.

Jagger opened his hand. The Walkers tumbled out in a daze. They were surrounded by the gorge, *under* Castle Corroway, with Jagger lying next to them in the river, moaning and sputtering.

"We're on the *Moray*!" Cordelia said, stamping her foot on the deck.

"Jeez," said Brendan, "I didn't think I'd *ever* be happy to be on this boat again—"

"Look!" Eleanor pointed up. The stone casket that had

held *The Book of Doom and Desire* was descending from the sky. And above it…

"*Walkers!*" the Wind Witch screeched.

She was coming down on a column of self-generated air, her rotten wings stinking up the ship. Against the gorge's sheer cliffs, she looked like an ancient god.

The stone casket reached the deck and stood there upright. Eleanor turned to Fat Jagger, who was lying half submerged in the river. "Jagger! Save yourself! Hide!"

Jagger nodded, took a deep breath – so deep that the Walkers felt it tugging at their hair – and slipped underwater. The ship rose as the river did. His giant body became a shimmering black shape that extended far in front of the *Moray* and behind it.

"Fools," said the Wind Witch, landing on the ship a safe distance from the casket. "You don't think I can kill your fat friend any time I like?" She used a gust of wind to open the casket and expose *The Book of Doom and Desire*. Then she turned to the Walkers and folded up her wings.

It was just her and them.

"I have something here," Dahlia Kristoff said, blowing a piece of paper across the ship into Brendan's hand, "and

I want one of you to open that book and put it inside. It's not complicated. I've made my wishes very simple."

Brendan read the paper: *Dahlia Kristoff shall rule the world forever.*

"Simple?" laughed Brendan. "You sound like one of those psycho villains in an Avengers movie."

"Yeah," said Eleanor, who had read over her brother's shoulder – pretty well! "Taking over the world is too much work! Who'd want the responsibility?"

"Somebody like her," said Cordelia. "A megalomaniac."

"What's a manga-lowly-maniac?" asked Eleanor.

"Megalomaniac. They have a delusional fantasy of great power," said Cordelia. "People like Alexander the Great, Adolf Hitler—"

"Silence!" barked the Witch. "Which of you will use the book?"

Cordelia looked at Brendan. Brendan looked at Eleanor. Eleanor shook her head. Her siblings followed suit.

"If you won't open the book, I'll *make* you open it!"

The Wind Witch pointed her arms at the Walkers. Suddenly Cordelia was lifted up as if she were in a harness – but the only things pulling on her were tendrils of air.

The witch raised an arm above her head and waved it… and Cordelia was blasted by a murderous wind into the ship's mainmast!

"Open it!" The Wind Witch darted her arm and slammed Cordelia against the wood.

"*Open it!*" The witch slammed Cordelia again – she shook her head, or maybe her head was just lolling back and forth—

"*Stop!*" Eleanor pleaded.

The Wind Witch dropped her arms. Cordelia slid to the deck, limp, with the mast scraping her face.

"You—!" Brendan ran towards the Wind Witch. He didn't care what magic she possessed; he was going to take her out.

The Wind Witch smiled and twirled her hands. A barrel on the deck split open, becoming a spinning Catherine wheel of curved wooden beams and two ribbons of metal. The beams cracked diagonally and shot towards Brendan like spears. Brendan dived, but one of them pierced his side, in the exact same spot Slayne had slashed earlier.

"*Aaaaagh!*" Brendan grabbed the hunk of wood. Blood welled up around it. He tried to pull it out, but the Wind

Witch kept it in place with a jet-engine gust of air. The blood was spreading now, creeping along the deck like it was being blown by one of those Xlerator hand dryers.

"Now, littlest Walker," said the Wind Witch, turning to Eleanor, "are *you* ready to do the right thing?"

"*Don't do it, Nell!*" screamed Brendan.

Eleanor stood her ground, shook her head.

"Very well," the Wind Witch said, "then you owe me a finger."

Eleanor bit her lip, trying to be brave—

And suddenly the sky grew dark.

A thundercloud appeared above the *Moray*: a thundercloud that took Dahlia Kristoff by surprise. It was silver and blue and black, almost like a floating lump of coal, and as Dahlia watched it, the cloud stretched to cover not just the ship but the trees, the river, the sky. It was almost like the strange quiet moments before a hot summer storm, when night invades day.

And then…

A voice came out of the cloud.

Deep. Wet. And powerful.

"Dah-*lia*! What. Have. You. *Done?*"

The centre of the cloud coalesced into a black figure with orange eyes.

"Father?" Dahlia said.

"You will never call me that again!" said the figure. "I am the *Storm King*!"

73

Confronted by the fearsome sight in front of her, Eleanor couldn't do much. Couldn't speak. Couldn't turn away. Couldn't blink. If this man had ever been Denver Kristoff, he wasn't any more.

The Storm King had a twisted, purple face the texture of hardened candle wax. It came into view as he floated down with the swirling black cloud shrouding his body. Spidery blue lightning crackled around him. His long mouth extended past where a normal human mouth stopped, curling up on one side and down on the other, as if he were smiling and frowning at once. Eleanor remembered what Penelope had said about Kristoff looking the same way, but it seemed that this Storm King was a much more advanced version of what she had described, like the difference between a suntan and skin cancer. Kristoff's nose was nothing but a collection of fleshy flaps hung over his lips. One of his orange, catlike eyes was higher than the other, perched near his forehead…

But within those eyes was a spark of understanding. As if Denver Kristoff were trapped inside the Storm King, under the transfigured flesh, and knew how hideous he was.

"What happened to you?" Brendan yelled, refusing to keep quiet even in his near-death state. "You were a pretty good-looking guy in those pictures… I bet the ladies were all over you back in the day! But now you are one ugly — *aaagh*!"

A burst of blue lightning leaped from the Storm King's hand and surrounded Brendan's face. The lightning danced and circled Brendan's head as he screamed in pain. When the lightning dissolved, there was a horrific result…

Brendan's face was an identical match to the Storm King's.

"*Oh no… no…*" gasped Brendan, catching a reflection of his new face in a twisted barrel hoop on deck. "*What did you do to me? I want my old face back!*"

"My features were brought on by my extreme use of the book," said the Storm King, "but I can give them to you free of charge. You appear to be at death's door… why not abide by the old cliché, '*Die young and leave a bad-looking corpse*'?"

"*Noooo!*" Brendan cried, hiding his face with his hands – then moving them away because the texture of his new face felt too creepy.

The Storm King turned his attention to the Wind Witch. She was whirling her hands in the air, trying to whip up a gust to blow him off the *Moray*—

"*Fool!*" the Storm King roared.

Two blue bolts rocketed out of his hands and knocked her on to the deck. Eleanor watched from behind a barrel, terrified.

"Why do you continue to search for the book?" the Storm King howled. "Look at me! My face is only a reflection of what the book has done to my soul! Is this what you want to become?"

The Storm King threw up his hands. His cloud cloak split in the middle and revealed his torso.

Eleanor would never forget: Kristoff's chest resembled a purple, extra-mouldy slice of Gorgonzola cheese. Huge chunks of flesh were missing. Sores covered the skin that *was* there. Blue sparks, accompanied by warping, whooshing cracks, danced along his damaged body.

"Using that book may grant you all you desire," said Kristoff, "but there is a dark price to pay. Look at me!"

"But you're still alive," the Wind Witch countered, shielding her eyes on the deck of the *Moray*, "and I am dying! I can't keep myself going with common magic any more. If the book's power can keep me alive, isn't that more desirable than something as shallow as human appearance?"

"It's not only what it does to your body," said Kristoff. "The book will chip away at your soul, so all that remains is a hint of goodness, a fragment of humanity, buried beneath pure evil and darkness. That's why I always vowed to protect you from it! I loved you so much I even killed poor Penelope Hope to save you from the book!"

Dahlia's voice turned suddenly sweet: "But Daddy, remember when we first used it together? And you would write down whatever I asked for and place it inside the book… and I would get all those wonderful presents… remember how happy I was? Remember how happy *we* were?"

The Storm King softened a little. Dahlia hadn't called him Daddy in many, many years.

"That was my mistake," he said. "I never should have showed you the book's power—"

"But those are the best memories of my life. Using the book, making my dreams come true. Making all the bad things go away. Why don't the two of us forget all of this and go back home, to Kristoff House? I've got rid of the Walker parents; we can do the same with the children… We'll have the house to ourselves, except now we'll use the book together… and rule forever." Dahlia paused and added softly—

"I still love you, Daddy."

The Storm King trembled, as if he couldn't remember the last time anyone had said they loved him. Eleanor thought he might cry—

But Dahlia glanced at the slip of paper that was now stuck in Brendan's spreading blood on the deck of the *Moray*. Her eyes filled with something needier than love: greed. The Storm King noticed.

"What's that?" he asked suspiciously.

Eleanor looked at *The Book of Doom and Desire*, still sitting in the casket on the deck, and got an idea. But she didn't have much time. The cloud above the Storm King was starting to pulse. *He's getting mad.*

"Don't be weak, Daddy. Let us use the book together—"

The Storm King sent a tendril of black cloud across the *Moray*, towards the scrap of paper.

"Daddy, stop. Don't look at that—"

He brought the paper to his face, blew off the blood with a flick of his wrist, and read it.

"I knew it!" he shouted. "You have no real love for me or anyone else! You only care about the book!" He used the tiny black cloud to tear the paper up, causing the Wind Witch to scream—

"HOW DARE YOU DESTROY MY DREAMS?"

The Wind Witch's arms cartwheeled madly, causing a huge wave to crash over the ship.

"YOU'RE WEAK, FATHER!" she cried, unfolding her wings and flying up to the mainmast. "TOO WEAK FOR SUCH POWER! AND YOU TAKE IT OUT ON ME!" River water swept the Storm King against the edge of the deck and held him in place, pounding his face, invading his mouth and lungs. Unconscious Cordelia and a bloodied Brendan were tossed around like toys. Eleanor was nowhere to be seen.

The Storm King slashed his arm through the rushing water so it exploded away from his face. He torpedoed up at the Wind Witch and opened his oversize mouth. He didn't need wings to fly.

A kilowatt-level swathe of blue lightning tore out of the Storm King's face and hands, frying the air around him. The Wind Witch blocked his bolt with one of her own. The explosion blasted the Storm King out of the sky, sending him tumbling back to the *Moray*. The Wind Witch flew into the black cloud above.

On deck, the water dissipated. Brendan found himself lying beside Cordelia. He looked at the wood protruding from his side. A metre away, the Storm King was preparing to attack again.

"Wait!" Brendan yelled.

The Storm King looked at him.

"Look… I know you've got to deal with your daughter issues. But before you leave… please… give me my old face back."

"And why would I do that?"

"Because like you said, deep inside," said Brendan, "you're still Denver Kristoff. There's still some good in there."

A flash of understanding appeared in the Storm King's eyes. He extended his hand. Swirling black clouds came out of each of his fingertips. Brendan felt them gather at his mouth and slide inside his nose. He saw the orange light in the Storm King's eyes get brighter. When the black fingerlings of cloud slipped away... Brendan's face was back to normal.

He reached up, felt his skin, and smiled at the Storm King.

"Thanks so much. Now when they see me lying in my coffin, everyone at school won't be grossed out."

Denver Kristoff slowly nodded—

And then he shot up into the cloud to take care of Dahlia.

"Phew," Brendan said, rocking his head aside, looking towards the stone casket...

The Book of Doom and Desire was gone!

And so was Eleanor.

"Nell?" Brendan called weakly. "Nell—"

Brendan went quiet as the first explosion of lightning erupted above. Inside the cloud, the Wind Witch and the Storm King had begun a titanic battle.

74

Meanwhile, a few dozen metres away, inside the tiny bit of the Kristoff House chimney that still stuck up above the water, Eleanor looked at the same sight. The cloud seemed alive, throbbing with blue-and-white light, and a horrible burning smell drifted down…

But Eleanor had a job to do.

In her hands was *The Book of Doom and Desire*. She had carried it over the ropes to Kristoff House and climbed inside the chimney while the Storm King and the Wind Witch fought. Now she was stuffed in this dirty little square space. *Sometimes it pays to be the smallest,* she thought, patting the chimney walls. Soot came off on her fingers. She smiled. That was part of the plan.

Eleanor opened the book without looking at it and

ripped a page out as quickly as possible before closing it. By treating the book like a bear trap, she managed not to get enchanted by it. She looked at the page. A simple, blank page.

Now comes the tough part. Time to write.

She flashed back to that horrible thing that had happened to her at school, when she'd messed up reading in front of the whole class. She pushed it aside. *None of that matters now.* She put her soot-covered finger on the paper. Screams sounded from the cloud above. Eleanor closed her eyes. She remembered what Cordelia had told her ages ago, outside Kristoff House, about how maybe she should try reading backwards. The key wasn't to read backwards. It was to read *blind*.

She blocked out the world, blocked out the screams, blocked out the confusion and echoes of those kids... and wrote.

Then she reopened *The Book of Doom and Desire*.

Just a little. Just enough to get the paper in.

She slipped it inside—

And a huge rush of wind sucked her out of the chimney and up towards the roiling cloud.

75

Eleanor thought it was the Wind Witch. Or the Storm King. Or both. She was certain they were bringing her up into the cloud to rearrange her body with lightning. It would be a brutal death, but Eleanor felt calm – because she had tried to do something heroic. She got closer to the cloud…

And then it started to spin.

Eleanor saw a tiny white dot at the centre of it. The cloud was swirling around the dot, changing its shape, starting to resemble an enormous Dunkin' Donut without the colourful sprinkles. Tremendous creaking winds accompanied this, and Eleanor began spinning, making circles over the *Moray* as she stared up at the shifting cloud. Now its sides were puffed out against the gorge; Eleanor saw the Wind Witch and the Storm King trying to fly away, but they were trapped in the same spiral as her. The cloud was growing, and the dot was growing – it was more of a disc now. Eleanor began to lose track of where she was. She looked down—

Castle Corroway was dozens of metres below. The Resistance forces from Tinz had clearly won the battle, but were scattering in terror at the sight of the turbulence above. None of the soldiers were getting sucked towards the cloud; whatever force was consuming Eleanor, Denver and Dahlia, it appeared to be very selective.

The cloud was moving higher, racing upwards as if it would eventually soar into space, nearly covering the sky from horizon to horizon.

"Cordelia!" Eleanor called. Her sister suddenly appeared beside her, twisting like a trapeze artist, still unconscious, her hair flying out behind her. In an instant, she was gone, far above. Eleanor was still rising – and the cloud was still growing. She looked down and saw the last thing she expected…

Kristoff House! Untied from the *Moray*, flying upwards, spinning in mid-air. The broken windows and seaweed and cracks and dents and holes in it made it look strangely weary, like an old friend returning from a long journey. *It's a great house*, Eleanor thought, *at least when it's got a family inside.*

It rushed past her with a *whoosh*.

Eleanor looked back down and saw Fat Jagger.

He was sitting up in the river, taking deep breaths, looking at Eleanor with a goofy grin. He waved to her and blew a kiss.

"Thanks, Jagger!" Eleanor yelled. "Hope I get to see you again!" She had an idea, now, where she was heading.

Kristoff House reached the centre of the cloud. The Wind Witch and the Storm King circled it, getting close to the front door.

Then something slammed into Eleanor from below.

It was Brendan, flying upwards, spinning in mid-air, terrified.

"What's happening?" he yelled. Blood was coming out of his side, spiralling up instead of falling down.

"We're going home!" said Eleanor, and then things got very weird inside her head, almost too weird to describe. It was as if barriers were breaking down in the world and in her mind. She saw Kristoff House at the centre of the giant cloud-torus, and then she saw her mother, lying in a hospital bed, holding her as a newborn, with her father standing over them: an image she couldn't possibly remember, even though she knew it was true. Then she saw Denver Kristoff, not as the Storm King, but as himself with his blocky beard, sitting alone in his attic, about to open *The Book of Doom and Desire*; then she saw younger versions of Cordelia, Brendan and herself playing on the swings at Alta Vista, their primary school; this was followed by an image of Kristoff House as it had been when she first saw it, on Sea Cliff Avenue, backlit by the sun, part of the rhythms of San Francisco, of life; and then she saw the chalk outlines of her parents. All the while she got closer and closer to Kristoff House, and then the entrance was right in front of her, and the door was open, and there was seaweed dripping off it, and Cordelia's unconscious body slipped through it, and Brendan rushed through, clutching his injured side, and behind the door there wasn't a hallway any more, but a flat white surface – the same colour that had started as the centre of the doughnut-shaped cloud and turned into the white disc – and Eleanor remembered how she had asked her dad once, *What's at the end of the universe?* And he'd said, *There is no end. It just goes on and on...* but this seemed like the end.

And then Eleanor hit the whiteness – *shooooooooomp!* – and her world went just as blank.

76

Cordelia wasn't sure what she was seeing. Half of it was clear: the blackness of the inside of her eyelids. But then, every few moments, the blackness was replaced by a *face*.

It was a marble face, stern, with a wavy beard. *I've seen that before,* Cordelia thought. *Greek... Plato? Aristotle?*

Suddenly she leaped to her feet. "Arsdottle!"

She kissed the marble bust whose name Dahlia Kristoff could never pronounce. Yes! She was in the great hall of Kristoff House—

And the house wasn't destroyed!

The track lighting was still in the ceiling. The coat-rack was by the door. Nothing was broken, shattered, turned to debris by the Wind Witch... Cordelia's mind spun. *What is happening?*

Then she saw Brendan and Eleanor.

They were lying on the floor, blinking, dumbstruck, just as she had been. But not injured! Their wounds were all gone. It was like nothing had happened.

"Bren! Nell!" Cordelia hugged them. Brendan made a noise halfway between a laugh and a cry. Eleanor clung to Cordelia, pressing into her hair.

"You made it!"

"Yeah, but... what happened?"

"We're *alive* – that's what happened!" Brendan said. He felt something jab his hip. He pulled out his PSP, laughed at it, and dropped it as he wrapped his arms around his sisters. The tear streaks on his cheeks were curved by a huge grin. "We defeated the Wind Witch with that giant portal thing! But... how?"

"Well, it began with the book," Eleanor started to explain – and then she went silent. Because someone was standing over them.

"*Mum!*"

If Bellamy Walker had wanted to press assault charges, she could have. Eleanor grabbed her knees. Cordelia burrowed into her shoulder. Brendan hugged her so hard she almost fell over.

"Hold on, what's happening – what's got into you three?"

"You're alive!" Cordelia said – and then she looked aside. "*Dad!*"

Dr Jake Walker was coming down the hall, carrying a pizza. "What's going on—?"

Cordelia, Brendan and Eleanor gave their father a triple bear hug, making him scramble to keep the pizza box from falling. "Hey! What's – oh, you guys are sweet—"

"What did you *do*?" Mrs Walker asked, interrupting.

"What do you mean?" Cordelia said. She noticed the logo on the pizza box: PINO'S.

"Did you mess with the shampoo in my bathroom?" Mrs Walker said. "Did you crank-call someone? Did you toilet paper a house? This isn't normal behaviour. You did something wrong."

"Good point," Dr Walker said. "And Brendan and Eleanor, how did you disappear from the living room? You were there a minute ago. Is this a *Punk'd*?"

"Uh…" Brendan said, looking at Cordelia.

"Yeah…" Cordelia mumbled, trying to think how

exactly she could tell her parents that she and her siblings had just returned victorious from a battle for the fate of the world. And brought them back from the dead.

Eleanor spoke up: "We were doing an experiment."

"Oh?" Mrs Walker asked. "Like the experiment where Brendan taped silly straws together and flooded the house?"

"No, this was an experiment about loving your parents. We saw it on a TV show Anderson Cooper. You're supposed to go into a room and pretend that your parents are dead, and then when you see them, you hug them like they just came back to life. Like you never want them to go ever again."

"Uh…" Mrs Walker said.

"Anderson Cooper," Dr Walker said.

"What's important is that we love you, and we're totally ready to eat pizza and watch TV. Whatever show you want. Just as long as we're together," said Eleanor.

Dr Walker squinted. "Are you *sure* you're OK?"

Eleanor embraced her father. Dr Walker gave his wife a look. Mrs Walker shrugged: *I guess we should take what we can get.*

Dr Walker took Eleanor's hand. Cordelia winked at

Eleanor. Brendan patted his little sister's back. As they all walked towards the living room, the house looked a little bit smaller… or maybe the Walkers had grown.

There was only one thing that bothered Brendan as he sat with his siblings while his parents ordered *Duck Soup* on demand. He whispered to Eleanor, "What if Dahlia comes back?"

Eleanor didn't answer. For once, it felt good to have knowledge that her siblings didn't. She watched TV with a tight-lipped smile as Brendan and Cordelia got more and more desperate: "What did you *do*?"

"Come on, Nell, *tell us*!"

"What are you three talking about?" Mrs Walker asked.

"Nothing," Cordelia said quickly. She kept waiting for the doorbell to interrupt like last time… but it never came. *Duck Soup* ended without a Dahlia Kristoff guest appearance.

"That was fun," said Dr Walker… but he noticed his children were already leaving the room. "Where are you three going?"

"Upstairs. To read," Cordelia said.

"Yeah, me too," said Brendan.

"Me too," said Eleanor.

"OK," said Dr Walker, "Cordelia I understand… Bren and Nell?"

"Books can be a great adventure," said Brendan.

"*What?* Who are you and what have you done to my son?" asked Mrs Walker.

"Mum," said Brendan, "you're supposed to encourage reading, not make fun of it. Deal, Nell and I got caught up in these books, uh, and we wanted to… um… discuss them." After he finished Brendan realised he was telling the truth.

"Are you telling me you formed a book club?"

"That's right," said Eleanor.

"That's so cute!" Mrs Walker clutched her husband's arm. "OK, go upstairs and have your book club. I'll dig out my laptop and pay a few" – she glanced at Dr Walker sadly – "bills."

The Walkers were barely up the stairs when Eleanor said innocently: "So you're probably wondering how I got us all home."

"Nell," Brendan said, "if you don't tell us everything right now, I'm going to go Wind Witch on you."

Eleanor began: "First I realised *The Book of Doom and Desire* could help us…"

She led her siblings to the second-floor bedroom that would be hers – that *was* hers, in a way, because Kristoff House no longer felt new. "I was up there," she continued, pointing to the ceiling, "stuffed inside the chimney with the book in my hands, when I wrote us to safety."

"How?" asked Brendan.

"Because if the Wind Witch wrote on a piece of paper that she wanted to rule the world and expected it to come true… maybe I could write down what I wanted and *it* could come true."

"What did you write with?" asked Cordelia. "Did you have a pen?"

"I used the soot," said Eleanor.

"The soot?" asked Brendan.

"The inside of the chimney's covered with it. It's just like charcoal. But I had to think about what to write. And I had to make sure I wrote it in the right order or else I could get us in real trouble."

"Yeah," said Brendan. "Like if you wanted to write, 'Brendan stops the Wind Witch', but you dyslexed it up so it said, 'The Wind Witch stops Brendan.'"

"Exactly," said Eleanor. "It was really hard, but I concentrated more than ever and finally wrote, 'The Wind Witch was sent to the worst place ever, and the Walkers were sent home. Back to the night it all started. With their parents alive.'"

"That's a lot!" Brendan said.

"Yeah. I made sure it was in the right order and slipped the paper into the book. And then the cloud started spinning, and that's how we all ended up back here."

"You used the power of the book against itself!" Cordelia said. "I'm so proud! I wish I could've seen it. Stupid unconsciousness."

"Don't worry," said Brendan, "you'll be awake next time."

"There's not going to *be* a next time! We won. The Wind Witch is gone. Banished to the worst place ever," Cordelia said.

"Do you think I should've been more specific?" asked Eleanor. "I mean, what if she's somewhere she could get out?"

"That's right. We don't know where this 'worst place'

is," said Brendan. "For me it would be Top Shop."

"For her it's probably some horrible novel of Kristoff's she'll never escape from," said Cordelia, "and I missed all the action."

"Hold on, Deal," said Eleanor. "You were the one who figured out we were *in* Kristoff's books. You saved our lives more times than we can count. And you got to meet Will. That's not exactly missing the action."

"But Will's still dead," said Cordelia. In all the excitement of getting home she hadn't been thinking about him. But she missed his grin – and his F. Scott Fitzgerald hair – and the way he was always so right about things. Except when he became captain – but that probably wouldn't happen again. "It'd be better if I'd never met him at all."

"Don't say that."

"Why?" Cordelia asked. "He never really existed anyway. He was just a fictional character. Now the only way I can see him is if I read *The Fighting Ace*."

"There might be another way to see him," Eleanor said.

"Don't mess with me. Will's—"

A ping on the window silenced Cordelia. Eleanor kept quiet. Another ping. Someone was throwing pebbles against the glass from outside. Brendan moved next to Eleanor. "You didn't…"

"I wrote a few other things in the book," Eleanor admitted.

Cordelia went to the window and nearly smacked her head on the window frame. Standing below, in his bomber jacket, was Will Draper.

"Cordelia!" he called. "Look at me! Here in the real world! This isn't a silly novel, is it?"

"*Will!* What are you—" Cordelia turned to look at Eleanor.

"I wrote, 'And bring Will Draper back too.'"

Cordelia gave Eleanor a quick squeeze (*"Thank you!"*) before turning back: "Will, are you OK? What do you remember?"

"Slayne stabbing me in the back, the dirty coward. Then me waking up in those bushes and seeing your profile in the window. Hey… am I in 2013? In San bloody Francisco?"

"Yes! My sister—"

"I don't want to hear about it. I know a stroke of luck when I see one. May I come in?"

"Yes—" Cordelia started. "Wait, *no*! My parents are here!"

"So? I introduce myself, throw in a bit o' the old British charm – I'll fit right in." Will stepped towards the front door—

"Will! They're suspicious already! You *can't*!"

The pilot stopped. "You really don't want me to?"

"Now's not the time. Come to school tomorrow. I get out at three thirty. We can talk then." Cordelia blanked out for a second, imagining what it would be like to sit through school after what she'd been through: to pay attention when her history teacher talked about the Treaty of Utrecht; to have serious conversations with her peers about how unfair it was that you had to be sixteen to audition for *Idol*. How could she be normal and not explode, or laugh, or both? Knowing she would see Will would help her get through it.

"I'll write down the address," she told him, grabbing a pen.

"Where do I go in the mean time? Am I to sleep in the street?"

"Here," Eleanor said, pushing her sister aside. "You can take this." She let an envelope flutter to the lawn.

Will opened it. There was cash inside.

"Nell!" Brendan said. "Isn't that your birthday money?"

"It is," Eleanor said, "but I won't be needing it any more."

"Why?" Brendan asked.

Downstairs, Will watched a red Corvette's headlights slide by on Sea Cliff Avenue. "Look at that! Automobiles have certainly changed!"

"Here's my school's address," Cordelia said, letting a piece of paper flutter down to Will. "Now walk that way to California Street, get the number one bus to downtown, and ask for a Days Inn. I'll see you tomorrow."

Will nodded, tipped his hat (although he didn't have one), and left. Cordelia expected him to look back, but Will had learned long ago from Frank Quigley that when you part ways with a girl, especially a pretty one like Cordelia, you keep your eyes straight ahead.

Once he was gone, Eleanor got up to leave.

"Where are you going?" Cordelia asked. "There's more to discuss!"

"Yeah…" said Brendan. "Like what happened to the Storm King? Did you send him away too?"

"I forgot," said Eleanor. "But I wrote down one last wish."

"What?"

Before Eleanor could answer, Mrs Walker screamed in the kitchen. The Walkers raced down and found their parents staring open-mouthed at her laptop, hitting refresh like robots.

"Guys…?" Cordelia asked. "What's wrong?"

"There's… ah… some kind of glitch with the bank," Dr Walker said, holding up his phone. "I'm on hold with them."

"Mum?" Brendan asked.

Mrs Walker's eyes were filled with tears of happiness. She answered in a quivering, hopeful voice: "It appears that we have ten million dollars in our savings account."

Brendan and Cordelia turned to Eleanor: *No*.

Eleanor gave them a slight nod and a smile: *Yes*. But she quickly turned back to her mother and feigned surprise.

"That's *crazy*! How could that happen? Maybe you guys played lotto and you don't remember?"

"Look at this," Dr Walker said, still on hold with the bank. He put an envelope on the kitchen table. "Our first piece of mail at this address."

Mrs Walker opened it. It was a letter about the lawsuit

at the John Muir Medical Center, where Dr Walker had worked.

"'In exchange for silence on this matter, the plaintiff has pledged a settlement of… *ten million dollars*'?" Mrs Walker asked.

"Yes, thank you very much, goodnight," said Dr Walker into the phone. He hung up. "It's real?"

"Look at this, honey! It's real! I told you that countersuit would scare him! The money must've already been transferred!"

Dr and Mrs Walker cheered and hugged each other. Their kids joined them in short order. "Awesome, Dad!" Eleanor said. "Can I get a horse now? Please?"

"Why not?" said Dr Walker.

"Yesss!" said Eleanor. "And we can name her Majesty?"

"Where in God's name are we gonna put a horse?" Mrs Walker asked.

"With ten million dollars we'll build her a stable on the roof!" said Dr Walker. "Along with a special horse lift to take her to the park!"

As the family laughed, Cordelia tried to take a mental picture. There was only one thing wrong – she felt a little cold. And when she covered herself with her grandmother's old wool throw, it didn't help, as if the cold were coming from inside her instead of out. But she'd been through a lot; there were bound to be lingering effects.

The fact was that these moments – when the Walkers weren't fighting, and they weren't late for anything, and they were just together and comfortable in a way they could never explain – were rare. And a lot of money from a magical book might make them even rarer. It might, indeed, bring its own problems, and those problems might be terrible.

But for now, for tonight, everything was as it should be.

Epilogue

Meanwhile, far below Kristoff House, on the rocky shore known as Baker Beach, right in the path the house would take if it ever did slide into the ocean, a wet hand grabbed the top of a huge boulder.

The hand was thick and tough. Seaweed hung from it. The sharp rock tried to cut it open, but the hand was too strong.

A second hand joined the first, and with a hoarse moan the owner of them heaved up, flopping on to the boulder. The brute waves of the Pacific crashed behind like static. Waking up in the bay after a journey between worlds will deaden the senses.

Next was a head-first skid down to a patch of sand. Then a crawl to the cliff below Kristoff House. Then a painful climb. Fingers scraped. Thorny vegetation dug in. The hands didn't flinch. Salt was spat. Pain was pushed deep, to be covered by hate that shone as brightly as the Golden Gate Bridge to the left, or the onyx sea below.

Finally the hands hauled the owner into the backyard of Kristoff House. The face looked at the familiar structure. Noted a family, in the kitchen, sharing hot chocolate.

I could kill them all, thought Denver Kristoff. *They'd be dead within seconds, for killing Dahlia. No one takes my daughter away from me.*

But now was not the time. Kristoff had a place he could go, a place that made Kristoff House look like a shack. His mouth was still twisted into a horrific double rictus, and his nose was still flaps of flesh, so he would need a mask – but at this place, he would be welcomed for a sacrifice he had made in the past… and able to plan his next move.

The Bohemian Club at 624 Taylor Street. Home of the Lorekeepers. Just a few blocks from where Will Draper was heading.

It's a real place in San Francisco, you know. You can visit any time you want. It's no secret.